CW01457569

THE DEAD CITY ROLLERS

THE DEAD CITY ROLLERS

R. T. STROUD

Matador
9 Priory Business Park,
Wistow Road, Kibworth Beauchamp,
Leicestershire. LE8 0RX
Tel: (+44) 116 279 2299
Fax: (+44) 116 279 2277
Email: books@troubador.co.uk
Web: www.troubador.co.uk/matador

ISBN 978-1783065-882

British Library Cataloguing in Publication Data.
A catalogue record for this book is available from the British Library.

Typeset in 11pt Aldine401 BT Roman by Troubador Publishing Ltd, Leicester, UK
Printed and bound by CPI Group (UK) Ltd, Croydon, CR0 4YY

Matador is an imprint of Troubador Publishing Ltd

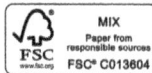

MIX
Paper from
responsible sources
FSC
www.fsc.org   FSC® C013604

To Dilys

WE'RE WELSH, WE'RE PROGRAMMED TO SELF-DESTRUCT.
TRY AND STOP OUR CULTURE?
GO KILL YOURSELF, MOTHERFUCKER.

THE DISASTERS

Alistair didn't know it yet, but in five days he'd be putting both barrels of a shotgun into his mouth and slowly, ever so slowly, wrapping his thumb around the trigger.

The thing he'd find so surprising was how the body goes into a kind of pre-emptive shock, how the mind shuts down from fear, failing you, failing to find you a way out of a really fucked up situation.

It is funny how life works sometimes. For instance, if Alistair knew what he'd be doing five days down the line, he'd look at you and laugh. Right now he was more concerned about the weather.

Swansea gets rain, you see. Swansea gets rain by the bucket load. A lot of it was falling on Alistair at present as he trudged home, his hood up and his head down. Above him clouds hung low, blanketing the city with their clinging pre-winter drizzle.

As well as not knowing his future five days hence, Alistair also didn't know he was currently being watched. His watcher was an immobile figure lying deep within a Brer rabbit-thick and litter-strewn hedge.

Immobile that is except for the eyes that tracked Alistair. It would indeed be hard to see this man, swaddled as he was in camouflage clothing.

To be fair to Alistair, he didn't notice a lot in the rain; he just concentrated on keeping his hood up and his head down.

Besides, he was busy contemplating his ego in relation to the weather. It was either that or contemplate how his knackered old trainers seemed to be acting like sponges.

Alistair's thoughts went something like this – it always seemed to be raining when he walked around the city on these thrice-weekly deliveries, the first heavy drops coinciding with the beginning of his run and only stopping as he got home. The bloody wind as well always seemed to be changing direction, ensuring he had to walk directly into it. Alistair was convinced the weather did it on purpose just to annoy him, like the butt of an Aesop's fable. He wasn't sure if thinking like this meant he had incredible delusions of grandeur or a persecution complex. It was something he'd have to ask Ebin when he got home.

Ebin was the last person on his run. Just two more deliveries to go and then he'd get in, fight his way over the mountain of junk mail, drop off the drugs and then sneak past the weirdo's room, for his Wednesday night bath.

From the bushes the pair of eyes watched him slip and do a prat-fall Charlie Chaplin would've been proud of.

Donald Gooberman remained lying bush-deep and still as death until the figure had pulled himself to his feet and let out a number of loud and varied curses before squelching off out of view.

The swearing man had seemed skinny, as much as it was possible to tell, swaddled as he had been in a pair of baggy combat trousers with a sodden, hooded top hiding his features. *He did have a potty mouth though*, Donald thought.

Whoever it was hadn't broken their stride or shown any sign of noticing him, hidden as he was in the middle of a hedge.

People were never that observant in the rain and Donald had taken a lot of time applying his camouflage paint.

Donald Gooberman liked the rain. It masked the noise you made moving through the undergrowth.

When the street was empty, Donald awkwardly turned his bulk around and continued crawling deeper through the wet bushes. He dragged an olive-drab jerry can after him.

Over the last week, between chopping and crawling, Donald had managed to create a wide tunnel – fifteen feet through the bushes. The tunnel stopped just short of a gravel embankment that ran down to the railway line.

Donald carefully parted the last bit of foliage and looked over the railway line at the new and very expensive housing estate.

The uniform square gardens ran right up to the track. If

Donald had known about houses, he would have called them Mock Tudor.

Donald's target was in the kitchen of the largest house. He'd been there at this time all week. Watching the target, Donald felt another one of his headaches building up. It always started with a tightness in the scalp and, in the bad old days, ended with him screaming and punching walls.

On instinct Donald found himself scrabbling through his pockets looking for the tablets. He stopped, remembering the pastor locking him with those bright green eyes and taking the little brown bottle away.

The pastor was right to do it. This mission was too critical for him to be deadened by his meds.

Pastor Morris was indeed a very clever man; he had stressed to Donald how important it would be to plan the attack correctly. Taking the time to understand the target's habits and find out when he was most vulnerable. Planning was the most important thing, the pastor had stressed.

Donald secretly thought the most important thing was camouflage, but had kept his mouth shut. After all, Pastor Morris had given him this nice new knife and a lot more encouragement than his mother would have.

3

Finally home, Alistair forced the door open. The constant rain of the last few weeks had made the old, wooden thing swell. He shook off as much of the excess rain water as possible.

They should really get more money from Danny for having to walk around delivering drugs in the rain. Some sort of inclemency bonus. Towels would do, big soft towels, like the ones people pinched from posh hotels. It was a good point and as soon as Danny stopped being pissed off at them all, he would bring it up.

Alistair couldn't help but smile; here he was twenty-three years old and his ambition was a pair of dry socks, some decent trainers and to be paid partly in towels. This was another part of the realisation he'd had earlier. Lying there, after falling on a slick layer of leaves, Alistair decided he needed a change. He needed to stop feeling so goddamn incredibly down as he had been of late.

When, a few months before, this awful feeling of sadness had pervaded him, he had just got wasted a lot. This self-medication had kind of worked for a while and it had been a good summer. Now the oncoming winter turned everything grey; the sky, the buildings and above all the people. Autumn had made his spirits fall like the slippery bloody oak leaves and Alistair had found his mind constantly turning back to the girl he had killed three years ago.

If Ebin had been there, at that moment, he would have said

Alistair was over-dramatising and called him a prick. Ebin would then spend the rest of the day winding him up. There's a word for people like Ebin, and it's not a good word.

Shouldering the door shut, Alistair clambered over the thick carpet of junk mail that no one ever got around to picking up, before heading upstairs for his last delivery of the day.

Ebin and Clancy were sitting in the lounge, which was also Ebin's room, bonging and playing *Mario Kart*, pot smoke pea-souping around them. Alistair paused in the doorway to let his eyes grow accustomed to the gloom. As always, the place was a tip. The few bits of carpet you could see, below dirty clothes and old magazines, were irredeemably stained with carelessly kicked bong water. The cheap table in the middle of the room was also covered in detritus; its centrepiece was a cracked plant pot, sans plant, which was now an overflowing ashtray. Ebin and Clancy were obliviously sitting on a brown, spring-blown sofa below a giant *Ween* poster.

Clancy gave him his customary monged-out smile. "You look happy," he said.

And Clancy was correct; Alistair was happy.

The epiphany had happened while he was picking himself up from the floor. The epiphany itself was simple – there was more to life than this and it was up to him to find out what that more was.

Ebin, by way of greeting, called Alistair *a soppy-looking bastard,* before taking the big lump of pot off him, ready for the evening's business. He did this in much pain, showing off a bandage on his right hand.

Clancy turned back to the bong, while Ebin explained how he'd been trying to break into the weirdo's room and had slipped with the chisel, cutting his hand open.

That was the problem with being on the dole and constantly skint: it was difficult to keep yourself entertained. They did try their best though. For example, there was the weekly TV-licensing-man run. This involved one of them ringing the doorbell and then timing how long it took the others to gather up and hide the TV,

Super NES and video. Their current record was sixty-three seconds; Ebin reckoned with more practice they could get it down to less than a minute.

Ebin would fill much of his time with different obsessions. He was currently obsessed with Donald, the muscle-bound army freak who had moved in a month ago. The dirty, bastard, money-grubbing landlord would often fill the spare room with a revolving litany of mentalists.

The current in-patient had been briefly introduced as Donald. Donald was a hell of a big chap. He was bouncer-big, with what had once probably been muscles all but subsumed by fat. He had a childlike face below short-cropped, ginger hair. Ebin said he looked like Chunk's stunt double out of *The Goonies*. He had said this quietly somewhere he was sure Donald wasn't likely to hear.

They only ever saw Donald occasionally and when they did, he always seemed to be sneaking around acting all furtive and stuff, normally dressed head to toe in combat fatigues. The guy was an absolute nutter; last week he'd gone bananas and smashed up his room. Ebin had wanted to call the police until Alistair had gestured at all the drugs around. Ebin had muttered something before squeezing behind the couch for an hour.

Ebin was currently appraising the two-ounce block with a critical eye. He turned it over in his good hand.

"Do you remember when we were kids and your folks would take you to get shoes?" he addressed Alistair.

Clancy sighed and Alistair started edging towards his Wednesday bath.

"The care and attention you'd be shown by the lady working in the shoe shop. Do you remember that?"

Alistair started shuffling backwards; he could see where this was going.

"They would measure your feet in that big metal contraption. The one that looked like it could crush you."

The doorbell rang.

9

"Then, when they had your size, your exact size, mind you, they would disappear and come out with a pile of different shoes."

Clancy concentrated on making another mix, his lighter flickering over the length of a cigarette, charring it black.

The bell rang again.

"Now that was service," Ebin continued. "What happens when you try to buy shoes now? All you get is a youth chewing at you. It's all about money; the idea of customer service is out the window. It's a problem rife at all levels of society."

The person outside was getting impatient.

"Take this pot, for instance. How can I cut this up into a load of five bucks when my hand is like this?" he asked, waving his bandaged paw. "Why should I anyway? You know what I sell and should provide it all cut up accordingly." Ebin turned back to the TV. "There's a knife in the kitchen and if you could get the door while you're on your feet."

"I am not carrying the amount of pot I have to carry cut up into deals. I'd go to prison forever, and customer service? Customer fucking service? That's rich, talking about customer service. You two are the worst dealers I know. You've got to let the fucking customers in to be fucking dealers. It's Wednesday and I need a bath." Alistair stormed out. "And answer the fucking door."

Behind him Ebin and Clancy started laughing.

4

Zachariah Plum was busying himself in the kitchen, valiantly trying to keep pace with the TV chef. This new hobby was a real pain and was definitely not something he'd be boasting about.

Cookery wouldn't do anything for his image or, as he was discovering, something he cared about. It was just something to do in order to pass the time until the plan was complete and he could leave this God-awful city for ever. He was sure it had never rained this much back home.

Zach looked up as the doorbell was repeatedly rung.

Swearing under his breath and giving up on his soufflé, he took off his apron, wincing as he did.

He looked at himself in the mirror, before straightening his hair.

Zach really hated this look. They'd said it would be a good way to impress the locals. He'd been sure they'd just been winding him up though. A three-year bloody wind up, brilliant. *The locals weren't that stupid*, he'd thought, *nobody could be*. Unbelievably, it turned out they had been.

The only ones who hadn't gone along with it were the girls. They'd just smirked when he'd introduced himself as Zach the Mac or Big Boy Z.

The doorbell rang again.

With one last look to check his hair was in place, he left the kitchen. Zach winced again as he opened the door to the hallway.

He was sure he'd cracked a knuckle, the one on his right little finger. It was swollen badly.

That stupid, trouble-making girl, he mused for the tenth time this week. If only she'd just gone away when he'd asked her, rather than cussing him out in front of the ladies. What else could he have done? Any perceived weakness would have gotten back to Mardy in a flash. The ladies loved to gossip, loved to stir things up when they could and he was too far along this road to risk Mardy getting in a mood with him.

The front door was the first thing to catch Zach's attention as he entered the hall. Burning doors tend to do that.

"Motherfu—" Zach started before the smell hit him.

The letterbox was, or rather, the greasy brown bag trapped in the letterbox was smoking, black and heavily.

Zach darted forward holding his breath and flapping his apron at the flames. This inadvertently fanned them, causing the bag to split and spray its contents, napalm-like over the floor.

Several individual fires were created in the deep-pile carpet. Zach danced back and forth stamping all antsy pantsy, not stopping until the fire was out and he was just left with the gagging smell and a pitching smoke alarm.

Bursting out into the fresh air, he slipped on the front lawn. Zach froze, legs akimbo. There, exuding menace at the end of the street, was a souped-up, green car. The two men sitting in it were staring at him; the little one with the faded Hawaiian shirt and sunglasses was giving him a big toothy grin while the other man just glared.

"Oh shit," Zach breathed, before turning around and, with as much dignity as possible, marching back into the smoky house.

5

Upon seeing his target move away from the kitchen window Donald slithered through the bushes and down the gravel bank. He paused for a moment, checking both ways, before crossing the railway line and flattening himself against the garden fence.

His headache was thumping mortar-like now. He ignored it though; it was unimportant.

The promise, that was important. But he'd broken it; he'd failed to protect her – which was why, with some effort, he climbed into the deserted garden and started moving towards the back door. The olive-drab jerry can heavy in his hand.

6

The souped-up, green car idled. The thrumming of the engine the only sound in the cul-de-sac.

"I don't know if I like him or not," Stone said, a moment or two after Zach had disappeared back into his house and slammed the door.

Stone sat slouched in the driver's seat; he was rake-thin and decked in a once sharp suit, *Ted Baker* or one of those. He watched the closed door. A wisp of smoke was coming out of the letterbox.

Stone picked his teeth reflectively before looking over at his big partner. "I mean, he makes a bit of an effort with his appearance and all, but I don't know whether he's being a bit racist."

His partner looked at him in surprise. He held the stare while adjusting his cufflinks; they were in the shape of rugby balls. "A *bit* racist? Of course he's being racist; he's a white guy who makes his living from the profits of prostitutes, which he does dressed up as a black pimp from the seventies. I mean I find that offensive on so many levels. What possible debate could be going on in your head over whether you like him or not?"

"Well, I appreciate the aesthetic effort he's making."

"*Aesthetic effort?*" Keyes sighed, shifting uncomfortably in his seat. The seatbelt was, as always, digging into his chest. He really hated this car. "What do you mean by aesthetic effort? What, the pink Cadillac he's got parked on the drive? You're insane. He hits women, for God's sake, and it's not even a real afro."

"How do you know?" Stone said, interlacing his hands behind his head.

"We saw her in the hospital, remember? You were bitching about how much you hated hospitals."

"No, about the afro."

"It's obviously a wig; the thing's a different colour from his eyebrows," Keyes continued. "That's detective work, that is."

Detective Keyes hadn't always been a detective. He use to play prop forward for the Whites, back when top level rugby was still an amateur game, which, with the exception of the odd kick back or pile of tickets to sell on, meant you had to get a proper job after your knee joint is shattered in a ruck.

The first of the pizza delivery scooters entered the cul-de-sac.

"Detective work?" Stone tutted. "This isn't detective work. Why are we even here? It's not as if he beat her up in public or anything. Why do we care? We should be dealing with that Post Office thing, rather than fannying about with this."

"You know damn well why we're here." Keyes sighed, still fidgeting, this time with his tie. It was his old club tie, SRFC running obliquely across it. "If you don't want to be here go."

Stone started to say something before noticing the other's face start to darken, stopped and in a more conciliatory tone said, "Fine, we'll stay here and annoy Zach for a while then."

They lapsed into silence and watched two more scooters turn onto the road.

*

It had been just over a week ago when they had walked through the deserted corridors of the hospital to meet the nervous old timer. It was late – early hours of the morning late. The only sound came from the tapping of Johnson's cane as he paced back and forth outside one of the rooms. Keyes thought it was the most he had ever seen the ancient desk sergeant move.

"What's going on, Johnson?" Stone demanded curtly; he hated hospitals, having spent so much time bringing his daughter to them.

The old sergeant shushed him with that universal *you can't talk loudly in a hospital* gesture, before coming over all deferential.

"Boys, I'm sorry for getting you out here at this time in the morning."

Keyes contrasted this unfamiliar image of Johnson with the grumpy, surly one he had come to know and be annoyed by in work.

"What do you want, Johnson?"

The old man paused for a long time, silence streamed back into the hospital, as some internal process went on in his head.

"I think I need a favour," he said, leading them through a door.

The room was small and darker than the neon-stripped corridor. Keyes could only make out a vague shape in the bed. As his eyes adjusted he realised it was a woman; he was pretty sure it was a woman, at least. Under a shock of bright pink hair was a face swollen and bruised the colour of aubergine.

Detective Keyes picked up the file from the foot of the poor girl's bed; it looked tiny in his hand. "Trish Reed. Why is that name familiar?"

"Didn't we have her in the station a while ago?" Stone said. "She threw red paint all over that posh bitch in a fur coat, some sort of animal rights thing. She had that fucking dog, remember?"

"I remember you kicking it."

Stone laughed at the memory. "Yeah, I hate dogs. So, who is she to you, Johnson?"

"She used to be a friend of my granddaughter's."

"Used to be?"

"Some people get sucked into a certain life." The sergeant shrugged sadly.

"Who did this?" Keyes demanded.

"Zachariah Plum – which is why I need a favour."

"Ah, you want him to go in the book," Stone said, picking something from his teeth.

16

The last place you wanted to be was in the Keystone Cops' book. Burning bags of dog muck through your letterbox and pizza delivery boys turning up at your door was just a childlike way of saying it's starting, wait and see what we're going to do next.

Johnson nodded, before looking, sadly, at the bed. "I've tried to help her in the past, for the sake of her family, you understand, but to no avail. This is it; once you've put Zach in your book, I'm done with this girl."

"Knowing how much my large partner hates to see beaten women, I think that could be done," Stone said, kneading the old policeman's shoulder and making him visibly wince. "You know, Johnson, you really didn't have to drag us out here at this time of night for the freak show in the bed; you could have just asked."

Johnson broke free, turning to face them both directly, some of his patriarchal desk sergeant gruffness coming back. "This stays in the room."

Stone winked at him. "The boss will never know."

Keyes hadn't taken his eyes off the bed.

*

Zach's door was staying resolutely shut, despite being repeatedly knocked on by the gathering knot of pizza boys.

Suddenly, to a man, they jumped back.

Something had started to rhythmically pound on the other side of the door, something that sounded huge.

Slowly, a large crack appeared in the centre of the door, increasing exponentially.

Everyone backed away further.

The detectives leaned forward.

The door splintered open.

Zach appeared head first and tried to crawl across the lawn. He was followed by a huge figure wearing army fatigues. The huge figure pounced on him and started swinging punches.

Detectives Keyes and Stone looked at each other.

Detective Stone was the first to start laughing. "Zach's really having a bad day; his house smells of dog shit and now he's getting beaten up on his lawn."

"The place is on fire as well."

Stone was still laughing as he got out of the car and walked over. "That's enough of that now, gentlemen," he said, pushing his way through the stunned delivery boys.

"Zachariah Plum, I am arresting you for assault and arson." Keyes chuckled, a few feet behind.

Zach's assailant looked up at them. The expression of anger on his face turned to one of confusion, before he jumped up and started to run down the road.

"Stop," Keyes shouted noncommittally, while bending down over the bloodily pulped pimp.

Stone sprinted after the suspect. Keyes followed a few seconds later shouting, "See, it is a wig."

7.

The hostel lay in one of Swansea's forgotten corners. It hadn't always been forgotten; it was just as if one day there had been a meeting and everyone had decided to build in the opposite direction.

The hostel had no outward look of habitation, there was no bright JESUS SAVES sign, no markings to say that it was *The Mount Pleasant Hostel for the Young and Disenfranchised*, named after the equally run down chapel next to it. The only thing that would have looked out of place to the sharper observer were the surveillance cameras on each corner of the building, 360-degreeing the area.

The hostel was nearly deserted at the moment. The court order stated that those it catered for could only stay there for three and a half days a week.

Today was moving day and the large drab-grey dormitory was empty, save for a person-shaped lump in one bed.

Trish, still all black and blue from her beating, drifted awake to start the last week of her life. She groggily looked around the bare dormitory. The small amount of grey light chinking through the barred window showed that she was the last one in there. The bastards hadn't woken her up again.

Trish felt disorientated; she knew it was moving day, but the grey light did nothing to tell her what time it was and whether she should be here or at the Hare Krishnas' hostel. Her eyes, heavy

19

with sleep, started to close again. If only she could get more comfortable and stop the throbbing in her face, which was still swollen and sore. It had been a bad beating. Over what? Fuck knows. She remembered getting in an argument with someone and the next thing she knew she was waking up in hospital, the next few days spent drifting in and out of consciousness.

The door at the end of the dormitory creaked open on its ancient hinges, flooding the room with more light than had been afforded by the small window. The spherical shape of Brother Dowling was backlit in the doorway; he was humming some upbeat hymn.

Trish lay there quiet and still. Out of all the freaks helping the pastor, this squat, sweaty, bespectacled man was her least favourite. She watched him walk past, towards the back of the dormitory. He moved with a strange, one-leg-dragging gait. Trish stayed still; hopefully he'd be so intent on getting into the secret passage, she would go unnoticed.

Brother Dowling stopped, then turned very slowly and squinted at her, his eyes distorted by those stupid jam-pot spectacles. He looked around the rest of the dormitory before coming to sit on the edge of the bed, the springs giving under his weight.

"You should have gone by now," he said, in his unusually effeminate voice.

Trish was fully clothed under the blankets and tried to roll away from him. But the slug-man's weight pulled the sheets snug to the bed.

"Did you oversleep again?" he asked, drawing himself closer to Trish, the smell of stale sweat engulfing her. "They aren't very good friends, leaving you all the time." He shook his head sadly. "I feel bad for you, Trish, I really do. Look at your face; you have been given a right going-over. What you really need is someone who is here for you and can look after you." An octopus-slimy smile crossed his face as he brought a shaking hand up to stroke her hair.

Trish went for the eyes, nails flashing cat-like. Brother Dowling spazzed backwards off the bed clutching his cheek and whimpering all high pitched and girly.

"I… I was only going to tell you about Jesus."

Trish stood over him, tangled in blankets, but free enough to lift her foot and grind the grin off his greasy face.

"Enough." The bellowed order filled the room, stopping Trish mid-stamp and Brother Dowling mid-blub.

Trish stood there, foolishly balancing on one leg, a sheet hanging from her foot.

"You can stop now, Trish," Pastor Morris said, softly.

Trish made sure she put her foot down on Brother Dowling's chubby fingers. He let out a little yelp.

The pastor looked down at him, disgust playing briefly across his sallow face. "You should be getting on with your tasks," he ordered.

Brother Dowling didn't even look in Trish's direction as he scuttled out of the room.

The pastor watched him go before turning to Trish. "Would you like a while to sort yourself out?" he asked.

She shook her head, feeling embarrassed at her outburst. Brother Dowling talked about Jesus a lot.

"It is time to leave now, Trish," the pastor said. "It is late and your dog has been barking in the graveyard for an hour."

Trish went to gather her few things from the knot of sheets and put her boots on.

"Please allow me to walk with you a while," Pastor Morris said, stepping out of the doorway and gesturing her past with a half-bow.

Pastor Morris gave her a cigarette as they walked around the side of the hostel. Trish had never seen the pastor smoke. She winced fitting the cigarette between her split lips.

The pastor lit it, regarding her with his piercing green eyes. "Your face seems bad."

Trish just stared at the ground.

"They helped you though? The police, they came to see you in hospital."

She looked in surprise at the pastor.

"I know a lot of things." He smiled thinly, not taking his eyes off her.

Trish shrugged, she couldn't remember the police being of any particular service; they had just seen her as a scruffy junkie who'd probably got what she deserved.

"Did they ask about this place?"

Trish shook her head. "They just asked what happened and if I wanted to press any charges."

The pastor's eyes continued to bore into her.

"Uh… but they didn't sound as if they really wanted me to," Trish continued.

Pastor Morris nodded to himself. "I am worried about you, Trish. I am worried about all of you out there in harm's way."

Trish didn't say anything as they entered the overgrown graveyard.

"It is important that you are careful. There is a presence in this city and you are not safe." He glanced upward at the old chapel. "None of us are."

Out in the graveyard a shape moved.

Trish concentrated on her cigarette, while the pastor continued to talk. She had a good few hours of waiting around town before she met Alistair.

The shape out in the graveyard got closer; Dog came wheeling up, displaying some long dead, half-eaten, unidentifiable carcass.

Dog had stopped taking food off humans right after it had run under that bus, off its doggy head on drugs. Bongo had been devastated, having only given the acid to him for a laugh. Despite the vet's advice he had stubbornly refused to have Dog put down, instead creating a new set of canine back legs out of pram wheels.

Dog squeaked around the two of them, excited, salivating and in need of a good oiling.

Pastor Morris smiled and patted Dog's head. "It may not seem like there is anyone who cares, but that is wrong. Believe me, Trish; even you have a Guardian Angel."

Something in those words gave Trish comfort as she left the hostel, for what would be the last time.

Unseen, a car pulled out from the top of the road and followed her.

onald stood naked in the middle of his room. His bloodied camouflage fatigues were folded neatly on a chair in the corner.

A thousand shards of himself were reflected in the broken mirror as he laced the needle back and forth. Donald was using a long piece of fishing line to close the deep and bleeding cut in his chest; the pain was making him want to black-out.

A lot of the blood had got onto the broken mirror. It seemed to get everywhere, squeezing through the zig-zagged stitches, making his hands slippery and dripping onto the floor.

The mission had not gone as planned.

The infiltration itself was well executed; he had crossed the railway line and climbed straight over the garden fence, dragging the olive-drab jerry can after him. His timing had been perfect; the target had been just opening the back door and was gingerly putting something in the bin. Donald charged across the lawn and windmilled the jerry can into his head.

He dragged the inert body into the house. The air was thick and rank with smoke, making Donald gag. *So far so good*, he had thought, breathing through his mouth. The pastor would be pleased he'd put his trust in him.

*

"Make me pleased to have put my trust in you." Pastor Morris had said those exact words to Donald while handing over the large,

serrated hunting knife. Standing there, in the run-down, damp-smelling chapel, Donald had unsheathed the knife in awe, mesmerised by the light playing off the vicious blade.

Above them in the rafters, pigeons flapped around.

It had been good tactics to come and see the pastor after Trish had been beaten up and left bleeding down that alley.

*

The ambulance had taken her away, leaving Dog whining and straining at its string. Donald knew at least he could help Dog and so had brought it back to the hostel, tears of impotence in his eyes. The mutt was edgy, probably in some sort of doggy shock, its tail stuck firmly between its rear axles.

The door to the hostel was heavily reinforced with metal plates. This, like the rest of the building, looked long disused. Above the door was a surveillance camera in a wire-mesh cage. Donald wasted a moment or two looking for a bell, before giving up and banging hard on the door. After knocking several times, Donald became worried no one was home.

Just as he was about to leave, the door was opened by a scruffy man, with matted ginger dreadlocks and an equally unkempt beard. He looked startled to see Donald standing there.

"What do you want?" he demanded. "'Ere, what you doing with Trish's dog?"

The man stepped outside, squaring up to Donald, even though he clearly lacked the height and body weight. Donald stepped back, surprised at the man's aggression.

"She's hurt," Donald said quietly.

That stopped him.

"What did you do to her?" the dreadlocked man demanded.

Behind him shapes moved in the darkness of the hostel.

"Nothing," Donald mumbled, feeling tears on his cheeks. "It wasn't my fault. My alarm didn't go off and I didn't get here in time and by then she had gone and…" His words tripped over themselves as they came out.

"Where's Trish?" the man said, shoving him violently.

Dog started barking.

"She's been taken to hospital," Donald sobbed. "I was trying to protect her," he went on, pulling in gulps of air. "I'd promised Bongo."

"You know Bongo?" the man, who Donald would later find out was called Jason, asked.

"I promised him I'd protect her. He said there was an evil in the town, but I didn't believe him and now Trish is in hospital."

On hearing this, Jason glanced up at the camera above them, before awkwardly putting out his hand and patting Donald on the shoulder.

"Come inside, there's someone who you should talk to about this."

The interior of the hostel was dark with all the chairs stacked neatly on the tables. It reminded Donald of a school dining room during half term. The place seemed deserted, but Donald couldn't help but feel he was being watched. He tried to dry his eyes as he followed Jason through the tables and up a winding staircase. Dog was left at the bottom, where it started snouting around for scraps.

The stairs went up a long way, ending on a tiny landing with one door leading off it.

"Wait in there." Jason gestured. "The pastor will be up in a while."

Donald opened the door and entered.

The office wasn't much bigger than the landing. A large, ornate oak desk had been squeezed into one corner and a row of blank TVs lined the wall. In front of the desk was a single fragile-looking chair. Donald stood by the chair and waited.

A few minutes later the door was opened by a tall, anaemic-looking man wearing a dog collar. The man had mad brown hair pointing off in a myriad of directions and the most piercing green eyes Donald had ever seen.

"Hello, my son," he said gravely, after appraising Donald for a few moments.

Donald snapped to attention.

The pastor walked around the desk and squeezed in behind it. "Um… at ease?"

Donald relaxed.

"Brother Jason told me that Trish has been taken to hospital and you were kind enough to bring back her dog." The pastor produced a pack of cigarettes and offered one to Donald who shook his head. He smiled and put them back in his shirt pocket. "What happened to Trish?"

He asked it in such a gentle caring way that Donald nearly started to cry again.

The pastor came around the desk and helped Donald into the chair. "My son, we need to stay calm and collected if we are to help Trish."

Donald nodded dumbly.

Pastor Morris smiled. "I want you to start from the beginning and tell me everything."

And so, Donald had started to tell him everything about the last three weeks. He began by telling him about the mission Bongo had given him.

*

Bongo was Donald's friend from the ward.

Bongo hadn't been the military type. He was a thin, pale husk of a man; the kind of guy you wouldn't want covering your back in a fire-fight. It had been Bongo though, in a lucid moment, who had tasked Donald with his mission.

It had been after lunch, just before the midday meds had fully kicked in. Donald had been alone in the Recreation Room drawing a picture. Bongo had come up to him, dressed in his ward-issued pyjamas, all dull eyed and vacant. He had walked around the room once, glancing out of the window, before very quickly squatting down next to Donald.

"She's in danger," he whispered, his voice sounding scratchy and under-used.

Donald put down the crayon and stared at him, having never heard Bongo speak before.

"She's in danger," he repeated, staring at the door nervously.

"Who is?"

Bongo's eyes darted around again and then he leaned in closer. "My girlfriend's in danger," he said, spreading musk over Donald with his rancid breath. "She's in a lot of danger."

Donald had seen Bongo's girlfriend visiting. She had bright pink hair and a kind face.

"What do you mean?" Donald asked, himself in a whisper now.

"There is an evil in the city; Trish is not safe."

"What sort of evil?"

Bongo ducked down as a nurse walked past the door. He watched her go, before turning back to Donald, his eyes changing, seeming to have more focus.

"There's no time for that. You think you're a soldier and a soldier's job is to protect people. So you must protect her."

Donald started to say something, but was hushed.

"Look, I'm stuck in here for a long time and she won't leave town without me." Bongo gripped Donald's arm tightly. "So that leaves you! You're going to be let out soon and then you are going to protect her until I can escape."

Donald had promised there and then, his heart swelling at being tasked with such an important mission.

*

Pastor Morris had sat with his eyes closed and hands steepled, while Donald had gone through his story. Covering everything from his weeks of following Trish, to the power cut in his flat that

28

led to his alarm not going off, to chasing after the pink car as it had sped away from the Central Hotel.

After Donald had finished his story Pastor Morris had sat silently with his eyes still shut for close to a minute. Donald wondered if he had fallen asleep.

The pastor opened his eyes and, faster than Donald could flinch, reached over and gripped his hands with incredible strength.

"You are at a crossroads, my son," he said, fixing him with that piercing stare. "Let me ask you a question." A faint accent, Donald couldn't place, played across his words. "Do you think *evil* in any form should prosper and grow fat in this fair city?"

Donald was pretty sure the answer was no.

"No," he said with confidence.

Pastor Morris' grip increased on Donald's hands.

Donald was sure it had been the right answer.

"What would you do to fight evil where you saw it feed and grow?"

"Everything I could."

"Everything? Would you burn it? Pull out its roots and salt the ground?"

"Everything," Donald repeated, louder now.

The pastor released Donald's hands and collapsed back into the chair like he'd taken a punch. A brilliant smile suddenly played across his face.

"In that case, I've got a mission for you."

*

Donald had come back to the hostel a few days later; the door had again been opened by Jason who had led him down a corridor and into the main chapel. There the pastor had given him his shiny new knife and the name and address of Zachariah Plum.

And so it was, after a week of surveillance and planning, Donald was able to liberally fling petrol around the pimp's kitchen.

Donald struck a match and flicked it onto the work surface, watching with pride as the blue flame shot across the chopping board and lit the place up. He then turned his attention to his target, who was gone.

Donald panicked for a second, before noticing the trail of blood. The target had made it to the end of the hall and was scrabbling to pull himself to his feet and open the front door. Donald marched towards him, the heat on his back getting intense. He had helped Zach out of the house by smashing his head through the door.

It had gone all wrong outside. Donald was surprised to see so many people standing around staring at him, all of them open-mouthed and holding pizzas.

There were also those two policemen.

They'd told him to stop.

Donald had run.

The policemen were very fast and managed to corner him at the bottom of the cul-de-sac. Donald had tried to explain that he was on their side and that he was fighting evil, but they had just laughed. Panicking now, he pulled his shiny new knife, only wanting to scare them off.

The smaller of the policemen had guffawed loudly, before, with considerable speed and strength, grabbing him by the wrist and twisting the knife out of his hand.

After that everything had gone hazy, like the blackouts he used to get in hospital. Donald remembered lashing out and the pain ripping through his chest, as the policeman very calmly slashed him with the knife.

Then all Donald could remember was running. Running back up the big hill to his little room.

He had learned an important lesson today. It was the last time he would reason with the police.

Donald grunted in agony as he picked up his duffle bag and headed out the door. It was time to get away, to go In-Country. He had let the pastor down, he had let Trish down and now Donald had only one place left to go.

He was going home to his mam's.

9

Alistair was swaying gently in the Coach House's toilet, busily trying to take his mind off the smell. He was thinking about who designed toilets; did anyone?

Most jobs gave you a chance to specialise. There were doctors who dealt with throats or noses and others who just looked at lady bits; so why not architects who solely designed toilets? After all, there was evidence of the workmanship and pride that had once gone into these bogs.

Whoever it was had taken their time over the tiles lining the walls. Not only was there mortar, concrete, or whatever that white sticky stuff between them was called, but also tiny tacks, nailed in to help secure them. However, the workmanship was now buried under the carved messages of love for women or the Swans and someone who seemed to worship "Satin".

Perhaps somewhere a toilet architect lay in tears.

Two of the tacks were at Alistair's eye level. He always used them as a measuring post; the longer it took to focus on them the more wasted he was. At present four of the little buggers floated in front of his vision.

Alistair smiled to himself.

*

He'd realised earlier, while lying on the pavement in the rain, that there was more to life than this. It was perhaps something he had always known, but sprawled there, with water running around him, it had struck home as hard as the concrete. Nothing would change until he changed himself – nothing would change until he changed himself. How obvious was that?

Later, while soaking in his Wednesday bath, Alistair lit a joint and, with a large grin on his face, started coming up with his own twelve-step programme – a twelve-step programme for betterment. Some of the details had yet to be finalised, for instance, the number of steps needed, but it would be around twelve. Alistair had planned to start tonight, straight after his bath.

He didn't even really enjoy going out to the stinking, sticky, sweat-dripping club that was Dirty Dora's, yet every week he would.

So that was the first step. He would still go out; after all, what else was there to do in Swansea on a Wednesday? But he wouldn't do any speed or whatever else was shoved under his nose or slipped into his drink.

That was Step One.

Step One had been made easier with the help of alcohol. The drink for the evening was Munting McJunting cider, a massive bottle of the stuff cost two pounds and probably worked out cheaper than water. Alistair happily started to plough through it while being pestered by Ebin and Clancy.

"You're not doing any speed at all?" Clancy had sounded intrigued. "But why?"

"Come on, take some," Ebin cajoled, having no intention of letting Alistair go a whole evening without wiping away white snot.

"No," Alistair repeated, one step at a timing it.

"Are you working for Danny again tomorrow?" Clancy had enquired. He couldn't seem to get his head around the idea of not doing speed on a Wednesday.

"That's not the point. I'm going to improve myself. You're all going to see a whole new me," Alistair announced, taking a triumphant glug of cider.

"A good improvement would be to start cutting up the pot

when you bring it home," Ebin said, waving his wounded hand for the fortieth time that evening.

Downstairs the bell rang.

"A good improvement would be not being such a gaylord," Clancy said, getting up to answer the door.

It was always brisk business on a Wednesday.

Clancy shuffled back into the room with two people in his wake. They both paused, letting their eyes grow accustomed to the smoky gloom that was the lounge and Ebin's room.

"Wee Gay Andy will know," Ebin said, by way of a greeting. "Isn't Alistair gay, if he doesn't do some speed tonight?"

Wee Gay Andy was a member of the surprisingly large Goth community that infested the city. With him was a slightly chubby female, gothic in looks save for her wiry, ginger hair.

"Look, you idiots, enough with the homophobic shit," Wee Gay Andy said, sitting down.

Ebin laughed at him.

Alistair leant over and pinched him on the arm saying, "You are not a vampire."

That was the way Alistair liked to greet Goths – he saw himself, in part, as a grounding force.

Wee Gay Andy and the fat, silent, ginger girl scored a five buck and headed off after the customary one joint. Andy didn't go out much since his money trouble had started.

The pre-Dirty Dora's ritual went on, with the number of people in the lounge and Ebin's room rising and falling.

Ebin and Clancy knocked out pot and the occasional crappy wrap of speed to all the heavies, punks and college kids in the area. Most of the pot was sold in just shuffles – five quid, thumbnail sized, deals. It couldn't really be said they were building a business empire.

In the midst of all the evening's dealing, bonging, licking, snorting and bombing, Alistair sat immaculately on Step One.

He hadn't even been tempted after seeing Trish sitting outside the Coach House. She looked up and smiled as they approached the pub. Dog was lying next to her, with that ear-down, resigned look universal to beggars' mutts.

"Skanky fuck," Ebin muttered and went into the pub with Clancy and the rest of them. Alistair let them go.

"Hey Trish, how's it going?" Alistair asked. She looked like crap.

"Yeah man. Not bad."

Alistair and Trish had played out this weekly charade for a long time. Even though it seemed that Trish was there begging, Alistair knew that she would be gone as soon as he went inside the pub. He remembered how Trish had always hated the city centre at night. Alistair knew though she would put up with it to get the money off him.

Alistair squatted down to be at eye level with her.

Dog looked up at him dolefully and got a stroke.

"What happened to your face?"

"I got beaten up."

"Who by?"

Trish shrugged.

"Well, it doesn't look good. You've had it checked out, have you?"

"Yeah, I had to get stitches." Trish angled her face up to show the sutures.

"You sure you're ok?"

There wasn't a lot else he could say. He'd stopped offering her somewhere to crash a long time ago. She'd always give him this cold *Is that what you want for the money?* kind of look.

Alistair put the notes into her hand and got up to go into the pub. "I'll see you later; you know where I am if you need anything or want to talk or something."

As always Trish looked away.

"Alistair," she called after him. "I do need something; I need you to help me get Bongo out of hospital."

"What do you mean 'get him out of hospital'?"

"He's been in there three years now and he's still the same. I could do a better job than them."

Alistair came away from the door and back down to eye level. "Trish, he's in there for a reason."

"Because of you."

"Look it's—"

"You owe me this; this is how you make up for all that shit. Fuck this money," she said, throwing the cash at Alistair. "This is how you make up for killing Ceri."

Ah Ceri, there we are, that's the card to play.

Alistair picked up the four tenners and put them back gently in Trish's hand before sitting down next to her. They both sat in silence, back in the past.

"What would you do?" Alistair finally asked. "Take him between hostels? Have him sitting in the street like this?"

"No, I really need to get out of this city. Things are… well, they're just not right. And I need Bongo with me before we go."

"Where would you go?"

"France, Spain, somewhere warm, it doesn't matter, I've got money." She smiled, carefully putting the cash away.

Alistair smiled too. "Yeah, come on then, I'll help bust your boyfriend out of the nut house. What do you want me to do?"

Trish gave him a big smile now. "I don't know yet; just for you to say that. I know where you are and I'm working out a plan."

Alistair got up, pushing himself off the wall. She grabbed his hand and squeezed it.

"Thanks man, sorry for bringing up Ceri. That was way out of line. It wasn't your fault, you know."

Alistair had to look away.

*

Alistair dragged himself back to the moment, back to the four tacks blurring in front of his eyes and away from girls long dead.

They had met eight or nine people in the Coach House, including whoever Ebin was dating this week. Now everyone was spread between three ashtray-loaded tables. Ebin was involved in a speed-fuelled debate about who would win a fight between a zebra and a giraffe, completely ignoring his punky new girlfriend, who was concentrating on her pout. This one was called Amy apparently.

Clancy sat next to him and was busy chewing his lips while chain smoking. All around the table, there were a lot of in-depth-looking conversations going on. That and sniffing.

Alistair sat down rather more heavily than he intended, banging his knee and putting an elbow in a pool of beer. The girl next to him turned and smiled, not in a nasty way, but more in a trying to share the joke kind of way. Alistair assumed that she was friends with Ebin's punky new squeeze.

Alistair felt he should strike up a conversation and ask her about school or something, but nothing came to mind. The only girl he ever really talked to was Trish and now it looked like she would be going.

He didn't know if what she said had been serious, but in a way he hoped it was. It would be good to be able to move on; he'd been stuck in the past for a long time.

The girl kept glancing at him. Alistair though thought sod it to coming up with conversation topics. Instead he sat back in his chair and let the concoction of voices sweep over him, the booze and pot turning it into a pleasurable buzz.

Everybody, except pouty in the corner, seemed happy, which in turn made Alistair feel happy. He was changing, becoming a better person. Hadn't he turned down speed tonight? One step at a time and all that.

It was then that the most captivating girl he had ever seen walked into the bar and Alistair did start to change.

10

Trish left her spot in front of the pub a few minutes after Alistair had gone. She felt bad about bringing up Ceri like that, but getting Bongo out of the hospital was her only concern. Then they could get on the road and get away. Those thoughts were for later though. Right now she needed to get a bed.

The Hare Krishnas hostel was about twenty minutes away and Trish hoped it wasn't full for the night. Having to move back and forth between the two hostels was a pain in the ass. However, with all the media interest and police pressure at the time, it had probably been the judge's only option.

Trish hated it though; she never felt safe walking through town at night. Dog didn't like town either; he was sticking close to her, his tail and ears were low, wheels squeaking slightly.

"Always go down the back alleys," Bongo had told her once, as ever his voice was close, reassuring. *"It's the best way to avoid all the wankers."*

She missed him; she wanted him here now. They'd be together soon though. Bongo was getting better. Hadn't he seemed better last week as they walked through the hospital gardens? And even if he wasn't totally better, he only needed to be well enough to jump the wall. Then they could both just disappear somewhere. She had almost a grand and a half stashed in her childhood savings account; money from Alistair, money to give them a head start.

Trish came to one of the many alleys that dissected the city

38

centre. She hesitated, looking into the darkness, willing herself to go on, but strangely deciding against the idea.

It was odd. Trish normally wouldn't have thought twice about going down there.

She turned, intending to carry along the road, but a fight spilled out from a pub and she didn't want to walk past it. She stepped into the darkness, feeling more hesitant than she ever had before. Dog, seeming to pick up on her vibe, let out a little whine before following.

Trish slowly walked further and further into the darkness. The noise from town deadened by the alley's damp walls. Behind her the street was already curving away out of sight.

Trish jumped sideways as a bin bag rolled, like the first stone in an avalanche, off a large pile of other ones. It settled in the middle of the puddle-cracked lane.

Dog should have made her feel better, but the mutt was flaky at best. Sometimes it would be nervous, other times aggressive. The vet said it could be post-traumatic stress; Trish thought it was flashbacks.

Dog rubbed himself against her leg before going ramrod straight. Even in the darkness Trish could feel his change in demeanour. He let out a low growl, guttural and fierce, before charging off into the darkness.

Trish followed him, an incredible *let's get the fuck out of here* feeling pervading her. She could hear Dog's wheels squeaking off somewhere in the distance, followed by some frenzied barking, a yelp and then… silence.

"Here boy, come back to us," she shouted. "Keith, call your fucking dog."

Trish didn't know where the name Keith came from, but it sounded a manly enough name to keep people away.

Behind her there was a noise of a bin bag being kicked. Trish increased her pace.

"Keith, call your dog."

Light footsteps started following her.

She ran, fear travelling up her spine. The footsteps broke into a run.

In front of Trish the alley opened out onto a deserted street.

Fifty feet away.

Forty-five.

Forty.

Thirty-f—uck.

Creatures exploded, purple around her. Grabbing and clawing. Dog was barking wildly from somewhere. Trish hit the pavement. Blows rained down onto her head.

Then weightlessness. An incredible feeling of weightlessness. In her semi-conscious state, Trish thought that this was it, this was death, just a peaceful floating sensation.

"I think I hit her too hard," a voice said.

"Just be quiet and pick your end up more," another voice said, puffing with exhaustion.

They stopped; she heard a car door opening.

"Come on, come on," a third voice was ordering.

Trish was bundled into the back of the car. Forced down into the footwell, one of the men's legs sprawling over her. The smell of Dog pervaded her nose. His frightened whimpering was close to her ear.

"Is this definitely the one?" the third voice asked.

"Of course it bloody well is. Now come on, I need a drink."

"Ok, ok… What on earth?"

Trish heard a thump on the roof, followed by smashing glass. Her next sensation was being forced down deeper into the footwell, as the car accelerated away.

FOUR DAYS LEFT

awn was cresting over the hill, soon to burn away the fingers of river fog shrouding the valley below. Even though his centre didn't open until ten, Franklin London had already been awake for two hours. He noticed there was a nip to the air this morning; winter was on its way.

Getting up early was a hard habit for Franklin to break. For sixty-five years he had risen before dawn and put in a full day's work on the farm, regardless of whether there was a nip to the air or not.

That had all changed though. Between the monopoly of the supermarkets and the interest on bank loans, his farm had been losing money hand over fist for years.

So he and the wife had diversified. Marjorie had always loved to bake and opened a small tea shop. This, as Franklin reflected, was a blessing at the time. It had been important to keep busy rather than brooding over the death of their son.

Franklin had diversified too, becoming the biggest exporter of wolves' piss in Wales.

Franklin's spurs chinked on the cobbles as he walked across the paddock. Behind him, in the large wire enclosure, were ten, now fed and watered, wolves.

Some people thought it was strange that Franklin always dressed as a cowboy. It was not as if the wolf centre was particularly Wild West orientated, situated as it was in the Gower. It was just that, now he had diversified, Franklin could, except for the early mornings, cast off the shackles of farming life.

Franklin had always loved cowboys. Once a year on his birthday, his father would take him the fifteen-mile journey into Swansea. There they would have a meal in the Cardoma before going to the pictures. They were black and white in those days and for two shillings you could see a movie, ride on the tram, get a bag of chips and go on and on about how cheap everything was. Out of all the films Franklin had seen, he loved Westerns the most. He'd got more than one beating for lassoing sheep instead of working.

That's why he kept the wolves. It was the idea of freedom that went with them; the same freedom cowboys must have felt. A more complicated man might have thought they were making up for the lack of freedom you got having worked on a farm for sixty-five years. Franklin London wasn't that complicated though – he was a farmer.

Besides, the kids loved the wolves, which meant the parents would pay the admission price, let their sprogs go on the adventure playground and eat his wife's cakes.

Franklin could understand why kids loved the wolves. They really were amazing creatures. He turned to admire them again. They padded around their cages restless, slinking back and forth as if waiting for there to be an opening in the fence. The years of capture had not dulled their memory of freedom one iota. The big alpha male stopped padding and stared down across the valley, his ears pricking up. In the distance an expensive-looking car was coming up the waterlogged track, spraying mud in its wake.

Franklin London sighed; it would be another one of those idiot drug dealers, he thought.

2

The back of his car fishtailed out, bringing Karl Reno back to the moment. Karl should have been tired; he hadn't slept for the last twenty-four hours. What time had he left the club? About three? About four? Something like that. With the amount of coke Karl had sloshing around his system, time kind of lost its meaning. He'd been doing over a ton all the way along a series of deserted motorways, before passing Swansea, getting onto the smaller country roads and then, finally, turning up this muddy farm track.

He really was fried; looking at himself in the driver's mirror he realised how dishevelled he was. The well-tailored lines of his new suit were crumpled, he had bags under his eyes and a nose that was redder than it should be. Even his hair, which was normally perfect, seemed to be greased flat.

Karl knew he had a long day ahead of him and had been trying to keep his buzz going, but doing a line off the steering wheel at 120 mph was quite tricky.

The new suit had been worth the money. Karl believed strongly that you had to spend money to make money. It had been a successful night in **[REDACTED]**, Batty Boy, Daryl and the rest of their crew had obviously been impressed, and now Karl was on the brink of something big. Finally, he could bypass his boss and all those other morons working for him like Danny and Zach the bloody Mac. All it took was a little bit of time, the right clothes, the right attitude and the patter – definitely the patter.

He had spent a long time last night chatting with Batty Boy and Daryl in the roped-off section at the back of the club. All of them getting loaded on champagne and coke, Karl impressing upon them the business they could be doing together. Just how ripe Swansea was for an influx of hard drugs. Hard drugs and coke – definitely coke.

It was a different world in **[REDACTED]**. The way that crew dressed and carried themselves made them look like the serious players they were. It was light years away from all the idiots in Swansea. As Karl powered his car around another mud-saturated corner, his mind drifted back to the way Tony, one of the meat heads working for the boss, had smirked at his new haircut. *"Fucking hell, son. What are you trying to be? A camp Rod Stewart impersonator?"*

They'd all learn though; there was going to be a reckoning. Yes indeed, Karl was going somewhere and it wasn't just to pick up ten gallons of wolves' piss from that inbred fucking farmer.

3

Fifteen miles away and about four hours later, Alistair woke up feeling like crap. Ebin's base snoring was coming from the bed. Alistair, by passing out in it, had opted for the couch. He pulled a half-smoked joint off his t-shirt, stared at it, before shrugging and sparking it up. He quietly smoked while fingering the large burn hole in his top, unable to get up the energy to be annoyed. It had been a really, really good night for a Wednesday in Swansea.

*

Dora's Nightclub lay on the edge of the docks and was a ten-minute shamble from the Coach House. A hundred years ago, the building had been headquarters for some grand company that had splashed its affluence all over the ornate, granite-fronted building. Eroded letters on the pillars proclaimed *"Belgium–Congo Trading"*. Above the entrance was a statue of some stern-looking dude in a waistcoat. The old gripper's legacy had now been turned into the sweat-dripping, sticky-floored, neon-lit shit-hole known, without much affection, as Dirty Dora's.

On the way down there, Alistair had taken up station at the back of the group. He found his eyes lingering on the girl who was going to change his life. She wore a black dress that radiated more class than was normally seen in Dirty Dora's. The dress complimented her long, flowing black hair, but it was the smile that was really captivating. She had the most amazing smile; it reminded Alistair of things past. He was walking a little way behind the girl and just couldn't stop his eyes drifting back to her. She walked on her own slightly out of the group.

This new girl didn't seem to fall into any of the well-defined categories as Ebin's lot. She wasn't a heavy, a Goth, a punk or a college kid; she was just there looking beautiful. In the pub Alistair had noticed the quiet confidence that she seemed to possess. Even meeting a large group of amphetamine-loaded drunkards hadn't seemed to make her uncomfortable or concerned, unlike most of the nervous little things Ebin seemed to go for.

As they walked towards Dora's, Alistair was amazed at the effect she had on everyone. The boys had become louder and more primal, whereas the girls had become poutier. Ebin and Clancy became involved in a play fight, which lasted until they got to the club.

Alistair had remained aloof from the ritualistic cock showing; he was sure that girls preferred blokes who weren't rolling around in the gutter. Besides, he was still worried about Trish and the bruises on her face; they had looked really bad.

The Breeders were playing from the speakers as they entered Dora's.

As happened every Wednesday, Alistair only remembered how much he hated clubs when he got in them. He couldn't dance, lacking both rhythm and, weirdly enough, balance. Ebin reckoned he danced with the rhythm of an albino.

Alistair also hated spending his evening screaming over the music into someone's ear. Luckily they were able to get a table at the back of the club, away from the dance floor and the four huge speakers.

Over the years of Wednesday nights in Dora's, Alistair had developed a very specific role; he always seemed to get lumbered with everybody's coats and bags, while they went off and danced.

Alistair had been rolling a joint with Clancy when she came over. Clancy's eyes lit up, convinced that she had been impressed with his wrestling skills. Alistair just felt a bit sad. If he had a penny for every time girls approached him, eye lashes a-fluttering, to get a free smoke, he would have around thirty-three pence.

The girl sat down next to them and blessed Alistair with one of her smiles.

"You're Alistair, right?" she shouted, close to his ear.

He had nodded.

"Can I borrow some skins?" she asked, pulling out a large lump of pot.

*

Alistair sat on Ebin's couch smiling at the memory, letting his brain wander back over the events of last night, putting them into order and savouring each bit. The music had become slightly more muffled as the club filled up, so they didn't have to shout.

Her name was Maggie. She had said this demurely, dropping her eyes and explaining it was the favourite prime minister of her parents. Maggie really did have a lovely smile and she had used it a lot as they talked and got stoned for most of the night.

If it wasn't for his aching head and the shaky, pukey, hungover feeling he had, everything would be great. Great, except for a nagging feeling he had forgotten something.

There was definitely something he had to do.

*

He had been wrapped in conversation with Maggie for over two hours.

Maggie – the more he said the name the better it sounded.

She had been in the middle of telling him how she wasn't a student, but was thinking about it next year. She hadn't been back in the country for long as she'd been travelling. Alistair noticed her features cloud over when she mentioned the travelling; he was going to ask what was wrong, but something told him not to.

That was when Lettuce fell on them.

Lettuce also worked for Danny Howells and could be best described as a rat-faced, little turd. He leered at Alistair and Maggie before giggling and scuttling away.

"Cool, I found you," Ninja said, walking up.

Wherever there was Lettuce, there was Ninja, Ninja being the dominant half of the double act.

"Great," Alistair murmured unenthusiastically, while making frantic *fuck off I am talking to a girl* signs with his head.

If Maggie thought anything of the meeting, it didn't show on her face.

There were a couple of reasons why Alistair didn't want to talk to Ninja and Lettuce that night. For a start, he would rather be talking to sweet, wonderful, out of his league Maggie. Also, there was that sliding scale women kept in their heads. As Alistair understood it, you started off at a certain level, but every time you did something stupid, like fighting in the street or talking to Lettuce, you would slide slightly down the scale. No matter what you did after that, whether it was flowers, chocolates or candle-lit serenades, you could never get back to the original level.

"Nah, man, I'm glad we found you." Ninja smiled, his wonky teeth looking green under the neon light. "Danny told me to tell you something…" He paused. "Danny said there is a…" He paused again, his face looking strained, as he tried to remember the exact message. "There's a geography lesson around his, tomorrow at ten."

Lettuce confirmed, "Ten in the morning."

"What? A geography less— Oh, you bloody idiot," Alistair moaned.

Lettuce had messed up, big time, on their last run to pick up pot in **[REDACTED]** and this was Danny's way of punishing them all.

The clock on Ebin's video showed well after ten as Alistair remembered this. With great difficulty he dragged his sorry ass off the couch. Ebin, being technically unemployed, had nothing to do until that evening's round of dealing, so Alistair left quietly, dragging the bastard's duvet off him and hiding it in a cupboard.

Alistair liked geography, but not at ten in the morning and not because Lettuce was a moron. What choice did he have though? When Danny Howells got an idea into his head, it stayed there, like shrapnel. Danny Howells was definitely the kind of chap you didn't want to annoy and Alistair was worried because he was running so late.

His head ached as he hurried up to his room to find a coat. It was then he noticed the blood all over the doorframe and handle of the nutter's room. Alistair tiptoed past it, rushed down the stairs and over the pile of unopened junk mail. He burst out of the front door and straight into two men.

The men didn't move.

"Your face looks nasty, Detective Stone," Alistair said politely to the shorter of the two. Alistair hadn't seen either of these bastards for a while and noticed how Stone was looking older.

Detective Stone gave him a maniacal grin in return.

"Hello Alistair," Detective Keyes, the larger detective growled, an air of menace behind his politeness. "I was wondering if you could help us with our inquiries."

4

"He's a big gentleman? A bit shorter than me, wears a lot of camouflage?" Detective Keyes asked.

"Top of the stairs, it's the door with blood all over it," Alistair directed, before rushing past them.

The Keystone Cops watched him stumble off up the hill, before shrugging at each other and entering the house.

Stone went in first, still mucho-pissed; his left eye was purple and swollen shut. Stone hated taking cuts and bruises home to his wife. And he really hated explaining to their daughter how *silly daddy had walked into a cupboard again*.

Stone also hated to be outdone by any of the shit-heads in this city.

Even back as a near-raw recruit, Detective Stone had hated to be outdone. Two weeks into the job, he and his puppy walker had been alerted to a burglary in a block of flats over in Dyfatty. They'd got there fast, getting up the stairs and out onto the landing as the suspect was leaving the premises.

The suspect had run back inside with Stone right on his heels. The burglar had got onto the balcony before trying to make a three-storey jump. Stone had followed him over the railing without hesitation.

"What the hell were you thinking?" his training officer had shouted, between puffs, when he'd finally got downstairs.

"I'm never going to let one of these idiots do something I

can't," Stone had replied calmly, while underneath him the idiot thrashed around holding his legs, white bone showing.

And really that was the mantra for Stone's police work. You can never be outdone, outpaced, outthought by any of them.

That's why they had the powerful-looking green car tricked out to be the fastest ride in town. That's why most people thought he was an utter bastard and that's why he was here now.

Keyes ducked his head under the doorframe and followed his partner up the stairs, already braced to pull him off the recently identified Donald Gooberman.

Identifying Donald Gooberman had been one of the easiest half-hours of police work in his career.

*

Detective Keyes had got back to the station after searching the area around Zach's house for the, as then, unidentified assailant.

Stone had wanted to stay out longer.

"Look, I reckon that he's gone to ground along the railway track somewhere," Stone insisted, as they stood in the middle of the road.

Around them, onlookers were rubbernecking the blazing house.

"I mean he couldn't have gone far, not with me stabbing him like that."

"That was quite nasty actually."

Stone just pointed at his eye; it was already starting to close from where he had been punched.

Keyes looked at his watch; *the ambulance and fire engine should be here by now.* "Look, we'll keep the crowd back and wait with Zach," he said, absentmindedly prodding with his toe the prone, handcuffed body lying face down on the road. "Then, when we get back to the station, we'll find this guy."

The flames, blown by the wind, were starting to spread to the neighbour's house.

Keyes was beginning to wish he hadn't told radio control not to rush getting the ambulance and fire engine here.

"We can't go back to the station," Stone said, gingerly touching his face. "Brogan will want to know what happened to me and why you decided to burn down all these houses."

"Look, it was that lunatic who set the fire."

"Yeah, but you were the one saying 'Oh no rush, like, boys' when requesting the fire engine."

"That was only to annoy Zach."

"I don't think he heard you. In fact, I think he might be dead."

Luckily Zach wasn't dead. He was possibly brain dead, but not proper dead. They took off the cuffs and rolled him into some semblance of the recovery position as an ambulance pulled into the cul-de-sac. The ambulance was followed closely by a fire engine.

The Keystone Cops stood around for a while being berated by a short, stocky, moustached fireman. He was wittering on about the number of houses they'd have to damp down and how another crew would be needed out here.

"I'm bored now," Stone said, dismissing the fireman. "I'm going to the hospital with Zach. You deal with Brogan."

Keyes knew his partner really wanted to go to the hospital to see his daughter; she'd been taken back in a week ago. Even so, he couldn't help being peeved at getting lumbered with all the paperwork.

Keyes had driven back to the police station to get an ID on the GI Joe-looking suspect and to hopefully avoid his boss, Chief Inspector Brogan.

It hadn't been hard to find Donald Gooberman.

Starting with the theory that their vigilante friend was probably well known to Social Services, he hit the phones.

"Hello Social Services? My name is Detective Keyes. Do you have someone on file that is around six foot five, very violent and likes to dress up as Rambo?" he asked cheerfully. "You do? And he's recently been released from hospital back into the community? Well, isn't that great."

Armed with the name and address of Donald Gooberman, Keyes was mid-dial to his partner when three raps on the door stopped him.

"I am glad I caught you," Chief Inspector Brogan said, entering the room.

Brogan was a short, balding bird of a man; he looked a lot like Clarence Boddicker. Stone, who got the reference, would always mutter *"bitches leave"* when they were dismissed from his office.

Keyes' heart sank. He should have left the office as soon as he had got off the phone. Now he was going to be stuck writing out a report for two bloody hours.

Brogan loved paperwork – things written down, crossed, dotted and duplicated. Often, he would explain at length about the necessity to meticulously document their actions, *"as it was important to always be above reproach"* – officious little twat.

Everything about Chief Inspector Brogan was officious, from his immaculate suit to the pens lined up on his desk, to always knocking three times on their door. Stone reckoned he was gay. Not a camp sort of gay, but the type that had a lot of Nazi memorabilia and would strap you down in a pig-snouted leather mask.

"I have had the fire chief on the phone and he does not seem happy," Brogan said, looking at Keyes over his glasses.

Keyes always found it hard to keep eye contact with his superior. The man had exceedingly hard eyes. He started to say something, but stopped as Brogan held up a hand imperiously.

"I informed him that I would not discuss the matter further until I had received a report from the attending officers. As one of those attending officers, Detective Keyes, I expect that report on my desk in the next hour." Brogan turned to leave. "Oh, I also expect a written update on the Post Office robberies."

Keyes watched Brogan disappear before putting his head on the desk. Stone normally did the typing.

Between, ever so slowly, typing up the two reports, he put off his partner from finding Donald until the morning.

"Spend some more time with your kid, then go and see the missus; I'm stuck here for a while," Keyes said down the phone.

Stone had ranted and sworn, but not that much.

*

So here they were hunting down Donald Gooberman. The trail of blood leading up the stairs helped. The house was dirty and smelt of stale pot smoke. Normally, Keyes would have enjoyed rousting Alistair and intimidating the fuck out of whoever else lived here, but, with the look in his partner's eye, he decided to leave it. In a way he felt sorry for Donald. If Zach hadn't been beaten up so publicly and if Stone hadn't been hit in the face, they'd probably not be visiting now.

They walked silently up the stairs, as close to the wall as possible, limiting creaks from the floorboards – *Donald, we're coming to get you, son.*

At the top of the stairs was a door covered in dry blood.

Stone turned to his partner. "We should knock," he whispered loudly, a crazy-ass smile flecking across his face.

The door splintered under the weight of his boot, before he charged in screaming. Keyes followed, having to duck under the doorframe.

The room was bare except for a few pieces of furniture, a broken mirror and puddles of drying blood. Keyes sighed, before leaning back on the wall and watching as his partner trashed the room and swore.

anny Howells lived on a rough estate at the top of a fuck-off winding hill – Swansea was pissing covered in them. Townhill hadn't always been a bad area though. Once there had been a community, a culture of everyone being in it together. Then somewhere in the eighties, around the time of Thatcher, that had changed; everyone became in it for themselves – changing a community into something akin to a shanty town.

Alistair pushed open Danny's squeaking garden gate and walked down the steps to the prefab council house, his head throbbing. He took a moment to compose himself by Danny's expensive, armour-plated door. The door was, by all accounts, bomb proof, riot proof and, most importantly, police battering ram proof. As usual it was open.

The fact that no cloud of pot smoke enveloped Alistair as he entered the house meant the lecture hadn't got into full swing yet. He walked through the tidy little entrance hall into Danny's lounge and was met by four pairs of stares.

Danny had arranged all his furniture around a blackboard. Lettuce and Ninja were slouched down on the settee, giving Alistair stinking looks. Kieran, the other runner, was sitting straight backed on a chair, looking bored. And then there was Danny – squat, hard Danny, dressed as always in a tracksuit. He was bald, which accentuated his odd-shaped skull. Alistair guessed callipers had been used at some point during his birth. Overall, Danny had the appearance of a perpetually annoyed PE teacher.

Danny was already halfway through a bottle of sherry and didn't seem too happy at Alistair's tardiness. Alistair flopped onto the nearest chair and gave everyone his biggest and best shit-eating grin.

"Right, now we are all finally here," Danny said, looking directly at Alistair, "I can begin the lesson."

Everyone shuffled around in their seats, preparing themselves for a long morning of watching Danny getting drunker and drunker whilst talking crap. It was his way of punishing them for the cock up they had made. Or, more correctly, the cock up Lettuce had made.

*

It had been on their last big drug run. Alistair despised their big drug runs. Once every two weeks he had to get up early, along with Lettuce, Ninja and Kieran, to catch a train to **[REDACTED]**. They would carry an envelope stuffed with money and a load of plastic squash bottles filled with wolves' urine.

After running around for a couple of hours in **[REDACTED]**, they would make the return journey. This time loaded down with enough blocks of pot to make a decent-sized igloo.

The day of Lettuce's cock up had started off as usual. The four of them were squeezed, knee to knee, around a table in the packed train. Alistair was up close against the window, trying to ignore everyone else. He was wondering why they always had to use a train. It was one of Danny's half thought through ruses. Danny reckoned that with the drug-filled duffle bags they would pass for students going home for the holidays. Looking at the other three sitting by him, it was unclear what Danny's idea of a student actually was.

When they had first got onto the train, Alistair had offered to look after the money, but Lettuce had just laughed at him, saying that he could carry the wolves' piss instead – he could be wolves' piss boy today. Lettuce said this before climbing over Ninja, whose head was buried in a martial arts magazine, and stumbling off towards the toilet for one of his "special" cigarettes.

Alistair sank down in his seat and regarded the bottle of vodka Lettuce had left on the table. It was going to be a long old day and it would, as Alistair theorised, pass quicker if he was drunk.

Lettuce was quite a while in the toilet and when he returned Alistair had to blame the ticket collector for drinking most of the vodka. Ninja looked up from his magazine and offered to help Lettuce get him if he came round again.

Luckily the guard didn't come round again and, a mere four hours later, the little group made it from the train to the station bar without incident.

As per normal, they had to spend a long time in the bar waiting for the payphone to ring and for a gruff voice to give them an address.

Alistair was sipping his third pint, which, combined with the vodka, was making him feel woozy. Ninja and Kieran were keeping themselves entertained by frisbeeing beer mats across the bar at a table of students. The students were trying not to make eye contact – *perhaps they are going home for their holidays*, Alistair thought.

The payphone by the bar rang as Lettuce stumbled out of the toilets, having had another one of his "special" cigarettes. Alistair, rather unsteadily, got up to answer the phone and scribbled down an address.

They headed out from the station in a cab.

Two minutes later they were screaming back to the station in order to find the envelope of money Lettuce had left in the toilet.

*

Nick Forbes was hurrying away from the train station. A lot had happened to Nick that morning. The journey down to his job interview had been intolerable. There had been four drunken yobs sitting across the aisle from him, who had spent most of their time arguing over a bottle of vodka. Nick was going to call the ticket inspector, but the ticket inspector seemed somehow the subject of the argument.

Then, after arriving in the station, he had been met with an hour delay to the London train. Dispirited, Nick had waited on the platform, knowing that he still had time to make it to his interview. An hour later it was announced that the delayed train was now actually cancelled. Fuming, Nick got up and went to the toilet, before finding someone to complain to, in the strongest possible terms.

It was there in the toilet that his luck seemed to change. Entering the loos, he nearly bumped into one of the lunatics from the train, the little rat-looking one. While washing his hands, Nick had noticed the bag on the floor. Part of him was wary, remembering the threat of the IRA. However, the bag was open slightly and semtex wasn't normally stuffed in an envelope, nor did it have the Queen's head on it.

What should he do? He didn't need to count the money to tell there was an awful lot of it. All the options flashed through his mind. Should he take it to a guard? Or to the police? Perhaps there was a secret camera somewhere and this was one of those TV programmes. Nick breathed in deeply and licked his lips. It was probably something to do with those people on the train. He was sure the small rat-like one had been carrying a similar bag. *Bugger it*, he thought. Bugger it and bugger them. He licked his lips again, before picking up the bag, walking straight out of the station and towards his first ever proper beating.

*

Lettuce was quiet and pensive in the taxi. He had fucked up big time. If he didn't get the money back, Danny would go mental at him.

"Where did you leave it?" Alistair asked again. Danny would go mental at them all.

"You're in so much shit," Kieran warned, stating the obvious.

Alistair could tell that secretly Kieran was loving this. He held himself in higher regard than the others and as such viewed this as their fuck up rather than his. He was like a mini version of that Karl Reno prick, with the same attempt at snazzy fashion and annoying supercilious attitude.

Ninja was looking scared as well. Scared and angry. "Stop the cab," he screamed, flinging the door open and leaping out before the car had come to a halt.

Alistair watched in horror as Ninja ran up to some posh-looking guy in a suit and carried out a really vicious assault, before grabbing something and diving back into the taxi.

"I saw him looking shifty and almost running away from the station." Ninja laughed, holding up the bag in delight. "Clever, eh?"

Alistair was looking at the crowd gathering around the man on the ground. The man looked like he had a nasty head wound. The crowd was looking and pointing at the taxi. Alistair realised that they weren't moving.

The taxi driver was staring, open mouthed, at them in his mirror.

"Oh we're students; it's a game we play for rag week,' Alistair blurted.

The crowd was coming towards them.

"It's called find the bag, Tristan over there on the floor had it, but now we do," Alistair babbled as way of explanation. "We get sponsorship," he finished lamely.

The crowd had surrounded the taxi.

"*Fucking move,*" Ninja shouted.

The taxi jumped forward accelerating away into traffic.

"This is Simon. He does media studies."

"Do I look like a fucking student?" Ninja said.

Alistair figured at least twenty people had taken the taxi's registration. So they'd swapped vehicles twice before arriving at the address he'd been given.

The address they got the pot from always changed. Alistair guessed that there must be a stream of similar people coming and going throughout the day. He also got the feeling that his lot always came last.

This time they pulled up in front of a non-descript terraced house in a non-descript terrace. After double-checking the address, Alistair knocked.

Lettuce fell through the front door when it was opened.

A smartly dressed black man, with the incredibly thick neck of a bouncer, ushered them into a small lounge. Two other well-dressed and very large black men sat around, smirking slightly. The lounge was all brown, orange and seventies-looking. Alistair noticed a picture of an overweight middle-aged couple and their podgy son on the mantelpiece and he hoped there wasn't a family gagged and duct-taped upstairs.

Lettuce smiled at them. "This place smells of cereal," he announced as way of a greeting. "Can I have some cereal?"

Everyone stared at Lettuce.

Alistair didn't like the **[REDACTED]** guys. They thought they were big league and he guessed they probably used words like *professionals* or *businessmen* to describe themselves. This, in Alistair's opinion, was a sign of watching too many gangster films.

He remembered how enthralled Karl Reno had been when he used to do the runs with them. The plonker had even started wearing suits and sunglasses.

Ninja, still staring at Lettuce, put the bag on the table.

Alistair plonked his bottles of wolves' piss on there as well. The contents of which would soon be winging their way around the world, splashed over numerous illegal cargos in order to scare off any sniffer dogs.

The lounge was starting to get hot and claustrophobic.

Normally the whole process lasted about ten minutes. Their

money was counted, before being taken away with the wolves' piss. After that a phone call was made and then the drugs arrived five minutes later. This meant the drugs and the money were never in half a mile of each other at one time. This cut down on the repercussions of being raided or the chances of someone trying some sort of silly-bugger double cross.

That was the way it normally happened.

This time though a thought struck Alistair – no one had actually checked inside the bag Ninja had taken. He had a flash forward to the big men opening it up and a load of dirty washing falling out.

Alistair made a split-second, alcohol-fuelled decision and dived for the bag.

This elicited the wrong reaction all round.

Everything happened quick-draw fast.

The *professional businessmen* went for the guns under their long coats.

Ninja, bless him, was across the room in a second, his butterfly knife open and against the biggest fuck's eyeball, throwing star aimed at another one.

Lettuce too moved with incredible speed and had his Stanley knife against the thick neck of the black guy who had let them in.

Kieran, rounder bat raised in the air, was calculating their odds and looking scared.

Alistair managed to slide off the table and land upside down on the floor. He unzipped the bag slightly and peered inside, before looking at the scene he had created.

It seemed strange to Alistair. You go twenty-three years without seeing a real gun and then three are pulled on you all at once.

He stood up very slowly, all eyes on him. "I was just checking," he said, gingerly placing the bag back on the table.

Silence filled the room.

"You're a hell of a twat," Lettuce laughed retracting his blade.

"What do you reckon, Batty Boy? I think these boys need some better weapons," one of the *gangsters* growled.

"Complete fucking amateurs," the one known as Batty Boy agreed, before removing the gun from Ninja's head.

"I'd have taken your fucking eyes," Ninja promised, slowly folding the knife and stepping back over an upturned chair.

Alistair would later admit it was quite a cool scene.

A very long ten minutes followed before they were outside the house loaded down each with a duffle bag and rucksack full of pot.

Alistair had jumped at the idea of going to the pub in order to settle his nerves.

It had been around then that Lettuce had cocked up, leading to a pissed-off Danny giving them this geography lesson.

It was only when they found a pub, and piled the bags of pot under the table, could Alistair relax and stop shaking. It was the first time he had ever seen a real gun, let alone had one pointed at his head.

Lettuce too must have been affected by it all, at some rat-like level. He suggested that they all drop some acid to get over the shock. Alistair had tried to take control, saying it would be best to leave off the acid until they got home. Lettuce had shared a wink with Ninja before saying that Alistair was right.

Halfway through his second pint, Alistair went to the pub's very nice toilets. Returning to the table, Lettuce and Ninja were giggling expectantly, with Kieran just sitting there in his normal aloof way.

Alistair sat down. "Look the police," he said, pointing out of the window.

Everyone turned, not noticing Alistair deftly switching the pints.

"Oh sorry, it was just a van." Alistair shrugged gulping down the pint.

"Nice drink?" Ninja enquired.

Alistair fixed him with one of his biggest and best shit-eating grins. "Yes, it really was, thanks."

"Fucking hell, man, you've just had four drops of acid," Lettuce announced, bouncing up and down with excitement, his rodent-like features contorted into a look of pure joy. "We got you, you've been dosed good and proper," he laughed, downing his pint in jubilation.

Kieran just shook his head tiredly.

"Four drops?" Alistair asked, sounding concerned. "How many have you guys done?"

"Two each." Lettuce bounced. "It'll be a fun ride home."

"Yes, it will," Alistair agreed.

It was an hour later, waiting for the train home when Lettuce disappeared with his rucksack and duffle bag full of pot. His only goodbye message being, "Look at my fingers."

A day later Danny received a phone call from a panicked Lettuce asking where he was.

"How the fuck should I know?" Danny had screamed down the phone.

*

Hence the geography lesson.

"Before we start you'll need this," Danny said to Alistair, passing him a clipboard and some crayons.

"For fuck's sake," Kieran mumbled to himself.

Danny was deliberately treating everybody like they were pupils in the sort of class that the teachers called special, but everyone else called rems.

They had to copy a map of Britain from the board and then colour it in with the crayons. Alistair enjoyed this. He coloured the land green and the sea blue. Danny had polished off the sherry by this time and was merrily getting into the swing of teaching. He checked all their maps, complimenting the little sailing boat Alistair had drawn, bobbing just off the Isle of Wight.

Their next task was to label Swansea in red and **[REDACTED]** in yellow. Danny also made them label where Lettuce had ended up.

It took Lettuce three attempts to label Swansea on his map. After his second attempt he started giggling. This annoyed Danny who threw the empty sherry bottle at him.

After Lettuce had finished picking bits of broken glass off himself and gotten the right place on the map, Danny made them all draw a train. They all drew one of the old types, with lots of steam coming out of the top. Kieran thought all this was below him, as he demonstrated by the poor standard of his colouring.

After being made to take notes about train routes and timetables, they had a test. Even Lettuce passed.

Ninja got annoyed that Kieran and Alistair got the highest marks and accused them of cheating. This riled Alistair as he had nearly done A-Level Geography.

Danny, who by now was jollied full of booze and slurring his words, calmed everything down. "Boys," he said, "you're all winners. Except for you, Lettuce, you're a little prick."

6

Pastor Morris was staring through his grubby office window, across the overgrown cemetery. He felt tired having not slept all night. He felt scared.

The graveyard looked bleak with many of the long-neglected gravestones pointing at higgledy piggledy angles. The pastor caught his pale reflection in the grimy glass and thought, not for the first time, how much he'd changed and again questioned if he could be as strong as he needed to be.

Donald had appeared late last night banging at the hostel door. The pastor had been alone at the time.

Pastor Morris walked through the deserted building and opened the metal door. Donald stood in front of him, camouflage fatigues soaked through with blood and his eyes wet from crying.

Donald seemed even more distressed than the first time he had come to the hostel.

"She's gone; they dragged her into a car," he sobbed, crumpling forward for a hug.

The pastor stood there, gingerly hugging back, his clothes soaking up blood, thinking that Donald wasn't doing well in the guardian angel stakes.

He had taken Donald up to his office and calmed him down as

best he could. The big man looked shrunken into himself, with tiredness and probably lack of blood. Between sobs Donald told how he had failed Trish and how the figures in purple cloaks had dragged her into a car.

After Donald had finished recounting his story, the pastor had to sit on his hands to stop them shaking.

❋

Pastor Morris turned away from his gaunt reflection and regarded everyone in his office.

"I have brought you here as time runs short," the pastor said, looking over the three men.

Aled stood in the corner of the room, dressed in an old army surplus coat, as always with that far away, startled look on his face. Aled's sandwich board was propped in the corner, annoyingly covering the bank of monitors. Today it proclaimed in large black letters:

THE
LORD
COMETH

Internally, the pastor despaired. He had explained at length to Aled the danger that they would soon be in and, as tools of the Lord, they would have to be sharp, ready and alert. Despite this, Aled still insisted on having at least two hours a day in the town centre, with his sandwich board, handing out leaflets and generally being ignored.

Next to Aled, sweating heavily as usual, was Brother Dowling.

Taking up most of the room though was Donald, still looking sheepish from his failure to protect Trish.

Stretching the gardening analogy still further – if evil was a weed, these three were the gardeners. The pastor sighed inwardly at this thought.

Donald haltingly told them about his attack on the pimp and how he had lost the knife to one of the policemen, who had, in turn, given him the cut across his chest. Whilst recounting this, Donald didn't make eye contact; he just stared down at the woodworm-rife floor.

The pastor couldn't have cared less about the pimp; it had been little more than an exercise to test Donald's mettle. After seeing the state of the pimp in the hospital and from Aled's report about the gutted house, Donald would be a useful, if yet blunt addition to God's tool box.

"I am sure we can do you a little better than a knife in future," the pastor said, sharing a look with Aled. "How did you escape from the police?"

Donald went on to describe his sprint in front of a train and his successful use of camouflage and less successful use of fishing line.

"I then sneaked into my mum's garden to leave all my stuff, before going back out," Donald said.

"Why did you sneak back out?" the pastor asked.

He knew the answer, but needed Donald thinking – thinking about all the little details so nothing of importance was missed.

"Mum wouldn't have let me go back out again," Donald said, a childlike lilt entering his voice. "But I needed to make sure Trish was alright. The friends of the man I beat could want revenge on her."

"Do you think the people that took Trish were friends of the man you beat?" Pastor Morris asked.

"No, they were different."

"Where did you start following her from?"

Donald paused, his brow crinkling. "I can't remember."

"Damn it," the pastor snapped, slapping the desk. "Who in the name of hell do you think you're talking to, slouching like that? Now you stand up straight and you pull yourself together. This isn't a game; this is a girl's life and if you want us to save her, you'd better be a man."

Donald snapped to attention. "Sir, yes, sir," he shouted a few decibels short of a bellow.

"Where did you start following her from?" the pastor repeated, pacing now.

"Sir, I failed to rendezvous with her outside the hostel, sir." Donald was standing ramrod straight. "I located her outside the Coach House pub and followed her from there."

"How did you know to look for her there?"

"Since I have been following her, she meets Alistair outside of it every Wednesday night."

Ah, something he didn't mention before, the pastor thought. "Who's this Alistair? How do you know his name?"

"He's her friend." Donald shrugged. "They talk for a while and then she goes off. I know his name because he's one of the people living in the house I was staying at."

"What does he do?" Brother Dowling asked.

"I think they all deal drugs," Donald said.

"Did he give her any?" Brother Dowling sounded concerned.

"No, I saw him give her money though."

"What happened then?" Pastor Morris asked.

"They talked for a while before she headed off towards the Hare Krishna hostel."

Aled muttered under his breath at the mention of the Hare Krishnas.

"I followed behind her through town, but my cut had opened up and I started to fall behind. Then she went down one of the alleyways." Donald was starting to sag and go all sad-eyed again. "Trish always walks fast through town at night."

"Why would she go down a dark alley?" Pastor Morris barked.

"There was a fight in front of her, on the street, some men outside a bar."

The pastor nodded – continue.

"It's then I saw them. A car pulled up really close to the mouth of the alley and two men got out and ran after Trish before the car drove away."

"Describe them."

"I only saw them for a second and they all wore purple hoods and cloaks."

Pastor Morris looked at Aled and Brother Dowling. Dowling was sweating more heavily and suddenly looked scared. Aled, well, Aled just had a little smile twitching across his lips.

The pastor turned back to Donald. "Did anyone else see them?"

Donald shook his head. "Everyone seemed to be watching the fight. I ran after her down the alley as fast as I could. When I got there Trish and her dog were being dragged into a car. I jumped on the car and I think I damaged the windscreen, but then they just sped off."

"Can you describe the car?"

Donald's brow furrowed for a moment. "It was big, one of those Land Rover types, I think."

The pastor looked like he was going to shout again, but his features mellowed. "Thank you, Donald. You look exhausted. Go and lie down in the dormitory."

He would make him run through the story again, but it would do for now. After all, Donald was going to have a busy day tomorrow.

"We won't find her alive," Aled said, after Donald had left.

Pastor Morris considered this for a moment. "Time does indeed grow short for her, but we are not done yet. You saw the state of Trish. Those bruises she had on her face – they wouldn't like to kill a beaten girl." Pastor Morris smiled reassuringly, looking at them both, judging the two men.

Aled, he could tell, was getting himself keyed up, excited for the fight to come. Brother Dowling though remained silent, probably going over whatever Trish fantasies were washing around inside his dandruff-covered head.

"But it is important to remember we are on the side of God," Pastor Morris continued. "Also I think it is a matter for the police to get involved with."

71

"Go to the police?" Brother Dowling gasped, taking his glasses off and rubbing his forehead vigorously. "They are not to be trusted. You have said so yourself," *rub, rub, rub,* "you wouldn't have been chased out of your last parish so readily if the police had not been in league with them." He shook his head in disbelief. "And now you want to go and advertise where you are and what we know?"

The pastor smiled, outwardly calm. "Our friend Donald will be the one to go to the police. His little stunt yesterday has made him known to them. Hopefully they will look for her to find him."

Aled and Dowling looked at him blankly.

The pastor held back another sigh. "It's not so easy to kill someone when the police are looking for them." He smiled his reassuring smile again.

"What if the police are in on it?" Brother Dowling asked, his thick lips quivering.

"At the moment there is nothing to tie Donald to us," the pastor said before pausing. "And, in the grand scheme of things, he is expendable."

7

K arl Reno pulled up outside Danny's house, running late. The farmer had insisted on going through, in detail, how to spread the wolves' urine correctly and how long it lasted before the scent faded. Karl couldn't give a shit. He hadn't given a shit the first time the farmer had told him or the dozens of times since then. He had, as he always did, just paid the hundred and fifty quid and opened his boot.

"For that much money, you can load the piss into my car yourself," he'd told the goofy-looking inbred while glaring over his sunglasses.

In turn, the farmer had just glowered.

He'd then gone home to shower and change, but must have just crashed out, waking, twenty minutes ago, still dressed in his crumpled suit with greased-flat hair.

Now here he was outside Danny's council house on this shitty estate. Reno wasn't even happy parking his car here, which was stupid; Danny's house should have its own insurance grouping.

Danny Howells was another fuck-up in a city of fuck-ups. He still lived on the same estate he had been born on, probably even in the same shitty house – Karl couldn't remember.

The boss always said how Danny had the balls and the attitude to go far; it was just that he lacked the brains and, now with age and a kid, the will.

Danny was quite happy being a big man on this shitty estate, making a modest living and being left in peace. To Karl that was a life worse than death. There was a city here for the taking.

Karl looked at himself in the rear-view mirror before getting out of the car.

He was a star in the ascendance.

*

Last night Batty Boy had said the same thing to one of the girls squeezed into their VIP booth.

"This man here's a star in the ascendance," he had shouted over the thumping base, smiling at Karl.

Karl had never been in a VIP section before. Karl hadn't even been in a club that had a VIP section before.

Daryl leaned forward chinking glasses. "In the ascendance."

One of the girls, model-pretty, started kneading Karl's crotch under the table.

Karl had driven down to **[REDACTED]** earlier that evening; Karl drove fast. Once there he had spent thirty minutes, fucking around, in the city's one-way system, before finding the Indian restaurant where they were meeting.

Batty Boy wasn't alone; he sat at a table in the back with another equally well-dressed man.

Batty Boy offered him a seat and introduced him to Daryl. "This is the guy I've been telling you about," he told his friend.

Karl smiled and gave Daryl a firm handshake, no nerves at all, the coke having bulldozed its way through that weakness.

Daryl regarded Karl for a long moment, seemingly weighing him up. Daryl could have been about forty, but it was hard to tell. He had a perfectly trimmed pencil beard and a thick gold watch that probably cost more than some of the houses in Swansea. To Karl both of these men radiated wealth and sophistication, the kind of things that Karl ached for. Even Batty Boy, who must have been the same age as Karl, looked and acted like he was from a different world. Karl couldn't help but feel that Swansea was struggling in some Second Division while the guys from **[REDACTED]** were in the Premiership.

They ordered and talked, asking Karl about Swansea and the layout of his organisation. To Karl it felt like the final job interview.

Daryl did most of the talking, his outward friendliness belying an inward mocking hostility that, between the coke, the compliments and his base stupidity, Karl failed to pick up on. A mistake he would soon be bitterly regretting.

Later, during dessert, Karl had asked Batty Boy, "So who exactly do you work for then? Are you guys like Yardies?"

Both men fell silent.

"Do we look like fucking *Yardies* to you?" Daryl demanded, suddenly turning nasty.

"Well, no," Karl stammered. In all honesty unsure what a Yardy actually looked like.

Batty Boy started laughing, breaking the tension. "No, man, you could say we're just one big happy family."

*

Karl knocked on the heavy metal door. The boss had insisted it be put in and had, eventually, bought it as a Christmas present for Danny. It was Kevlar-coated, reinforced steel, with a peep hole, seven dead-locks and a security chain. The damn thing was tank proof, bullet proof, bomb proof and, as usual, open.

"Oh, it's you." Lettuce grinned gummily as Karl entered the now smoky room.

Karl despised Lettuce.

The talk Danny had been told to give seemed to be over. Karl looked around the room in disgust; all the idiots were seated around a kiddie's chalk board with a picture of Britain drawn on it.

Karl wanted to smack his forehead in despair.

Everyone grinned at him.

He despised them all.

"This is it, is it?" he asked Danny.

"What do you mean?" Danny replied evenly.

"This… this is the talk the boss asked you to give these morons?" He gestured at the board. "What the fuck is it?"

"Ask us where we go to get the drugs from," Alistair piped up, noticing how tired Karl looked and also the white speckling over his crumpled suit.

Karl Reno was another person with too many gangster videos in his collection.

Karl turned to him with a look of disgust on his face. "What did you say?"

"Ask us where we get the drugs from," Alistair repeated, slowly and clearly, in the voice he reserved for halfwits. "Look, I'll show you," he said, getting to his feet and barging past Karl, who was a couple of inches taller than him.

"Can I use your pointer?" he asked with an over-exuded air of politeness.

Danny gave a little bow and a smile before handing it over.

"Right, this is where we are now. And here is where we go to get all the drugs and drop off those bloody bottles of piss." Alistair smacked the little board as he said it. "And now…" Alistair surveyed the room. "Ninja, how would you get from here to there?"

Ninja smirked at Karl before taking a moment to look at his notes.

"I would use a train," he said, after a brief pause.

Everyone except Kieran and Karl laughed.

"And you think this is acceptable, do you?" Karl spluttered at Danny.

"They know what their job is," Danny retorted, bored. "Now don't you have something for us?"

"The bottles are in the car."

"Well, go and get them," Danny ordered with a dismissive gesture.

"I'll help," Kieran said, before following Karl out of the door.

"Piss boy," someone shouted after Karl.

"How did it go in **[REDACTED]**?" Kieran whispered eagerly, as they walked out to the car.

"It went well. They're a good crew and it's on."

"When?"

Karl turned around to make sure there was no one around. "We'll talk later." He grabbed hard onto Kieran's arm, pulling him close. "You need to stay cool about all of this."

8

onald swallowed his nervousness as he entered the police station. Pastor Morris had told him there was no need to be nervous.

The pastor was a very kind man. Earlier, when Donald was called back into the office, Pastor Morris had complimented him on how well he had done hurting that pimp and how they needed him to help Trish again.

Pastor Morris had explained that Donald would need to go to the police station.

At first, Donald had been against it. The policemen he had met recently hadn't conducted themselves in the way policemen should – one of them had stabbed him.

Both the pastor and Brother Dowling had soothed Donald, explaining that this was the only way.

The rest of the morning had been spent instructing him on exactly what to say and how to act when he got there. Pastor Morris had, for some reason, been very specific about not mentioning the fact that the men wore purple robes.

Donald walked up to the front desk and smiled, exactly as they had told him. The sergeant behind the desk had grey hair and looked a lot older than those other two policemen he had met. Donald thought he was probably too old to catch criminals now.

"I would like to report a missing person," Donald announced loudly and clearly.

"Would you now?" the sergeant asked slowly. "A missing person, you say?"

Donald noticed the sergeant was backing away slightly.

"If you would like to wait in the room behind you, sir, I will ring the detectives who deal with missing person cases," the sergeant said, picking up the receiver.

The pastor had told Donald something like this might happen and not to go into any room or wait around longer than was needed.

"Her name is…" Donald tried to continue, only to be stopped by the sergeant holding up a finger to quiet him.

"Her name is…" Donald tried again.

"It's Sergeant Johnson here from the front desk. There's someone here who'd like to see you." The sergeant smiled at Donald, pointing to the room again. "A missing person case… it's got everything to do with you and your partner. Now if you could hurry because the large gentleman is wai—"

The sergeant had difficulty in finishing the sentence as Donald reached over and ripped the phone out of the wall.

"The missing person is Trish Reed. She has been kidnapped and needs to be found quickly or bad things will happen. She was meant to be staying with the Hare Krishnas, but never made it to them." Donald talked faster, backing towards the door. "She is five foot seven with pink hair and a dog with wheels instead of legs," he finished, before running out the door.

The sergeant hit the alarm.

Donald watched from some bushes on the roundabout as the two policemen from yesterday burst out of the station and looked around wildly for him.

9

Karl Reno leaned out of his car and pressed the buzzer; he waited for a moment before pressing it again. Nothing happened.

"Look, I know you can fucking see me," he said into the camera, which was mounted above the mansion's high and wrought iron front gate.

The camera just stared down.

Karl pushed his hand down on the horn knowing it probably couldn't be heard up at the house.

After a few more minutes of swearing and honking, the gates finally swung open. Karl flicked a V at the camera, before driving up the lengthy driveway to the front of the house. A metallic blue beamer, which Karl didn't recognise, was parked on the gravel by the fountain.

Tony and Ivor, the boss's two assistants/guard-dogs/enforcers/gate-operators stood outside the house. They were both dressed in tailored suits, their muscles bulging like puppies in an Armani sack.

"Where the hell have you been?" Tony demanded. "The boss has been trying to get hold of you all night."

"He's not in a good mood," Ivor chipped in. "Someone beat up Zach and put him in a coma."

"Where is he?" Karl asked, trying to push past the two.

"He's in hospital; they rushed him in yesterday."

"Not Zach, the boss."

Tony put out a barrier-like arm. "He'll see you in a while; he's got some proper people he's talking to at the moment." Tony put the emphasis on the word *proper* while rolling his eyes – he could multitask.

"Poor guy's house got burned down as well," Ivor continued. "He really liked the house. Do you remember how happy he was when he bought it?"

"He'd even plumped for the platinum package," Tony agreed.

"It really was a nice house." Ivor nodded.

Tony and Ivor lapsed into a moment's silence for the house. Karl walked past them and into the lobby.

Mardy Davies was a poor kid done good. He had been born and brought up on the same estate as Danny, but now lived a stratosphere above him. Mardy had his sticky little fingers into more pies than that fat kid from the nursery rhyme.

Mardy, like a lot of people who had suddenly made money, thought he knew how to flaunt it; from the tiger fountain outside, to the hallway that was on a par with an Egyptian burial chamber. Mardy wanted you to know he was rich.

Karl went through the hall and into the lounge-cum-waiting room, helped himself to a drink from a crystal tumbler and stood by the window.

From the lounge he could see across the well-kept lawn into the swimming pool. Mrs Mardy Davies was in there doing laps, her blonde hair tied back and feet hardly breaking the surface. Karl sipped his boss's expensive brandy and watched his boss's expensive wife.

Emily Davies came out of the pool and put a big towel around her. Turning towards the house she saw Karl and flashed a coy little smile at him. He raised his glass to her, only turning when he heard voices in the hall. The boss was seeing off his visitors. Karl stayed out of sight; the boss didn't like *proper* people to see his other employees.

Karl watched from around the corner as farewells were

exchanged. The three *proper* people looked as overweightly-opulent as his boss. Mardy would be giving them his best bone-crushing handshake.

A few minutes later the boss came into the lounge. He was wearing a silk smoking jacket, a large unlit cigar stuck in his big, fat, moustached face.

"Right, lad," he said, heartily smacking Karl on the shoulder before leading him into his office and sitting down behind his expansive mahogany desk. *"Nice bit of tropical hardwood this,"* he had said when it had first arrived years before.

"You took the piss around to Danny's?"

Karl nodded.

"And Danny has told them how to be proper representatives of our concern."

Karl had never heard his boss use the word business. Whether it was the supply of pot, the women Zach ran, the backroom gambling, that crappy club in the docks or that time three years ago they had taken a heroin dealer out on that boat and weighed him down with all the chains in the world – it was always a concern.

Karl paused for a minute. "Well, Mr Davies, the idiots will know better than to get lost with that much product again."

Mardy nodded.

"Look, to be honest, boss, you'd be better off restructuring it. We could get better people to do the work."

Mardy Davies cut the end off his cigar using the miniature gold guillotine on his desk, the end falling, Anne Boleyn-like, into a little basket.

"That's the point; they are all idiots and they work for next to nothing. As long as Danny is keeping a rein on them, we'll leave it at that." The boss changed the subject. "We tried to get in touch with you last night; where were you?"

"I was with this new girl I've been seeing," Karl said, his lie practised.

"Courting, eh? No wonder you look so tired." Mardy laughed loudly at his apparent joke. "I presume the boys told you what happened with Zach. Now, Tony rang the hospital this morning and he's regained consciousness, so take the boys down to see him and find out who did it and why. Everything is going well at the moment, so I want to find out why my boat is being rocked." The boss lit his cigar. "Those men who just pulled off in that expensive-looking car are property developers; they are looking at doing up all of the docks. Turning all those old buildings into nice new flats. They used the word *gentrification*, which was a word I'd not heard before. Do you know what it means?"

Karl started to open his mouth.

"It means a lot of money to whoever owns land down there. And as you know, I own this city." Mardy blew a self-congratulatory smoke ring. "So I don't want there to be any sort of rocking of my boat."

Karl got up to leave.

"And take some flowers or something for Zach. The poor guy lost his house."

10

There was a small amount of grey light pin-holing its way through unfamiliar curtains as Trish drifted awake. She felt sleepy; her eyelids were heavy and started to close again. If only she could roll over and get more comfortable; it was just that her arms seemed to be stuck.

Trish groaned, before forcing her eyes open and trying to tug her arms free. They wouldn't budge. She tried to call out for Bongo, but didn't have the strength; her throat was just so incredibly dry.

Things started coming into focus a bit.

It was the same pretty room, with rose-pattern curtains, she had been dreaming about – at least Trish thought she'd been dreaming. There were a lot of thoughts and questions trying to form in her mind, before dissipating again, like smoke blown through cotton wool – if only she wasn't so tired.

Where on earth was she? Where was Bongo and Dog? Why did her arm ache? She concentrated hard. Bongo was still in the mental hospital; Trish remembered that much. She also remembered leaving the hostel. It had been dark and she'd been the last one to leave; everyone else had gone without her. Bongo would never have done that.

Dog had been outside prancing and wheeling, all his doggy friends were gone and he was happy to see her. Together they had left the hostel and then… then? Alistair. She had seen Alistair, smiling with those sad eyes of his.

It was after she had left him that something else had happened; what was it? She couldn't concentrate anymore.

As Trish slipped back into unconsciousness she wished her arm would stop hurting and that Bongo was with her.

11

Alistair staggered out of Danny's house, accidentally wasted again, having spent the last three hours getting stoned and drunk. Alistair wished he'd been like Kieran who had made his excuses and left early. This wasn't part of his twelve-step programme.

Danny, sherry-full and weaving, had eventually stood and thanked them for being so good during his lesson, but now it was time for them to all fuck off as he had business to do. Alistair assumed that the business in question was passing out on the sofa; a weakness that Danny would not show to his subordinates – because, to be fair, no one respects a quitter.

Outside, he had shaken off Lettuce's offer of going back to his for a mull, opting instead to go for a mooch.

Getting wasted and talking shit had brought back that all pervading, restless feeling. It had been gone for a while. Well, since the moment last night he had first seen Maggie smile. She had taken the feeling away for that short period of time and even now she kept bobbing up in his thoughts, pushing out the memory of the girl he had killed.

It was over three years ago now and it saddened Alistair that he had trouble picturing her face anymore. He remembered vividly, though, what she had done for him and, in turn, what he had ultimately done to her.

Alistair had gotten to know Ceri a lifetime ago. He'd been a different person back then; freshly kicked out of home, his emotions see-sawing between little-boy-scared loneliness to acting like a prick.

Heroin had been the drug at the time; the city was awash with the stuff. Alistair, skint and jobless, had started selling it; real small time like.

*

Alistair used to go round a dilapidated house, on one of the dilapidated streets above the city centre. That's where Moses Jones kept shop.

There'd always be a *waiting room* full of restless people, close enough to smell the stuff being cooked up next door. It never bothered Alistair though as he never touched it. Perhaps that was why Moses liked him, even though *liked* wasn't the right word. Perhaps in part Moses respected him as he was solely in it for the money.

Moses was bordering on being overweight, a fact highlighted by the skeletal look of most of his customer base. Alistair reckoned he must have been in his forties, but dressed, almost comically, like a teenager, with high-end, expensive tracksuits and badly bleached blond hair.

"Always make them wait," Moses told Alistair once.

Moses spoke with a cockney accent, sharp and clipped, rather than the slurred speak of those that surrounded them. Moses liked doling out these helpful tips. He saw himself as some Fagin-type character or more precisely as the other one from *Oliver*, the nasty one with the dog.

"Like, if you say you'll be there at three, get there at four," Moses said.

"Oh, I normally do that anyway, but not on purpose."

"Listen, son, this is a serious business. You have to use your nonce unless you want to end up in pokey."

Alistair had nodded sagely; pretty sure that *nonce* meant head and *pokey* meant prison. He really didn't want to be making money from selling this crap though. It wasn't a good thing to be doing, but he did it anyway.

Selling a little more.

Moses took him on mentor-like, tutoring him, telling him all about the trade, telling him everything – except who their actual boss was. Nothing more than a wink and *"Oh, Mr Big, he's in the car trade."*

Selling more. Selling a lot more.

Making money for Moses.

Making money for Moses' boss.

Dealing big time.

And then he met the girl he was going to kill. Ceri, poor Ceri.

*

Poor Ceri – for a while, she'd offered him a different way. Yet he was still here, still in this shit-hole city, still muleing around drugs.

Alistair decided he needed to go for a wander and think about where he was heading.

Movement over progress – get it carved on your *fucking* gravestone.

It was after wandering for a while that he found himself in the middle of town, fuzzy headed and having managed to think himself into a really bad mood. Alistair was debating whether to get some food when there she was, coming through the crowd, spotlighting him with that million-watt smile.

Maggie was dressed differently from last night. Her hair was tied back, drawing attention to her long neck. Alistair caught a flash of flat stomach, showing where her top ended and her trousers started.

He just drunk her in. She looked better in the daylight than in the club, which in itself was a rarity. This made Alistair feel incredibly self-conscious. He felt like someone who had slept in his clothes all night and, upon waking, had done a lot of drugs, which, of course, he had.

Their eyes met through the crowd.

"What are you doing here?" he found himself spluttering.

"Stalking you," Maggie said, looking serious. "Whenever I meet someone in a club I start to stalk them." She started to blush. "Sorry, that came out scarier than I meant it to. God, you probably think I'm some sort of freak now," she apologised. "I'm actually heading home. I stayed at my friend's house last night, remember, Bethany?"

Alistair didn't.

"Well, now I've got to get a bus back home."

Alistair remembered how she lived out in the sticks. "No car?" he asked.

She shrugged. "My parents can be a bit weird and they don't let me drive their car at night."

"Bummer," Alistair said, before realising no one said bummer anymore.

A silence started to stretch, one of those silences when you are waiting for someone to say anything; so Alistair did. "Hey, I was going to get something to eat. You want to come and watch?"

That got a laugh and they fell into step together.

Alistair told her that he had had fun last night.

Maggie said she still felt a mess.

Alistair said she looked beautiful before catching himself.

She blushed and bit her lip – *isn't it sweet when girls do that?*

They got a sandwich, which Alistair offered to pay for. Maggie said it was unusual to still meet a gentleman, but not to worry as he was on the dole.

Alistair nearly laughed in her face; he wanted to say, *"I'm loaded; you don't think I shift all those drugs around for free, do you? Three years of this shit and I've got a stack of money sitting in Danny's safe. What do you think my outlays are? Food, booze and giving money to a homeless girl because I'm racked with guilt."*

Instead he just said, "Thanks."

Maggie and Alistair sat outside, in the weak sunlight, by the new, expensive council-built mini-amphitheatre. Originally, it had been a small flower garden, a bit of green in a lot of grey, but people being people, had made it stink of piss and strewn it with condoms. Hence the new concrete mini-amphitheatre.

They sat on the top step watching the ollie-ing skateboarders, who, much to the disgust of the local paper, had taken it over.

"Thanks for last night," Maggie said, between mouthfuls. "You're the first person I have talked to properly since I got back from abroad. It was fun." She paused. "It's just living out of town and not knowing anyone anymore, it was... well, I enjoyed it." She smiled at him; not one of those great million candle ones, but a softer sadder one.

The girl sure had a lot of smiles.

Alistair felt he should say something, but only crap came out. "You know why they wear those chains, don't you?" he asked, indicating towards the skaters.

Maggie shook her head.

"Tiny dogs," he continued, between the mouthfuls of sandwich.

"What, like Chihuahuas?"

"Oh no, much more muscular than the simple Chihuahua. They use terriers. Just pull them out of their stupidly baggy trousers and they're off being pulled up hills and stuff."

"What if the dog sees a cat?" Maggie asked.

It was a good point that Alistair hadn't thought about before.

After the food, they wandered around the town centre, holding hands. It was weird, but they just got up and held hands as they walked. It was just so... so nice.

Finally, they arrived at the run-down, pigeon-guaned bus station. The buses out to banjo-country left from the far end.

She held his hand as if waiting for something.

The queue of people started getting on the bus. Alistair paused before, clumsily, asking if she wanted to go out.

"Where would you take a girl in this fair city then?"

Good point; he hadn't thought it through that far.

"There's a comet storm forecast and Ebin reckoned it would be worth seeing. Shit, no, that's not a good date."

Maggie smiled coyly. "That sounds like it would be a great way to spend a first date."

Isn't it sweet when girls say that?

12

"Look whose ride I'm about to vandalise," Detective Stone said, excitedly.

He double-parked, before trotting across the road, oblivious to the horn of an ambulance.

It was the first thing that had been said since they'd left the police station. Donald Gooberman had managed to piss Stone off big-time. The fact that a six-foot-five mental patient, daubed in camouflage paint, was not only able to run around their city but walk into their police station and nonchalantly report a missing person made them look bad.

*

They had been sitting in their cluttered little office when the phone had rung.

"A missing person? Fuck all to do with us," Stone had said dismissively, before sitting up alert and signalling for his partner's attention. "He's what? Keep him there, we'll be down now."

By the time they had charged through the building, the alarm was going and Donald had vanished.

It did not look good.

Chief Inspector Brogan had used those exact same words twenty minutes later as he paced back and forth behind his unnaturally tidy desk, occasionally looking at the two seated detectives.

Stone was sure that having them sitting while he stood was another bloody management technique. It meant they had to look up to him. Brogan was full of those little tricks. The man was born to be a bureaucrat, from his propensity – or perversity – for correctly dotted and crossed paperwork to the pencils arranged to square drill exactness. The guy really needed to be blown.

"It does not look good," Brogan had scolded them. "A man wanted in connection with a serious assault walks in here and then just walks out again."

"Johnson, on the desk, described it more as bolting, sir," Stone corrected, before loudly slurping his coffee.

Stone and Keyes always stopped for coffee when summoned to their boss's office. That was one of their anti-management techniques, as was the slurping.

Brogan ignored them and carried on pacing. "This is the sort of thing that leads to the lack of confidence so prevalent amongst the public today."

Stone and Keyes shared a smirk. It meant their telling off was coming to the end. Brogan always finished on this topic; he was very big on the idea of public confidence in the police.

Brogan sat down. "Who did this Donald Gooberman report missing?" he asked, staring directly at Keyes.

The big man found himself looking away; Brogan had a stare that bored into you.

"According to Johnson, he reported a homeless girl missing. Her name was Trish Reed."

"That's the girl who was beaten up by Zachariah Plum," Stone chipped in.

Keyes noticed a flicker of something unreadable across their boss's face.

Brogan nodded. "And did he say who kidnapped this girl?"

"Apparently, all he said was men."

"Did he say how long ago this happened?"

Both detectives shook their heads.

"In that case, that can go on the back burner for now. Your priority, as of this moment, is to find this Donald Gooberman and then place him under arrest."

"But, sir, surely even if he is insane, the report of a kidnapping should be looked into," Keyes said.

Brogan sighed condescendingly. "You have enough to do without concerning yourself with an unverified report from a wanted fugitive with a history of mental illness."

"But, sir—" Keyes started to protest.

"Between your woefully unsuccessful investigation into those Post Office robberies and now this vigilante roaming the streets, a homeless girl's disappearance comes pretty far down the list of priorities."

Keyes stared at him. "Sir, a kidnap comes pretty high on my list." It came out in a growl.

"Detective!" Brogan barked, hitting the table hard. "The girl is a non-person in this city. Kidnapped? She's just been beaten up by a pimp for God's sake. I am not wasting man hours looking for a homeless prostitute who was seen getting into a man's car."

Keyes found himself standing, fists balled.

Brogan stared up at him not flinching.

Keyes felt his partner's arm round him restraining.

Pulling.

"We'll get on to Donald, sir," Stone said.

Leading.

They were outside now.

"Easy, buddy," Stone chided. "We'll find Donald and see what he actually saw."

Keyes hit the wall, taking out plaster.

13

Donald had stayed secreted on the traffic island for an hour, before slipping away and heading back to the chapel.

As instructed, Donald took his time to get back, making sure he wasn't followed by anyone. He entered the chapel grounds via the back. He had to cross some allotments before slipping through the hole, which Al had shown him, in the rusted iron railings and creeping into the graveyard.

Pastor Morris was waiting by the altar with Al when Donald entered the chapel. Al's sign was leaning against a pew; it said:

> # GOD IS
> # COMING TO
> # GET YOU

"You did well at the police station," the pastor told Donald after he'd recounted his experience with the police. "But there is still a lot of work to do. Aled, I think it is time that you show Donald around our operation and get him fully fitted up. Meanwhile, I have got to get Brother Dowling prepared, in case we get a visit from the police."

Al grinned at Donald. "You're going to love this."

Donald followed Aled through the church and into the hostel. Al pulled back a worn bit of carpet and opened a trap door. He led Donald down into the dank, spider-webbed basement. It was very dark.

Al turned to Donald, close to him now. "The pastor is a great, God-fearing man and he trusts you. Otherwise we wouldn't be down here, but before we go any further, I need to know that you are fully committed to fighting evil." In the darkness his eyes seemed to glow. "If we go on further, then there is no way back."

"I am fully committed."

Al held his stare for what felt like an eternity, before turning and pushing hard against the wall. "Then let's go."

The false wall gave way to a clean, brightly lit corridor, which led downward for another fifty yards.

"We are under the church now," Al tour-guided him. "They converted the crypt during the blitz to store books from the city's library. We keep other things in it now though."

The end of the corridor was blocked by a thick metal door. The door reminded Donald of the ones you get on submarines. Al spun the well-oiled handle and put his shoulder into it. The door opened into a large cavern.

"It's something, isn't it?" Al went on. "Come in, this is our operation room."

On the wall was a big map of the city and countryside around it. Below the map was a large olive-drab radio. A shelf full of smaller radios, the size of backpacks, was next to it.

"These babies have seen action as far back as Malaysia; they're not new, but they're sturdy. We've run the antenna up onto the roof and can get radio cover for miles."

Al walked on, past a bank of monitors identical to the ones in the pastor's office.

"Over here we have got our medical supplies and, if push comes to shove, a rudimentary operating table."

Donald hadn't moved from the door. Al stopped and turned around, following Donald's gaze.

"Ah, and these are our weapons," he said hefting one of the machine guns off the table.

14

Zach the Mac, Big Daddy Z, the Beaten-to-a-Pulp Pimp, had spent the morning drifting in and out of consciousness, Donald Gooberman having reciprocated on him with interest.

Zach's jaw was wired shut, his eyes were blackened closed, both arms were plaster-casted up in slings and he was pissing into a tube.

The sound of the door opening and an argument entering the room brought him round.

"Look, bitch, I've told you, he's our brother," a voice, not dissimilar to that little prick Karl Reno, was saying.

Zach looked, through his puffy eyes, to see the nurse deciding. *Hey, if these three thugs want to be his brother I'm damn well not going to stop them.*

The nurse left, muttering about how their mother must be proud.

Zach sat up as best he could, which wasn't very good at all.

"Sorry to hear about your house," Tony said, the bunch of flowers looking tiny in his big paw.

Zach tried to talk, the wire round his jaw and lack of teeth making it difficult; Zach gurgled.

Ivor walked around the bed and bent over, putting one of his cauliflower ears close to Zach's shattered maw. He nodded for a moment before shaking his head. "No, they didn't manage to save anything."

In Ivor's line of work, you learned to understand what people with no teeth said, or at least the gist of what they were saying, which was normally, *"Oh God, oh God, no, not my fingers."*

Zach tried again. "Mmmm mmmmm mm mmm?"

Ivor shook his head. "They couldn't even save your car. I think one of those bastard coppers lit a rag in the petrol tank before they called the fire brigade."

"It really was a lovely car," Tony commiserated. "That Stone is a horrible piece of work."

"Right!" Karl nearly exploded; they were meant to be fucking gangsters, not some sort of gay and lesbian support group. "Who did this to you?"

"Mm mmm mmm mmm, mm mmmmm mmmm mmm mmmm mmmm mmmmmmmm mm m mmmmmmm."

"Just one man, eh?" Ivor translated. "He came over the back wall. He was dressed up like a soldier."

"Did you recognise him?" Karl probed.

"Mm."

"Are you sure?"

"Mm mmmmmm m'm mmmmmmmm mmmm!"

"Of course he's fucking sure. The guy was over six foot five and wearing army fatigues," Ivor snapped.

"Well, that will help for starters." Karl looked at his watch. He was done here.

"Do you remember that time we got wasted?"

The voice from the doorway made them turn.

"And there was that woman, who was hardly even a woman, more some sort of troll and I wouldn't have touched her with yours, but she was desperate, so we used that branch from the ugly tree? Well, she had triplets."

The speaker, one of the bastard coppers, was slouched in the doorway. Behind him, like a doorway eclipse, his partner stood, hatred radiating off him.

"Boys, it's your daddies," Detective Stone said, leaving the door frame, coming in then hugging both Tony and Ivor, blubbering about how he had missed them growing up; he then tried to check if Ivor had washed behind his ears.

The Keystone Cops knew all about this lot, knew about them like dogs knew about cats. There was one cat in particular they'd like to get to know a lot better, the oh-so-allusive Mr Mardy Davies.

They'd been close once, but nope, no cigar.

Stone finished hugging them all, before turning to the bed and letting out a scream. "Fuck," he cried, jumping back into the corner of the room, theatrically making his fingers into a cross.

Keyes followed him into the room.

"What the fuck is it?" Stone was shouting.

"Well, Detective Stone, according to this, it is Zachariah Plum," Keyes said, reading the clipboard at the bottom of the bed. "Apparently, he is suffering from a severe bout of the bumps. Jesus, Zach, it looks like your face has been turned into a giant twat."

The Keystone Cops never used their first names outside the office. It was another level of separation, another way of insulating themselves from these people.

"Right, you two," Stone said, to Tony and Ivor, ignoring Karl. "You know anyone about this tall, dressed up like Rambo, likes to make pretty fires?"

Tony and Ivor busily concentrated on the steel between their toes and the leather.

"It's what we were trying to find out," Karl said curtly. "Now do you mind fucking off? We are trying to visit our friend."

Tony and Ivor sidled away from him.

Outside at her work station the nurse looked up at the sound of splintering chair.

"Sorry about that, officer, it's just the young ones today… well, you know," Tony said.

"That's ok, Tony." Keyes patted him good naturedly on the shoulder.

"We brought you a present," Stone cheerfully told Zach, while proudly producing a plastic bag from his pocket and sitting heavily on Zach's legs. "It's your teeth."

Zach let out a groan.

"We had to pull some of them out of the pavement," Stone added conversationally, before getting up and putting the bag of teeth under Zach's pillow for the tooth fairy. Stone's smile faded, turning into a glare. "Who was that guy who gave me a black eye?"

Everyone stayed silent.

"Sod you then."

"We'll try something different," Keyes said, ignoring his partner. "Where is Trish Reed, that girl you beat?"

"Mmm mmm mmmm mm Mmmm Mmmm?" Zach mumbled through the metal in his mouth.

"You haven't seen her? Are you sure?" Stone chided.

Keyes leaned forward. "Listen, Zach, this is very important. Why did you beat her up?"

Zach just turned his head away. Keyes started to turn red, very subtly at first, but it didn't go unnoticed by Stone.

"Zach, you'd better help us or you'll probably need those bones reset again," he said, looking sideways at his partner, all humour having gone out of his voice.

Tony noticed too.

Tony, at some level, had principles and he didn't want to be helping those two vicious bastards, but he liked Zach and the poor guy had already lost all his stuff. "Is that the scruffy girl with all that shit in her hair? Looks like a gypo?" he asked, taking all eyes off Zach.

"If by *shit in her hair*, you mean pink dye? Then yes, that is the girl we are inquiring about," Stone said jovially, one eye still on his partner.

"Oh yeah, I heard someone gave her a little bit of a hiding," Tony continued. "Apparently, she had taken to begging outside the Central Hotel and getting arsy if none of the businessmen, going in and out, gave her money." Tony was picking his phrases carefully; he even made the scutty Central Hotel sound like an international five-star conference centre. "Well, as I heard it, this girl is really nuts, very highly strung and she gets in a fight with Brandy, one of the... ladies. Well, you know how women fight and they had to be pulled apart." He stopped to look at his shoes. "Well, somewhere in the pulling apart she got a little bruised."

"She got hospitalised," Keyes said coldly.

"Well, that was the last time she came close to the hotel," Tony finished. "And now we had better be off."

Tony and Ivor picked up the unconscious Karl Reno and walked out of the room, only to be called back in by Detective Stone.

"Not leaving the presents?"

They both came back in, putting the flowers and chocolates on the bed.

"Before you go, I want you to apologise to the nurse for lying to her about you all being brothers and calling her a bitch. If you don't I will come and get you and bring you back to do it," Keyes ordered gravely.

The big man was a stickler for manners.

"Bye boys, you be careful out there in the big world. Your daddy's missing you," Stone shouted after them, happily.

Stone turned to Zach. "Well, we should be off as well. Before we do though, you don't happen to know where the toilets are in this place?"

"Mm mmm mm mmmm mmmmmmm mmm'm," Zach begged.

Stone slowly lowered the bed covers.

"Are you sure? If you do know, just say."

"Mm mmm mmmm mm mmmmmmmm mmmmmmmmm," Zach swore, as Stone relieved himself.

"What was up with you in there?" Stone asked when they were back in the car. "I thought you were about to throttle that idiot pimp."

His partner remained silent.

"It's about that girl, isn't it?" Stone sighed. "Look, Zach put her in a pretty nasty way, but he's had his comeuppance, so that's over with now."

"She's still missing," Keyes said.

"Yes, but what can we do?" Stone asked. "Brogan told us to leave it and he's mad enough about the Post Office thing. So stop asking all these questions about this missing girl. I don't want to piss him off any more than we have already."

Out of the corner of his eyes Stone could see the big detective starting to huff.

Stone turned all pacifying. "Look, after we find Donald Gooberman, we can start looking for this girl."

Keyes still stared out of the window, arms crossed.

Stone sighed. "Ok, look, if it will cheer you up any, we'll find the kidnapped girl at the same time. But we really need to find this army nut job before those assholes," he said as they drove past Tony, Ivor and the still unconscious Karl Reno. They were trying to work out who'd slashed their tyres and put dog-muck under the door handles with a stick.

"Kids today, eh?" Stone shouted out of his window, before wheel-spinning out of the car park.

Keyes stayed quiet and mad, his mind elsewhere – *Trish, where are you, girl?*

15

"Her arm's starting to look bad." The male voice was tinged with anxiety. "I think it's become infected." He sounded middle class and middle age.

"I can't believe you even got a simple job like that wrong," a woman scolded. "For goodness' sake, how many times have you done it in the past? Surely it was one of the first things they taught you."

"Normally, when I put a needle in someone's arm, they're not trying to scratch my eyes out," the male voice replied defensively.

"It doesn't matter now anyway; she is only going to be with us for one more night."

"She was never meant to be here that long," the man complained.

"You saw the state of her face. We couldn't possibly go presenting her to everyone like that."

The man started to say something but was cut off.

"Look, it is important that we do things correctly." The woman tutted. "What on earth will everyone think if we make a pig's ear of this? I mean you've already lost her dog."

"The damn thing bit me as I was getting it out of the car."

"Good."

The conversation brought Trish around. She had been dreaming of Bongo and the last time they had been together.

It had been unseasonably warm that day, the summer having marshalled itself together for one last sunny burst. Trish remembered there was a slight breeze and smiles on people's faces. She'd visited Bongo on the ward and had been able to take him out for a walk around the hospital's well-manicured grounds, Warren, the large black nurse, following at a discreet distance.

Bongo had looked good. There was more colour to his face and he was putting some weight back on. She didn't like the way his hair was cut, but that would be an easy thing to rectify. Bongo had seemed more alert. He still didn't make eye contact with her or speak, but Trish could definitely sense that he was aware of what was going on around him.

As they walked along, next to the perimeter wall, Trish made a decision. Three years of this was enough; she could do a better job of fixing Bongo herself. Looking behind her, she saw the nurse chatting to a female carer, not paying any attention to them. Trish looked at the wall; it was only a seven-foot scramble. Bundle him over and then get away from this fucking city, with all its hostels, twats, drugs and fear. It was a great idea, but Trish knew it needed to be planned in more detail than simply giving Bongo a bunk up.

Later, after their walk, the nurse took Bongo away, leaving Trish in the best mood she had been in for a long time.

Just as she was about to leave, another nurse told her that the doctor would like a word.

After being led through a maze of corridors and up endless flights of stairs, Trish was ushered into Doctor Linton's room.

Being the head clinician meant that Doctor Linton had the biggest office at the top of the hospital. Overflowing shelves of textbooks took up each wall, which Trish, who had never been one for reading, ignored. Instead, she was drawn to the window; the view stretched across the grounds, over the oh-so-jumpable wall and down to the town and the sweep of the bay, which, in the sun, looked all blue and shiny.

"It really is an impressive view," Doctor Linton said, close behind her. He had a deep Welsh accent.

She turned to look at the diminutive, grey-headed man, who was dressed smartly in a suit.

He smiled, showing small, yellow teeth. "It is good to meet you at last," he said, holding out a hand.

Trish shook the doctor's hand, unused to such formality.

"Would you like to sit down?" he asked, gesturing to two chairs by the window.

Trish perched herself on the edge of the chair, feeling awkward at being treated in such a way.

Doctor Linton went on to talk about how Garrett was doing – no one in the hospital used the name Bongo.

The doctor spoke enthusiastically, reminding Trish of a little, Welsh Johnny Ball.

Garrett, he explained, was suffering from drug-induced psychosis, his behaviour, at present, being best described as a series of peaks and troughs.

"The troughs, if you like, are becoming shallower and Garrett is communicating with the nurses and patients better, which is a good sign." The doctor smiled kindly over his glasses. "Garrett is, of course, still very withdrawn and seems unsure of his surroundings, but the self-harm and violent behaviour have dropped off." He glanced at his watch. "Unfortunately, it is difficult to tell if this is an actual improvement or if we are finally getting the balance of his medication right."

Trish smiled to herself, convinced that the only medication Bongo needed was to get out of here.

The old coot continued, animatedly describing the medication they had been trying. Trish wasn't listening though; she was planning where they would go first, somewhere where the sea was always blue and shiny.

Doctor Linton finished talking and led her to the door. As she was about to leave he thanked her for sticking by Garrett so well, stressing how important it was to his recovery. He put a hand on her arm and asked, with a look of concern on his face, how she was and if there was anything he could do for her.

Except for Alistair, Doctor Linton was the first person to ask her that for a long time and the old geezer sounded as if he meant it.

"Yes, Doctor, I'm doing really well." She smiled, not adding, *now that me and Bongo are going to get out of here.*

*

"She's mumbling something about the sea," the male voice said.

"The drugs must be wearing off; we'll have to use the other arm this time," the woman decided. "Try not to get this one infected as well."

"You do it then," the man grumbled uselessly. "Damn, now I've forgotten the wipes to sterilise the arm."

"It's not really going to matter if you sterilise it or not, she'll only be here until tomorrow night."

"No, while she is in my house I have a duty of responsibility to her," the man said, leaving the room and closing the door.

"Excuse my husband; he's just a little prick with a needle," the woman joked.

16

Pastor Morris was in his office staring intently at the grainy black and white image on one of the monitors. The image showed Richard Dowling sitting in the dining room.

Brother Dowling had company.

The surveillance camera had been placed high on a cupboard and masked by boxes; they had done this just after Donald left for the police station. It gave a clear view, over Brother Dowling's thinning pate, of the two men sitting opposite him.

They had turned up at the hostel's front door, identifying themselves as policemen. He had, of course, been expecting the police to connect Trish to the hostel. It was just he hadn't expected them to turn up quite as quickly. If only they'd had more time to practise.

Brother Dowling had asked the policemen to come in and seated them screen centre; so far so good.

It was just when the questions began flying that things started to become undone. The pastor's second-in-command was looking as guilty as hell.

"We haven't seen her since she left that night," Dowling repeated, the camera's microphone making his voice oscillate piercingly.

"Who's we?" the smaller, wirier detective asked quickly.

It was the smaller detective who handled the introductions and had, so far, done all the talking. The pastor assumed he was the brains.

"Myself, or any of the other volunteers here," Dowling clarified, wiping his brow for the umpteenth time.

The pastor had debated long and hard about dealing with the police himself. He looked different now, but it would still have been a risk.

"And she would have gone straight to the Hare Krishnas' centre?" the smaller policeman asked.

Even on the tiny surveillance screen, the detective's eye looked badly bruised. Pastor Morris assumed that must have been the one Donald hit.

"Sometimes I wonder where these poor souls go when they are not here." Brother Dowling shrugged.

The policemen stayed silent; it stretched.

"Often they come here in a terrible state," Brother Dowling continued.

The pastor shook his head; he'd told Dowling, *Just solely answer what they ask, don't say more than you have to.*

"Did Trish often get in a *terrible state*?"

"Trish was… highly strung, whether that was from drugs it is hard to say."

The larger policeman leaned forward imposingly. "Are a lot of the people who come here on drugs?" he demanded.

He was the brawn.

"Once, a long time ago, it was heroin, but then there were all those deaths." Brother Dowling shrugged. "In a way it was almost a blessing in disguise. That horrible drug hasn't been a problem in Swansea since."

Another long silence stretched.

"Unfortunately, human nature being what it is means a lot of the people we cater for are… highly strung."

The smaller detective pulled something out of his pocket and placed it on the desk. "Have you seen this man?"

It was probably a photo of Donald, probably taken from the cameras in the police station. Even so, the pastor squinted, nose to screen, unable to make out what was on the desk. He cursed the primitive equipment he had been reduced to. In his last parish things had been so much different.

Dowling rubbed his glasses with a handkerchief, before picking up the picture. He studied it for longer than a glance, just like the pastor had told him to, before shaking his head. "Is he related to Trish?"

"We are trying to find that out," Detective Stone said, taking the picture back and subconsciously wiping his hand on his trouser leg.

The larger policeman gave his partner a sidelong look; Pastor Morris couldn't put his finger on what that look conveyed.

"How did Trish seem when you last saw her?" the large detective asked, softer than before.

He wants to concentrate on the girl. His partner just wants to get the person who hit him. It's the big one who wants to help Trish. He's a possible ally, the pastor thought.

"Again, highly strung," Brother Dowling continued. "She was very nervous. Trish had just come out of hospital and seemed very on edge."

"In what way was she nervous?"

"She wasn't happy to leave on the Wednesday night; she said there were men after her." Dowling left that hanging in the air, just like he had been told to by the pastor.

"Men?" the larger policeman asked, genuine interest showing on his face. "Did she think they were the same men who put her in hospital?"

The pastor re-evaluated him – brains and brawn; he had pre-empted the next thing that Brother Dowling was going to say.

"I asked her that, but she said no. She said there were three men in a blue car, a very expensive-looking Range Rover-type. Trish said she had seen them twice in the last day and she was scared they wanted her for something. Of course, I dismissed it at the time, thinking she just wanted to stay in the hostel, but now... You don't think?"

Very good, the pastor thought.

The other policeman fidgeted and looked boredly around the room. "No other description?"

Dowling shook his head. Pastor Morris had told him not to mention the purple robes. Not just yet.

After ten more minutes of questioning the smaller detective got up to leave. "Well, thank you for your time," he said.

"If you think of anything else here is my card," the huge detective said as he stood, his bulk filling up much of the screen.

Neither of them offered to shake Richard Dowling's hand.

"One more thing before we go," the smaller policeman said, turning around.

It was a hackneyed move, the pastor thought, *reminiscent of a Columbo episode.*

"Where is the preacher of the church this building is connected to?"

"Pastor," Richard Dowling corrected. "He's a pastor."

"Pastor then."

"Out among his parishioners, I would imagine. Pastor Morris is a very busy man."

"I'm sure that his parishioners are glad he is watching over them," the detective said, seeming to look directly at the camera.

t was dark when Karl Reno smiled into the camera and pressed the buzzer. This time the gates were opened straight away. He started the long walk up the driveway, having, at her insistence, parked his car three streets away.

His head still ached from being hit with the chair.

*

Tony had clucked over him while they waited for the RAC outside the hospital. Tony reckoned he needed a couple of stitches.

Ivor too came over and tried to prod the gash in Karl's face, saying if there were any splinters lodged inside the cut, his head could go septic.

Tony had nodded sagely in agreement.

Karl had told them both to *fuck off* and had waited in the car.

*

He bet the bastards were all having a good old laugh at him tonight. Tony had said the boss wanted to go to the casino. He could see Mardy now, sitting in one of the private rooms, all red-faced and sweaty, smoking one of those huge cigars and playing for high stakes against saps. Mardy, with his little entourage and a couple of the girls from the Central, drinking scotch and talking about what an asshole that Reno kid was.

As he walked up the driveway, Karl fumed at this image. They were all idiots, especially the boss – backward-looking fuck; holding on to the past like it was important. The business was ripe for expansion. *He should be implementing the ideas I come up with instead of laughing at me,* Karl seethed.

Things were going to change though and after his successful business meeting down in **[REDACTED]**, things were going to be changing very quickly indeed.

*

He had met Batty Boy a year ago, while trying to supervise the idiots on one of those chaotic drug runs. Every part of it was all just so, well, amateurish, even down to using the train. Karl hated trains.

"Look, we could drive down," he'd told the boss.

Mardy had just shaken his head, before leaning forward and conspiratorially tapping his nose. "A car could be stopped by the police, whereas they never check trains."

"What the fuck are you talking about? They never check trains?" Karl had wanted to shout. *"That doesn't make any sense."*

He had held his tongue though and bided his time.

Karl didn't have to bide for long, as it was on that trip, after a hellish four hours on the train and a squashed taxi ride, that he had met Batty Boy.

Karl had been impressed from the moment he saw him, standing in the lounge of that day's house, all aloof and supervisory. Karl reckoned that they were about the same age, but realised that he was about ten years behind in everything. Take the fashion stakes, for example: although simply dressed in a black cashmere sweater and jeans, the cut and quality of Batty Boy's clothes were a world away from what Karl was used to.

Karl couldn't help feel like some sort of provincial bumpkin in comparison. Indeed Batty Boy hardly bothered to contain his contempt as the Swansea boys fell through the door.

It was as they were leaving that the courtship began.

The idiots were lugging the merchandise out, when Batty Boy had put his hand out stopping Karl and said, "We don't just sell this shit," while pushing something into Karl's hand.

From the hall there had been a crashing noise as Lettuce's bag took out a shelf-worth of china.

Intrigued, Karl had pocketed the gift until they were on the train heading back to Swansea. Leaving the idiots to get progressively more wasted, he had gone to the toilet. There he had opened the little wrap and for the first time in his life had a taste of coke.

"Coke?" Mardy had shouted. "Who is going to pay forty quid a gram for posh speed?" He was really working himself up. "I've told you before, no hard drugs in the city."

That was one of the boss's stupid, nonsensical rules. Since he had taken over the running of the city, post the heroin deaths, all you could get was pot, speed or acid.

The subject was a bee in the boss's bonnet. He reckoned as long as there was no major drug problem, there would be no major police interest in them.

Karl had stood there listening to Mardy Davies ranting away and remembered the simple conclusion he had come to on the train: his boss was a coward and every day Mardy didn't open up the market would just confirm it in Karl's mind.

*

Karl was smiling broadly as he rang the doorbell. Karl Reno was going to have it all; he was in the ascendance, baby.

Emily Davies opened the door, holding two glasses of whisky, still wet from showering off her husband's stench.

Karl took in her long legs and the little negligee.

Yes, indeed, Karl thought as he moved towards her. *I am going to have it all.*

"What the hell happened to your face?" Emily asked.

THREE DAYS LEFT

"**A** girl's going to see the comets!" Ebin moaned, broken-record-like – he'd been bitching about it since yesterday.

Alistair ignored him; Ebin was just peeved that he'd have no one to bring, having unceremoniously dumped that pouty little thing outside Dirty Dora's the other night. Besides, it was cold and too early in the morning for Ebin's bitching.

They had just finished signing on and Alistair wanted to go back to bed; he really didn't do mornings well. Even when Alistair had to go on one of those blooming drug runs, he normally wouldn't have to get up earlier than ten. Whereas signing on day, bloody hell. Ebin reckoned it was a government plot to piss off the honest, hard-working, dole bludgers.

Alistair had been woken even earlier this morning by a persistent ringing on the doorbell. Thinking *fucking useless pair of dealers*, he had rolled over and tried to get back to sleep, only to be roused again by Ebin running past his room shouting, "Code Three, Code Three, this is not a drill."

Code Three, in Ebin speak, meant that there was a TV licensing inspector at the door.

Alistair, being TV-less, had put a pillow over his head.

Even having been roused early couldn't dampen Alistair's spirits. Maggie was coming around later and they were going to see the meteor shower.

Ebin had heard about the meteor shower from *The Sky at*

Night, which he always maintained that, with the exception of *University Challenge*, was the only programme you could find on TV pitched above GSCE level.

Ebin, like most children, had been into healthy, Blue Peter-type activities, such as astronomy and stamp collecting when he was younger. Unlike most kids though, he had kept up his interest in astronomy and was able to name every star in the sky.

"Nah, man, you know I'm just kidding with you," Ebin said, breaking the silence as they left the dole office. "It's been a long time since I've seen you with a girl; we all thought your flower must have grown back."

Alistair smiled. "You're right, it's been a long time. There is something about this one though." He paused, trying to work it out in his head. He shrugged, failing. "She's… I don't know, different."

Ebin stopped and looked at his friend, a warm smile on his face. "Do you know how gay you sound sometimes?" he asked, before walking off. "Come on, faggot," he called over his shoulder. "Let's go window shopping."

They almost made it as far as the first window, before Ebin stopped again, pushing Alistair up against the wall and clamping his hand around his mouth.

Alistair considered that this would have been deeply sexy and arousing if Ebin had been a beautiful woman and not an oik.

"There he is," Ebin whispered excitedly, through clenched teeth, taking enough of his weight off Alistair so he could look up.

"We're not actually hiding from him, leaning against this wall," Alistair mumbled, through his mate's palm.

"Yes, we are."

"He's twenty feet away. He's looking at us," Alistair said, while trying to get Ebin's grubby hand off his mouth.

"Then we must talk to him," Ebin declared, pushing himself off the wall and heading over.

Crazy Al stood on the street corner staring at them. Today, the front of his sandwich board proclaimed:

Alistair couldn't place where in the Bible that verse came from.

Crazy Al clenched a wad of leaflets in his hand, which he tried to give out to all the passers-by. For some reason, the passers-by couldn't see him.

Crazy Al had apparently once been in the army or something. Al had mad eyes, pupils pin-prick small and slightly glazed. Eyes that looked through you, like God was standing behind you; it was really disconcerting.

Basically, Crazy Al was one of those people who look like they will smell of piss.

He had been around less and less recently, so Ebin jumped at the opportunity for a natter.

"Must it be whenever you see him?" Alistair sighed, following a few paces behind.

"Yes, whenever I see him," Ebin agreed. "I am trying to save him."

Ebin always made a point of stopping to discuss moral and spiritual topics with Crazy Al. "Hi Al, how are you today?" Ebin asked cheerfully. "I was just wondering if you believe in ghosts."

Crazy Al smiled a smile that was meant to be friendly, radiating the Lord's love, but came over as scary and desperate. Alistair guessed they were probably the only people that had talked to him all morning.

Al's smile widened, revealing brown teeth. "Ghosts?" He looked thoughtful.

It always started amiably, Alistair thought.

"I believe in one ghost."

"Casper?" Ebin asked, poker straight.

"No, the Holy Ghost," Al said, as if talking to a child.

"Just one? Why not others?"

It always started going downhill at this point.

"If you will admit that there is one ghost, then surely it is possible that there could be more."

Al sighed. "The word *ghost* is deceptive. It is the spirit of the Lord among us, not the spirit of someone who has died."

Ebin nodded thoughtfully.

"You see," Al continued, "Jesus was never a ghost; He died and then rose again."

"Ah, like a zombie." Ebin seemed to finally understand.

Alistair had to turn away.

"No, not like a zombie." There was a slight edge creeping into Al's voice. "He died and then rose to save us."

"Like the living dead?"

Alistair looked around for the best piece of cover.

"Yes, exactly," Aled beamed. "That is a very good way of putting it. Jesus was like the living dead."

"What did he eat?" Ebin asked.

"Eat?"

"Yes, I thought the living dead ate brains. Did Jesus eat brains?"

A nerve above Al's eye started to twitch. "No, why would He eat brains?"

"That was never really explained." Ebin looked at Alistair. "Why do zombies eat brains?"

"Jesus was never a zombie," Al screeched. "Jesus was Love. He came to Earth to save us all."

"Why are people dying all over the place then?" Ebin asked.

"That is not God's fault."

"Then whose is it? If He loves us, why do you get little black kids starving to death? I wouldn't let one starve to death in front of me and I don't particularly like kids."

"It is written in Psalm 147, 'He gathereth together the outcasts of Israel. He healeth the broken in heart, and bindeth up their wounds.'"

"What the hell doeth that mean?" Ebin asked. "It is also written, 'Peter had a ball, Peter had a blue ball. Jane had a ball, Jane had a blue ball.'" Ebin was shouting now. "Just because it is written down doesn't mean it's fucking true. There are a lot of fucking stories." He was ignoring Alistair tugging his coat. "You lot have been killing each other for centuries over which of your ancestors told the best story."

Alistair found himself backing away, trying to drag his mate after him.

"God is love; if God is love, He loves even me. God is love; if God is love, He loves even me," Al started mumbling to himself, eyes dancing all about the floor.

"It is like that shit with the Hare Krishnas; what the fuck was that all about? People are homeless so you start fighting with the Hare Krishnas over who gets to provide them with soup and coffee in the evening? Like a group of kids. Why didn't you all work together rather than attacking them and setting fire to their van?"

"God is love; if God is love, He loves even me." Al was shouting it now, pulling his hair. "God is love; if God is love, He loves even me."

"Time to go," Ebin said.

"God is love; if God is love, He loves even me. *God is love; if God is love, He loves even me.*" Al finished at the level of a scream; he pulled his gun and started swinging it in the direction of the retreating forms.

Every time this happened Ebin would stop at a distance that he considered safe and continue the theological discussion. Even though Alistair was sure the gun was fake, he still found himself ducking down, mindful that real ones had a greater range than fifteen feet.

"Anyway, it's not wrong to question God, is it?" Ebin was

shouting now. "If He is all forgiving and we are all, without one single exception, His children who He loves, then He will forgive me and I will go to heaven, won't I?"

"No, no, you won't, because you are a cunt," Al screamed, waving his gun at them as they departed.

Puffing their way back up the big, winding, fuck-off hill to the house, Alistair decided to forgo sleep and resort to drugs. He didn't like guns and, to get in a crap pun, found his nerves shot out. Ebin's philosophising was also a contributory factor to him not wanting to stay clear headed.

Every two weeks, Ebin would get in some stupid argument with Al, who obviously had mental health problems, and it would end up with Al reciting the bit about God loving him and then pull out the fake gun.

Alistair found it all quite sad really. He also found it a bit sad that no one in Swansea cared enough to look up from their shopping.

"You know, it is not that I deliberately try to wind him up," Ebin was saying. "I really hope there is a God."

Ebin argued that he was a soul seeking an underlying truth, a belief system in an altogether frightening and random universe. In order to be free to do this, he should be able to engage Al in conversation to see if God was the answer to his myriad of questions.

Alistair believed that the underlying truth was that Ebin liked being a twat to people and you couldn't find enlightenment from someone who was mad, carried a gun and called you a cunt.

2

Karl Reno was driving through the gates and up the gravel drive to Mardy Davies' house. Unlike last night this was a proper visit. He had Tony sitting next to him in the front and Ivor taking up most of the back seat. It had been a busy morning for them.

＊

Karl had woken early; his head was still throbbing from where he had been hit by that chair. The whisky he'd been drinking with Emily didn't help much either. She had wanted to know exactly what had been said by Batty Boy and the **[REDACTED]** crew.

Karl told her it could wait; they only had a little while before her husband came back. Emily had been insistent though and had quizzed him on every little detail of his trip. They hadn't even had a chance to do anything. She'd spent the evening taking his hands off her knee and making him go over all the details again and again. Karl had got annoyed by this and had ended up drunker than he intended.

His head really hurt. It took two lines in the bathroom to get rid of the DT shakes.

He arrived at the Central Hotel feeling a lot better.

It was quiet in the dusty lobby; three of the girls milled around, smoking their way towards the end of the shift.

Ivor sat on a moth-bitten sofa, his bulk making the cushions sag. "You look like shit and you're late," he said as way of greeting. "We were meant to be here early to show our faces."

Karl checked his watch, 9 am. This was fucking early.

"Zach would always show his face before nine o'clock," Ivor continued. "Even if he had been up all night, he'd always swing past here on the way home."

"Yeah, well, he hasn't got a home now, has he?" Karl snapped. "Or much of a face, for that matter. Where's the other one?"

Ivor looked disapprovingly at him before pointing towards the payphone in the corner; Tony was finishing a call.

"You look like shit and you're late," Tony said walking over. "You were meant to be here early to reassure the girls that even though Zach is in hospital, we're here if they need us."

Karl rolled his eyes with exasperation. "God forbid one of the whores didn't feel safe."

One of the whores flicked him off behind his back.

"Anyway, now you're here we can go," Tony said. "I've been on the phone to a friend in Social Services and they gave me the address of Donald Gooberman."

"Who the fuck is Donald Gooberman?" Karl demanded.

"Have a wild guess," Tony said, waving goodbye to the ladies.

They'd driven out of town before stopping outside a crummy-looking house above the Uplands.

Karl popped the boot.

Tony and Ivor took a moment to select their sporting equipment; Tony going for a nine iron and Ivor the more traditional baseball bat.

"Let's do this cleanly," Tony cautioned, hiding the golf club under his coat.

Karl put his finger on the bell until he heard movement and the door was opened.

Tony and Ivor got ready.

The door was opened by a scruffy-looking, non-Donald Gooberman figure dressed in Bermuda shorts and a hooded top.

The guy must have been in his early twenties with spiked brown hair and a nose ring. He stood there expectantly for a moment. "TV licensing?" the scruff bag asked. "We don't have a television, I'm afraid. We are readers in this house," he informed them haughtily before slamming the door.

Karl and Tony shared looks as running footsteps were heard disappearing up the stairs.

"Shall I knock again?" Ivor asked, getting ready to break the door down.

Karl nodded a big yes.

"Try knocking again, properly," Tony ordered, aware of how many people were walking past.

Karl put his finger back on the bell. They stood there waiting for sixty-three seconds.

"Right, now you can break it down," Tony said.

At that point the door was opened again by the same scruffy guy, looking red-faced and out of breath.

"As I said, we don't have a TV, but it's ok to check now if you want," he said, earnestly.

"We don't give a shit about your TV," Karl shouted. "We are looking for Donald Gooberman."

Ivor towered forward menacingly. "Big guy likes to set fire to people's houses."

"You're not from the TV licensing board? So I didn't need to hide the TV just now? Who are you then?"

"We are looking for the big guy who wears combat fatigues." Karl was starting to lose patience with this idiot.

"He's not here. The police were looking for him yesterday. Pair of bastards smashed his door down, which is really going to piss off the landlord. Now fuck off," the idiot said, trying to slam the door.

They easily pushed past him and started off up the stairs.

"Room at the top, you can't miss it, there's no door," he shouted after them.

The house was skanky, with threadbare carpets and a smell of stale pot smoke. On the top floor, a broken door led into a deserted and trashed room. Karl noticed that, for some reason, cellophane had been spread over the windows.

"What you going to do? Look for clues?" The scruffy guy laughed from the doorway, before disappearing to leave them to, rather embarrassedly, look for clues.

*

When they got into Mardy Davies' house Tony and Ivor trotted off to go through the fridge. Karl watched them go with a look of disgust on his face; you could almost hear the greedy bastards salivating.

He turned to watch Emily come down the stairs. She was wearing tennis whites, which accentuated the tan on her long legs; a coy smile was on her lips.

"He's in the drawing room. He hasn't been home long." She gestured him through.

Mardy was sitting in an overly stuffed leather armchair. From the look of him he'd spent the morning slaughtering a game of golf. He was dressed like an ass. Danny Howells sat in another armchair, dressed in his tracksuit bottoms and his big, fat, stupid gold chain. The room was heavy with cigar smoke.

"We haven't had any luck tracking him down yet," Karl said as way of greeting. He had decided to get the dressing down for not finding that Gooberman freak out of the way first.

"Is a man like that hard to find?" Mardy asked, with puzzlement in his voice.

"You could try to find out where he lives," Danny said – shit stirring.

"Of course I found out where he lives," Karl bristled. "It's the first place we looked, besides Keyes and Stone are after him as well. Plus, I've got to look after Zach's operation while he's in hospital."

Danny smirked.

"Why don't you find him?" Karl growled.

Danny's face turned all serious and mad – *speak to me like that again, pal.*

"I meant to talk to you about Zach," Mardy cut in, ignoring the staring contest. "When you've got a moment, tell him he no longer works for me."

"He what? Why?" Karl asked, slightly taken aback.

"I don't want someone who can't protect his own home running one of my concerns," Mardy answered. "You can run things for now until we work out something more permanent."

Out of the corner of his eye Karl could see Danny smirking again.

"That's not the big news though," Mardy said. "The big news is I want him out of town in the next week. I don't even want him associating with my city anymore."

"But…" Karl stopped himself; there was no point in arguing with the boss.

"Now, I know you've got a lot to do, so I'll let you get on," Mardy said, waving his cigar in the general direction of the door. "Oh, and before you go, pull Tony's head out of the fridge and tell him that our friend, the stationery shop owner, will be waiting for him to collect my winnings from last night's game."

"Don't bother with Tony. I'll pick up the money on my way to the hospital," Karl offered, thinking that it would give him a chance to see if Kieran really did have greater potential than just muleing around pot.

The boss nodded, seemingly pleased with Karl's work ethic.

"He's a good kid," Mardy told Danny when they were alone.

"I've said it before, but I don't trust him," Danny replied. "He thinks he's smarter than he is. But more worryingly, he thinks he's smarter than us."

The boss took a reflective drag on the cigar.

3

"I 've just come back from shopping, deary. I nearly ran some lunatic over; he was wearing one of those sandwich boards."

Donald Gooberman came awake with a start, banging his head and having a moment of panic, unsure where he was or why he was surrounded by darkness.

"I saw Mrs White at the shops. She told me that poor Mr Marshall lost heavily at cards again last night," his mother said from above him, before pausing conspiratorially. "Margery says he is losing more and more often."

Donald sank back down, realising he was safe in his garden.

It had been a late night.

*

Al had spent three hours teaching Donald about the guns. Donald had started to say that he had learned all about guns in the army, but Al had grabbed him by the neck, which was quite a stretch for the little man, and snarled for him to *"Shut up and not dare say that. There were better men than you in the army and they were in it for real, and some of them died for that honour"*. Al's eyes had gone distant after he said this, leaving Donald scrabbling at his vice-like grip, trying to get air in.

Al had come back to the room with a start and let him go, looking shaken. "I apologise," he said, before continuing as if nothing had happened.

Al explained that, as time was short, they would stick to just two weapons – the machine gun, an AK-47, and the ancient Browning revolver.

Al had spent a long time explaining about weapon safety, for instance, if it doesn't fire for some reason, don't look down the barrel.

Donald marvelled at how the wiry little man seemed in his element dealing with these weapons, showing him how to put in a mag, take it out, strip the guns down and put them back together again.

Finally, just as Donald couldn't wait any longer, Al took him to the end of the room, where there was a narrow passage hewn out of the rock. Electric strip lighting ran down it, illuminating a distant target and a wall of sandbags.

"We are very deep underground so no one will hear us," Al said. "Now put the stock tight into your shoulder and aim down the barrel, that's right, now what you don't want to do is—"

Firing the gun was different from what Donald seemed to remember; the recoil knocked him back a pace. Al was shouting something about waiting, but Donald was too excited, the paper target obliterating in front of his sights.

Aled had been annoyed at Donald for not waiting for all the instructions, but had to admit that it wasn't the most complicated device to work. As long as you kept the safety on, most of the time, and remembered not to look down the barrel, you were pretty much set.

Donald had spent the rest of the afternoon blissfully blasting shit.

The only distraction to his afternoon had been when a buzzer went off from over by the bank of monitors.

Al had gone over and switched them on, before urgently calling to Donald. "There are two men at the front door. Are they those two policemen?"

Donald had looked at the grainy black and white picture and nodded, feeling a rush of panic starting to build. "That's the one who stabbed me. I was sure that I wasn't followed. How do they know I'm here?"

"Relax, they're not here for you, they're trying to find Trish."

Al moved to another monitor, this one showed an empty room. Donald watched as Brother Dowling opened the door and spoke briefly to the two detectives, before letting them in.

"We won't fire the guns for a little while," Al decided, staring intently at the TV screen.

Later on, the pastor and Brother Dowling had come into the room followed by three other people. Donald recognised Jason, the stinking hippy-type with the horrible ginger dreadlocks, as the one who had let him into the hostel; that seemed like a lifetime ago now. The other two were familiar from his surveillance of Trish. They were homeless too and often used to hang out together in the city centre with all their dogs.

The pastor had introduced Donald to everyone. Again praising him on the sterling work he had done.

Donald smiled, but felt disconcerted looking at the rabble that made up this little army.

Jason, of the three homeless people, seemed to be the most with it. At least he carried himself with a modicum of alertness. The other two looked, at best, slightly out of it. Gavin was small, even childlike in looks, with a frizzy mass of dirty blond hair and a wispy goatee that, presumably, he'd grown to make himself look older. Muppet was a lot taller and very lean with a skinhead and a face full of piercings.

Donald decided that Pastor Morris was lucky to have professionals like himself and Al. He crisply saluted them all to underline that point. None of them saluted back; they just shared looks.

"Uh, thank you, Donald," the pastor said, before moving in front of the large map.

Donald looked at the map properly for the first time, the guns having got in the way before. He noticed that there were photographs of men and women on the wall next to it along with newspaper clippings about missing people. In some of the photographs, the person was looking directly at the camera, while in others the picture seemed to have been taken without their knowledge.

One of the photos was of Trish. She wasn't looking at the camera, but rather seemed to be in conversation, a smile playing across her lips. It was a good picture, the photographer having managed to get a shot of Trish flicking her hair out of her face. Donald stared at it, realising for the first time just how beautiful a girl she was.

Pastor Morris tapped the picture with a stick. "Trish, as you all know, is missing." The pastor paused, surveying the room. "She is not the first among you, among us, to disappear and as you know these missing, our friends, our brothers and sisters, are probably only the tip of the iceberg." The pastor's powerful voice demanded attention. "But things are starting to go our way. We grow strong, we are armed, trained and ready. We are going to save Trish and get revenge for all those they have taken."

Everyone in the room cheered, the force of the pastor's belief driving them on.

"We believe that Trish will be killed tomorrow night to coincide with a forecast meteorite shower, because, and I damn them to hell for this, they love the dramatic." He paused again. "However, this works in our favour. It gives us more time to find her and save her."

Pastor Morris then went on to brief them on the plan of action. Using the map, he split everyone up into groups to search for Trish. One team would be down at the docks whilst the rest of them spread out around the outlying countryside.

"Today we will not take any of the weapons. For now, we must not do anything that will get us noticed. Today I just want anything suspicious reported in on the radio."

Jason raised his hand. "What exactly are we looking for?"

The pastor regarded him for a moment. "I guarantee that Trish will not die tonight, but they will need to prepare. So just look for preparation, anything that looks wrong."

"But—"

"Now go," the pastor ordered them.

Donald was paired off with Al. They had driven out into the countryside in a beaten-up, yellow minibus, dropping off people as they went. Each group carried a heavy backpack radio and an OS map.

Al had finally parked up in the yard of a tumbled-down farm. "There are tons of these abandoned farms all around the Gower," he told Donald. "It'll be the countryside we'll be concentrating our search on tomorrow. What they are going to do to Trish requires a lot of privacy."

Donald was going to ask what would happen to Trish, but fear closed his throat with a grip stronger than Al's.

They climbed over a sty and headed uphill.

"We'll get to the high ground and follow the ridge along. Keep your eye out for anything suspicious."

They walked uphill in silence for a while, until the ground levelled out giving them a view over the peninsula; behind them Swansea glowed, distant and streetlight orange.

"Stop," Al ordered.

Donald froze.

"Look at that."

"What?"

All Donald could see was the moon reflecting off the sea and, up in the sky, a load of stars.

"All of this beauty," Al marvelled.

He then went on to ask Donald his knowledge of our Lord God and Saviour.

Donald spent the next five long hours walking across the countryside, listening to Al. He had been glad when they had called it a night and insisted he was dropped off at his mum's.

"You'd be better off back in the hostel," Al had said, as he pulled up by the building site.

"No, I want to check on my mum before bed," Donald lied; his headache was back, black and raging.

"I'll call round for you tomorrow then." Al had nodded, before forcing some leaflets into his hand and driving off.

Donald waited for the minibus to disappear before crossing the building site, lifting up the corrugated iron and crawling into his hole. He had fallen straight asleep.

*

The hole had been something Donald had started just before his stay in hospital. It had taken two days of hard work to dig a trench, six foot deep and seven foot long. He had dug this in the corner of his mother's garden. It was partially shielded by the privet bushes. Donald had then taken some timber from the building site behind the house. He had placed it, crossways, two feet down into the trench and piled earth and topsoil back on, making sure to leave enough of a gap for him to climb down into the hole. Donald had been very proud of his new home, which was big enough for him to lie down in. He even had enough head room to sit up if he wanted. There were even a couple of niches hollowed out for candles so he could read his survivalist magazines.

The one problem had been the dirt. He had spread as much as possible on his mother's garden. She had been quite pleased, at first, thinking that he was making himself useful for a change.

There was still a lot more soil though. His mother had suggested burying it. Donald sometimes got annoyed that she didn't take his work seriously.

Eventually Donald had started spreading the soil around the building site at night. Wanting to improve his home, he had even dug a tunnel through to the building site, so he could come and go as he pleased, without having to take his shoes off to go through the house.

*

Above him his mother had moved on to talk about Mrs White's sciatica. His mother had got into the habit of bringing her chair outside to sit in the garden and talk to the hole; Donald was sure she only did it to annoy him.

From the house the doorbell rang.

4

The little bell chinged gaily, as Karl Reno walked through the door.

Paul Marshall looked up from behind the counter and his heart fell. There were two of them. One of them he didn't recognise, but the other one was that little twat, Karl Reno.

Karl Reno was smiling nastily.

Mardy Davies must be especially pissed off to send that vicious bastard, Paul thought.

Paul Marshall was a quiet, unassuming man. He had built up his stationery business over the years and now had two shops in the city. Paul had a friendly nature, which had helped to build a good customer base. Something that was important in the cut-and-thrust world of stationery supply.

Paul didn't drink, had never used drugs and believed firmly in family values. His only vice was gambling, something he did compulsively and badly.

It had never really been a problem though; the business did well, his wife was happy and his daughter had a pony in the stable.

It was only recently things had changed. If Paul was honest, the words *spiralling out of control* could be used.

Last night he had lost again. It had been at poker this time. Betting heavily, to try and win back what he lost, had left him several thousand pounds down. It was an amount Mardy Davies wouldn't add to his tab.

Paul hadn't been really worried though. It was a bad patch; things would pick up and he would cut down on the cards. Besides, his daughter was away from school, doing her work experience this week, and had insisted she wanted to work in a stationery shop.

Paul knew from the outset that she was pulling a scam; she could twist him around her little finger. He lamented the fact that she was at the age now where she could use those skills on other men too. She'd even started going out to clubs and recently he'd become convinced she was seeing someone. Prying though had only led to the sound of feet running up stairs and a door slamming.

Amy had been in a poutier mood than usual for the last few days. So Paul assumed that it had finished between her and this mystery boy. Hopefully, learning about the stationery business would improve her mood.

"Honey, why don't you go and buy some more tea bags?" he asked calmly, not taking his eyes off the two pseudo customers.

"Oh, and who are you, darling? You are just the sweetest little thing,' Karl purred, his smile turning predatory.

Paul came around the desk. "She has nothing to do with any of this."

The man he didn't recognise walked past him around the little shop.

"Go and get some shopping, sweetie... I've got business to talk with these gentlemen."

"Daddy, what's wrong?" Amy asked, the question coming out in a whine.

Karl brushed her cheek. "This does concern you, sweetie. It can be a... I don't know, a life lesson."

She recoiled from his touch, her father springing forward, only to be grabbed roughly from behind by Kieran who smashed him back into a shelf of his stock.

"*Sit down!*" Karl roared at the girl, who immediately did as she was told. He knelt down by her. "Now, you see Daddy has a hobby, he likes to play cards."

The girl kept on looking at her father, her eyes growing moist.

"Now, playing cards can be an excellent hobby if you do it right," Karl continued, in the same gentle tones. "However, your daddy, despite all his other strengths, is a fucking awful card player."

Kieran sniggered at this.

"And now your dad owes some money to my boss, which he hasn't paid back. *Why haven't you paid it back*?" Turning to Kieran he asked, "Where's the bat?"

"I left it in the car," Kieran said, looking embarrassed.

"Go and get it then," Karl ordered.

"Sorry about this," Karl apologised, as Kieran scuttled out of the door.

An uncomfortable silence filled the shop as they waited for two minutes.

Finally, Kieran returned with a metal baseball bat. He took a couple of perfunctory swings in the air towards Paul and his daughter. The daughter started crying loudly.

"Now stop it," Karl told Kieran in a quiet voice. "You're scaring this little thing. What's your name, honey?"

"Amy," the girl sobbed.

"That's a pretty name."

"Now you leave her alone," Paul shouted coming forward again.

Karl stood and backed off, holding his hands up in a gesture of surrender. "Kieran, give him the bat."

Kieran stared.

"Give him the bat," Karl repeated.

Kieran and Paul looked at each other before Paul snatched the bat.

"Now you've got the bat. You can either take it and start smashing up your shop or we take the bat off you and start smashing up your daughter," Karl explained.

Paul paused for a while letting it sink in, doing the maths, deciding.

Kieran had nonchalantly backed away from him and was standing behind Karl.

"Alright, let her go first though," Paul conceded, all world-weary and deflated.

"Amy, you go and get those tea bags and we'll be gone by the time you come back," Karl said gently.

A nod from her father and she started out of the door.

Kieran grabbed her arm lightning fast. "Don't go trying to get any help or anything like that now."

She ran off down the road crying, her ears filled with the sound of Daddy smashing his shop up.

5

The door was opened a few inches before being stopped by a security chain. Detective Keyes smiled at the old lady.

"Mrs Gooberman?" he inquired politely. "We're the police."

"You don't look like the police," she replied curtly.

"I can assure you we are," Keyes said, producing his warrant card and holding it close to the door.

"What about the other one?" the old lady demanded, after a lengthy inspection of the ID.

"He's a detective too." Keyes nudged his partner.

Stone ignored this, as he seemed busy staring at his hands, turning them over very slowly.

Keyes sighed inwardly. He was about ready to stop using acid as a crime-fighting tool; every bloody time they broke it out, Stone would sneak a tab; the boy surely did love his acid.

*

They had spent the first part of the morning re-reading crime reports from the three Post Office robberies. All their running around had come up with diddly-squat. Keyes was sure there'd be another one soon. In the meantime, they could put in the book that they were still investigating it – a *bit of crossing the Ts and dotting the Is a day keeps Chief Inspector Brogan away.*

Then it was back to Trish. That was if she was even missing, as

Stone kept on repeating. They only had the say so of an ex-mental patient after all. But Keyes knew something was wrong. There were definitely a few hinky characters popping up. Richard Dowling at the hostel had set their freak alarms off. The sweaty, greasy man looked guilty of something.

Stone reckoned he probably had a room full of dead men, all posed around his dinner table. Whatever it was, the weirdo had held something back when they interviewed him.

"Let's go and find some homeless people," Stone had said, getting up from his desk. "See if they know where your girlfriend Trish is hiding."

Keyes guessed that this sudden enthusiasm for the investigation came from the boredom of paperwork, rather than concern over Trish.

They had looked around the square in the city centre, cruised past all the Spars and normal begging spots without luck.

Prowling around the old docks in the run-down, shitty area of town was when they hit pay-dirt.

"Over there," Keyes said.

Stone had parked by a large area of Luftwaffed-to-waste ground.

The policemen got out of the car, ducked through a hole in the fence and pushed through some bushes. In the distance were two figures, sheltered under the overhang of what had once been a building.

The two figures immediately scoped them as police officers and started moving away.

"Stop where you are," Keyes shouted over at them – game face on.

The two men shared glances.

"If you make us run, when we catch you I'll break your kneecaps," Stone yelled.

The two men waited until the police had picked their way across the waste ground.

Keyes appraised them quickly, Larry and Moe – *hey guys, where's Curly?*

Larry vibed as the smarter of the two; he had sharp eyes, behind his ginger dreadlocks.

"What do you want?" Larry asked suspiciously, electing himself as the spokesman.

Moe looked around nervously. He was the smallest, weasliest-looking of the two. He had dirty blond hair, a stupid goatee beard and an incredibly young-looking face.

Keyes good-copped it. "Just a chat really." He smiled, squinting up into the drizzle. "Nice day for it."

"What're you doing here?" Stone demanded, getting up close in Moe's face – *go nuts at the smallest guy and the hard man knows where he stands, without having to test the boundaries and lose face.*

Keyes put a restraining hand on his partner's shoulder. "We were hoping you guys could help. There was an incident in the street over there last night, behind Dora's Nightclub," Keyes lied earnestly. "You sleep here? Maybe last night?" He gestured towards the shelter under what was left of the building.

"No, man, there's a hostel, we were there."

"You spend most nights in the hostel?"

"Different hostels," Larry said. "The Christians and the Hare Krishnas both run one."

"That's good; it's not the weather to be out in." Keyes turned to go, stopping. "Well look, we're here now so I'll ask anyway. There's this girl, Trish Reed, pretty girl, pink hair, got a fucked-up dog with only two legs. Well, she's saying that she got attacked outside Dora's."

A look of recognition passed between Larry and Moe.

"You know her or anything about her?"

Larry paused and glanced at his colleague. "No, never heard of her. You're saying that you talked to her yesterday though?"

Keyes' eyes narrowed. "If you've never heard of her, what do you care?"

The homeless men shared looks.

Keyes' demeanour changed; he seemed to swell and grow

larger. "Why are you lying? You've shared hostels with the girl and you don't recognise her? For fuck's sake, you dolt, she's got a dog with two legs."

"We haven't seen her all week. Brother Dowling said she was missing, I don't know, we were scared."

"What of?" Keyes demanded, getting closer.

Moe spoke for the first time. "You can't tell him."

Keyes ignored him, closing Larry down. "What are you scared of?"

Larry looked around desperately.

"Don't tell him," Moe pleaded, a panicked edge in his voice.

"Shut the fuck up," Stone ordered him.

"No, you can't tell him," Moe repeated.

"I said shut the fuck up," Stone said, pushing him.

Moe stumbled backwards almost tripping. He regained his balance and reached into his coat, pulling out a metal object; he shook the gun at them wildly.

It all happened very fast.

Larry froze for a moment staring at the scene. "Shit, man, we weren't meant to bring the guns out," he said, before splitting, roadrunner-fast.

"This is a new one," Stone said to his partner.

Steel came into Moe's voice. "Back off towards your car," he ordered.

"What are you scared of?" Keyes asked calmly, watching the gun.

"Look, fuck off," Moe shouted.

Stone winked at his partner. "Don't tell us to *fuck off*, tell those two policemen behind you."

Moe turned and the Keystone Cops jumped on him.

He was strong for a little guy. Stone hung onto his arm, trying to force the gun out of his hand, while Keyes held him by the throat.

"Got the gun," Stone shouted, falling backwards into a bush.

Keyes kept his hands around the throat. "Now I'll ask you again," he started to say.

Moe made little choking noises.

Stone pulled himself out of the bush. "Hey, this is real. Where you get a real gun from?"

"Fuck you," Moe managed to spit.

"Fuck me?" Stone asked, punching low. Moe sagged and choked.

"It looks like he's a bit of a hard man, eh?" Stone said, massaging his knuckles. "A couple of hours tenderising should change that. Go get the kit."

"Let's find out what he's doing with a gun first and what he's scared of."

"Fuck it, this thing he pulled on us is real. He's getting the kit first."

"If it's real, we should follow protocol and call out the armed response team," Keyes said, as he dragged Moe, by the goatee, back through the bushes and held him against the car.

"No, no armed response team, I hate those racist bastards," Stone said, while rummaging in the boot.

He finally found what he was looking for.

Keyes changed his grip, clamping one of his big hands over Moe's nose. "How much do you reckon he can take?"

Stone stood a little way back, resting his chin between his thumb and forefinger like a doctor making a tricky diagnosis. "The guy's probably got a strong toxic tolerance." After a moment's deliberation he announced his conclusion. "I would normally recommend three tabs." He opened a plastic baggy he'd brought out of the car. "But because the fucker pulled a gun on us let's round it up to five."

Keyes whistled through his teeth. "Are you sure? I mean—"

Stone ignored him and moved forward, pushing the tiny bits of paper into Moe's mouth.

*

That had been an hour ago. Keyes looked at his partner. If Stone was coming up now, Moe was probably feeling very claustrophobic in the boot of the car.

"Is your friend alright?" Mrs Gooberman asked, having taken the chain off the door.

Stone had started giggling.

"He's just happy because he got promoted today," Keyes explained, entering the house. "We'd like to ask you some questions about your son."

"We'd like tea," Stone spluttered.

"If that's no trouble, ma'am," Keyes continued.

"With lots of sugar."

While Mrs Gooberman pottered around the kitchen, Stone and Keyes sat in the cluttered lounge, looking out into the large garden.

Keyes noticed the solitary deckchair on the lawn facing away from the house.

Stone was staring at a picture above the fire.

"That's a picture of my late husband." Mrs Gooberman had entered the room silently, carrying the tea tray. "He was in the services."

"The picture frame is all shiny," Stone told her.

Keyes ran his hand through his hair, their sign that he was going to take the lead in this interview. Stone was too busy putting sugar into his drink to notice.

"Have you seen your son recently?" Keyes began.

"Donald? I don't like talking about Donald," she said, before viciously stirring her tea.

"It's important, Mrs Gooberman."

She sighed. "Ever since the incident Donald has been a bit strange. He was better after he came out of the hospital. The council even found somewhere for him to live. I thought that was very nice of them."

"Have you seen him recently?"

"I haven't seen him for a long time, Detective," she said, a hint of sadness entering her voice. "Now my programmes are on." She turned towards the television, indicating the conversation was over. "It is time for *Murder, She Wrote* and I do enjoy my crime programmes."

"I bet you do." Keyes smiled, thinking she knew a damn sight more than she was saying.

He got up to go, his bulk filling the room. "If you happen to see him, tell him to be careful," Keyes said. "Your son has been butting heads with a lot of dangerous people and he will, one day, come up against someone bigger and stronger." He returned to the sofa, gently taking the spoon off Stone and putting it on the table, before helping him up. "Or someone innocent, then it will be too late to help him."

Mrs Gooberman gave him a very sad smile.

Stone waved goodbye and thanked her for the tea.

Outside, Keyes planned the next move. Wishing, gun or no gun, Stone hadn't dosed Moe up, Keyes decided the best plan would be to watch Brother up-to-his-greasy-neck-in-things Dowling for a while.

It was a good plan. It would keep his partner out of the station until he'd come down a bit and Moe could have another couple of hours flipping out in the boot. Then they could interview him and find out what was going on.

"Why's the boot open?" Stone asked, cutting into his thoughts.

6

Alistair was annoyed with himself. He had meant to tidy the house and Maggie would be here in half an hour.

After the earlier run in with Crazy Al, he had resisted the urge to get wasted and instead had a bath and a shave. If only Ebin hadn't shoved a joint under his nose after the bath, the house would be tidy by now. Instead he had been sitting in Ebin's room getting wasted.

Alistair felt both nervous and excited about Maggie coming round. It was odd, he realised; they were two emotions that had been foreign to him for a long time.

It was also a good afternoon because Mordechai was back from university. Mordechai had palled around with Ebin for years. When Alistair had first met him, he'd asked if it was a Jewish name; Mordechai had nodded, some Jewish scientist had told the world about the Israelis having nukes and gone to jail for it. His crazy parents liked the idea of the truth winning out, so had changed his name. Poor kid had been in infant's school at the time and wasn't even Jewish.

Ebin too had been nervous. He was worried in case Mordechai had turned into an arrogant student twat. Luckily, he was still the amiable loser of old, just slightly happier. He'd just met a girl at university and was pretty sure he was going to fall in love with her.

At the moment, Ebin was in the middle of taking the piss out of Mordechai.

Alistair thought it was jealousy. Ebin was looking for more than his current life offered him and resented success in others.

"So what if I'm a fucking student, it's better than being a fucking hippy," Mordechai shot back.

"I am not a *fucking hippy*. I, unlike the rest of you, take an interest in broadening my mind," Ebin said.

Ebin, in his quest to get more out of life, had spent a couple of months reading about Buddhism. He had even tried to lend Alistair one of his books. Alistair had diligently looked at the front cover, before deciding that you should never trust a fat prophet.

"Anyway, I have discounted Buddhism as a viable belief system," Ebin continued imperiously. "It seemed cool enough, but thinking something is cool is not a reason to change your life."

Alistair reckoned it was his comments about fat prophets that had spoiled it for him. He hoped so at least.

"It's like a *Scooby Doo* cartoon," Ebin continued. "When you see *Scooby Doo* for the first time, you think it is absolutely great and then when you see it again as an adult... well when you are older," Ebin corrected himself, looking at Mordechai, "you remember how you liked it, and you still do, but now you laugh for different reasons."

"That's crap. I saw *Monkey Magic* again on Sky a couple of months ago. It really was poor," Mordechai spoke up, the adult crack having annoyed him.

Ebin smiled patronisingly. "You're missing my point and you probably didn't like *Monkey Magic* as a kid."

"I did like it as a kid; he had a pet cloud and everything. I saw it again recently though and it was crap. So you are wrong."

Alistair sighed; he had seen this pantomime many times before. Ebin would come up with a half-baked idea and then defend it to the death, rather than be proved wrong.

"How old were you when you saw it?" Ebin pressed on.

"I don't know, three or four maybe," Mordechai said.

"Well, I obviously didn't mean when you were that age. You don't have the same taste at four as when you are seven. I mean, I used to watch *Play School* when I was four, but then, when I got to the age of seven, I thought that it was crap. Well, I didn't know that word then, so I thought it was poo poo or something."

"So are you saying that I still have the same taste now at the age of twenty-three as I did at the age of seven, but not at the age of four?" Alistair asked to show he was paying attention.

"In essence, yes." Ebin brightened. "It is like the time me and Mordechai showed Clancy *An American Werewolf in London*."

Clancy, who had been completely oblivious to the conversation, looked up. He had only been back from work for an hour and was having cereal for tea. Milk flicked off the end of his shoulder-length hair.

"Eh?" he said, through a mouthful of cornflakes.

"You look disabled." Ebin sounded disgusted.

"You have never seen *An American Werewolf in London*?" Alistair was amazed. "Everybody in the world has seen it."

"I have seen it," Clancy said, spraying milk, spit and cornflakes over himself. "What a bad film."

"You even sound disabled." Ebin scowled.

Alistair couldn't believe it. "It's a great film, the bit where he changes into a werewolf, how can you say it's bad?"

"Exactly my point," Ebin shouted, excitedly winning his audience back and knocking an ashtray over. "You see, Clancy saw it for the first time at the age of twenty and thought it was crap. When we saw it, however, we were a lot younger and really liked it. So those feelings influence the way we look at it now."

"What has that got to do with anything?" Mordechai asked. "We were talking about Buddhism and now we are talking about horror films."

"I stopped listening when he started to compare Buddhism to *Scooby Doo*,' Clancy said, finishing his cornflakes.

"The original point I was making," Ebin sighed, "was that *Scooby Doo* is really cool, like Buddhism, but I wouldn't necessarily join their gang and go around searching for ghosts."

The search for some sort of spiritual thing didn't just stop at dickish comparisons to cartoons or getting madmen to swear at them.

One day over the summer, they had gone to a Hare Krishna convention. It had been flyposted on the multitude of boarded-up, closed-down shops, alongside adverts for local punk bands, album releases and Socialist Worker's posters.

The Hare Krishnas had even had a procession through town to advertise it, staying, of course, far away from Crazy Al's corner. Some of them still bore scars.

Seeing a load of blokes dancing around like that had perked everybody's interest.

Clancy thought they must have been cold without hair. Alistair thought they looked pretty. Ebin wanted to ask them spiritual questions and Mordechai just followed along for a laugh.

So they all went to the Hare Krishna evening. Or *"hippy shit"* as Mordechai had called it.

They turned up at the rented church hall fashionably late because Ebin had insisted on everybody getting stoned to fully appreciate the meaning of Harry's words.

Alistair's first impression was they had walked into the wrong church hall. The Hares weren't weedy and pale, with a vegetarian sheen, as one might expect. Most of them were massive, with heavily tattooed forearms and the look of ex-squaddies about them. In truth, it looked like a Combat 18 meeting.

The four of them found seats at the back of the hall.

On the small stage there was a heavily tattooed skinhead jumping around, his orange robes flying behind him. As far as any of them could make out, he was pretending to be a butterfly.

"Is that Harry?" Clancy whispered.

At the side of the stage was an incredibly tall and bony, orange-robed man. He was explaining to the audience why the skinhead was dancing.

Alistair was quickly bored and started looking around for the table with all the cake on. You should always be able to get cake at a place like this. It was like fetes, there were always stalls with the Styrofoam cups of squash and loads of cake.

Perhaps Hare Krishnas don't eat cake, Alistair reflected. *They are vegetarian after all*. But how much meat was there in cakes? Not much, except maybe in steak turnovers, which Alistair had always thought would be a great idea for a cake.

Unable to see any cakes, he stared around looking at everybody in the hall. There was, except for normal people, a real cross section of society. There were a lot of aging hippy women, who all probably believed in the power of crystals. A handful of punks and about twenty of those little round insecure girls, who think if they dress like something out of a vampire movie, they become more interesting individuals.

Alistair was glad he wasn't a Goth. It was dangerous. In the evening you became almost invisible to motorists. The only advantage he could see was not having to do much laundry.

Alistair sat stoned in the church hall, pondering why black doesn't reflect headlights and why there was no cake.

Mordechai and Clancy were getting restless too; they decided to go for a joint on the swings opposite before going to the pub.

Filled with assurances that there would be food at either the swings or the pub, Alistair went as well. Ebin said that they were heathen and he would catch up with them later.

7

The enemy had its tentacles everywhere. Pastor Morris knew that well. However, he still held on to the hope that those two policemen searching for her would help. *Perhaps send out the message that you can't take this one, she is on the radar, she has been missed, people do care.*

He knew deep down it was a vain hope.

Trish was running out of time. The pastor could feel it. By now her bruises would be healed up. Any that weren't could be covered by makeup. And then they'd be able to put her on show at the ceremony.

Going to the police had been a costly gamble. Jason had come back earlier from his patrol of the docks; he'd been out of breath and panicked. The pastor had calmed him and listened to the story of how those two policemen had picked up Gavin and shoved him in the boot of the car.

Then later that afternoon, the two policemen were back. Their car was parked a little way up the road from the hostel. The pastor had watched it through one of the CCTV cameras. It had sat there for two hours.

Pastor Morris had been scared. What had Gavin told them? Paranoid thoughts entered his mind. Perhaps the two policemen worked for *them*.

The power of the enemy was legion. Memories came back from his old parish. Before the pastor's death, they had even turned his own congregation against him.

It was indeed easy to be scared and for a moment lose sight of God's overarching plan for you. It was after the car had gone Pastor Morris realised this.

He'd been down in the Op Centre staring at the map. There was no way he could cover such a large area with his little group. This left him with only one choice.

It was time to ask for help.

Asking for help was a hard decision and the pastor prayed for a sign. When, a few minutes later, Al and Donald entered the church, bringing Gavin with them, Pastor Morris had rejoiced.

Gavin was now beardless and his face was a bloody, tattered mess.

The pastor had tried to calm him and find out what he had told the police, but Gavin was babbling and crying.

"It looks like he is on drugs, possibly LSD," the pastor said, looking accusingly at Jason.

Jason put his hands up in a *nothing to do with me* gesture. "They must have given it to him before they put him in the boot of the car."

Donald had started telling a story of how he had taken acid, while on a boat going up the Mekong Delta, but the pastor had cut him off, instead asking Al what had happened.

Al explained that he had been on his way to pick up Donald and had seen the two policemen going into Donald's mother's house. He had then heard the muffled screaming and banging coming from their car.

Al had jimmied the boot and found Gavin covered in blood. "It looked like he almost scratched his face off," Al said.

After a while trying unsuccessfully to get some sense out of Gavin, they bandaged up his face and restrained him in one of the rooms off the Op Centre.

It was time to get help.

*

The night was cold and clear as the pastor stood outside the Hare Krishnas building with Brother Dowling, Al and Donald.

Al was really not pleased to be here.

Since the summer, the Hare Krishnas had built a new hostel, with a café downstairs. The café was prettily decorated with flowers and even a little, babbling waterfall. It was open to the public, offering the unique chance to try different lentil dishes while talking to a Hare Krishna. As always it was deserted.

Deserted except for the twenty Hare Krishnas who sat around the little tables, their conversation suddenly hushed.

Pastor Morris studied their faces. Some of them looked at Al nervously, while others held barely restrained hatred behind their eyes. He recognised many of them from their time staying at the Mount Pleasant Hostel for the Young and Disenfranchised, before converting to life in the orange robes.

There was a lot to read behind all their eyes.

Only Pragnesh Lankhani looked at him with the eyes of someone who has found inner peace.

Pragnesh Lankhani was their leader; he was tall and skeletal, even towering over Donald. He hadn't been christened Pragnesh Lankhani, but you don't get many Hare Krishnas called Dave.

"We need to talk," the pastor said. "Someone else has been taken."

"I don't see of what help we can be. There is no militant wing of the Hare Krishnas," Pragnesh Lankhani said softly.

Behind their leader the rest of them started chanting, "Hare Krishna, Hare Krishna, Krishna, Krishna, Hare, Hare."

"Her name is Trish Reed. Many of you here will know her and she will die tonight, I can feel it," the pastor implored, as the chanting got louder.

"Hare Krishna, Hare Krishna, Krishna, Krishna, Hare, Hare, Hare Rama, Hare Rama, Rama, Rama, Hare, Hare."

"We don't need these… these people," Al spat. "We should go, before I lose my temper again."

Pastor Morris held out a restraining arm, before smiling and stepping forward.

8

Trish was shaken awake and her hands were untied. She came out of her dozy, comatose state quickly, the pain in her left arm sobering her.

Trish tried to let out a scream, through her gag, as she was lifted off the bed by at least two pairs of hands.

"Ah, she kicked me," the now familiar voice of the bitch, whore-woman screamed.

Trish's blindfold slipped and she saw two figures dressed in purple from hood to toe. For a second, Trish thought of the Ku Klux Klan; it confused her, she wasn't black.

One of the robed figures, the woman, was on the floor holding her face. Trish dived at the man, slashing at his mask.

The three of them landed in a heap on the floor, Trish on top, fighting wildcat-wild.

She got to her feet, stamping down hard on the prone bodies. If they hadn't taken off her heavy army boots she would be crushing bone.

She turned and with one final kick was out of the bedroom door and straight into another hooded figure.

Trish let out a scream as she was pushed, mightily, back into the room, falling, skull crackingly, onto a small table.

Hands grabbed her from all around, clawing at her, pulling her onto the bed.

The hooded figure at the door calmly lifted a needle and

entered the room. "You should have injected the scrubber again before untying her," he said, looking at the half-beaten man and woman pinning Trish down.

The last thing Trish remembered was recognising the voice and feeling as cheated and as lonely as she ever had done.

9

Unlike the others, Clancy had a job. He worked in the hospital. Sometimes he would steal things of interest. The last thing he had nabbed was a child's prosthetic testicle.

Clancy also had a car. It wasn't particularly reliable or road worthy, but he loved the old thing, in the same way as you would love the old, incontinent family dog.

They were currently chug-chugging their way down the country lanes – *comet shower here we come*.

Clancy's car made a lot of worrying clanking noises, which were currently being drowned out by *Take Warning* booming through the speakers, Clancy having got his Dead Kennedy/Operation Ivy tape stuck in the tape player about a year ago. While trying to get it out he had broken the on/off switch; it now played on a loop whenever the engine was running.

Alistair and Maggie were sitting in the back of the car. Ebin was squeezed in next to them, as he refused to sit in the front, or the death seat, as he called it. Mordechai had called shotgun.

"Mate, your car is shit. It is even the same colour as shit," Ebin shouted over the music.

In an effort to fix the on/off switch, Clancy had somehow managed to break the volume control.

"Look, as I've said before, it's purple, a very dark purple," Clancy replied angrily.

It was the easiest way to annoy him; he loved his old car.

"It's not; it's the colour of my poo," Mordechai said.

He liked annoying people too.

"You should see a doctor if your poo is purple," Clancy said.

"Shit, shit, shit," Ebin shouted, just above the noise.

Alistair was staying out of it. He had Maggie squashed up close to him and he didn't want her associating him with such a lowbrow conversation.

*

Maggie had come round to their house earlier on in the evening, ringing the doorbell and standing there looking radiant, flashing one of those heart-stopping smiles. Alistair had stood there for a second staring at her.

There was something about this girl; he didn't know what, but she made him feel somehow connected again.

She had stood there for a moment, before asking if she could come in. This had embarrassed Alistair, in the same way as having got accidentally wasted did.

She hadn't minded though and had sat down for a smoke with them all. Alistair had noticed how the others had been mesmerised by her also.

They'd all talked for a while. That fun, pointless stoned talk that people do, swapping stupid stories and remembering excellences past. At one point Clancy had asked about her travelling. Maggie had said she'd been around Thailand for a while, but didn't elaborate, before asking him about his job, all the time stealing glances at Alistair.

*

And now, as they drove down darkened country lanes, listening to one of the best punk albums ever made, Maggie put her hand in his, interlinking fingers, leant in and brushed a kiss against Alistair's cheek.

10

They had been dropped off by Al at the same tumbled-down farm as yesterday.

"Just follow the same route as we've already done and you'll all be fine," Al told Donald, before driving off, in the chapel's decrepit old minibus.

Donald was accompanied by Jason and Muppet.

Muppet was lean, had a skinhead, a face full of piercings and a leather jacket with *"God Save the Queen"* scrawled on the back, a sentiment Donald couldn't agree with more.

Muppet looked around for a moment, before a broken-toothed smile spread across his face. "Tom Morello's guitar put it best, when it said *'arm the homeless',*" he whooped, raising his AK-47 in the air.

He crossed the road, jumped the sty and went bounding off into the bushes shouting, "Get some. Get some," and making machine-gun noises.

Jason walked after him lighting a rolly. Donald didn't know who Tom Morello was. Muppet had run out of breath halfway up the hill and soon fell into step with Donald and Jason.

Donald was on point, hunting the enemy, just like back in Phnom Penh. He moved silently from tree to tree, stopping to listen for any sound of danger ahead in the darkness. Jason and Muppet followed behind, sharing a bottle of Munting McJunting cider and smoking a joint.

Donald had tried to warn them that a sniper could zero in on the cigarette glow, but they had just laughed and said something rude.

It could have been worse though, Donald had thought. The Hare Krishnas were on patrol in the countryside to the north of the city. Between their chanting, their drums and finger cymbals, they were just asking to be lit-up in an ambush.

Donald didn't really like the Hare Krishnas and he knew Al definitely didn't. Al had been in a bad mood since they had left the café.

The pastor though had been elated. He had preached to the unconverted.

❋

He had preached to them with Bible black fury, his eyes burning, his voice dripping with fire and brimstone – reaching crescendos and crashing back down.

Donald had been mesmerised by his performance, as had the Hare Krishnas, their chanting at first drowned out before petering away.

The pastor had talked for twenty minutes to a silent audience. He had covered love, hate, forgiveness, charity and chastisement. Eventually, stopping and wiping his brow.

The leading Hare Krishna had gone into a huddle around one of the tables with some of his older-looking associates. Donald had strained to hear what they were saying, but could only make out heated muttering.

Finally, Pragnesh Lankhani had risen and come to stand in front of them. "We will help as we can. But first, Aled must apologise for attacking us and for what he did to our soup wagon."

"One moment," Pastor Morris said, before going into his own huddle with Al and Brother Dowling.

Donald sidled over to listen.

"No, I refuse," Al was saying. "It was God's will that their soup wagon was smited. I cannot apologise for doing something God wants."

"God didn't want you to smite them," Brother Dowling almost shouted. "I told you at the time, there is nothing in the scriptures about petrol bombing a van, besides, Trish needs us."

Al was about to say something else before the pastor cut across him. "This incident with the van happened before I came to you. It does not concern me, it is in the past, and we now need to deal with the present. Aled, I command that you stand up in front of them, like a man, and apologise." He looked at his watch. "Time is running out for Trish."

Al had stared at him before slowly nodding in agreement. He straightened up and turned to face the assembled Hare Krishnas. "I apologise for my behaviour in the past and for any pain I inflicted on any of you," he said haltingly. "I cannot change any of what happened, but I can help Trish; I would like you to help her too."

Pragnesh Lankhani had nodded at this. "Then we will help as we can."

The pastor had smiled. "We must move quickly."

Which they did.

Pastor Morris and Pragnesh Lankhani had turned the café into their main base of operation. Soon they were gathered around a large Ordinance Survey map of the city and surrounding countryside.

Donald helped as well, mainly by not mentioning that Al had his fingers crossed throughout the entire apology.

The pastor had made sure that all the equipment they would need had been loaded into the chapel's decrepit old minibus.

They had even brought the bulky old military radios with the huge aerials. Unfortunately, there weren't enough to go around, so only the patrols far out in the country had one.

Jason and Muppet had said, since Donald thought he was in the army, he could carry the fucking thing. Donald started to tell them how, back in the jungle, Charlie had always targeted the radioman first, but they ignored him.

11

They pulled in to the yard of a tumbled-down farm, one of the many abandoned ones that dotted the countryside.

Alistair was debating whether to tell everybody about the financial trouble farmers were in. Whoever had owned this farm probably hadn't diversified properly when push came to shove. It was quite an interesting subject. For example, farmers have the highest suicide rate of any occupation, with dentists coming a close second. Alistair decided against it though as they piled out into the muddy courtyard.

The night was really clear and crisp. Everyone's breath was coming out like smoke, except for Mordechai who actually had joint smoke coming out of him.

"About eleven it's meant to start," Ebin said, taking charge. He had three blankets wrapped around himself, covering the two hooded tops, three pairs of trousers and a scarf. One thing about being on the dole was that you really learnt to appreciate warmth; that and the joy of layers, it was like being old.

The mud squelched under foot as they climbed over a sty and walked up the path. Alistair passed the joint to Maggie who, for now, had stopped holding his hand.

The path headed steeply uphill, sentinelled by trees, before turning into a field.

They had to climb over another sty between some high thorn bushes. Mordechai climbed over it by slipping and falling on his face in the mud.

The field was full of corn stalks, cut ankle high. In the distance there were some cylindrical objects that looked like large, docile animals.

Clancy and Ebin were having an argument over whether there was such a thing as rape seed oil. Clancy thought that it was something Ebin had just made up.

"I need a piss," Mordechai said.

At least the boys are on their best behaviour, Alistair despaired to himself, as Mordechai ran up the hill.

Maggie reckoned the cylindrical objects could be very quiet, very fat cows with no legs. "They breed them like that so there is more meat." She smiled.

Ebin and Clancy were still arguing.

Alistair started to light another joint, while vaguely hoping Mordechai wasn't pissing on one of the legless cows – they had enough problems.

Seconds later, they were all running and slipping to avoid the rolling cow or, as Alistair discovered diving with Maggie to the right, a large rolled-up ball of hay.

Forty feet up the hill, Mordechai was doubled up in hoots of laughter, congratulating himself at his comical use of the laws of gravity.

"You cunt," Ebin shouted. "Cows and sheep and, er… chickens need it for the winter." Ebin's knowledge about farmyard animals was cursory at best.

They spent a while drinking from their bottles of Munting McJunting cider and playing with the hay, trying to crush each other or running on it as it rolled down the hill.

Soon the bushes at the bottom of the field were full of the bales of hay.

"Right, I'm bored now," Ebin said.

In the top corner of the field was a small concrete shed, about seven feet high, with a flat roof. It looked like the sort of Action

Man command centre that kids made by turning over a cardboard box and cutting holes in it.

They used one of the concrete windows for leverage to climb onto the roof. Maggie had some trouble getting up. Probably because she was a girl, Ebin kindly informed her.

In the dark, she heard him being hit.

Mordechai had more problems than Maggie getting up. Mainly because Ebin and Clancy kept on pushing him back down and flicking lit cigarette butts at him.

Soon everyone quietened down. They lay cocooned in blankets on the concrete roof. Above them the still heavens stretched away into infinity.

"Ooh, there's one," Maggie said, noticing the yellow streak burning itself out across the sky.

After that there was one every few seconds.

Maggie put her hand under the blanket and held onto Alistair's. She put her head against his shoulder and whispered, "Thanks for this."

12

The pain shooting through Trish's arm brought her around and, for a moment, she felt like she was floating. Trish turned her head left and right, but couldn't see anything. She'd been blindfolded again.

Slowly, Trish realised that she was being carried, face down, by at least four pairs of hands. She tried to thrash, only to have the grip on her limbs tighten.

She was moved roughly to face the right way up. There was a smell here – familiar, she just couldn't place it.

Her feet touching the ground, Trish immediately kicked out with her free leg, connecting and crunching something hard.

"Ah," a new voice squealed.

Trish kicked towards the sound, connecting with nothing. The inside of the blindfold flashed purple for a second as her infected arm was twisted and tied behind her back.

Trish's feet were also tied.

"Brothers and Sisters, we are gathered here to witness the demise of this girl," a different voice spoke close to Trish's ear. The word *girl* was spat out in disgust. "She has been accused of attacking a member of our Society, with both forethought and malice. And you, my Brothers and Sisters, are present to witness the punishment."

There was a general murmuring at this.

"Bring forth the accuser."

The blindfold was removed from Trish's face.

It took a few moments for her eyes to adjust, to take it all in.

It was only then that she started screaming.

onald froze, raising his hand and clenching his fist, so the other two would do the same. Jason and Muppet just ended up careening into the back of him, swearing and spilling cider.

"Did you hear that?" Donald whispered to the other two.

"You spilt my drink," Muppet accused.

"No, wait, I think I heard something too," Jason said.

They stood still for a few moments, looking, listening and in one case complaining. Above them, the stars shone brightly and were criss-crossed with meteorites.

Nothing.

Still nothing.

Just as they were about to move again, Donald noticed the glow of a light, flickering and dancing, maybe half a klick away, downhill, in a dell, behind some trees. He looked at the other two and without a word started leading them towards it.

14

Franklin London went to the bedroom window of his farmhouse and pulled back the curtain. The howls from the wolves were filling the air.

They had been in a strange mood; prowling back and forth, even growling at him when he took their food out.

"Come back to bed, Frank, you know what they get like," his wife said, looking up from her knitting.

Franklin put on his heavy, ancient dressing gown. "No, I want to check on them."

Downstairs he pulled on his boots, put on the courtyard lights and went outside.

The light illuminated the wolves across the courtyard. They were prowling back and forth. Geronimo, the big alpha male, was up on his hind legs scratching at the metal fence, his howl coming from some deep down, primeval place.

For the first time ever Franklin went towards the cage cautiously. They weren't this bad even during a thunderstorm. They seemed to calm a bit as he got closer. Geronimo stopped his attack on the fence and started to slink back and forth, ears down.

Franklin made a quick inspection of the cage. He noticed some earth had been scratched away from outside it. In his experience, foxes could be bastards for breaking into hen houses and the like, but a fox breaking into a pen full of wolves? He shook his head.

Out in the darkness, further than the yard lights reached,

Franklin heard a squeaking noise, almost like a child's rusty swing. It came again. He peered into the blackness, but the noise had stopped.

The wolves seemed calmer now.

Franklin went back into the house, closing the door but leaving the yard's lights on. Upstairs, his wife was still knitting away.

"Everything alright?" she asked.

"Seems to be quiet out there now," Franklin replied, looking out of the window at the still yard, unable to shake an uneasy feeling.

"I wouldn't worry about it," his wife said. "The wolves always get a bit funny when they're sacrificing someone up at the old quarry."

15

The faceless, purple-robed figures stood unmoving as Trish sobbed out the last of her scream. Behind them, a ring of torches flickered their shadows, bogeyman-like, onto the quarry wall.

Looking down Trish saw she was dressed in quite a revealing white dress. Around her feet, wood was piled shin high.

She placed that smell – petrol.

There were so many of them. Why wouldn't one of them step forward and stop this?

One of the monsters came towards her. Trish pulled at her ropes. Trish thrashed. Trish pleaded.

The figure stood directly in front of her, before turning to the assembled audience. They were chanting something quietly; odd syllables, grating, unfamiliar.

"This is the one I accuse." The figure was a woman, speaking loudly. "As is my right as a Sister of this Society," she said, speaking proudly.

"What have I done?" Trish pleaded, her voice loud above the muted chanting.

The woman didn't seem to hear. "This… this thing attacked me like I was a common whore."

The woman removed her hood and turned to stare at Trish. Her face was filled with an incredible look of satisfaction.

Trish remembered the woman now and felt any strength she had left sag out of her.

"It was just paint," she moaned. "Just a coat, I didn't mean to."

The woman gave her a look of pure contempt. "You little bitch," she hissed, only loud enough for Trish to hear. "That mink cost more money than you have ever seen."

Another figure, this one robed in darker purple, overlaid with a yellow sash, put a restraining hand on the woman's shoulder, before turning her back towards the assembled audience. "It has been decided, you may extract the revenge that rightly belongs to a Sister of our number."

Trish recognised his voice and started crying again. He walked towards her and ran his hand through her hair, gently, almost father-like, which Trish found the most insulting thing of all.

He started to replace her blindfold.

The last thing Trish saw was the woman advancing on her, burning torch held aloft.

16

"We've found her! We've found her," Donald's voice came urgently through the radio, distorted and warped by static. Pastor Morris leapt up from his chair and grabbed at the microphone.

"They're burning her! The bastards are burning her!"

"Where are you?" the pastor demanded, his voice sounding surprisingly calm.

"They're burning her. I can see her thrashing."

The pastor looked at Pragnesh Lankhani, before sighing and changing his voice. "Calm down, soldier," he barked. "Help will be there. Now where are you?"

"Above some sort of quarry, there are dozens of them, just standing there watching."

Pastor Morris pointed towards the Ordinance Survey map, which Pragnesh Lankhani rushed to pore over. "Have you been spotted? I repeat, have you been spotted?"

"Negative."

Donald seemed to have composed himself a bit.

"Sit tight, son, we want you to observe. I repeat, sit tight."

"She's burning."

The pastor covered the mic and looked sadly at the Hare Krishna. "We are too late this time. There will be others though." He went back to Donald. "Sit tight. Stay where you are. There are too many of them for you to do anything."

"Negative, I've got to do something."

"Jason stop him," the pastor ordered.

There was silence on the other end of the radio; it stretched for what seemed like an eternity.

"He's out," Jason said breathlessly over the radio. "Muppet's decked him."

"Ok, Jason, wait where you are. Radio silence until they leave. We'll take it from here."

"It's too late for that. Shit, there's a light on us."

"Jason, get out of there."

"Shit."

Machine-gun fire garbled over the static.

Someone was shouting, *"Get some. Get some."*

Then nothing.

17

Dawn would be coming soon.

A fresh breeze drafted through the glassless window, blowing away some of the accelerants' fumes.

The building, like a lot of the grand Victorian buildings down by the docks, had been abandoned for over a decade. All boarded up, window smashed and pigeon filled.

It had survived the end of an empire. It had survived depression, recession and the Luftwaffe fire storms.

It had survived a lot.

A match flared for a moment, before the old place whumped up.

TWO DAYS LEFT

onald came to all disorientated, his head aching with flash-bang intensity. For a moment he thought he was in the hospital.

And it was a peaceful moment – but only a moment.

His memory came back, flood-like in its force.

He remembered seeing Trish down in the quarry, writhing, as she disappeared in the flames, all those people standing around, watching, doing nothing.

Donald had shouted into the mic. What? He didn't know. The next second he was throwing off the heavy radio, selecting fully automatic on the AK-47 and starting down the slope towards her. He remembered the other two grabbing at him, wrestling with him and then… He was here and Trish…? She was gone.

Jason and that Muppet had stopped him saving Trish and, for that, Donald was going to kill them.

Donald tried to sit up, but couldn't move, tied as he was to one of the tables in the operation room. Donald strained at the ropes, images of Trish bombarding his mind. He pulled, he thrashed, he screamed it all out.

Pastor Morris appeared and put a cool hand on Donald's forehead. "How is your head?" he asked. "You've been out for quite a while. Brother Dowling was starting to worry."

Donald began to sob.

"I am sorry for your loss, my son," Pastor Morris said calmingly. "We will all miss Trish, but we did what we could."

"You killed her. You… you, you bastard." Donald very rarely swore.

The pastor's tone turned harsh. "She was already dead and if they hadn't stopped you running down there then you would be too." He paused, his voice growing softer. "Donald, it was a successful mission, we found out where they meet. I drove out there. I parked up and got number plates as they left. We are so close to them now, Donald, and it's thanks to you."

Donald found the pastor's words soothing and felt part of the hatred leaching out of him.

"Now if I untie you, will you be calm?"

Donald nodded and the pastor untied him. He sat up and gingerly felt his head; there was a bandage around it.

The pastor insisted that they prayed together. It made Donald feel uncomfortable, but they knelt and prayed for Trish. Pastor Morris finished with, "And as you are my witness, Lord, we will get revenge for Trish and the other fallen ones."

They both said their *amens*.

Afterwards, the pastor led him up to the deserted dormitory. Early morning light was coming through the windows.

"I want you to rest here now. There will be a long day ahead of us later."

Donald smiled and thanked him.

After a while, Donald crept downstairs and left the hostel. He had one final mission to do, a mission that filled him with fear. Donald had to go and tell Bongo about Trish and how he had let her down.

First, though, he needed to go home and get a disguise. The nurses wouldn't be very pleased if he turned up wearing his army uniform.

2

etective Stone looked tired; his daughter had taken a turn for the worse yesterday evening, poor mite. Keyes had told him not to come in, he'd cover it with Chief Inspector Brogan, but Stone had been insistent. *"Got to keep busy, you know."* Stone hated hospitals.

They had decided to break up their morning.

"I'll let you look for this stupid girl, if we can then get back to finding that asshole Donald Gooberman," Stone said.

"Look, are you sure you don't want to disappear for the day?" his partner urged, worried Stone was going to end up hurting someone.

"Fuck that," Stone had muttered. "Go pull her file and then we'll go and see that scrubber's family."

Keyes gave him a long look before leaving his partner to stalk around their little office, while he pulled Trish's file.

Trish had a file. It wasn't a particularly big file, containing only details of a couple of cautions: possession of amphetamine, public urination and assault.

The assault charge had come from an incident a month ago, when she had thrown paint over some woman's fur coat.

"Fucking hippy," Stone had blustered reading this.

Transient had been type-smudged under the word ADDRESS. Stapled to the file was a scribbled note giving the details of her parents.

Mr and Mrs Reed lived in Sketty, which was, for want of a better phrase, a leafy suburb. At least in the summer it was leafy; now it was more a branchy suburb.

They had a well-kept little garden at the front of the house and even a drive.

"Good kid gone bad," Stone mumbled, while shaking his head.

Keyes couldn't work out if he was taking the piss or not.

The door was opened by a well-dressed woman in her late forties; she looked like she had been very pretty once.

"Mrs Reed?" Stone asked in his gravest voice.

She nodded.

"Police, I'm afraid it's about your daughter. May we come in?"

Mrs Reed sagged against the wall, hands up to her mouth to stifle a whimper.

Keyes wished Stone wouldn't always keep doing this.

"Is your daughter Trish Reed?" Stone asked in his sober voice, as they were led into an overstuffed lounge.

"What's wrong?" The mother's voice was shaking and so were her hands.

"When did you last see your daughter?" Stone said, ignoring the question.

"Why what's happened?" The woman was close to crying.

Stone winked at his partner and was about to ask another question when Keyes butted in. "We are sure that your daughter's fine, Mrs Reed. It's just that we have had her reported missing by someone."

"Missing? What do you mean?"

"A friend of hers came to the police station, saying that he hadn't seen her for a while. We often get this sort of thing. A couple has an argument, one of them needs a break, it really is nothing to worry about," he said, while leaning forward and holding her hands between his big paws. They were cold and lifeless. "It really is just a routine inquiry," he assured her.

"We haven't seen Trish for a couple of months. The last time that we saw her, she called around at three in the morning needing money."

Mrs Reed's breath was heavy with gin.

"Was she with anyone?"

The woman paused for a moment. "Not that I saw, she didn't look well. She had lost a lot of weight."

"What about friends, could she be at a friend's house?"

"The only boy I ever saw her with was that Bongo."

The woman pronounced the name Bongo like she would have pronounced the word shit.

"Where is this Bongo?"

"He's in the home on the hill now, drugs put him there."

"The home on the hill?" Keyes was confused.

"Yes, Officer, Cefn Coed Mental Hospital. It was the drugs that put him there."

Keyes and Stone shared a look. Keyes pulled out a picture of another resident of Cefn Coed, the illustrious Donald Gooberman.

Mrs Reed didn't recognise him. Even though he did look like a *"very smart young man"*. The woman talked older than her years.

After a few more questions, they got up to leave.

Keyes stopped at the lounge door. "Before we go, is there a photo of Trish we can borrow?" he asked. "It would be very helpful and I promise I'll return it to you when we find her."

Mrs Reed hesitated for a moment, before going over to the mantelpiece. She removed a picture from it. The picture was of Trish. She couldn't have been more than sixteen when it was taken. She was wearing a baggy knitted jumper and Keyes noticed a silver cross around her neck. Trish was smiling an innocent smile in the photo, unaware of the breaks life was going to throw at her.

He thanked Mrs Reed and they left.

Keyes knew she'd end up plastered by the time hubby came home. A nice drive and little garden; not much of a panacea for having your only daughter drift away from you.

Keyes had left her his card.

"She didn't even know her daughter had been beaten up and put in hospital," Keyes thought out loud as they drove. "Why didn't Trish call them to ask for help? Or I don't know…" He trailed off.

Stone hit the dashboard. "Fuck that, if she'd wanted them to know she could have rung them. She probably wouldn't want to see the father anyway. That's probably why the girl's living on the street in the first place." He turned his head from the road to look at his partner. "If you want, we'll go back tonight when he's back from work. We'll go bad cop, bad cop on the cunt. Ask him why he felt the need to touch up Trish when she was a kid. Then we'll ask that drunken sod of a wife why she didn't cut his dick off for fucking her daughter." Stone rubbed his eyes, all anger having left his voice. "Or it could be that they are just nice, normal, hard-working people who had a fuck-tard for a daughter."

He turned back to the road, seeming older in the light.

3

The house was quiet and still. Alistair lay in bed staring vacantly at his alarm clock. He'd have to be up and out on a run soon. He found it hard to care. He'd been unable to sleep for most of the night, his first date with Maggie running in a loop through his head, trying to work out if he had cocked up or not.

*

Clouds had formed, the breeze picking up, heralding the end of the comet shower.

They had upped sticks and headed back to the car, Ebin and the rest of them fucking about, Maggie and Alistair walking in front, talking softly.

"I'm sorry about tonight. It was a bit of a crap first date," Alistair said.

Maggie stopped, letting go of his hand. "Oh my God, you actually thought we were on a date?"

"Well I just assumed th—"

"Stop being a soppy bastard," she laughed, taking up his hand again. "So far this has been a lovely first date. Thank you for asking me out."

Ebin went screaming past, a ball of hay crashing after him.

"It's definitely different from the cinema," Maggie said.

They got back to the house and all adjourned to the lounge

and Ebin's room. Clancy busied himself making a mull, while Ebin and Mordechai busied themselves smirking at Alistair and Maggie.

"Here, why don't you show Maggie up onto the roof?" Ebin said, nudging Alistair conspiratorially.

"Yeah," Mordechai giggled. "Show her the view from the roof."

Ebin had a theory about the roof. Anytime he brought a girl home, he'd take her up onto it to admire the view.

Ebin reckoned it was a win–win thing to do. Either they did it, which showed they liked you enough to do something dumb. Or they didn't and would make it up to you in a different way, because they felt stupid – God bless him, he was a cunt.

"I'd love to go and sit up on a cold roof," Maggie said, sarcastically. She might have said it sarcastically, but she got up all the same, a wicked smile on her face. "Come on then, show me this roof."

Alistair hesitated for a moment, before getting up and motioning her out of the room. He couldn't help but notice how not one set of eyes left her.

Getting onto the roof was not an easy thing. Alistair had to unscrew one of the landing windows and stand on a chair to shimmy out onto the slippery tiles. Maggie followed quickly on his heels, not seeming too fazed that they were three storeys up.

They sat up there for a while, looking over the city. It really was a great view.

"Do you come here often?" Maggie asked, biting her lip at the cheesiness of the question.

"Quite a bit actually. It's quiet. I like it up here."

"So tell me, Alistair, what exactly is your story?" she said, regarding him fully.

"What do you mean?"

"I don't know, tell me something about yourself."

Tell her what? How good old Moses Jones had taken him under his wing, tutored him in the intricacies of dealing brown? How on that fateful day he'd taken two wraps round to the squat, one for Ceri and one for Trish and Bongo to fight over? Tell her how Bongo had ended up in a coma and he had killed Ceri?

He shrugged. "Recently I've been... I don't know, wanting a change. Swansea's getting me down. I've even started a twelve-step programme of self-improvement."

"Really." Maggie smiled, not unkindly. "What step you on?"

"Now sitting here with you? One more than I was this morning."

"Thanks."

"What about you?"

"What do you mean?" Maggie said, trying to parrot Alistair's accent.

"Well, you don't seem to fit in properly."

Maggie cocked her head to one side and looked at him. "What an incredibly odd thing to say."

"I mean in the club, when we met. You just didn't look as if you belonged there."

"Where do I belong then?"

"Somewhere better."

"Thanks, I think. You're right though. When I was away, I lost touch with a lot of people. All my friends went off to university and, I don't know, it's changed. I'm thinking of following them maybe. I want to go to Bristol and study something. I'm going to go up there for a look around, in a few weeks, maybe."

It was odd; Alistair had only known this girl for a second, but her saying she was leaving pulled at something inside of him.

"And leave this," he said, gesturing over the city, covering the feeling well.

"It's not this pretty all the time," she said, getting up and starting to walk along the ridge of the roof.

Alistair put an arm out to stop her, suddenly scared; the roof was like oil in places.

She turned to look back at him. She looked as sad as hell. "Do you ever feel like you're on the edge? Like you're walking a tightrope and there is nothing good on either side of it? It's all crap?" Maggie smiled sadly and turned away, stepped up to the edge of the roof and spread her arms like in that dumb ass *Titanic* film.

And Alistair was more than scared now. He started to get up, to move towards her. It looked like she was going to jump.

The moment stretched and then she turned and came back to him. "I think it would be best if I go now," she said, not looking into his eyes.

By the time they got to the door downstairs everything was back to normal.

"Sorry about up on the roof." Maggie smiled, doing that biting her lower lip thing. "Sometimes you need to force yourself to do something you don't want to do, but that needs to be done."

"That's ok. You had me going for a second though."

"Good," she said, before leaning forward and kissing him hard.

He kissed her back, but she pulled away, holding him at arm's length. "I've got to go now. Thank your friends and I'll see you soon."

"Wait, I'm sorry if—"

"No, don't be. I really like you, Alistair, but I've got to go now, ok. I'll see you soon though," she said, turning and rushing away into the sodium-orange night.

4

They drove through the large front gates of Cefn Coed Mental Hospital, killing two birds with one stone: *"I'll let you look for this stupid girl, if we can then get back to finding that asshole Donald Gooberman."*

The security guard came out of his little hut to see who they were. He was old; the very thick glasses he wore made his eyes look all weird and buggy. Detective Stone didn't even acknowledge him, just flashed his warrant card, before wheel spinning off.

The long drive curved upwards through some well-kept woods, which thinned out to show the hospital, surrounded by lawns and rose beds. In a spray of gravel Stone parked the car, all angled wrongly, directly outside the front door.

One of the patients came towards them, shuffling, slippered, bedecked in a badly fitting tracksuit, an inane grin on his face.

"Get away from my car! You fucking zombie," Stone shouted, pushing him violently.

The patient emitted a low moan and ran away with his fingers in his ears.

"Let's try and stay calm, shall we?" his partner cautioned.

"I don't want slime all over the car," Stone snapped.

"Just calm it down a bit."

They walked through the front door of the hospital and into a large, high-ceilinged hall. A pretty nurse sat behind the reception counter.

Stone produced his ID. "We're here to see Doctor Linton," he said rudely.

Keyes gave him a stinking look.

The nurse, flustered, checked the computer in front of her. "Do you have an appointment?" she asked.

Stone gave her a disgusted look. He then pulled out his ID again. "This says we don't need an appointment."

The nurse gained a bit of her poise. "Doctor Linton does not like to be disturbed."

Stone marched past her without another word, followed reluctantly by his partner.

The nurse rushed after them complaining.

She rather frostily led them through a maze of passages and up a load of stairs, until they came to the doctor's office.

Keyes had got in front of his partner by this time and used his bulk to stop Stone marching in there and attacking anyone.

Keyes knocked politely, waited a moment and then entered. Stone shoed off the nurse before following.

Doctor Linton didn't even glance up at them. Instead, he held up a finger, gesturing for them to wait as he carried on writing.

Keyes took a moment to study him. Small, grey receding hair, glasses perched on his nose at an arrogant angle.

Keyes cleared his throat, but the doctor kept on writing.

Keyes held out a hand to restrain his partner from jumping over the desk.

Keyes walked over and sat on the desk. It creaked under his weight. Doctor Linton looked up in shock.

Keyes grinned politely.

"How dare you burst in here and act like this!" the doctor exploded.

Keyes held up a finger to stop him, then leant over, picked up the paperwork and dropped it on the floor.

The doctor stared speechlessly.

"I am Detective Keyes and this is my partner, Detective Stone."

He looked at the pile of paper on the floor. "It might be alright to keep your nurses waiting, but don't try to act that way with us, little man."

The doctor turned purple with anger, but was smart enough to keep his mouth shut.

Keyes continued. "We are here due to an ongoing two-pronged investigation." *You want to see an arrogant demeanour, little man?* "Firstly, we are investigating a missing girl. Her name is Trish Reed. We have information to suggest that she has a relationship with one of your patients. His name is Bongo, or Garrett Hughes as you would probably know him." A quick call back to the station had got Bongo's full name and an extensive list of minor convictions and associates. "Later on, after we have finished questioning you, we will, of course, want to talk to him."

Keyes put a picture of Trish on the desk.

The doctor looked at it, recognition flashing across his face. "I know Trish; she is very loyal to Garrett. I was talking to her just last week. I mean she didn't look well at the time. But disappeared? How has she disappeared?"

Keyes was surprised at how quickly concern had replaced anger in the doctor's face. He couldn't help thinking that maybe he'd gotten the wrong impression of him.

"When I talked to Trish last, I asked how she was feeling and she said she was 'doing really well'."

"Did she seem to be acting strangely at all?" Keyes asked. "Or mention that anything unusual had happened?"

"Unusual? Nothing springs to mind. Unusual, such as what?"

"Anything out of the ordinary? People following her perhaps?"

"You think something has happened?" The doctor seemed incredulous.

"We did have a report to that effect."

Doctor Linton turned to look at the sweep of the bay out of his window. "I don't know what to say, Officer. I know it has been a hard three years for the poor girl, especially as Garrett hasn't really been making any progress," he sighed. "If anything, and I know it sounds harsh, I hope she has come to her senses and moved on somewhere else."

Keyes got off the desk and sat in one of the chairs opposite the doctor. His partner remained standing by the door. "Her disappearance was reported to us by a one Donald Gooberman."

"Donald?" the doctor asked.

"Yes, Donald," Stone said, speaking for the first time. "He's been in a bit of trouble lately and see this black eye of mine? Well, that has got him in my personal bad books too."

"Under our current system and due to certain pressures, it was deemed that Donald was fit and ready to be let back into the community," the doctor said, his authoritative air coming back on strong.

"Certain pressures being a lack of beds?" Stone tutted, in disgust.

"Donald was assessed by my medical team and it was decided that as he had made significant progress, and with the correct medication, he would be able to function as a perfectly normal member of society."

"Well, my eye and the man he put in the hospital say he's not functioning very well as a perfectly normal member of society. And when we have him in custody, I guarantee that I will be personally pushing for an inquiry into this hospital's practices."

"How would Donald have known Trish?" Keyes asked, verbally stepping in-between the two men.

The doctor turned to look at him, dismissing Stone. "Donald was friendly with Garrett, in as much as Garrett is able to form any social bond at the moment."

"May we see Garrett?" Keyes asked politely, wanting to get his stewing partner out of the room.

"It is not usual," Doctor Linton said. "But this does not sound like a usual situation." He hesitated for a moment, before pressing a buzzer. "I must warn you though that Garrett has his good days and his bad days."

A few minutes later, a large, mother-hen-like matron came in and was introduced.

"Well, Garrett has currently got a friend visiting him and they are out on the lawn," she said, when hearing their request. "We'd have to see how tired he is."

"This is quite important," Keyes said earnestly.

"Well, hopefully Donald hasn't tired him out too much." She turned to the doctor. "Donald has come to visit Garrett. He looks an awful lot better; he isn't even wearing any camouflage paint."

Keyes and Stone looked at her and then they looked at each other, before running for the door.

5

Danny Howells sat in the conservatory overlooking Mardy Davies' lush and expansive lawn. He absent-mindedly fingered his thick gold chain and wondered why exactly he'd been called round for the second time in two days.

Mardy sat next to him in a wicker chair. They were both smoking cigars in the reflective way that cigars are meant to be smoked. The rain was pittering and pattering on the glass roof above them.

Danny had been sitting out in the conservatory for about an hour, waiting for his friend to join him. Mardy had been finishing up a meeting with some members of the County Council, something about expanding his club, the shitty-looking one down by the docks.

The boss had been buying up land around there for years, convinced that in the future the docks would be regenerated like other cities. Danny doubted it himself, but in all honesty, his friend had that knack of being right about things. Mardy Davies had a good head for business.

*

Even when they were kids, Mardy always had a bunch of different scams going to make money. There had been a bottling company's warehouse down the hill from the estate. They had been going past it one day when Mardy noticed that a skylight was open, a small one, high up on the roof. They had been about seven at the time, him, Mardy and John.

They had climbed onto the roof.

Danny had always been the biggest boy in his year and Mardy had the stocky frame that followed him through into adulthood. This left John; short, scrawny, bespectacled John. Short and scrawny enough to fit through the skylight and get out bottles of pop.

Mardy though had said no, arguing that the skylight could be closed tomorrow. It would be better for them to loosen some of the roof tiles from the inside, thus giving them access whenever they wanted.

It was that kind of thinking that got Mardy Davies a conservatory, overlooking an expansive lawn.

*

"What do you think about him?" Mardy asked, bringing Danny back to the present.

They were discussing Karl Reno.

"I think he should be strung up and shot with his own shit," Danny replied.

"I just don't know why he has to act like that. Paul Marshall is a decent man, a fucking lousy card player, but a decent man."

"It was a bit over the top," Danny agreed.

"I know it's important to act tough, but you don't need to smash up his shop and terrify his daughter like that."

"How old is she?"

"About sixteen, sweet little thing too," Mardy sighed. "I don't know if it's old age setting in or just the weather, but I am getting a bit sick of all this." He examined the end of his cigar. "As soon as the council vote to invest money in the docks, which after today's little talk they will, I'm legitimising, getting away from baseball bats and all the rest of this nonsense."

Now Danny realised why he'd been called round: Mardy wanted a sounding board. "Would John allow that?" he asked. John was only brought up when they were alone.

"He'd have to agree," Mardy said, catching himself. "Right now though, I'm more concerned about Karl."

Danny noticed the quick change of topic. Danny was very loyal to John. John had got him his kid back. He let it go for now though, turning back to that little twat Karl Reno. "I've said it before, but he thinks he's cleverer than he is, even cleverer than you, which isn't clever."

"What can I do though? He got results. Marshall was on the phone this morning saying he had the money." Mardy tapped ash into a gold-leafed ashtray. "I sent Ivor round this morning to pick up the money."

Behind them there was a knock and Tony lumbered into the conservatory.

"I've just had that stationery shop owner on the phone nearly in tears," Tony told his boss. "You're never going to guess what's happened."

6

Karl Reno's phone rang. He recognised Tony's number. He turned it off.

Karl was busy.

The **[REDACTED]** crew were coming to town.

Reno wanted to look professional for them. He'd told Kieran to buy a *fucking* suit. He'd told Kieran to drive, he'd told him to stay silent, stay in the car – he'd told him to chauffeur.

Kieran had been well chuffed.

Reno looked around the deserted car park. Batty Boy was running late.

They'd arranged to meet here, outside Swansea on neutral ground. In the distance, miles down the valley, you could just make out the city; a drizzle was falling.

The **[REDACTED]** crew were coming to town. Soon there'd be no more answering the phone to Mardy, no more of his monkey work. Karl was going to become the organ grinder.

No more monkey work – like that thing with Zach the Mac.

*

The same nurse had been on duty. She stared at him malevolently as he'd walked into Zach's room. Zach was sitting up. He looked better; he could talk a bit now, even though it all came out slurred, like he was still punch drunk.

"How're you feeling?" Karl asked.

Zach gave him a *how do you think I'm feeling* look.

"That's too bad," Karl said. "You've got to be out of town by tomorrow."

"Huh?" Zach managed, his face radiating surprise.

"Mardy wants you out of town by tomorrow." He shrugged. "Them's the breaks."

"Them's the breaks," Zach repeated, slurring the words. "You know you'll be sorry."

"I don't think so," Karl laughed. "What are you going to do, you fucking cripple? You've been banished."

Banished, he liked that word.

"You'll be sorry," Zach shouted after him as he left.

*

Banished, that was a good word. Karl was going to banish a lot of people in the next few days, at least the lucky ones.

A car was coming; he heard it way before he saw it, the deep bomp, bomp, bomp of the base shook the ground.

It was a top of the range beamer. It turned into the car park. Batty Boy and Daryl sat in the back.

The **[REDACTED]** crew were here.

Zach smiled – no more monkey work for him.

Little did he know that this was just the advance party.

The rest of the slaughter crew were on their way.

7.

Alistair dramatically fell through the door and staggered past Carter into the kitchen, before drinking water, heavily, from the cleanest glass.

Carter liked Alistair's falling through the door ritual.

Carter lived in one of the terrace houses, a long walk up a slippery, steep hill above town. From his back bedroom you could see the fights kicking off along the strip as the nightclubs chucked out. This meant Carter could see his own bedroom window, while he was stamping on someone's head.

Carter loved fighting. In his bedroom he had a four-foot-long wooden lamp stand with one notch carved in it for each *"fucker I decked"*. There were a lot of notches.

"You look like you've just got off the fucking sunshine bus," Carter said, laughing loudly, as Alistair gulped down water.

Carter always made the same joke and always laughed loudly at it. Being a psycho, Carter could laugh loudly at whatever the heck he wanted.

Carter had been a dealer since back in the day, whenever that was exactly. Except for the two times hanging out at Her Majesty's pleasure.

He sat there now, wearing only a dirty pair of boxer shorts, with his scraggily hair falling onto his bare muscular shoulders.

"You should move somewhere closer to town," Alistair said, noticing Carter was out of breath. He'd probably been masturbating too vigorously, Alistair thought, because, Carter was indeed a vicious wanker.

Alistair hated this weekly delivery. It meant being around the speed-fuelled, paranoid-as-fuck Carter.

A few months ago he had to push the drugs through the letter box. Carter was all barricaded up inside, coming off a four-day amphetamine jag, gabbling a paranoid, blue streak – how he knew they were after him and were out to get him.

The fucking idiot even had an escape ladder in his bedroom.

Today though, Alistair had bigger things on his mind than Carter. He couldn't shake this nagging feeling that he'd done something to scare off Maggie. It had been as if she couldn't wait to get out of there last night.

Carter returned to whatever vacuous show he was watching. Alistair stood at the kitchen window finishing his glass of water. The whole city was spread out below him, all of it looking tired and grey. The only colour in the whole vista was a merrily burning fire in an oil drum out the back.

"What're you burning?" Alistair asked.

"Nothing," Carter said, quite viciously.

Alistair flashed his best *couldn't give a shit anyway* smile, before joining him on the couch to watch some poor-looking people crying in front of an audience.

Alistair stared at the screen with little interest, for a while, before digging around in his little black bag and pulling out a large lump of pot.

"Here you go. Also, you owe for the last two weeks' worth as well."

"Whatcha mean the last two weeks' worth?" Carter snapped, mad as fuck, psycho eyes flashing.

"You haven't paid any money for the last two weeks," Alistair sighed. "And I need it today."

Sod it; I'm not scared of you.

"You saying I'm behind?"

Stare him down. "Yes, I'm saying you're behind."

The staring match stretched.

Alistair's hand slid onto his cosh.

The staring match stretched.

Carter broke eye contact.

Carter lost.

"Here you go then," he said, digging into the recesses of the sofa and handing over a big wedge of notes.

Alistair counted it, taking his time, like the top-dog gets to. The first notes were crispy clean, the rest red splattered, tanning brown.

"Fucked up my knuckles the other night," Carter said, showing off his war wounds and trying to win back his dominance with a new fighting story.

"This twat owes me money, you know Andy? That Goth cunt, he's been avoiding me for weeks."

He stopped, water bubbled as he lit the bong.

"I'd taken a few tabs of acid to go down Dirty Dora's like, loads of fit women there, man." He nudged Alistair conspiratorially. "On the way home, I decides to give the little twat a visit," Carter continued between lungfuls of watery smoke.

Alistair normally had a few hits of the bong when he called in on Carter. However, he planned to forgo this, still step, step, stepping it as he was.

"Anyway, I gets to the house right and put the door through, takes a couple of kicks like, but it goes through."

Carter's leg flew out to demonstrate his technique.

Alistair nodded, in as reflective a way as he could be bothered.

"Then there's Andy, coming down the stairs with a baseball bat." He paused for dramatic effect. "I tell you, mate, I nearly shoved it up his fucking ass."

Alistair acted suitably impressed.

"So I has him up against the wall, then his bitch girlfriend starts screaming, so I slaps her, shuts her up like." Carter demonstrated on thin air.

Alistair moved away slightly; something about Carter's story was bothering him.

"Anyway, I start smashing the house up with the baseball bat and Andy reckons he doesn't know who I am or anything about my seven quid. So I starts hitting him."

While Carter continued his fight with the air, it occurred to Alistair what was bothering him. "Which house does Andy live in again?" he asked.

"Just past the Vivian Arms, the house with no door," Carter said, annoyed that his story was interrupted. He swiped again at the atmosphere. "So eventually he remembers that he does know me and… Oh, here's the money," Carter finished his story, triumphantly smiling at Alistair, as if he was waiting for a round of applause.

"I thought Wee Gay Andy didn't have a girlfriend," Alistair said, trying to keep a straight face.

And that was the problem, Alistair thought, after leaving Carter's and heading down the steep hill towards Brynmill and his next drop-off: the plain, unadulterated, stupidity of those that surrounded him. It really was unbelievable. Sure, he was just a small cog in a large criminal machine. And God knows what the likes of Danny, Karl and those two big fellas, Tony and Ivor, got up to, but stupid? Gee whiz. If they conducted their affairs in the same way as the people Alistair worked with, then goodness knows how there was any crime in the city at all. No matter how dumb the local constabulary was, they should really notice the guy with a head full of acid kicking in strangers' doors or someone like Lettuce stumbling around loaded down with bags of pot.

Compared to the level the others worked at, Alistair came over as a Moriarty esq. figure. When out on a run, he always tried to vary his route as much as he could be bothered. Also, whenever he remembered, he'd keep an eye out for anything suspicious.

Over the years of doing this, Alistair had developed a number of little games to keep him alert. Often he would walk through town pretending to be a spy; Alinski, spy extraordinaire, traversing Moscow with vital information and stolen microchips in his little black bag.

Other times, he pretended to be a racing car.

Today though he wasn't concentrating on anything. Walking through the Uplands, lost in the thoughts of last night, Alistair didn't see the police cars and all the billowing Scene of Crime tape, until he almost collided with an overweight policeman.

"How are you today, sir?" the policeman asked, casually moving in front of him.

8

The street had been taped off. A number of uniformed coppers milled around a badly parked car. Even from a distance the blood, splattered all over it, stood out.

"The day just gets better." Detective Stone smiled, getting out of the car. He was in a great mood, despite losing Donald again.

*

They had burst out of the hospital and run across the lawn towards the solitary figure of Bongo/Garrett. Stone had been in front, getting there first. He had shaken the patient, asked him where Donald was, called him a *"Vegetable"*, before shouting *"Fuck"* and running towards the woods.

Keyes was rushing after his partner when Bongo put a hand out to stop him.

"They've taken her, burnt her all up and left nothing," Bongo said.

Keyes tried to run past him, but Bongo's grip was akin to iron. He pulled Keyes closer, his reeking breath surrounding them.

"No one protected her, not Donald, not Alistair, no one. And she is dead. Dead." Bongo's hold went limp, his eyes welling up.

One of the hospital nurses appeared next to them; a large, bald, black man, who towered even over Keyes. "Donald had some bad news for Garrett." The name plate he wore said Warren. "I think Garrett should come inside now."

Warren gently took Bongo away.

"Where's Donald?" Keyes shouted after him.

Warren shrugged. "That boy sure did love to hide."

Keyes stood there watching them walk back across the grass to the hospital.

"Cheers for the help," Stone said jogging up, out of breath.

"He started talking," Keyes mumbled.

"I bet that was fucking helpful."

While heading back to the car, Stone's phone started to ring. He huffily pulled it out to answer. The conversation lasted for about a minute before Stone closed the phone and started whooping and spinning, like a bad Julie Andrews' impersonator.

He bounded up to his partner. "We gotta go."

*

"Are you two going to be the lead officers?" the overweight sergeant, who seemed to be in charge of the scene, asked.

Stone ignored the question. "What happened?" he said.

Good mood or not, you have to keep up your image in front of the help.

"It's been a busy day," Sergeant Toms answered, gesturing to the first lot of police tape.

"The Post Office across the street was robbed earlier and we've been dealing with that all morning. Then this happens." He gestured to the car.

Keyes surveyed the scene.

"Are they related?"

"I don't think so," the sergeant said, glancing at his notebook, like it was stand up in court time. "We've got a couple of good descriptions of the man who did over the Post Office; skinny guy in a ski mask. White, about five-nine, probably the same one you've been chasing for a while. Then there's the one with the car. Well, I saw that myself." He paused for a moment, scratching the end of his nose. "Very nasty business."

"Well?" Stone geed him along.

"I was here speaking to a possible witness; this scruffy-looking kid, who seemed very nervous for some reason. I was about to search his bag when it all kicked off." He paused for another scratch. "The victim had parked here and gone into the stationery shop. He was only in there for a moment and I didn't think anything of it. When he came out and was getting into his car, it all happened."

"Are you going to tell us?" Stone barked.

"As I was saying," Toms continued, slowly. "A big man bursts out of the bushes, grabs the victim by the collar and the victim is a fair old size mind you, smashes his head against the roof of the car, kicks away his legs and starts slamming the door on his head."

"What did you do?" Keyes asked, looking at the drying blood pooled around the car.

"Well, I shout out. Tell the scruffy kid to stay where he is and run over. So does Suzie." The sergeant gestured towards a young, plain-looking policewoman they had ignored up until now. "So the assailant digs around in the victim's pockets for a moment, pulls something out and hightails it into the stationery shop."

"Did you follow?" Stone asked curtly.

The sergeant gave him a cold look. "Course I followed, so did young Suzie. The guy bolted through the stationery shop and out the back. We lost him a little while after that."

"You lost him?"

"Lot of that going around," Sergeant Toms retorted, looking at Stone's bruised eye.

"Was the assailant dressed up like a soldier?" Keyes asked.

The sergeant went back to his notebook. Keyes was pretty sure he only checked his notes to annoy Stone.

"No, he was dressed very smartly. He seemed to be wearing a

suit. It is your guy though," Toms continued. "There's one witness who can positively identify him as Donald Gooberman." He pointed towards a little old lady standing by the wall. "She saw him hiding in the bushes and was going to ask how his mother was, but as he seemed so busy, with all his vigilante business, she didn't want to disturb him."

Stone headed off without another word towards the stationery shop, his large partner following behind.

Sergeant Toms shook his head. "It's better to stay away from those two, Suzie. They're a pair of lunatics."

9

They were going to find Donald Gooberman *heavy*.

Tony was driving his intimidating beamer; Danny sat in the passenger seat, their respective aftershaves clashing.

"I don't like it," Tony said. "Are we really going to go *heavy*?"

Danny was silent for a while. "That's what he wants."

"I know that, but it's not like we're dealing with superman."

"That's what he wants," Danny repeated.

*

Danny and Mardy had been sitting in the conservatory when Tony lumbered in.

"I've just had that stationery shop owner on the phone nearly in tears," Tony told his boss. "You're never going to guess what's happened."

Mardy put his cigar in the ashtray and massaged his temples. "He's not still going on about having to smash up his shop, is he? If he carries on I'll go down and make him do it again."

"He was very upset and he wanted you to know that it had nothing to do with him."

"What didn't have anything to do with him?" Mardy asked. He was tired and Tony did have a tendency to over-dramatise things.

"Well, that's the thing, it took me a while to get him to calm down and tell me—"

"And are you going to tell me?" the boss snapped.

Danny smiled into his drink.

"Alright, just because you've got a headache coming on, don't take it out on me," Tony said, sounding hurt. "Ivor went round to get the money off him and then got mugged."

"Ivor got mugged?" Danny blinked. "Who the hell would start trouble with Ivor?"

"What the fuck?" Mardy rose to his feet, ashtray flying into the wall. "Is someone trying to fuck with us? I have a reputation to uphold you know. Get Ivor here now. I want to know what these muggers look like."

"That's another problem, see," Tony said, uncomfortable in the face of his boss's anger. "Ivor's in hospital, he's in a coma."

Danny whistled. "Jesus, I thought he was meant to be hard."

"Who did this?" Mardy said, his face twisted into an expression of anger, his voice eerily calm. "It was the shopkeeper, wasn't it? Bring him to me now."

"No, it wasn't," Tony, who had drunk with Paul Marshall in the club a couple of times and quite liked him, said quickly. "It was that Donald Gooberman twat again."

"Well, go and get him then!" the boss screamed.

Tony gratefully turned to leave.

"Wait," Mardy ordered. "Danny, you go too. Ring Reno as well. I've had enough of this nonsense. I want this prick found today. I want everyone to go heavy as well."

"Seriously?" Danny started to say before seeing the look on Mardy's face. He shrugged instead and left with Tony, who was already on the phone trying to get hold of that little shit Karl Reno.

*

"I don't care what Mardy wants, I'll stick with the golf club," Tony said, changing gears as they started to drive up the steep hill to Danny's house.

Danny ran his hand over his stubbly skull. "That'll be fine with me."

"I mean, it's been so long I had to have a think where I keep it. Where do you keep yours?"

"Somewhere safe," Danny said as they pulled up to the kerb.

10

Suzie Gorman watched her sergeant walk away, muttering to himself. She was left standing on her own. The adrenaline of the chase was wearing off now. It was being replaced with the fear about what she had in her pocket.

Suzie hadn't been a policewoman for very long and every day she found her faith being tested to its breaking point. She had always thought being a policewoman would be about helping people, but between the work load, time spent writing up reports and just the general detritus you had to wade through daily, people seemed to be pushed to the sidelines.

*

A while ago she had discussed it at her Wednesday prayer group. It had shamed her to say, but she felt the milk of human kindness had run dry in the people of Swansea. This had only led to the same old arguments they seemed to have every week. Suzie had left feeling no better than when she had arrived.

It was on her way out that the reverend called her back. He asked if she had a moment to meet someone. Suzie could always spare a moment for Reverend Roberts; he'd been at the church since she was a girl.

Reverend Roberts led her through to his study at the back of the church. A man was sitting there facing away from the door; he stood to greet her as she entered.

"This is Suzie Gorman, the whole congregation is very proud of her," Reverend Roberts said. "She is with the police."

"A very necessary job," the man had nodded.

Suzie noticed he had the most piercing green eyes she had ever seen.

Reverend Roberts lowered himself into his chair and motioned the others to sit.

"This is Pastor Morris," he told Suzie.

The old reverend fell silent for a long time. The silence grew.

"Suzie," he said finally. "Pastor Morris does important work for God. I beseech you; if he ever needs any help, please give it to him."

Suzie had been a little taken aback, sure she was missing some underlying context. "What exactly is this important work?" she asked Pastor Morris.

"I am, like us all, just a simple servant of the Lord. My calling has put me on the path of helping some of the most wretched people in this city." He had leant forward and taken Suzie's hand. "It is a hard job and you would be a blessing to me if you would help."

Suzie found it difficult to break the pastor's stare; there was something about it. It drew her in, made her want to please him. She found herself nodding that she would help.

"Thank you, Suzie," the green-eyed man had said.

He had said this softly with an accent she couldn't quite place.

*

It had been a month later when Pastor Morris had turned up at her house. He needed to find a car; a pink Cadillac. He asked if she could help.

Of course, Suzie had been reluctant to get the name and address, but there was something about the pastor. She had done as he had asked, pulling the name and address of Zachariah Plum.

A week later Zachariah Plum landed up in hospital.

Pastor Morris had come to her house again this morning. This time he had a registration number. Again he needed her help. She knew it was the wrong thing to do, but there was just something in his eyes that was… well, almost hypnotising. It was amazing how the little scrap of paper in her pocket felt so heavy.

"Where's that scruffy-looking fellow?" Sergeant Toms asked, walking towards her.

11

The scruffy-looking fellow was, in fact, hightailing it up the steep hill towards Danny's house. He was going to drop off the money. Then, he was going to pinch a line from the Dead Kennedys' and inform Danny to *"take this job and shove it"*. He was sick of this shit. Sod the idea of twelve steps; he was going to take one giant leap.

He'd nearly been arrested back there.

*

"How are you today, sir?" the red-faced policeman had asked him.

"Fine thanks. How are you?"

There was a silence.

"What happened?" Alistair asked, to fill the silence, noticing all the other policemen buzzing in and out of the Post Office.

"Rather a nasty robbery, about an hour ago." The policeman inched closer. "An old lady was hurt rather badly. She's in hospital."

"Is she ok?" Alistair asked, generally concerned.

"We don't know." The policeman's tone was grave. "You haven't seen anything suspicious, have you?"

"No, nothing." *Ah, nothing except Carter sitting there in his boxer shorts, while a barrel of his clothes burned out back. Oh, and of course the money, with blood on it, in my bag. That's right, the blood-covered money next to a couple of hundred pounds worth of pot.* "I've been in bed all morning anyway," Alistair said, noticing his voice shaking slightly.

"What's in the bag?" The policeman's tone had an edge to it now.

"Nothing... Er, my washing," Alistair lied, badly.

"Sir, I am going to need to inspect the contents of the bag."

"It's very smelly washing."

"Sir, if you could just step over to the police ca— bloody hell!"

Alistair turned and was surprised to see the nutter from his house, slamming a car door on somebody's head.

"You wait here," the policeman ordered, while running towards Donald.

Alistair was too busy scurrying off in the opposite direction to see what happened next.

*

Sod twelve steps, one big leap, that's what he needed.

A fucking Post Office robbery! For fuck's sake, it was even the fucking Post Office closest to Carter's own house. That was it – epiphany time, road to Damascus time, whatever analogy Danny wanted to hear; Alistair didn't care, he was out.

Alistair had been doing this shit now for three years, three whole years of his life. Was that how long it had been? Three years since he'd met Danny Howells and inadvertently applied for this job.

*

It was while he was going through his bad patch, the death, well, his murder of Ceri, was still hanging, lead-weight heavy, on his heart.

He'd been laying low.

He'd been getting drunk.

He'd been getting as drunk as a skunk in a funk, burning

through money fast. Terrified the bastards could put it all together and come after him.

Alistair used to drink in the Fountain, a run-down pub, in a run-down estate, in a run-down area of the run-down fucking city. It was his Hole in the Wall.

That was when he had met Danny Howells. They had got talking. Alistair, all drunk, skint and lonely, had been invited back for a smoke.

After that Alistair went around a lot. Danny only lived around the corner and never seemed to want Alistair to pay for any of the pot. Looking back, Alistair realised that it had been a recruiting strategy.

Danny had just come out of prison for something. He never talked about what. He had just got his kid back from Social Services; something that by all accounts had happened surprisingly fast. Danny was now turning his energy to recruiting runners.

Danny had good connections, a pot supply having just opened up down south in **[REDACTED]**. So Alistair was being groomed as one of his new recruits.

It is amazing how hindsight is always 20/20.

Alistair had his final interview for the post one wet afternoon. He remembered how the rain had been beating down, double time, on the corrugated roof.

Townhill was full of these prefabricated, post-war houses, which were only meant to last for ten years. That had been back in the nineteen-fifties.

Danny's nine-year-old son was stuck inside the house and was bored, the rain having taken away any chance for him to go out for a crafty fag or to torture a cat. The little Damien-child had decided to amuse himself by coming up behind Alistair and hitting him on the head with an Action Man, while calling him a *"Wanker"*.

Out of good manners, Alistair didn't say anything for a couple of minutes. Eventually though, he had enough.

"Look, fuck off," he said, turning around to look at the little bastard.

Before he knew it, Alistair was up against the wall on tiptoes, one of Danny's rough hands around his throat. It all happened so fast that Alistair still had a joint in his hand.

Danny was the shorter of the two and was now looking up at Alistair, an animal snarl on his face. "What the fuck are you doing swearing at my son?" Danny growled. "Apologise to him now." The words were spat out.

Even though Alistair couldn't see him, he knew the little brat had a big grin on his face. That incensed him more than Danny was scaring him. "What're you going to do? Fucking hit me?" Alistair hoped that sounded more aggressive than he actually felt. Inside he was jellified. "Well, you do what you have to do, but I am not taking shit from any nine year old."

Alistair tensed himself, wondering whether Danny would put in a head or body shot first. Seconds past, Danny kept on staring; Alistair reckoned a head shot.

He felt the pressure around his neck slacken.

Danny stepped away and turned to his kid. "Be more polite," he said.

Alistair made sure that Danny saw him take a measured toke of the joint, concentrating on making his hands not shake.

Danny never mentioned the incident again. It was an hour later that he made the job offer.

Alistair had always wondered if the way he'd acted convinced Danny or perhaps he was already planning to make the proposal. Who knew? Perhaps is a horrible word; it is like harbouring that idea about other universes. Perhaps in another universe he had said no, or at least given it more thought, but in this universe he had said yes.

Ebin had gone on a rant about it once. How there should never be a perhaps, there should only be a definite. A here and a now, we don't have enough time for perhaps. You have one chance, one go and that's it. Deal with the responsibility and make your choices. That is the responsibility of life. There are no ifs or maybes, just time ticking past never to be relived.

And now, standing outside Danny's bomb-proof door, Alistair felt great. He was seeing Maggie again tonight and he was changing, he could feel it.

For once the heavy metal door was locked.

He knocked loudly.

There was no answer.

He knocked again.

Danny finally arrived, just as Alistair, cheesed off and wet from waiting, was going to leave. Danny and Tony pulled up outside the house. Tony sat in the car, engine running.

Danny got out and came down the little path to the house. He really didn't seem happy, gruffly inviting Alistair in and taking the money off him without any preamble.

"Look I'm busy at the moment so scarper until your next run," Danny said, going into the kitchen.

Alistair followed, deciding against using the Dead Kennedy line. "I am not doing this anymore," he said instead.

Danny started moving the washing machine.

Alistair cleared his throat. "I said I am not doing this anymore." His voice sounded deeper the second time. "I'm not sure how much notice I have to give, but I'll work for another two weeks then I'm out."

Danny ignored him. In fact, he seemed quite stressed as he was now pulling up part of the floor.

Alistair had decided it would be best to put his leaving into context, set the scene. Besides, it's not like it was the Mafia after all.

Ninja had left once. He had thought his girlfriend was pregnant. It seemed to be something he took incredibly seriously. Ninja had told Danny he needed a more respectful line of work, so had joined a call centre. It hadn't lasted long, with Ninja ending up getting into a screaming argument with a customer, smashing up his phone and being escorted from the building.

Danny was still scrabbling away in the corner of the kitchen. Under the linoleum was a small safe.

Alistair continued talking. He told Danny about Carter burning his clothes and the blood-stained money. He was going to mention Maggie and how absolutely amazing she was and how she was just really—

Danny opened the safe. It was stacked deep with money and also something else.

Danny pulled the gun out of the safe and turned around.

"Jesus, Danny, this isn't the Mafia," Alistair managed to croak.

12

The door was finally opened by Brother Dowling, who seemed shocked at Donald's appearance. "Where have you been?" he spluttered, while urgently ushering him inside.

After Donald had walked past him, Brother Dowling nervously scanned the graveyard. It was as quiet and overgrown as ever, but now there was an audible sense of oncoming doom attached to it. An involuntary shiver went up his spine before he slammed and bolted the heavy oak door.

"You're covered in blood, what happened? Where have you been?" Brother Dowling asked mopping his brow. "Why are you wearing a suit?"

*

The suit had been part of Donald's camouflage. He'd put it on, before going to tell Bongo that he had failed and Trish was dead.

Donald had picked up the suit from his mother's house. She had been overjoyed to see Donald inside again, like a respectable boy, and out of those silly-looking army clothes.

She had busied herself making tea, while he was upstairs changing into his suit. It was charcoal grey and smelt musty. He hadn't worn it since his father's funeral and had to squirm to get into it. Donald didn't want to go and see Bongo, so had gladly spent an hour drinking tea with his mother, as she filled him in on all the latest gossip.

"And you know that nice man, Mr Marshall, deary? He had his shop smashed up yesterday." She delicately nibbled a bourbon. "Everyone in the Post Office thinks that he owes money to some criminals, you know, what with his gambling problem and everything. It is his daughter I feel sorry for; she was picked on by them."

This caught Donald's attention.

"Mrs Williams saw her running away from the shop in tears, poor thing. No one called the police, you know. It does annoy me, all these petty gangsters, strutting around like they own the town and even threatening young girls."

Donald put down his tea to listen to his mother; he'd known little Amy for years.

"We were all saying how good it would be if there was someone to teach them a lesson," she went on. "Mr Marshall was in front of me in the bank today as well. He seemed to be getting out some money. I don't know what that is for though." His mother watched Donald carefully. "The bank teller said she'd need clearance to give him that much at once and the poor man became quite angry. He said he needed it by midday."

Donald drained his tea and got up to go. He'd have to hurry up to the hospital in order to be back in time.

His mother watched him go, for once, feeling quite proud of her son. She'd be the talk of the Post Office tomorrow.

*

It felt like it had taken a long time to walk up to the hospital, Donald's suit feeling itchy and claustrophobic all the way.

Donald was nervous. He had timed it so he would arrive just after the morning meds and a little bit before mid-morning meds. Donald reasoned that, if Bongo didn't take the news well, he'd only have to be upset for half an hour.

Sam, the old security guard, was still on the front gate. He recognised the hulking form of Donald, through his thick glasses, and let him walk up the long drive.

Inside all the nurses made a fuss of him, saying he looked well and they were glad he had stopped all that silly pretending to be in the army business.

That proves the camouflage is working, Donald thought.

Donald's old ward sister came bustling in; she always bustled.

"Why Donald," she beamed, before hugging him. "Don't you look smart?"

Very few of her patients came back in a shirt and tie. Some of them did come back in jackets though.

Donald had told her he had come to see Garrett, who, as luck would have it, had just taken his morning meds and was due a walk in the grounds.

Warren, the big, black orderly, had brought Bongo out.

They had walked for a while across the wet lawn with Warren following a little distance behind. Bongo didn't walk so much as shuffle, a long thread of saliva hanging from his mouth.

Donald had been struggling with a way of breaking the news about Trish, but he hadn't been able to. So instead, he just blurted it out. "Trish is dead, they killed her." Actually hearing the words being said like this, made them hit home. He felt his eyes well up with tears.

Bongo stopped his zombie-shuffle and turned to Donald. His eyes were all crusted and red, like he'd been crying for a lifetime. "I know, they come to me and they tell me these things." His voice was almost inaudible.

"Who do?"

"They come in the night, through the walls. I know it all."

"What do you know? Tell me," Donald pleaded, all snotty and tearful.

"Will you avenge her?" Bongo asked.

Donald, wetly, wiped his nose before nodding.

"Then you'd better run."

Donald had turned to see the two policemen running out of the hospital and looking around.

*

"The cameras picked you up entering the graveyard, but they only see so far. Were you followed?" Brother Dowling asked, nervously, as he bustled Donald along the hostel's corridors. "The pastor was worried when you disappeared like that. I haven't seen him this on edge ever," he confided.

Donald nodded, wondering why they were going down the corridor to the communal bathroom.

"He has been sitting in his office all morning with the door closed. Everyone else is down in the operation centre."

Brother Dowling unlocked a cupboard in the long, tiled communal bathroom and dug around, getting out a towel and opening a bar of soap.

"Jason and Muppet are worried you'll be angry with them. You won't be, will you?"

Donald had shaken his head in the negative, which seemed to please Brother Dowling. He pressed the towel and the already sweat-moistened soap into Donald's hand and pushed him towards the nearest shower.

"You need to wash off all that blood. Where on earth did it all come from?"

"I was hiding in a bush," Donald started to say. But in truth, his memory was hazy.

*

The bush he'd been crouching in had given him an unobstructed view of the stationery shop. His only distraction was when Mrs Beynon stopped to talk. She said how smart he looked in that suit and asked him how the vigilante business was going.

A little while later, almost on the stroke of midday, he saw a car stop and a man, with ugly features, enter the stationery shop.

The man looked like one of those petty gangsters.

When the man came back out, Donald had moved quickly, running up behind him and kicking away his legs.

It was then things went a bit hazy; Donald remembered this incredible feeling of hate well up inside him. Images of Trish burning and thrashing flickered in front of his eyes. And then, he was in the shop, covered in blood, handing back a brown envelope to Mr Marshall.

"Tell Amy, I'll protect her," he said.

Mr Marshall hadn't seemed that pleased to see him and asked a number of odd questions, such as, *"What the hell do you think you are doing?"* and *"Do you know who those people were?"* Mr Marshall then put his head in his hands and started quietly sobbing.

Donald, who had always felt a bit awkward when dealing with emotions, ran out of the back of the shop, as the police came in the front.

*

When Donald finished with his shower, there were a pile of charity box clothes waiting in a neatly folded pile. They fitted worse than the suit.

Donald put on the ill-fitting clothes and followed Brother Dowling down through the trap door and then into the operations room.

"Now you make sure you stay calm," Brother Dowling said, as he spun the lock to the door.

Inside Jason and Muppet froze, stopping what they were doing and eying Donald warily.

Donald looked at them in surprise. What had happened to their hair?

13

Two of their cases were within thirty feet of each other.

Detective Keyes had just heard from the hospital. The old woman from the Post Office robbery might not pull through. The skull-crushed Ivor might not pull through – *"operate on the old lady first."*

This amount of violence equalled a lot of police – meaning they could delegate; Keyes had to admit he liked that word.

Three hours in now, officers were going door to door, taking statements and canvassing. Crime Techs were dusting, scraping, lifting and bagging. While Keyes and Stone good cop, bad copped the stationery shop owner.

"So Mr Marshall, you have definitely never seen the victim before?" Stone asked, for the third time.

"Like I've told you, he came into my shop to ask for directions to the—"

"To the motorway."

"Yes, to the motorway."

"Why would a man who lived in Swansea need directions to the M4?"

"Well I suppose…"

Keyes let the answer drift over him. Marshall was lying. Lies and blood, that's all he'd been wading through for the last three hours. He was tired of it. It was taking time away from searching for Trish; *"They've taken her, burnt her all up and left nothing."*

They'd been into the Post Office once the Techs were done. The old lady's blood was thick on the counter.

The old lady's blood was sprayed up the wall.

The surveillance camera hadn't been working. They'd talked to the manager. He had said the old biddy didn't know how to change tapes, before asking how much had been stolen.

"When the Post Office manager comes down, handcuff him and take him to the cells," Stone had ordered someone.

That bastard was going to be having a bad day.

They moved on to Ivor's car. The car was due to be towed to the yard. Council workers lolled around, waiting to move in and clean the blood off the street.

Blood and lies – wading through it.

The old lady had been lying. "Do you know, I'm not sure if it was Donald Gooberman I saw in the bush."

"But Mrs Beynon, earlier you told my police sergeant that it was."

"Did I, dear? My mind isn't what it was, you know," she said, an amused twinkle in her eye.

Paul Marshall was lying.

"I think you're lying, Mr Marshall," Stone said. "Now Ivor isn't a nice person and he doesn't work for nice people. When they find out you are helping the person who killed him, then they are going to—"

"He's dead?" Paul Marshall looked terrified.

Stone nodded gravely – *as far as you're concerned, stupid.* "They are not going to be happy with you, Mr Marshall. Now tell us the truth, what really happened?"

"Ivor came in to collect money I owed to his boss, Mardy Davies." Marshall sagged. He was scared, tired and beaten. "I'd lost heavily at one of his private games. Ivor was coming round to pick up the money."

"So you hired Donald Gooberman to get him first?"

"No, God no, I haven't seen Donald for years, since he was locked up in the mental institution."

"Why would he try and help you then?"

"I honestly don't know. The bloody idiot just came in here and gave me back my money," Marshall said, pulling a blood-soaked envelope out of a drawer.

Stone took it off him and ripped it open, counting money.

He whistled. "You did lose heavily. Now, you know this money would normally be put into evidence until the case is cleared? How long would that be, Detective Keyes?"

"Until the case is cleared? Gosh, after the trial I'd imagine. Goodness me, probably for at least a year I'd say."

Paul Marshall turned green.

"However, you can take this back and we can leave you to argue your case with Mardy Davies." Stone waved the money enticingly. "You'd have to work for us from now on though. If we want any information about Mardy or if we want anything else for that matter, you've got to help us."

Paul Marshall turned greener. "I couldn't; if he found out, he'd kill me."

"That's the deal I'm afraid."

"I can't."

"That's no problem. Could you hand me an evidence bag please, Detective Keyes?"

"Wait. Ok, ok, I'll do it," Paul Marshall said.

Stone smiled. "If I give you this money back, that'll be it, we own you. Day or night we own you."

Marshall had licked his lips, eying the money. Marshall had nodded. Marshall looked ready to cry.

"Then you need to kiss my shoe," Stone said.

Marshall looked confused.

Stone put out his boot, toe up.

"Kiss it," Stone urged. "Show us you're committed."

Marshall hesitated.

Stone waved the money.

Marshall went down and kissed it.

"You belong to us now," Stone said, throwing the money onto the counter.

They left the shop, Stone whistling, his partner following after him.

Stone really must be in a good mood; normally he'd have spent longer debasing Paul Marshall.

*

He'd been in a good mood since the phone call that made him dance and twirl.

From hospital to hospital; they'd left the mental one and driven, wheel spinningly fast, to the children's one.

Keyes had waited out in the hall, while Stone went into his daughter's room. Little Megan looked pale; she was small for her age. Lucy was in there too, watching over her daughter. She'd aged since Keyes had seen her last. They'd become more insular since Megan had been diagnosed with leukaemia, that shitty, little, sneaky, fucking disease.

Megan needed a bone marrow donor.

The whole police station had tested themselves for bone marrow matches, but had come up unlucky. It was a hard old thing to match.

And that was the good news Stone had got. *They'd found a donor.*

Keyes watched from the hall, as Stone and Lucy hugged and jumped around the bed, looking as young and happy as when they had first met. It can be done next week. *Next fucking week!* No wonder he was in a good mood.

*

It was raining outside the stationery shop, making the scene even more miserable. The council workers had finished their roll ups

228

and were scrubbing the tarmac. The odd onlooker still rubbernecked from the other side of the tape.

Stone poked his partner and muttered, "Keep moving, don't look."

Sergeant Toms was pointing them out to Chief Inspector Brogan – God, something must be really wrong to see him out of the office.

Chief Inspector Brogan beelined it over, not a hint of a smile on his face. "You two need to come with me," he ordered. "Now."

14

Pastor Morris hadn't left his cramped, little office since earlier in the morning. He stared transfixed at the phone. The battle was beginning and they would have to move fast to survive. The evil – no, he could name them to himself now – the Society knew that they had been discovered. Muppet, opening fire into the quarry, had guaranteed that. And Trish was dead, burnt up, sacrificed like the others.

Had it been his responsibility that she'd been murdered? He ran the show, marshalled the rag-tag bunch of fighters, so yes, who else could he blame, God? No, God didn't bother himself in such petty affairs, the responsibility was his own and he could live with it easily. They had after all made contact with the Society. Even though they'd lost the small measure of good faith they'd managed to gain from the Hare Krishnas in the process.

*

The last report of automatic fire faded out and the radio had fallen silent.

"Guns!" Pragnesh Lankhani had exclaimed in horror.

"What did you think we'd do when we found her, chant?" the pastor retorted angrily.

Pastor Morris put his mic down and closed his eyes to offer up a prayer, before excitedly turning to the map. This was the closest they'd been to the Society.

An incredible sadness invaded the pastor as he found the abandoned quarry on the map. It was one of the many ancient ones, a historical scar on the Gower, from a time centuries ago when men would have cut the limestone by hand. It was small, remote and well known to him.

He closed his eyes again. This time offering up a prayer for himself. "There is no way we can get everyone there in time tonight." He said, his finger following a line, "This is the only road out. I think it would be worth having a look at our enemies and getting some number plates."

"We can have no further part in this," Pragnesh Lankhani said. "We are Hare Krishnas, not whatever it is you people are. We helped you to try and find the girl and we failed, but this is where it ends."

"Go to the police then. Tell them everything, see if they will help."

The bony Krishna looked at him with baleful eyes. "I too am a learned man, Pastor Morris, and I know the power of this Society you fight, and I know the depth of their roots, and the spread of their tentacles, so I cannot risk the lives of all my people."

"There are good policemen."

"I cannot get involved anymore," Pragnesh Lankhani said, turning his back on the pastor.

Pastor Morris had packed up the radio in silence and loaded it into the minibus, his mind galvanised and the fate of the Hare Krishnas sealed. There was no longer a fence to sit on.

He tore out of town in the church minibus.

He parked behind a barn, in an abandoned farm.

He beat the first of the stream of cars by five minutes.

He managed to take down forty number plates.

*

Now, sitting in his office staring at the phone, it was down to one person. He was waiting on the young policewoman to ring back.

When he had seen her this morning, the girl had been nervous and resistant. So he had, along with a lot of reassurance and persuasion, given her only one registration number. He had picked it at random.

And now he waited and waited.

It used to be so different. He wouldn't have been waiting on a scared girl to make the right decision; he would have had men and resources at his fingertips. At one time, Pastor Morris would have been able to get any information he had needed, instead of skulking in a cold, abandoned church.

That had all been a lifetime ago, when the Brethren were strong and powerful, before the purge and, of course, before his death.

Pastor Morris knew he had been lucky to get any contacts within the police force at all. Father Roberts, the old reverend, had been reluctant at first to introduce him to Suzie. Being a member of the Brethren though still opened a lot of doors, especially with older members of the clergy.

And now it was all down to her – Suzie Gorman.

Just one name and address that was all he needed.

And he needed it fast.

Sitting there now, staring at the phone, his mind kept drifting back to his visitor, the one who had entered the chapel, silently, as he'd been praying.

*

Once everyone had got back and they had bandaged up the unconscious Donald, Pastor Morris had gone to the chapel. He wanted to be alone, away from them all, at least for a while.

As always, it was cold and damp in there. The pastor looked sadly at the one, half-painted wall. A bucket, of now hardened paint, sat next to it.

Trying to do up this chapel had been his first job when he had taken this post.

He'd moved home after having to run, after having to fake his death. Some urge had drawn him back.

The Reverend Roberts had found him a chapel to take on. He'd been grateful; he'd told the old man so. Brother Dowling and Al were already in situ, running the hostel next door. The dust from Al's encounter with the Hare Krishnas still hadn't settled. Reverend Roberts had hoped that he would be a steadying influence on them.

He had tried. They had started painting the church, doing it up; they'd involved the homeless.

That was until the first disappearance.

Mad Vorn had been a long-term alcoholic. A lifetime in and outer: in and out of prison, in and out of the mental home and in and out of the hostel. He liked exposing his private parts to women.

One day he never showed up.

Pastor Morris remembered when Brother Dowling had told him. It had been an odd feeling, too insubstantial to put into words, but Pastor Morris knew straight away. It was *them*, they were here in the city.

That had been the first disappearance; there had been more.

God had guided him home for a reason.

"I'd look at hiring a different firm of painters if I were you."

The voice behind him had made him jump.

Pastor Morris spun around from his prayer and found himself facing a short man in a rain coat. The man was balding, with close-cropped hair. He wore rimless glasses on a humourless face.

"Excuse me?" the pastor spluttered, shocked and suddenly feeling very exposed.

"The wall." The man gestured. "It looks unfinished."

"Can I help you, my son?"

"Are you renovating it?"

233

"Renovating it?"

"The chapel, I assumed that it was deserted. It certainly looks like it from the outside."

"How did you get in?"

"It's a chapel, Father. The doors should always be open to those who need saving," the man said, coming closer.

"Do you need saving?" Pastor Morris asked, backing off, keeping the altar between himself and this man.

For a moment the man's expression changed, like he was suddenly far away. He refocused. "I think we all need saving, Father. And that's why I am here. Trish Reed? She is one of your flock?"

"Yes," the pastor said, realising that this was it. The Society knew he was on to them. There'd be no subterfuge from them this time, just straight out murder.

The man reached inside his coat.

The pastor sagged, not from fear but from knowing that they had won.

The man looked at him strangely.

The man pulled out a wallet. He produced a card with his photo on. "My name is Chief Inspector Brogan."

"Oh," the pastor croaked, gathering himself together a bit. "You're investigating her disappearance as well?"

"You know she has disappeared?"

"Two of your colleagues were here earlier, asking questions about her."

"Two of my colleagues?" the policeman asked sharply. "Here about Trish?"

"Yes, a Detective Keyes and a Detective Stone."

"Oh, well, Pastor…?"

"Morris."

"Well, Pastor Morris, I hope you will forgive me if I repeat some of the questions they have already asked."

Chief Inspector Brogan then went on to run through more or less the same questions as Brother Dowling had been asked.

The surprise that the Chief Inspector had shown, upon finding out that the other policemen had been here, struck the pastor as odd. He didn't know what to make of that.

Now, while he answered the questions, he took his time studying the man. This Chief Inspector Brogan was hiding something; it played behind his eyes, restrained there.

It made Pastor Morris feel unsettled; it stopped him from concentrating.

The policeman had just asked, "Are you aware of any acquaintances that she might be with?"

"Unfortunately, Trish didn't have a lot of friends."

The policeman froze. "You said *didn't*, why did you use the past tense?"

Pastor Morris suddenly felt very tired, he didn't want to lie anymore – *"They're burning her! The bastards are burning her."*

"I have a terrible feeling that Trish is gone for good, that we will not see her in this life again."

"What do you mean?"

The pastor smiled sadly. "There are a lot of dangers in this city, a lot of evil."

"That is why I am here, Father; it is my job to stop such things. Is there something you want to tell me?"

The pastor saw Al, in the background, lurking in the shadows of the door that led to the hostel. It brought him back to the mission. "No, I'm afraid I don't, Chief Inspector." He gently guided him out of the chapel. "Now I don't want to be rude, but we have a lot of preparations to get on with."

"Preparations?"

"My flock does not look after itself," the pastor said, leading the policeman towards the door.

*

The phone rang, making him jump, bringing him back to his office.

The pastor grabbed it.

Suzie Gorman had rung, fear and hesitation in her voice. She said hello and then went silent, a beep-beeping noise, telling the pastor she was on a payphone.

Come on, Suzie – help me get revenge for Trish – come on, Suzie.

More hesitation, then a name and an address, whispered urgently.

Then dial tone.

The pastor sat back and smiled.

15

They drove in convoy to the docks. Chief Inspector Brogan in the lead car, sticking one mile under the speed limit, Keyes and Stone tailing.

The building was a fire-fucked shell.

One tender was parked next to it. A few firemen milled around talking, while others rolled their hoses back up.

It was raining hard now.

Brogan pulled to the kerb and got out of his car. Stone parked halfway up the pavement.

"Why are we here?" Stone asked gruffly. "We've got enough to do, without investigating a fire as well."

Brogan's face turned hard. "This isn't just a fire and it is not something I could discuss over the radio. Now come with me."

The fire inspector was a squat man in his forties, with a thick moustache; he finished giving instructions to one of his subordinates, before joining the three detectives.

He shook hands with Brogan.

He glowered at Stone and Keyes, remembering them from Zach's house.

"I've just talked to the watch commander and he'll tell his men that this doesn't leave their fire station," he said.

Brogan nodded as if it was obvious that what they saw should remain confidential.

"I am not happy letting anyone into the building at the

moment," the fire inspector continued. "Until we shore up the walls, the whole place could collapse."

"The crime technicians are on their way now and I would not expect them to go into an unsafe building," Brogan said. "However, these detectives and I will need to go in to see the body." Brogan looked at Stone. "If that is alright with you."

"I'll race you," Stone said, not to be outdone by his boss.

"Wait, wait. The scaffold will be here within an hour. As will one of my recovery teams. They are the ones who are trained to go in, rather than you."

Brogan looked up at the clouds. "The longer we wait the more evidence will be washed away and I am not prepared for that to happen."

"Look, we used upwards of ten thousand gallons of water to dampen down this building, a bit of rain won't wash anything else away," the fire inspector told them stubbornly.

"Fuck it," Stone said, walking towards the entrance.

"Detective Stone, wait where you are," Brogan barked, before turning to the fire inspector. "If you say that it is unsafe, then we will wait. But, following our conversation about the suspected cause of death and the wider ramifications that cause of death might entail, I need to see the body as soon as possible."

The fire inspector pulled on his moustache uneasily, deciding. "Alright, but we take it slowly and we stick to the walls, and if I say we have to leave, we turn around and leave."

"Thank you."

He gestured them through the tape that led into the wreckage; soot clung to their clothes, pervading their noses and throats.

The staircase to the third floor was intact, but groaned as they walked up. The fire inspector led them to a corner of the building.

The worst of the fire had happened here, taking out the roof and half the wall.

Keyes looked out of what had once been the side of the building.

Across the road was Dora's Nightclub. The statue above the doorway stared back at him. *"Our Founder and Saviour"* was carved below it in weathered script.

A memory from his school days was triggered. It was a statue of Henry Morton Stanley, adventurer, explorer, the person who found David Livingstone in the jungle.

Keyes shook the memory away and turned back to the task at hand.

There was a body in the corner of the room, almost undistinguishable from a charred bit of wood, only the glint from a necklace making it stand out.

Stone walked across the room and looked at it. The body was long past being anything other than an *it*.

"Don't worry, the floor's safe," he said, noticing Keyes' reluctance to put his weight on the floorboards. Stone stamped up and down to demonstrate. "They knew how to build things back then."

"Careful, damn it," Brogan ordered.

Stone smiled at him and had one more little stamp, before turning back to the body. "Judging by its size and the necklace I'd imagine it was a woman once." He looked at the fire inspector. "Does the fire look deliberate?"

"This room is the starting point. As I told your boss, my bet is it was accidental. I'd imagine once an ID is made, it would turn out the woman was a transient." He knelt down next to Stone. "The person didn't move when the fire started, possibly due to smoke inhalation. But I reckon they were too out of it to know what was going on."

"How do you *reckon*?" Stone asked.

The fire inspector pointed at a foetal-looking mound of melted glass and a sliver of metal. "Needle," he explained. "This person was probably a squatter, took some drugs, passed out and kicked over a candle. This place would have gone up like a box of matches," he sighed. "Drugs definitely kill. You ought to hear some of the stories I know about sniffing glue while you smoke."

"I know who this is," Keyes said, having remained silent until now. He pulled out the picture of Trish Reed that he had taken from her mother. The necklaces matched.

16

Brother Dowling had come to get Donald from the operation centre. He led him up, through the church, and out into the graveyard.

"Al has gone to start the minibus," he explained, bustling Donald towards a hole in the fence. "The pastor has found out one of their names. You need to go and watch their house while they're at work."

Donald noticed that the minibus had been repainted; it was orange now. Al was waiting for him in the driving seat.

The minibus had snail-paced along in the beginnings of rush hour traffic. Al said that they had the name and address of one of the enemy, one of the men responsible for the death of Trish. And it was Donald's mission to keep an eye on the house, while the target was at work.

"He works late and the pastor said we have to get things ready," Al said.

Donald felt he should say something. "The van looks very pretty now," he said.

"Yes, I don't know what on earth the pastor's up to, but he is a great man and he has brought us this far."

"He is indeed great," Donald agreed.

"This is it," Al said eventually, stopping the van at the top of a cul-de-sac. "Number 13, the house with the green door."

Donald noticed they were in the Mayals, one of the posher areas of town.

"There is a copse of trees at the bottom of the road, you should hunker down in there." Al turned around in his seat. "The target is at work now; all you need to do is see who goes in and out of the house." He grabbed hard onto Donald's arm. "Your only mission is to watch. Don't attack anyone. Watch. If we mess this up, we are all dead."

*

Those had been the pastor's words earlier.

"If we mess this up, we are all dead," he had told Al and Brother Dowling, when he called them into his office.

Pastor Morris had looked tired. He had a twitch under his eye that wouldn't stop. This had worried Al.

Al had seen the warning signs before, in officers he had served under. The little cracks appearing, becoming bigger, until your officer was nothing but a liability.

It was like Captain Summers. Summers had been a liability from the start. He'd been responsible for them messing up their mission. If they'd killed General Leopold Galtieri, the war over the Falklands would have ended then and there.

Summers had cracked up as they were high-tailing it out of Buenos Aires, the Argentinean 107th Armoured Division hot on their heels. As the Argies closed in, Summers made bad decision after bad decision.

Al and the other sergeant, Faversham, decided he had to be dealt with.

Summers was long gone now, rotted away somewhere in the Argentinean jungle.

But the pastor is a great man and he has brought us this far.

*

Al got out of the minibus, opened the sliding door and pulled out one of the hefty radios. "If you see anyone, call it in," he said, passing the heavy radio to Donald. "You may have problems though, the radios have been on the fritz all evening. If you don't get an answer keep trying."

Donald hoisted the radio onto his back. "I want a gun," he said.

"You don't need one. If anything happens, split," Al said. "You are just watching. You are not going to attack anyone. Repeat it."

"I am just watching, I am not going to attack anyone," Donald intoned. "But I still want a gun."

Al looked up and down the deserted street before sighing. He pulled a pistol from his waistband. "The safety is on and there's not a bullet in the chamber."

Donald took the gun off him, caressing the steel lovingly.

Al got back into the van shaking his head. He sat there watching, as Donald crab-ran down the middle of the road towards cover.

The traffic had eased slightly as Al drove back towards the hostel. He was singing a hymn under his breath. His chorus of *"Bringing in the Sheaves"* was interrupted by the radio spluttering to life.

The pastor's voice came on full of fear. "They're here, they're outside, they're outside."

Al picked up the mic, but the signal had faded, as it had been doing all day.

He put his foot down.

17

They had a vacuum cleaner! An actual, working vacuum cleaner! Alistair had discovered it under the stairs, next to the ironing board. They had an ironing board!

He had got back from Danny's with four hours to spare, armed to the teeth with cleaning products.

And so, he had swarmed over the house; cleaning, tidying, scraping, burning and, in one case, leaving the fuck alone.

Ebin had helped too, well, supervised by mentioning bits Alistair had missed and telling him the correct way to hold a mop.

Finally, the house was done and Alistair had just got out of the bath. Something he was going to start doing more than on a Wednesday.

Now, all he had to do was hustle down to the shops and get a nice bunch of flowers. Then he could relax, with a celebratory joint and a game of *Mario Kart*.

It would indeed be a celebratory joint. After all he had survived handing in his notice.

*

"Jesus, Danny, this isn't the Mafia."

"What the fuck are you rabbiting on about?" Danny asked, not understanding.

Alistair had eyed the gun – it was the sort that an older cop, with only forty-eight hours left to retirement, would carry.

"Oh, the gun." Danny started laughing, big, belly-rolling laughter. "I'm not going to shoot you with it, you dozy twat." The laughter stopped as suddenly as it had started. "Ivor's in a coma, Mardy has gone mad, so we are getting serious, but you don't need to know about that." He prodded Alistair with the bit the bullet came out of. "And you haven't seen this, right?"

"With my eyes? I can't see anything, at least up close."

Danny nodded. "Good. Now fuck off, the last thing I want to hear about, right now, is your petty shit."

"Ok, I'm going and I know this isn't the right time, but my last two weeks start now. And I'll need all my back pay by the end of it."

*

There was a long queue in the shop and Alistair couldn't help feeling a bit gay standing in it holding a large bunch of flowers. Feeling a bit gay, how stupid is that? You are standing there with flowers for a girl. That's not gay; that's great. All the blokes are jealous because you have a girl and all the women fancy you because you're the sort of man who buys women flowers.

*

Maggie had rung him earlier on the knackered payphone downstairs, the evil, money-grubbing bastard of a landlord having installed it to squeeze yet more pennies out of them. Alistair hated it, as every time he had an incoming call, he had to talk through the beeps.

Alistair wondered for a moment how she had got the number. He had soon put that thought aside, as Maggie, earnestly, started to apologise for the way she had behaved the previous night.

"I'm sorry for running off like that. It was a really lovely evening and then… I don't know." She paused, a faint sigh carrying down the phone. "Look, I've been seriously messed about in the past and

I find it difficult with new people. But hey, that's something I'm dealing with. Anyway," she said, changing the subject, "are you doing anything tonight? We could meet up if you aren't busy."

"Yeah, I'd really like that."

"What say we try a date that doesn't involve dodging bales of hay?"

"What sort of date?" Alistair had asked.

"I don't know, cinema, flowers, a meal, dancing. You decide."

"Sounds good."

They had talked for a while longer; it had been good, it had been easy.

When Alistair had come off the phone, he saw Ebin sitting on the top of the stairs, looking at him gooey-eyed. "Got into her knickers yet?" he asked.

Alistair ignored him.

"Come on, seriously, you were this close to speaking in baby talk down the phone. You fucking woman," Ebin said, trailing after him. "God, if you're a woman that means she must be a lesbian or something."

Alistair spun round. "Look, enough, ok?"

"Alright, alright," Ebin said, putting his hands up in mock surrender. "As long as I know my friend has an outside chance of sleeping with a lesbian that's enough for me. Besides, if that little cutie doesn't sort out your dreams, then nothing will."

Ah, Alistair and his dreams. Or Alistair and his one recurring dream. The dream itself was vampire-based, just the standard running from a vampire sort of dream, nothing more complicated or special than that. It was just the way he'd wake up: sweat-soaked and thrashing with a scream in his ears.

*

Alistair had once made the mistake of consulting Ebin about his dreams, in a very off-handed way, of course. Ebin seemed like the best person to ask, as he had been reading a book on psychology and had, of late, been spouting some very clever-sounding lines of crap. Clancy reckoned he was trying to discover his inner child in order to abuse it.

"I had such a weird dream last night," Alistair said, casually dropping it into the conversation with Clancy and Ebin, before going on to explain about all the vampires and running and stuff.

"Oh I know why you're having that dream," Clancy said. "It's because we end up watching *Lost Boys* about three times a week."

Ebin shook his head. "No, no. It sounds more complicated than that. I was reading about dreams in my book. Many ancient races saw dreams as a window into the soul. And that dream certainly has a lot of imagery," he said, almost to himself, while flicking through his big book of psychology. "Oh here we are, dreams… there is even a bit on running from vampires."

Ebin studied the text for about a minute, his lips moving slightly as he read. Ebin stopped, composed himself, looking gravely up at Alistair. "Right, according to this it means you're a twat."

*

Alistair got to the till holding the flowers carefully. He had raided his under-the-mattress savings and reckoned he could stretch to the cinema, a full on proper meal and flowers.

It was then he saw something that made him freeze and go cold.

18

mily Davies watched her stupid husband head down the long gravel drive. He was drunk; he nearly drove into the gatepost. *That would be funny*, she thought, *Mardy wrapping his car round a tree.*

It would definitely make the plan a lot easier.

Tony had rung from the hospital. Ivor was still in a coma and he may not pull through. That's why Mardy was drunk and running off to see John.

Mardy would be asking for help.

John would say no. John would say, *"You know how things are meant to work in my city."*

Mardy would complain for a while, before coming home, having some more whisky and then putting the tape into the safe, with all the others.

Mardy didn't need any more whisky; he'd been drinking heavily all afternoon, this business with Ivor being in a coma having put him in one of his moods. It was terrible news about Ivor, this close to the plan being set in motion. The last thing Emily wanted was Mardy paranoid and on the war path with all his minions armed.

*

"Wait," Mardy had barked at Tony earlier in the day. "Danny, you go too. Ring Reno as well. I've had enough of this nonsense. I want this prick found today. I want everyone to go heavy as well."

When the two big lummocks had left, Emily went for a swim, while her husband had smashed up his study.

Later, when his anger had subsided, she had gone to check the damage. Luckily, the large Ming vase that held pride of place in his office had been broken beyond repair.

*

Emily waited for five minutes after Mardy had left, before ringing Karl Reno.

She really wanted to meet the new help from **[REDACTED]**. Emily wouldn't though, not yet at least; they probably wouldn't be happy finding out a woman ran the show.

That was one of the many problems with men. They were just too stupid to realise that, in most instances, a woman was in charge.

The phone was answered by Karl Reno. "Alright, love. How's it going?" he asked.

She rolled her eyes. "Can you talk now?"

"Yeah, I can talk."

"Is everything in place?"

"Yeah, I met them in the car park and got them settled in the house."

"How many of them came down?"

"Three."

"Good," Emily said. That would be an easy enough number to handle.

"They wanted to chill at the pad for the night, but I told them they'd be better off driving around, getting to know the area."

"Where are they now?"

There was a long pause. "Er… chilling at the pad."

She rolled her eyes again; Reno was an idiot. "Forget about them for now. Are you ready for the next part of the plan?"

"No, look, I've told you we don't need to do it."

249

"And I've told you we do."

"Why?"

"It's the only way he'll buy that Mardy has gone off the rails."

"But it's not; we've got the tape, that'll be enough."

"No, I know him, it won't be enough. He likes the idea of protecting people. He did something to protect me when I was in a similar state years ago. He'll do it to protect me again."

"Look, I'm not going to beat you up."

"You don't have a choice," she said angrily.

Reno was stupid and weak.

19

Al parked the van a couple of streets away from the hostel. He ignored his billboard and instead slipped on his army surplus coat. He tucked the AK-47, with the sawn-off stock, under it.

Behind the graveyard were the allotments. He scaled the low fence and walked quickly through them, eyes alert, heart racing – that old feeling coming back.

He slipped through the hole in the fence and squatted behind a gravestone.

The graveyard and church lay silent. A ground mist was rising, adding completely unneeded atmosphere to the moment.

Al moved forward, keeping low, going from gravestone to gravestone, aware of the surveillance cameras.

The last bit of cover belonged to an Eliza Pritchard *"Devoted Wife and Mother"*. She had been buried a fifteen-foot dash from the church's back door.

Al dashed.

He made it to the wall, pushing himself into it, ears straining for any noise that was out of place. Nothing.

The door at the back of the church was ajar, screaming trap.

Al paused, before slipping the safety off and selecting fully auto; he'd always been a stupid bugger.

Take a second to envisage the inside of the church.

Ready.

Go!

Al burst through the door, throwing himself down prone, gun up, prepared to empty the mag.

Silence.

Al got to his feet and started slowly along the corridor. Fear swallowed back and dispersed. That old feeling coming on strong. Listening, looking, gun aimed in front of him, set to rock and roll.

Silence, no one.

The building still shouting trap.

Time to move fast; he two at a timed it, up the stairs towards the pastor's office.

Get in there, sweep and clear. Get the cameras up and running to see who's where.

This done, Al flicked through the external cameras and then the internal ones, stopping when he got to the operation centre.

"What the hell?" Al breathed, hatred filling up his mind.

20

Mardy Davies was very drunk, as he skirted the bay, past the Mumbles and then around the headland.

The sky was starless. In the distance, a cross channel ferry was plying its way across the sea, illuminating the water around it.

Mardy pulled into the same car park they always met in. It overlooked a small beach of shingles and driftwood.

There was another car parked in the corner, furthest away from the entrance; it was steamed up and rocking slightly. Mardy watched it for a while as he waited for John to turn up.

Ten minutes later another car entered the car park, moving slowly, pulling up next to him.

Mardy checked the tape recorder was running as he got out of his car. He had known John since childhood, but lately he felt uneasy every time they met.

John had been a really weird, quiet kid. Mardy supposed the word for it now would be introspective.

Thinking back, they'd never had much in common.

*

Nothing in common except location. John had been brought up on the same estate as him and Danny. John had always lent himself to being protected. It had been an odd thing; Mardy had been the brains, with Danny handling the brawn and John… John had just been there following and watching.

They had tried to be big boys, like the scam they had stealing pop from the bottling plant.

The problem with the estate had been these black kids, the Farrell brothers. There'd been about seven of the pricks, all older and harder.

Jesse Farrell had been the oldest and hardest. He'd soon cottoned on to their pop bottle scam and had taken it over, giving them all a beating and making John go into the building for him instead, like some kind of bottle monkey.

The Farrell brothers had terrorised the estate back then; they'd been into everything from arson to burglary. And that was when John had changed, from the silent, skinny kid into the person he was today.

John's mother had been a cleaner in the local pub, his dad being long gone.

John and his mum always had less money than the rest of the people on the street. This, with all the industries closing down, was no mean achievement.

It hadn't mattered to the Farrell brothers though. They had gone in through the pantry window and trashed the place, taking the one thing of value in the house, a silver bracelet that had belonged to John's nan.

Mardy remembered it now, coming into the house with John after school and finding his mother sitting at her kitchen table in tears, crying over the stolen bracelet.

John hadn't said a word, just turned around and walked out of the house.

Mardy had followed to talk to him, young and unsure what to say to his friend.

John had stopped at the front gate, bending down to pick something up off the kerb. He then started marching straight up the road towards Aldo's Café.

Jesse Farrell had been standing outside with four of his brothers. They had started nudging each other and smirking as John walked up to them. Jesse started to say something, only to be hit in the face by the half a brick John was holding. Jesse had gone down screaming and bloody. John had fallen on top of him, repeatedly bringing the brick down with both hands onto Jesse's head.

He didn't stop until Jesse had stopped moving. John then got up, calm as you like, and looked at the other four stunned boys. They didn't make a move, even though they towered over him.

He then spoke to them, not a quaver in his voice. "If my mother's bracelet is not put through my letterbox in the next half an hour, I will come back and do this again to another one of you."

He then turned on his heel and walked home, Mardy speechlessly trailing in his wake.

Within ten minutes the bracelet was dropped onto the mat.

Three months later, when Jesse was finally discharged from hospital, the Farrell family upped and moved away.

*

The wind, coming off the sea, blew strong and cold as Mardy opened the door to his friend's car.

Chief Inspector John Brogan was illuminated by the light.

Mardy got in next to him and, for a moment, they both stared out across the beach to the dark sea.

21

The cul-de-sac was quiet, as Al sat at the top of the road watching number 13.

Donald was in the back by the minibus' sliding door. He had radioed in half an hour ago saying that the target had returned home.

Al was calm now, calm and happy. Pastor Morris was indeed a great man.

*

It had taken a long time for him to calm down back in the chapel.

After seeing the images on the video bank, he high-tailed it down to the operation room, pushed open the heavy door and stood there ready to cut the pastor down, images of the long dead Captain Summers flashing through his mind.

Pastor Morris just stood there meeting his gaze. Jason and Muppet cowered behind him, bald, except for little tufts of hair at the back of their necks. Both outfitted in orange robes.

"What in the name of little baby Jesus is going on?" Al demanded, white with rage, gun still covering them.

The pastor held out his hands, palms up, in a soothing gesture. "I noticed a car kept on driving past the chapel and hostel very slowly. I thought it was the Society and panicked," he said, by way of explanation for his earlier radio call. "Luckily, Brother Dowling calmed me down."

Towards the end, Captain Summers had opened fire on a llama.

"I think that they are on to us and because of that, it is time to move quickly and decisively," the pastor continued.

Al lowered his gun, slipping the safety on. "But why all this… this dressing up?"

Pastor Morris gestured for everyone to gather round.

"Last night, as you know, we were close to the Society," Pastor Morris told them. "However, we failed and our sister Trish paid for that failure. But let it not be said she died in vain, for we can now put a face and a name to a member of the Society." The pastor looked around the room. "His name is Martin Chandler. And this evil man is the editor of the city's newspaper." The pastor stopped, looking them all in the eye, one by one. "This man is an example of how deep the roots of the Society reach. They get in and influence everything. But not anymore; Martin Chandler is a link in the Society's chain and we are going to break him."

Pastor Morris then went on to explain the plan.

*

Sitting in the van now, engine ticking over, Al allowed himself a chuckle. He did despise those Hare Krishnas.

Down the street, Jason and Muppet walked in a line, their finger cymbals, hideously out of rhythm.

Their orange robes being caught by the breeze.

They went up the drive to number 13, pausing there a moment before ringing the bell.

Donald started to open the sliding door, but Al turned and put a restraining hand on his shoulder.

Number 13 was opened by the target.

Martin Chandler was middle aged and chubby, with a weak chin.

As they had been told, Jason and Muppet stood there for a

moment. Chandler went to ask them what they wanted, but was stopped as Muppet sprayed a long stream of mace in his eyes.

Donald slid the door open as Al accelerated down the cul-de-sac, skidding to a halt behind the target's maroon 4x4.

Donald was out in a flash, helping to drag the moaning editor into the minibus.

Jason was the last one in, slamming the door after him.

22

HEROIN-RELATED FIRE DEATH

The headline screamed banner-loud, before going on to explain how the fire service had discovered a body, while battling a blaze in the historic, but disused, dock area. An unnamed source had named the deceased as Trish Reed and told the paper that both the death and the fire were drugs-related and not being treated as suspicious.

The picture of Trish took up half the page.

The story continued onto the third page, turning to the city's police force and their historic failings in the fight against drugs. It listed all those killed in the spate of deaths amongst heroin users, three years ago.

There was a picture of one of the victims, Ceri Fletcher, twenty-one. They had used a photo from when she had been a schoolgirl. An illustration of innocence lost, Chief Inspector Brogan assumed. She really had been a pretty girl and the picture had captured it well, eyes alive and full of hope, with just the hint of a knowledgeable little smirk on her face.

Brogan remembered seeing her body afterwards. She had been the one, the only one he had felt guilty about. The other eleven bodies, all stuck in that hot-shot rictus, had given him nothing greater than a small feeling of satisfaction.

It had been Ceri that had torn his insides out.

She had done the same to Alistair and that poor kid carried it about his person like a rock.

∗

The local paper had been waiting on Brogan's desk when he returned from the meeting with Mardy in the car park. It had made him furious, even before he had gotten to the bottom of the article.

He needed to find out where they had got this information from. It had been gotten quickly and was, to a large degree, accurate. Except, and this was a big except, the death of somebody in these circumstances would always be treated as suspicious and there was *no* heroin problem in his city. He had personally seen to that three years ago.

Brogan would know if anything like that was trying to rear its head up again.

Mardy would have told him for one.

Mardy would tell Brogan whatever he wanted. He'd been there to witness the way Brogan dealt with the last of Swansea's heroin dealers. Or at least, deal with what Alistair had left of him.

∗

Mardy had reeked of whisky when he got into the car. They had both sat in silence for a while watching a ship out at sea.

Mardy spoke first. "You brought me out here to talk about this Donald Gooberman, didn't you? Well, he's put one of my men in a coma, so that makes him mine."

Brogan watched the ship sliding towards the horizon, until finally speaking. "I am sorry about Ivor, but he was attacked in public, which makes it a police matter."

"No. I can't have someone doing this to my people. How do you think it makes me look?"

260

"That isn't a concern. My men will arrest him in due course. How long do you think someone like that can hide for?"

"Well, he's been doing a good job up until now."

Brogan ignored the jibe. As far as he was concerned, the discussion about Donald Gooberman was finished. Besides, that wasn't what he'd brought Mardy out here to talk about. "A girl was found dead today. There was a fire in one of the old buildings down the docks. Once it was out they found her remains."

"What happened?"

"It's too early to say. They found the shard of a needle next to the body; they believe she could have been injecting, passed out and burnt the building down."

Mardy let this new information sink in for a moment. "Heroin?" He shook his head. "That's not likely. There has been none of that in the city for three years now, or at least nothing Tony and Ivor haven't run out."

*

It had been three years ago, after the spate of heroin-related deaths in the city, when Brogan had said *"no more drugs. This city will now be drug free"*.

Mardy had disagreed. "Don't be stupid, you won't get that ever, anywhere. Look at some of these people. You don't do glue because you want to do glue. You do it because you want to get off your head and there is nothing else available."

"What do you suggest then?" Brogan had asked.

"We control the supply; regulate it, minor stuff, things that won't end up in a load of dead junkies clogging up your morgue."

Brogan had been reticent.

Mardy had pushed; he'd always been a good salesman. "I've even got this man I use, a guy I know, called Zachariah Plum. He's a good man; I've started using him to look after some of the girls. He's got connections down in **[REDACTED]** and can get us an introduction."

261

Brogan had shaken his head no.

"Look, if we don't do it, someone else will and then we'll end up in the same position as before. At least this way, we'll know who's involved and if anyone starts selling anything we don't like, we can stamp it out."

In time Brogan had finally acquiesced and the drugs had started flowing back into the city. The pot came from **[REDACTED]**, while the amphetamines and acid came from a biker-run lab in mid Wales.

*

Even now, after all this time, the fact that there were any drugs at all still rankled the Chief Inspector. "I want you to pull all your people off Donald Gooberman," he said, "and get them checking if there is even a whiff of that filth back in my city, because my officers will be doing the same."

They held eye contact for a long time, until Mardy broke away and turned his attention back to the sea.

"Ok," he finally said.

"There was another Post Office robbery today as well. The little old lady might not pull through," Brogan continued. "It was strictly amateur and very violent. This is the fourth one in the last two months and it does not show us in a good light. My officers have to waste their time knocking on doors and asking questions. So come on, strictly amateur and violent. Who do you say?"

"Ask Carter," Mardy said, remembering back to the conversation he had had with Danny earlier that afternoon. "He was burning clothes in the garden and had money with blood on."

"How do you know?"

"I talked to Danny. He said Alistair was in a tiz and wants to quit. He nearly got searched by a policeman and it freaked him out."

"Alistair wants to leave, eh?" Brogan muttered almost to himself. He put it aside for the moment. "James Carter? Good. He also matches the description of someone who kicked down a young couple's door demanding money. I think it is time he is brought in for questioning."

"He has just had a big delivery of pot."

Brogan thought for a moment. "We'll hit him tomorrow then, give him a chance to sell some of it in the interim. I don't want my men focusing their questioning on any areas that aren't strictly relevant to the case. Does he still sell amphetamines?"

Mardy nodded uneasily.

"Good. I would like some drug-related seizure from him. If it does transpire the death of Trish is due to drugs, it would show we are being proactive, waging the war on drugs, so to speak."

The ferry had disappeared out of sight now.

"And Zach?" Brogan asked.

"Karl told him to leave the city and apparently he checked himself out of hospital this afternoon," Mardy said. He paused for a moment. "I'm not happy you made me throw him out of town. He was a good little earner."

"Zach severely beat up an innocent girl. I don't want that kind of behaviour from people in my employ. And Mardy, please don't question my motives again," Brogan said, before glancing down at the bag that his so-called friend held. "Now for the money."

"Here's your share of the monthly takings, John," Mardy said, handing over the envelope. It was very thick.

"You can get out now," Brogan said, putting his money into his jacket pocket.

Mardy opened the door, but Brogan stopped him.

"I need your car keys before you go."

"Why?"

"You have been drinking; I can smell it on your breath. I have no intention of letting you drive drunk. I'm a policeman, remember?"

Mardy started to laugh, but stopped when he saw his friend's humourless face.

"How am I meant to get home? Are you going to drive me?"

"I have got an unexplained death of a girl to get back to," Brogan said. He opened the envelope and got out a fifty. "I will treat you to a taxi though."

Mardy got out, slamming the door in his wake. The money not touched.

*

Ceri smiled back, as Brogan looked at the paper one more time, before getting up and leaving his office. He would have to see how the arrest of James Carter played in the local paper. Hopefully it would act as a distraction to this case.

The arrest would happen early tomorrow morning, while the idiot was still asleep. It would give enough time for his contacts at the paper to find out what a nasty piece of work this James Carter was.

A nice headline to the effect of *"Police Capture Post Office Animal"* should quieten the superintendent down.

If not, Mardy would have to give up another sacrifice; there were enough of them.

Brogan, Chief Inspector face on, knocked three times before stalking into Stone and Keyes' cramped office.

A sign had been tacked to the door; it said, *"Busy Detecteves – go away."* They had spelt detectives wrong.

It was late now, but both of them were still in there. Such a violence-heavy day tended to whack up the overtime.

As always the office was a mess. The large table, which took up half the room, was overflowing with pizza boxes and paperwork.

Stone was currently shouting down the phone at somebody.

"If the first draft's complete, send it over. I don't know, fax it. I want to see if we are looking at an accident or if I have to waste more time on this." He slammed the phone down. "Dickhead," he muttered, before turning towards his boss.

"I want an update on the progress of the Trish Reed case," Brogan said, by way of greeting.

Stone looked at his watch. "What now? I want to go and see my daughter."

"I do not require you to set up a slide show. I just want a brief outline of the case to date."

Stone sighed. "Fine, we've been running around all afternoon on the case. We've seen the family and, except for some crying, we got nothing from them. They'll be coming in tomorrow to formally ID the body, for what good that will do. They also put us in touch with her old dentist." Stone checked a spiral notebook on the desk. "A Ben Franks. He'll provide us with dental records. We went back around the area canvassing, but the fire happened about four in the morning, long after the nightclub was closed. Officers are going there tonight to talk to the staff and the punters. But I doubt if anyone saw a fucking thing." Stone swore because he knew it would annoy his boss. "And now we're going to write it all up."

"Who were you on the phone to?" Brogan asked.

"Oh yeah, that was the fire inspector. He has only got the preliminary fire report, but will send it over. He needs to run a few more tests, but reckons she started the fire herself." Stone looked towards the fax machine for a moment.

"And the doctor's report?" Brogan asked Keyes.

The big policeman was pale; he looked up vaguely, as if his mind had been elsewhere.

Stone answered for his partner. "Same thing, looks like death through smoke inhalation, but they have got to run a tox screening. I think it's going to pan out as a junkie death."

"Have you discussed this case with anyone else?" Brogan had the paper behind his back.

"Just you."

Stone was looking bored, which annoyed Brogan; he threw the paper onto the top of the debris-laden desk. "Can you explain this?"

Stone skim-read the article. "Wasn't us, chief. I didn't see any reporters around when they were putting out the fire, but you know how people talk and between the ambulance and fire crews, there were a load of people who could have blabbed to the press."

"Detective Keyes?"

"You're the first," the big man said, hollowly.

"Are you alright, Detective Keyes?"

"Tired, sir." The detective couldn't meet his eyes.

"We're fine, just been run ragged the last few days," Stone backed him up quickly.

"Well, try and get some rest. I want you both back in by six tomorrow morning. We are going to arrest the Post Office robber. It would be good to clear at least one of your cases this week, wouldn't it, gentlemen?" Brogan went to leave, aware he was missing something.

"Fuck's sake," Stone muttered, loud enough for his boss to hear. "That early? We weren't going to pick up Carter until after lunch." Stone smirked at the look of surprise on his boss's face. "Like it says on the door, we're 'busy detecteves'."

"Six in the morning," Brogan repeated as he turned and left the room.

Behind him the fax beeped.

Walking back down the corridor, Brogan couldn't help feeling that the investigation into the death of Trish Reed seemed to be solving itself awfully fast.

23

There was a knock on Alistair's door, quiet, gentle. He looked up, Maggie entered, knocking again as she did so. She was backlit by the hall light. Alistair realised that it was dark. He wondered how long he had been sitting on the floor like this.

Maggie put on the bedroom light and looked startled, as she saw his tear-streaked eyes.

"I didn't hear the bell," Alistair apologised, trying to wipe his eyes.

"It's alright, Ebin let me in. He asked if I had time to 'hop on the good leg and do the bad thing'. I said no, I was here to see you." She smiled weakly, hesitating for a moment before coming fully into the room and sitting, cross-legged, on the floor opposite Alistair.

She held his hands. "What's wrong?"

Alistair gulped in air, pulling himself together.

Maggie continued to hold his hands, biting her bottom lip, concern etched into her delicate features. "Hey, if you don't want to tell me, we can sit for a while."

"No, I do. It's this," Alistair said, turning the local paper over. In all truth he hadn't even read past the headline or the picture.

Trish Reed looked back at them from the front page.

Maggie skimmed the headline, glancing at the picture, before turning the page. "You knew her?"

Alistair nodded. "I hurt her badly once."

"How?"

Alistair broke eye contact, looked at the floor, looked at the ceiling, looked anywhere but at Maggie.

"How?" she repeated, holding his hands, squeezing them, pumping them.

Alistair looked back at her, pausing, before pushing ahead, laying out everything. "A while ago I killed her best friend and got her boyfriend hospitalised."

Maggie let go of his hand, sitting back, knees up into her chest.

Alistair continued. "It was back in the days when everyone was on skag. Like I told you on the roof, I was a different person back then. I was with this girl, Ceri." A smile fleeted across his lips at her name. It had been the first time he had said it out loud for years. "Well, kind of with her, she was really into the life."

"What happened?" Maggie asked, clutching her knees now, sitting away from him.

"I wanted her and me to get out, go somewhere else. There was nothing here for us. But she always said no. She said she was happy, hanging out with her friends, getting high." He paused, breathing deeply, fighting back tears. "She shared a flat with Trish and her boyfriend. I used to sort them out with stuff. I was dealing anyway so I got it for her cheap. I thought at least what she was getting from me would be good, clean stuff. It turned out I was wrong. I suppose it was bad timing. The guy I got it off, this guy Moses Jones, only had two wraps left. If I'd seen him later, he would have probably already sold them." Alistair shook his head at the dumb fucking luck of it all. "But I got them off him, took it round to theirs, one for Ceri and one for Trish and Bongo to fight over. I guess Bongo won, he had a brain haemorrhage."

"And Ceri?" Maggie asked. She'd started crying too now.

"She wasn't as strong; she died the next day in hospital."

"Did you see her?"

"Yes, I sat with her for a long time. I was the only one there. In all the time I knew her, Ceri never mentioned her family. So I didn't know how to contact them. It was just me and her, until she passed away."

"But they must have been at her funeral?"

"I don't know. I was hiding out at the time."

"Hiding out, why?"

"It was a long time ago, I'm different now."

"What were you hiding from?"

"It wasn't just Ceri and Bongo. People were dropping like flies. There was some bad stuff going round. All of it coming from Moses." Alistair sighed. "I went round to see him."

*

Alistair went round to see him, unsure what he was going to do, unsure what he was going to say.

Ceri was gone.

Bad thoughts were pounding through his brain.

Moses was leaving the house. He had a bag and he looked scared.

He spoke first. "Listen, Alistair mate, I'm busy right now, I'm out of stuff at the moment anyway."

All lies, all shit. "Where you going?"

Moses looked up and down the street, coming closer, raising his voice. "Look, pal, I'm busy, so fuck off alright."

Alistair grabbed his arm pulling him close, spitting out, "She's dead."

Moses' bluster went. "Look, they're all dead. Nine so far. Fuck knows what was in the last shipment, but they'll trace it back to me. So I'm disappearing. I'd disappear for a while too if I were you."

"We're not going anywhere," Alistair said quietly.

"Look, you stay if you want, but I'm out of here."

All the way over, Alistair hadn't known what he was going to do. That's what he would tell himself in the future. But deep down, hidden somewhere, he knew exactly what he was going to do. Why else would he have brought his cosh?

Moses tried to push past him. Alistair shoved him back against the door. Alistair bundled him into the house, cosh up, Ceri flashing through his mind.

*

"I don't remember much of what I did," Alistair told Maggie as they sat on his bedroom floor. "I mean people say that, but I really don't, it's just a blur."

"What happened to him?"

"He was murdered."

"By you?"

"Yes, I suppose I did. Not directly, but I stopped him running. He was on the news a few days later. He had been shot and his house was burnt down."

"Who did that?"

"Moses always used to talk about a Mr Big. I'm not kidding; he actually used the term 'Mr Big'. He thought it was funny, thought it made him sound like a proper gangster." Alistair tutted. "The paper said that the police suspected a local car dealer, a Stockard Clifton-James. Imagine that for a name? They reckoned this Stockard bloke had Moses shot to break any connection between the two of them, before he disappeared to Spain or somewhere. Apparently, that's where most gangsters seem to go. They were never able to trace him though."

They both sat in silence for a long time.

"Did you love her?" Maggie finally asked.

"Ceri?" Alistair shrugged. "She was the first person who had ever been there for me. I miss her a lot sometimes."

They sat in silence for a long time until Maggie finally stood up.

"Let's get out of here for a while," she said.

ONE DAY LEFT

1

I t was five o'clock in the morning, summer's-gone cold.

The three cars travelled in convoy, slowing and then knocking off their headlights as they turned onto James Carter's street.

After stopping, the occupants got out, eight in all; *hey, read his file, that James Carter's a psycho.*

The group took a second to get their bearings, before splitting up into two. No talking was needed. They'd gone over the plan in the police station.

Keyes and Stone quickly walked towards Carter's. Three uniformed officers scurrying in their wake.

Keyes counted house numbers. 50, 52, 54, 56, stopping at 58.

The group gathered, tense, breath crystallising in the air. Stone lit a cigarette.

"Put that out," Keyes hissed.

Stone glared at him, their eyes locking. Stone looked away, grinding the cigarette with his heel.

The second team, which had gone down the alley behind the house, came on the radio. "All in position."

Keyes turned to the door, hefting the two-handed battering ram like a toy.

He was through first, bounding up the stairs three at a time, "POLICE, POLICE, POLICE", his partner and one of the uniforms behind him.

Downstairs there was crashing and shouting as the back door went in.

Four doors led off the darkened landing. Keyes paused, his partner concertinaing into the back of him.

Light exploded, out of the door to the right, blindingly white.

Carter, wild haired and mad eyed, galloped at them, the light burning in front of him like a lance, Keyes and Stone jinxed clear.

The flash and scream happened simultaneously.

Everything went dark.

Keyes saw a movement and made towards the door Carter had appeared from, his heart beating in his ears. The screaming, like the shouts of his partner, indistinct.

The only illumination in the room was coming from an open window. A pair of legs was disappearing out of it, shadow-puppeting crocodile jaws.

Keyes moved forward, grabbing, missing, shouting out to the boys in the alley.

Carter, hanging from some kind of ladder, glared up at him with hate-filled eyes, before letting go and dropping backwards into the darkness, giving him the bird with both hands.

Keyes grabbed at the wire ladder, amazed how small and light it was. It was only then he saw the blood on his hands.

Crashing and shouting came from the alley.

Keyes turned back into the room, aware now of the earlier noise. He walked back onto the landing. A knot of policemen was gathered around a twitching body.

"The ambulance is on its way," someone shouted from downstairs.

2

Alistair awoke in the darkness; he could smell Maggie's hair against his face. He kissed the top of her head, just a gentle whisper of a kiss and, in the few moments before drifting back to sleep, he remembered last night.

*

Maggie had been right when she said they should get out of here.

Alistair had washed his face and cleaned himself up a bit, and then they headed out.

The night had been crisp, in a winter's coming sort of way.

Maggie said she'd treat him to booze. Alistair said he'd stick to Munting McJunting cider. Maggie said no, they were drinking whisky.

Bottle in hand, and at Maggie's insistence, they started walking.

The few people they passed seemed downbeat and muted, as if, city-wide, everyone was remembering things lost.

Eventually, they crossed Mumbles Road, crested the sorry, sad sand dunes and came out on the beach. The tide was far out, hazily lit by their backdrop of ten thousand street lamps. Maggie and Alistair settled down, out of the wind. Maggie faced him for a while, looking into his eyes.

"Are you ok?" she asked.

"I'm better now, being here with you," Alistair said, the line not coming out corny, just coming out true.

Satisfied with this, Maggie turned and snuggled into him.

They sat for a long time in silence, taking the occasional bitter pull of the booze.

"It's beautiful, mind," Alistair said, looking out over the sweep of the bay.

"When it looks like this, it is," Maggie said, untangling herself and again turning to face him. "But that's just because it's night and you've got all the lights. This really isn't a beautiful place."

Alistair was going to ask what she meant, but Maggie continued.

"You're going to need to get out of here, Alistair. It's not a good place."

"What's the alternative?"

"Tomorrow. Let's get out of here tomorrow. You remember when we were on the roof and I was talking about university? Well, let's do that tomorrow. Let's go on a day trip to Bristol. I can check the place out and you can have a day away from all this." Maggie was smiling at her sudden idea, obviously getting excited. "We can get an early train up and then, how do you put it? Go for a mooch."

Leaving Swansea? It did indeed sound like a good idea to Alistair. Leaving, and not just for a day trip. What was actually here for him? He'd lost Trish, which was his last real tie to the past. What did he have? What did he feel about it all? They were questions too big for Alistair to get his head around at the moment. He knew he would have to, but not tonight. Not right now.

They sat in the sand dunes for another hour, Maggie talking about what there was to see in Bristol and making plans for what they were going to do; trying to push the spectre of death, recent and past, aside. And Alistair in turn slowly getting warmed by the whisky and, as terrible as it sounded, feeling happier than he had in a long time.

"We're going to be leaving early tomorrow," Maggie said, as they got towards the bottom of the bottle. "It would make sense if

I crashed over yours." She looked away from him for a moment before looking back. "If that's ok with you."

"I think I'd like that a lot," Alistair said.

"Good. Let's get out of here then because I'm starting to freeze."

3

James Carter had been proved right: having that escape ladder hadn't meant he was paranoid. The fuckers really were after him.

It had been luck that he hadn't been asleep. Lucky he had all the speed sloshing around his system.

Lucky as well that the power had blown, when he'd shoved his lamp in that pig's face. The pig had started screaming, screaming like a girl, giving him enough time to get to the ladder.

The two coppers he'd beaten up down the alley, well, that hadn't been luck.

Getting past them had given him a clear run at freedom and he'd taken it fast. He'd charged down the alley, at the back of the house, around the corner and then hidden in the first doorway he came to.

He'd waited silently, until he heard the pounding of policemen running past, and then, very calmly, he'd walked between two neighbouring houses, crouched behind some bins, watching the road and his car parked opposite.

Carter always parked his car on a slight hill, which meant that at a time like this, he could simply get up from behind the bins, walk across the road, let the handbrake off and roll away, without having to start the engine.

This was one of the three exit routes Carter had planned for himself. A little paranoia could be a useful thing.

That had been half an hour ago.

Now, as he sped down country lanes, deep into the Gower, all times keeping a watchful eye out for any helicopters, the adrenaline subsided and he realised he didn't actually know where he was going.

His escape plan only went as far as getting out of the house. Anything past that was just safety in motion.

Fuck it though, he was free.

Carter fiddled with the cigarette lighter for a victory smoke. Fuck them all.

The blur that streaked in front of his headlights made him swerve.

The car flipped and all he saw was air.

4

The pastor stood alone in the darkened graveyard. His hands shook spastically as he smoked his first cigarette in three years. The smoke stung his eyes, aggravating his throat with pepper spray acidity.

It had been a long night and he still wasn't sure if the plan would work.

*

Al had shown amazing strength throughout the evening, ordering the others to march the newspaper editor, or the Sad Sack, as he called him, into one of the rooms in the hostel and leave him tied up on a chair to blubber.

Upstairs in the office, Al had done all the organising, while the pastor had just sat at his desk thinking about cigarettes.

Jason and Muppet were standing against the wall, sneaking nervous glances at their prisoner on one of the monitor screens. The pastor had been relieved he wasn't the only one out of his depth.

Al was pacing back and forth, stage centre; he was looking at Jason and Muppet. "He definitely saw you before you blinded him?"

They both nodded.

Al seemed satisfied with this. "Now you two get changed. I don't want to look at those horrible orange robes until tomorrow."

They shuffled off, looking relieved.

Al, Pastor Morris and Brother Dowling remained in the cold office.

"We'll let him sweat some first," Al said, looking at his watch. "Give it two hours. Then we'll get to work."

The pastor had spent the next two hours praying for strength.

The room had smelt of urine when they entered. Martin Chandler became alert immediately. Al walked around the blindfolded man, who moved his head, following the footsteps as they rang out on the bare concrete.

"What do you want?" Chandler asked. It came out in a plea.

Al remained silent, standing a few inches behind the tied man. Outside, he had told Donald and the pastor that he would do all the talking.

"What do you want?" Martin Chandler asked again, more forcefully this time.

Al leant close to his prisoner, his hot, stale breath prickling those sensitive hairs around the ear and back of the neck. "Was it fun?" he whispered, lover close.

The editor strained against his ropes, trying to get away from Al. "I don't know what you are talking about."

Al shushed him, rubbing his hand against the prisoner's flabby neck. "Was it fun when you watched her burn?" he said, caressing his face.

The pastor and Donald stood against the door, watching in silence.

Pastor Morris was trying to ignore the tools and knives, lying on the table, in the corner of the room. Donald looked mesmerised.

The man started crying, denying it, again through tears and snot. Al pulled out a dirty handkerchief and made the captive blow his nose.

"I want to know what it was like," Al repeated. "I won't ask again and I won't be lied to."

"It was horrible," Chandler gushed. "I tried to stop it, but there was nothing I could do, they burnt her." He dry sobbed, "Oh God, oh God, I am so sorry."

"There, there," Al chided, while walking over to the long table in the corner of the room.

The pastor tried to tear his eyes away from it, but couldn't.

"I am going to ask you again in a little while." Al's hands danced over the implements on the table.

"It's the truth," Chandler insisted.

"We'll talk again in a little while," Al said, selecting his tool.

Martin Chandler jerked violently, as the electric drill started.

Al walked across the room, reaching the crying man. He moved the drill inches away from Chandler's ear, bringing it across his face, close enough for him to feel the violent draught from the tool.

Al stopped the drill, leaving only the silence of the room. Once the drill had stopped spinning, Al pressed it gently onto the blindfold, where Chandler's eye was.

Chandler started to scream.

"Do you want to tell us about it all?" Al asked gently. "This is your last chance."

Martin Chandler cracked, the information flowing out of him as freely as the piss down his leg.

Pastor Morris almost collapsed into the doorway, breathing a sigh of relief. Al's bluff had worked; it was important to the plan that they let Martin Chandler go without a scratch.

Donald stood there looking crestfallen.

5

Carter dragged himself clear of the wreck. It was still the bitterly cold dark before morning.

He had cut his eyebrow open, but apart from that seemed fine. The car must have gone a hell of a distance down the bank. He couldn't even see the outline of the road above him, just trees.

Carter kicked the vehicle for a few minutes, mad with himself, mad with whatever it was that had jumped out in front of the car.

He remembered a shape, then air, the car, rolling over and over, in stand-outside-yourself slow motion. Then what? Carter thought he might have lost consciousness. The blood on his forehead was sticky and drying.

Where the hell was he? Where was the road?

It would be dawn soon; Carter decided he'd get his bearings then. If only he'd grabbed a jacket before escaping. It should have been something he carried in the boot of the car; *stupid, stupid, stupid.*

Fuck it though; he was still ahead of the game.

Off in the distance, Carter saw a light through the trees, a farm perhaps? A farm with transport he could steal.

Carter kicked the car, one more time for good measure, before crashing through the bushes towards civilisation. Drained, from lack of blood and sleep, he found it hard going.

Off thirty feet to his right, there was a squeaking noise, man-made and grating.

He stopped, listening, straining his eyes through the still trees.

The noise came again, closer now, like a rusting sign swinging in the breeze.

Carter found it unsettling. As he pressed on, the noise to his right started getting closer.

He headed onwards towards the light, increasing his pace as he went.

The sound got closer still.

There was crashing, bushes being ripped up and violently shaken. Just on the periphery of his vision.

Carter spun around; he saw a movement, fast and undistinguished.

Dawn would be here soon.

Carter couldn't help himself. He started to run towards the light.

He tripped over a log, ankle cracking and sprawling.

Carter let out a scream.

The squeaking noise was getting closer.

He lay there, scrabbling in the mud and leaves for a weapon, the bones in his foot protruding all bloody and jagged.

The squeaking noise was now on the other side of the log.

Carter tried to raise his head and see over the log. The pain though was too much.

His hand was reaching, groping, desperately for something.

The squeaking was now accompanied by a growl, deep and primal.

Carter's hands gripped onto a log, baseball bat thick.

The growl crescendoed.

Off in the distance towards the light, it sounded like there were wolves howling.

Carter had a good grip on the log. "Come on, you fucker," he shouted.

Carter swung his weapon, as a whirring mass of fangs, fur and wheels, exploded over the tree trunk.

Oh shit, rotten wood, was the last thing to go through Carter's head, before the teeth.

6

The nurse looked up, bleary eyed, from her station, as Chief Inspector Brogan strode through the double doors and onto the ward. He ignored her and instead kept on marching down the corridor.

By the time he'd been told about the abortive raid on James Carter's house, the injured police officer had been in surgery for an hour. It was the new girl, Suzie Gorman. The surgeon had stopped the internal bleeding and was now concentrating on saving the eye.

*

Brogan felt bad. He should have been at the hospital sooner.

It hadn't been the old desk sergeant Johnson's fault though; Brogan had deliberately got into his office before the morning shift came on, when the station was still and Mary Celeste quiet.

He always got into his office early, but this morning he had left his house while it was dark. Stone and Keyes should have finished their preliminary report on Trish by now and there would be a copy waiting for him on his desk. However, that could wait.

Brogan had gone straight to their office, unlocking the door with his master key. The filing cabinet was partly buried in the corner of the room. It had only taken a moment to jimmy the lock, but much longer to find what he was looking for in the badly organised filing system.

After finding what he wanted, Brogan left the room, relocked the door and went into his own office.

He had then sat at his desk, drinking a cup of black-tar-vending-machine coffee, while regarding the three files spread out in front of him.

The report from Keyes and Stone was in the dead centre of his desk. He hadn't touched it yet. It was thin, *too thin*, he thought, to sum up somebody's life.

He wanted to read the other two thicker files first.

File one: the Autopsy Report.

File two: the Fire Report.

Brogan took a pen out of his blazer and used it to push Keyes and Stone's work to the corner of the desk. Not even wanting to touch it, before he had read everything for himself and formed his own ideas.

Then he would compare his summary to theirs.

Brogan was still sitting at his desk two hours later; the plastic cup of coffee had been left un-drunk and was now ice cold.

The autopsy report lay open on his desk, as he re-read the details for the fourth time that morning, the fire inspector's work already read.

The autopsy report was clear and concise, without the normal meandering descriptions that filled such documents. It listed the subject's age, weight, height and race. There was a note stating that hair colour couldn't be determined due to extensive charring.

The report went on to state that there was no evidence of death throes and the carbon monoxide levels taken from a blood sample were into the lethal range.

Brogan had spent a long time looking at the tox screening section. High-end, pharmaceutical-grade morphine had been found in her blood work. The concentration in her blood showed she had been taking large doses for a short, undetermined period of time.

Perhaps that was it, Brogan let himself think. She had got her hands on a lot of very powerful drugs and had holed up for the week in the abandoned, draughty building.

The problem was he just didn't see it. There were too many anomalies. Trish was… had been a sociable girl and someone with that amount of pharmaceutical-grade opiate could get all the friends she craved.

Also, there was that crazy-looking two-legged dog that followed her everywhere; where was that? And then there was the autopsy itself. The more he re-read the details, the more it just didn't gel. The carbon monoxide in her blood was in the lethal range, which meant she had been alive, breathing in the smoke, while the fire was burning.

One explanation was that while the fire burned her up, she had been so off her face on drugs she hadn't or couldn't move to get away from it. Brogan just couldn't see it; Trish had been a damn scrappy girl. It all just didn't add up.

Then there were the drugs themselves. Where had she got them? High-quality stuff like that didn't come cheap. Had she stolen it? Was she hiding out from someone? Had whoever it was found her and covered his crime? *No, no, no, do not start guessing yet.* At this stage there were just too many possibilities.

The pathologist's report had been signed off by the city's chief medical examiner. This too surprised Brogan. He doubted Doctor Llewelyn would come off the golf course long enough to even see the body of a burnt-up junkie.

Brogan was about to re-read the report again, but he realised what he was putting off. Turned face down on the desk was a small stack of photos. They had been taken by the lab techs. He hadn't looked at them before, wanting to concentrate on the report. But now that was done and he couldn't put it off any longer.

Brogan found that his palms were wet as he turned the photos over. He knew it made no sense, having been standing in the same room as the body, the day before. But somehow, seeing the photos made everything so, well, final.

The first photo was a slightly out of focus close-up on Trish's face. The skull was bald and blackened beyond recognition; the lips pulled back in a grimace of pain, her teeth white and perfect-looking, in amongst the mess of death.

He looked at that picture for a long time, before going through the rest of the pile. They were also out of focus, either too close or too far away. Towards the end of the stack, Brogan was ready to strangle the damn photographer.

It was on the last photo that he stopped, reached into his drawer and scrabbled around for a magnifying glass.

He stared through the magnifying glass for a long time – *that's odd*.

Finally, he put down the photograph and turned to Keyes and Stone's preliminary report.

The first page had Trish's age, date of birth, description and other details on it. It struck Brogan as sad that someone's life could be summed up by a flimsy, typed page.

Stapled to the front page was the same picture of Trish that had got into the newspaper.

Next were copies of the post-fire pictures, Trish looking little more than a charcoaled log. Brogan flicked through the photos; he did this twice.

The photos were then followed by a page-long summary of the fire report and then the autopsy. Brogan read them both twice.

The final three pages were a typed description of the whole investigation, the whole afternoon's investigation.

Canvassing had brought up no witnesses to the event. There was a mention of Trish's missing days. From the report, it looked like Keyes and Stone had concluded that she was either holed up in the building or had been scoring. Stone had put in that the missing time was only known to Trish or her drug dealer.

The final page of the report outlined further lines of inquiry that the detectives intended to follow:

A search for the source of the drugs.

Re-interviewing the family.

Re-canvassing the area.

In other words they were saying, *"Well, that's your lot, folks."*

After Brogan read the report, he read it again. It was brush under the carpet sloppy. The girl had been written off before they had even finished investigating.

In truth, that was why he had picked Stone and Keyes to look into it. Yes, Keyes was a conscientious officer, but he was subservient to Stone's haywire mood swings. And Stone was a hater; he hated Trish and people like her. He hated the sort that had every chance and had flushed it away.

Brogan supposed it came from years of looking into the eyes of a daughter who might not live long enough to have the chance to flush it all away.

Brogan hadn't wanted them looking into Trish's life too deeply, as it was so tangled up with his own.

Now, in a couple of days, the report would be filed, shelved and forgotten, the local paper having moved on to the next thing we should be horrified by.

It was time to start the real investigation himself.

Brogan returned the reports to their filing cabinet and as he was leaving the office, Sergeant Johnson bumbled into him.

The old sergeant looked surprised to see the boss coming out of the Keystone Cops' office. Johnson had told him the news about Suzie Gorman.

Brogan had gone into his office to get the bottle of whisky he kept in his desk, before heading towards the hospital.

*

Brogan stopped outside the waiting area and looked through the door. The small room was packed with policemen, all looking nervous and impatient.

Brogan completely understood why they were here and what they were going through. One of their colleagues was on the operating table. There, they thought, because of a mistake they had made, all of them re-running events in their heads. Had they been looking the wrong way? Had they slipped slightly, going through the door? Why hadn't they been close enough to cover her back?

Only Keyes and Stone weren't in the room. They were out there, looking for Carter. They'd be mad as hell. They'd be ready to crucify the worthless bastard.

Sergeant Toms, the young girl's training officer, was sitting forlornly, looking at the floor, chewing a nail.

Even though Brogan could understand it, he couldn't allow it.

Brogan didn't burst through the doors or shout as he entered the room. It was a level order. "Out now."

The police officers looked up, wearily and abashed.

"I want him found and brought in without a mark on him," Brogan ordered. He paused, looking around the room. "Now go."

He waited until all the police had filed past him; Sergeant Toms didn't move. "She'll be alright," Brogan said, sitting down. He pulled the whisky from the recesses of his coat, passing it to the sergeant.

Toms seemed to focus on him for the first time.

"Drink," Brogan said. "I'm giving you the day off."

They sat in silence for a while, Brogan declining to take a pull from the bottle. He never touched the stuff.

Finally, Sergeant Toms spoke, exhausted and booze loosened. "You know, sir, I hope that the Keystone Cops catch that bugger first."

"I understand that, Sergeant, and I would be a liar if I did not agree. But no matter what happens, we must remember that we are police officers and must uphold the law."

Toms shook his head and drank deeply from the bottle.

7

The momentum of the train rocking back and forth had quickly put Maggie to sleep. She lay against Alistair's shoulder, looking surprisingly comfortable in the small seats. In the short time he had known Maggie, Alistair had noticed her ability to look comfortable and contented wherever she was, kind of like a cat.

The train journey was familiar to Alistair, having gone through Bristol on the way to pick up pot in **[REDACTED]** every couple of weeks for three years. Even so he still enjoyed the changing scenery.

The morning sun radiated through the window, the light playing off Maggie's black hair, giving it a myriad of hues. He kissed the top of her head and she stirred slightly, before cwtching closer.

He felt a completely different person from the night before.

*

This morning he had woken quickly from a vampire-free sleep. Maggie was sitting cross-legged on the bed, fully dressed, wearing her thick coat against the coldness of the room.

She poked him affectionately. "Time to get up and at 'em."

Alistair realised he was naked under the blankets and oddly felt embarrassed about it. He had waited until she skipped out to the bathroom, before getting out of bed and finding his cleanest clothes.

*

Alistair looked down at himself now and realised that, despite his best efforts, he still looked like a scruffy git.

Never mind though; he was with Maggie and everything was going to work out fine.

Or so he thought.

8

Martin Chandler's trousers were soaked with sweat, mud and piss as he was, blindfoldedly, pushed on, through what could only be woods.

It was far removed from editing the local paper.

Chandler, having spent most of the night crying and wetting himself, felt so very thirsty. Yet as he found, his body could still produce a snot-full of tears.

He fell, sprawling through the mud; he lay there with his heart jack-hammering in his ears.

Martin Chandler had covered uncountable tragedies in his paper, bringing the human element to a story. Embellishing stories, that had been one of his flairs; with a trick of the pen he could give it a more person-orientated feel. Lazy phrases, like "time going slowly", "life flashing before your eyes" and "stand-outside-yourself slow motion". But, as he lay there in the mud and the leaves, all he thought of was how this was the furthest he had walked for years. And, in the primeval way the mind has of insulating itself from danger, he found himself swearing to do more exercise when this was over.

Rough hands grabbed him from the floor and back to reality.

"If you think the walking is bad, wait until you have to start digging the hole," a hard voice laughed, close to his ear.

Martin Chandler started sobbing again.

*

He had spilled his guts easily and without being touched. Just the sound of that drill and the feel of the air, violently circulating an inch from his eye, had been enough.

He had caved in and blabbed straight away, telling them all about the Society.

He had sobbed it all out, every last bit of the information he intended to give them.

That wasn't enough for them though. His legs were numb from sitting in the one position for such a long time, being asked the same questions over and over.

"And who's your leader?" his interrogator asked again.

Martin Chandler gulped in air. "I don't know, I swear I don't."

"You need to confess, let it all out."

The man had a chillingly calm voice.

"I don't know. I have only been a member for two months."

"I think you're lying." Pacing now. "How many have you killed in that time?"

The editor turned, trying to follow the voice. "I haven't presented any to die, I was just there watching."

His head was wrenched back by the hair.

"You were there. You killed them. How many?"

"She was the third."

"You killed three in two months?"

Chandler nodded, letting out another blub.

"Who were they?"

"You never know who they are when they are presented, only what they did to deserve to die."

"And what did Trish do?"

"She attacked a member of the Society and embarrassed her in public."

"How?"

"The member didn't specify. You don't need to specify, just accusing someone is enough."

"The woman who *presented* Trish, what was her name?"

"I'm sorry, I don't know. We don't know who each other are. Those are the rules."

"You don't know any of their names?"

Back to this question.

"No, I've told you, those are the rules."

The interrogator/torturer let out a sigh. "When are you due to meet next?"

A light came on inside the editor's mind, a little ray of hope. It was all a bluff. They had been asking him questions for about an hour now and he still had all his digits and eyes. They couldn't do it; they couldn't torture him. It was all an act, pretending with drills and hair pulling.

"When are you due to meet next?" his interrogator asked.

Martin Chandler felt the power in the room shift. It was all an act. It was all pretend.

The question came again. Chandler tried not to smirk. "In two days' time. It will coincide with the second meteorite storm." *Sob, sob, blub, blub.*

"Where will you meet?"

"I swear I don't know. It changes, last time it was that old quarry, but after the shooting, people are scared. I don't know." *Ah boo hoo, ah, boo hoo, hoo.*

"Give me some names of the people in the Society."

And so it had continued for another hour, with Martin Chandler, between put on sobs and begs for mercy, giving them as little information as he could. *"I'm sorry, I don't know, we don't know who each other are. Those are the rules."* Those are the rules indeed. Ha, you couldn't very well network if you didn't know who anyone else was.

Eventually the questioning had ended and he had been left alone.

Possibly he slept for a while; it was hard to say. If he'd slept, then it had been the muffled voices that woke him. They seemed to be coming from a way away.

There were two people speaking, his soft-voiced interrogator and a new voice. Chandler strained his ears, concentrating.

"We can't let him go. He now knows that we are after them."

"What do you suggest then? Leave him tied up in that room for the rest of his life?"

It was his interrogator speaking.

"His life doesn't have to be that long."

Chandler started to hate the new voice.

"No," his interrogator was insistent, suddenly loaded with authority. "Who on earth do you think we are? We're meant to be Hare Krishnas for God's sake. First, one of us is firing a gun and then we kidnap a man, and now what? We go in there and kill him? No, he doesn't know who we are. I have decided that, after this evening's festival, we take what we know to the police."

"I think it's too dangerous to let him live. He could warn the Society about us."

"He is better off alive. We don't know how powerful this Society is or even if the police are involved. I say if we let him go now, he will warn the Society and that may be the best thing. Look at him in there. He's not a monster; they are all respectable, middle-class people. If they think there is a danger of them getting caught, then they will stop doing it."

"I think you're crazy," the second voice said.

*

Chandler had willed his interrogator to win, but up here in the woods, he knew he had lost. That ray of hope from earlier was all but gone now.

He fell again cracking his head and catching part of the blindfold on a branch. Light flooded in, dazzling him. He lay there, limp and exhausted.

If they wanted to kill him, they could damn well do it here.

But no rough hands came to pick him up and push him on.

He looked around slowly; he was alone in the woods.

With difficulty he sat up, catching in the distance the last glimpse of a bald head and an orange robe disappearing through the trees. Martin Chandler smiled in victory, exhaustion and relief.

He was alive and now he needed to get home and make a phone call.

9

Chief Inspector John Brogan had been a policeman for a long time. He had seen his fair share of colleagues in hospital and knew that, except for waiting, there was very little you could do.

He left the waiting room. Sergeant Toms would be enough to watch over her. The blood-sprayed policeman didn't look up from the bottle.

Brogan walked past the same nurse sitting behind her desk and turned right at the sign that pointed to the morgue.

He wanted, very badly, to chase something up.

The mortuary was, as in most hospitals, in the basement. Brogan walked down an echoing flight of steps, which led him into a labyrinth of corridors.

Three corridors led off from the stairwell. Above his head, pipes and wires were running, as criss-crossedly as veins. Brogan followed the corridor that sloped down steeply. The corridor branched off into three directions and Brogan was soon lost.

Not wanting to ask for directions, or even seeing anyone to ask, he eventually found a fire door, opened it, uncaring about any alarm, and walked around the hospital to the car park. From here he knew his way into the morgue by heart.

Annoyed by the time he'd wasted, he hurried down the ramp by the loading bay, through a heavy set of doors and into the coldness of the morgue.

All the time unaware of the two sets of eyes on him.

Brogan had timed it well and actually caught the city's chief medical examiner, Doctor Llewelyn, coming out of his office.

Doctor Llewelyn looked as if he was finished for the day, it being 10:30 in the morning and all.

Llewelyn was a small, mean-faced man, dwarfed even by Brogan. What he lost in size though, he made up for in ego.

"Officer… Brogan." The doctor gave him a thin, unconvincing smile.

Brogan smiled back warmly. "May I have a moment, Doctor? And I promise it will just be a moment," he said, inflecting that too polite, fawning speech that he generally found worked best with this horrible little man.

"Only if it is quick," the doctor sighed, not hiding the glance he took at his watch.

"Perhaps in your office," Brogan motioned.

Llewelyn tutted, before showing him in.

"While you are here," the doctor said, "I do not appreciate the manner with which your subordinates badgered my office for the report on that fire victim. I believe it was that frightful Detective Stone. I will expect you to pass on my unhappiness at his behaviour and I expect that, in future, he will wait patiently for our result."

Brogan held his hands up in a pacifying gesture. "I will pass the message on, Doctor."

Doctor Llewelyn nodded, seemingly sated.

"Can I ask why you were the one to perform the autopsy?" Brogan continued. "It seems a little… well, we both have subordinates to do the more onerous tasks that cross our desks."

The doctor gave him another thin smile. "It pays to keep one's hand in, that and present staff shortages."

"Can I ask if you noticed anything unusual about the body?"

The doctor eyed him coldly. "*Unusual*? Do you mean something I didn't include in my report?"

Damn, wrong question, Brogan thought, *back-pedal, back-pedal*. "I can assure you that *isn't* what I meant. You yourself mentioned pressure from my officers, I just wondered if—"

"If I did sloppy work? That seems to be the gist of your question, Officer."

Brogan sighed, angry at himself for slipping up and turning this into a conflict. But conflict it was so, *lean forward, look him in the eye and talk over anything that comes out of his mouth.* "That is Chief Inspector, not Officer, and if you want to talk in semantics, then yes, doctor, I am worried about you having performed a sub-standard autopsy."

Doctor Llewelyn started to puff himself up in a rage.

"Doctor," Brogan continued. "I have seen the photos of the cadaver and, to be honest, you would have been better off using a sketch artist. There was one shot in focus, one shot, Doctor, out of a dozen." He pulled the one good shot out of his coat, along with a magnifying glass, holding it, facing away from the doctor. "Did you find any evidence that Trish Reed had been restrained?"

"Restrained?" the doctor looked thrown.

"Yes, Doctor, restrained." Brogan turned the photo around and gave the doctor the magnifying glass.

Llewelyn stared through it, at the picture, before looking up at the detective. "I am sorry, but I do not know what I am supposed to be looking at."

"The left wrist."

The doctor peered through the magnifying glass. Brogan didn't take his eyes off him; he saw a shadow twitch across his features.

"Ah, I see what you mean," Llewelyn said finally. "That line running perpendicularly across the wrist." He put the magnifying glass down. "And you think it could be evidence of her being tied?"

Brogan nodded.

The doctor sighed and shook his head, as if he was about to admonish a naughty, stupid child. "You are right to an extent. We found melted fibres in the left wrist, but after testing we found that it was nothing more than…" He got up and opened a filing cabinet, taking his time to pull out a heavy folder. The doctor sat back down and flicked to the right page. "Ah, here we are… hemp fibre. Now from what I gather, this girl was one of those hippy, earth-child types. So I can only surmise that it was some sort of bracelet or strap and yes, it was only found on the one wrist."

"I see, thank you for your time." Brogan got up and turned to the door.

"Chief Inspector," the doctor called him back. "For future reference, if you wish to corner me and then harangue me with wild accusations, please contact my secretary first."

Brogan left without a word.

When Doctor Llewelyn was alone, he picked up the telephone and dialled a number from memory. "It's me, I think we may have a problem," he said.

Brogan left the bleach-smelling morgue and got into the relative freshness of the car park; he walked over to a bank of payphones and dropped in a few coins.

Brogan too dialled a number from memory.

The phone was answered almost immediately.

Brogan listened for a second before snapping. "No, it's not Emily, it's me. Why, what's wrong?"

Mardy, on the other end of the phone, told him how his wife was due to call about colour swatches for the bedroom.

Brogan knew Mardy well enough to know he was lying, but didn't have time to worry about it now.

"Carter has disappeared," Brogan said. He paused for a moment. "I'll tell you what that has got to do with you. He put three of my police officers down while he was escaping, one of them seriously. So I want all your people out looking for him."

Mardy started to say something, but Brogan cut him off. "I know they are meant to be seeing if anyone is dealing heroin in the city, get them to multitask."

"It's Emily," Mardy said. "She's left me."

Brogan felt his heart miss a beat, a stream of old feelings flooding back. He forced them to one side. "Right now that is not your priority."

Brogan hung up, not waiting for an answer.

10

Bristol rocked. It was cleaner than any place Alistair had ever been. The people were enthused with a life and colour that was somehow missing from Swansea.

What a great morning. Maggie had played tourist guide. Taking control of the map, she had led him up a steep hill, past trendy people shopping in trendy shops.

Alistair had felt seriously out of place. Maggie pulled that mind reading thing that she seemed to do and told him being with her made him trendy – trendy by default, if you like. And Maggie was right; she looked stunning, turning more than a few blokes' heads.

Their first stop had been a massive bridge, suspended over a deep gorge. The view was stunning and all, but Alistair found he only had eyes for Maggie. She was trying to, simultaneously, read the guidebook, while showing him where they were on the map. She was failing badly as the wind whipped the map, but looking as cute as a button while she did.

They had walked across the bridge, stopping at the halfway point, to spit off the side for a while.

"This is lush," Alistair had said, Maggie's enthusiasm captivating him.

She had come close to him, hugging him, groping him. "Hey look at that, you've just been molested on top of the Clifton suspension bridge," she said, her voice full of mischief.

Finally, they had gone for lunch. Alistair said he owed her a meal from the other night. Maggie had opted for Chinese, explaining there were no decent Chinese restaurants back home. Alistair had never tried chopsticks before and after a couple of minutes hoped he'd never have to again.

"I'm exhausted," Maggie said, after they had finished eating. "I guess I'm not used to walking this much."

"I'm used to it. I walk miles each week, normally in the rain as well. But not for long though, I'm ready to give the whole thing up." Alistair had smiled, while carefully placing his napkin on the table in a futile attempt to cover the mess he'd made on the table cloth.

Last night he had told her what he did, told her about his deliveries; he hadn't taken any pride in it.

"You're really going to give it up?" she asked, eyes sparkling, seeming pleased.

"Yeah, I'm done with it, I need a change."

She sat back, playing with the straw in her drink for a while. "Good for you, Alistair."

After the meal, Maggie and Alistair hit the university proper.

One of the people on Alistair's delivery runs was a student. So he was quite used to them. Why they couldn't do things in a quieter, less self-satisfied manner was beyond him though.

They had wandered aimlessly around the Student Union for a while, before getting directions to the new students' bit from a porter. Maggie had collected up armfuls of brochures or, as she had corrected Alistair, prospectuses. They had talked for a while to the woman who sat behind the desk. Maggie had asked her a lot of questions about university and, surprising even himself, so had Alistair.

11

Brother Dowling came awake with a start, wondering if he had heard the doorbell or just dreamt it. He was still groggy, feeling as if he'd just closed his eyes a second ago.

It had taken Brother Dowling longer than he'd planned to convince Donald to stay where he was and watch that dratted café.

*

"I don't like it," Donald had said, giving his expert military opinion.

They were standing on the rusted, rickety fire escape of a derelict building opposite the Hare Krishnas' café. A pigeon viewed them beadily from some old guttering.

"I'm too exposed up here," Donald continued, staring at the pigeon, which was somehow balancing on one withered foot.

Brother Dowling had sighed inwardly; it had been a long, tiring and spiritually questionable night. All he had wanted to do was sleep.

"Look, it's nice," he chided, still out of breath from climbing the fire escape. "You get a good view up and down the road. You can see both entrances of the café. And I thought in the army it was better to have the high ground."

Donald just shook his head, still staring at the pigeon.

"Come on, you must admit it is quite an elevated position."

Donald still didn't look happy.

"Is it the pigeon?"

The big man nodded his head vigorously.

"It won't hurt you."

"It's their feet. I don't like them."

"Look, it's gone now," Brother Dowling said, shooing it away.

The pigeon had fluttered up and landed a few feet further along the guttering.

It had been like trying to convince a child, a big, nutty child, to do his homework. However, he had eventually convinced Donald to stay where he was and watch the café.

Brother Dowling had then gone back to the chapel to drop off the minibus and check that Gavin was resting comfortably. The poor soul hadn't talked since he'd been let out of the policemen's trunk. The self-inflicted wounds on his face were gauze-wrapped, but still weeping a lot.

Finally, Brother Dowling had been able to go back to his house and rest.

*

The doorbell rang again.

Brother Dowling lay in bed for a moment, dozily getting his orientation; his sheets were wrapped around him, cocoon-like. Rubbing the sleep out of his eyes, he looked at his alarm clock, realising he'd slept through until the afternoon.

It had been a long night.

*

Watching as the fat newspaper editor cowered and urinated had been very uncomfortable. Watching as Al closed in on him with the drill had been… well, upsetting.

Pastor Morris had been insistent that they couldn't hurt the editor. Brother Dowling was sure that Al would have done

306

something really bad to the fat man if the information hadn't started flowing so readily.

The pastor's control was slipping. He hadn't been the same since the happenings in the quarry and now Al seemed to be starting to control decisions.

Luckily, the editor had started blabbing straight away, telling them of how the mysterious phone calls had started and how he had been invited to a meeting that would improve his life. Of course, Chandler initially thought it was a scam, but had finally gone along and after a number of induction rituals had joined the Society.

Al had questioned him repeatedly, but the editor had just repeated the same story – no one knew each other's names, but occasionally they would be contacted by phone to perform tasks.

As the questioning had dragged on into its fourth hour, Martin Chandler had even tried to defend the Society. Telling Al how, in today's culture, the law and the police didn't protect the honest citizen; there was no sanction for yobs or criminals, just a slap on the wrist or a foreign holiday.

"It is up to us to defend our way of life," Chandler had said. "Because no one else will."

"By killing?" Al had asked.

"If that is what it takes then yes."

Al, face all contorted in hatred, had looked at the drill and then back at his prisoner, back and forth, back and forth.

The pastor desperately gestured for him to leave the room; Al ignored him.

Later, when Al had calmed down, he and Brother Dowling stood outside the open door and read the lines, which Pastor Morris had written out for them.

"He is better off alive. We don't know how powerful this Society is or even if the police are involved," Al said, squinting at the crumpled bit of paper. "I say if we let him go now, you're right, he will warn the Society and that may be the best thing. Look at him in there. He's not a monster; they are all respectable, middle-class people. If they think there is a danger of them getting caught, then they will stop doing it."

"I think you're crazy," Brother Dowling had said.

Then, as dawn broke, he drove the van out to the woods. Jason and Muppet were in the back, shaven headed and dressed like Hare Krishnas. They were already both wasted and spent the journey telling Martin Chandler how they were going to bury him alive in the woods.

Brother Dowling couldn't help but question if they were all really doing God's will.

*

The doorbell rang for a third time.

Brother Dowling got out of bed, putting on his old, heavy dressing gown and stepping into his slippers.

He hadn't had many visitors since his mother had passed away three years ago and felt embarrassed answering the doorbell in such disarray.

The doorbell was rung a fourth time.

"I'm coming, I'm coming."

There were two men standing on the doorstep. Their matching uniforms stating they were from the gas company.

"Mr Dowling?" the taller man asked.

The taller man had a posh accent, an accent that just didn't jibe with the outfit.

Brother Dowling pointed down the road, his hand shaking badly. "No, he lives four doors up."

"Oh, sorry for bothering you," the taller man apologised, scratching his head.

There was a tense moment of silence, before Brother Dowling tried to close the door.

The two men charged forward.

Brother Dowling swung the door as hard as possible, not even seeing if it slammed shut; he turned and ran through the hall into his tidy little kitchen and scrabbled with the backdoor's safety chain, his hands all slick and shaking.

He pulled the chain free and flung the door open, as hands grabbed him from behind, forcing him back inside the house.

As the chemical-drenched rag was forced into his face and he started to go under, Brother Dowling thought, *they shouldn't be here; they should be after the Hare Krishnas.*

12

Before leaving the hospital, Chief Inspector Brogan had made one more call from the payphone.

He and the fire inspector went back a long old ways.

"It's me."

"Who is this? John?" the fire inspector asked.

"It's about the fire that killed the girl. I've got some questions."

"John, it's all in my report." A pause. "Look, when the big copper pulled out that girl's photo I recognised her and I know your past with her, but I'm sorry, it's an open and shut case."

"I've read open and shut cases before. I read one three years ago, remember?"

"I did that to help you, John, and I knew then that it would come back to haunt me."

"No, you did that to get yourself out of trouble. Who else have you 'helped'?"

"No one, the girl started the fire herself."

Brogan made a leap – Brogan exaggerated, "It's not turning out to look like a routine case."

"Why, what have you found out?"

Asked oddly, asked too eagerly.

"A lot and none of it has been well hidden."

The fireman sighed. "When I saw in the paper who the girl was, my heart sank. I have spent the last day hoping you wouldn't ring."

"Well, I have and I want to know the truth."

"John." It came out as a plea. "These are powerful people you are dealing with. Look, someone's coming. I'll meet you tonight at nine-thirty in the same old place."

The phone went dead.

Brogan drove back to the station slowly, his thoughts full of questions. His thoughts full of Emily Davies. Had she really left Mardy?

They'd nearly been an item, many years ago now, of course. He was still a bobby on the beat back then; he must have only been about twenty-two.

* * *

Emily collected glasses in her father's pub. She had just turned seventeen, but by God, she carried herself like a thirty year old.

Emily and her father were new to the city. The first time he'd rung the bell to call last orders, the locals had run out. They'd never heard the damn thing before; they thought there was a fire.

Brogan and Mardy had been smitten with her.

She had lit up Brogan's life back then. They had talked. They had talked a lot.

Her dad was a brute of a man and she often carried bruises.

"Report it, I can have him arrested," Brogan had said.

She said no.

All he'd wanted was to be with her, to make her happy.

Then he got the phone call; the phone call that changed everything. The phone call that had broken his heart. The phone call that had turned him into a murderer.

* * *

It was quiet back at the station; Sergeant Johnson sat, as always, behind the front desk. He nodded at the Chief Inspector.

311

"We haven't heard from the hospital yet," he said pre-empting Brogan's question.

"I am going to be in my office. I want you to get hold of Detective Keyes and Detective Stone. Find out how the search for this James Carter is going."

The old sergeant nodded. "By the way you have a visitor in your office."

"I'm busy, who is it?"

"She wouldn't give her name, only that it was a personal matter." The old sergeant harrumphed. "I said she could wait in your office."

Brogan shook his head, before walking up the stairs.

Emily Davies sat in his chair, facing the door, her eyes shielded behind a pair of large, sunglasses.

The office smelled of cigarettes.

Brogan sat down in front of his desk, feeling stupid for doing so.

He returned her stare.

"It's been a long time." She smiled, still with that beautiful smile.

"Yes, yes it has," Brogan agreed.

Brogan hadn't seen her for years; he'd forced himself not to. She hadn't changed a bit.

"What do you want?" he asked.

"I've left him," she said. "He's lost it. I told him to stay calm, but he's using coke all the time. He's just so paranoid."

She removed her glasses to show one eye, meat-pattied, closed. "I tried to tell him to calm down, but he's got people running all over town looking for this vigilante. He's become obsessed with him and doesn't trust anyone."

Brogan leaned forward, steepling his fingers on the desk. "Why have you come to me?" he asked. "Do you want to report a crime?"

"In a way, yes," she said, pulling out a small tape recorder and placing it in front of her on the desk.

13

Karl Reno sat in his car, seat back, reclining, while idly picking his teeth with a piece of card. In his other hand he held his mobile phone. He held it a few inches away from his ear; Mardy Davies was on the other end drunk and shouting.

Reno finished picking the last morsel of lunch out of his teeth, before smiling at himself in the rear-view mirror. "Ok, ok," he said, bored now and wanting to finish the call. "I'll look for her and call you if I find her."

Reno closed the phone, not waiting for an answer.

The boss was becoming an embarrassment; he was losing it, getting fucked over by a woman like that, for fuck's sake.

*

Tony had rung him earlier. Tony was dumb; Tony had sounded scared.

"Where are you?" Tony had asked, friendlier than normal.

"I'm busy, what do you want?"

"Mardy's... Mardy's not well."

"Call a fucking doctor then."

"No, it's... look, he's not well."

Tony went on to explain how he'd got back from visiting Ivor in the hospital. Reno couldn't give a fuck about Ivor and didn't even ask how he was.

Tony had got back to Mardy's mansion to find the front door wide open. *"It just all looked wrong, see."*

He had got out of the car, golf club in hand.

Inside, the house was trashed.

Tony had gone slowly from room to room until he came across Mardy, lying on the floor, his robe open, crying his eyes out.

"Emily has just up and left him, see. I knew it was real when I saw his safe was wide open and all her jewellery was gone."

"Just the jewellery?" Reno asked.

"Uh, yeah, as far as I could see, why?"

Excellent, Reno thought, *they hadn't noticed the missing tapes.* "Doesn't matter, where is he now?"

"He's collapsed on his bed. What should I do?"

Reno had smiled at this. He had thought long and hard about bringing Tony and Ivor in, but they were like dogs, loyal to a master, and he knew the fuckers didn't have any respect for him. No respect at all, until something like this happens, then they come asking for help and advice.

"Give him a drink or something. I'll try and find the wife," Reno said, hanging up without waiting for an answer.

Karl liked the power of doing that. When he was the boss man, he'd end all his phone calls that way.

And Karl knew he was going to be the boss man pretty damn soon. All the pieces were in place. Emily had left Mardy and, just as importantly, the **[REDACTED]** crew had come to town.

*

Batty Boy's car had pulled up, the bomp, bomp, bomp of base at a teeth-shattering level.

"Stay in the car, stay looking forward," Karl had ordered Kieran.

Batty Boy had not been alone. He'd been with two other men: Daryl, who Reno had met before, and Tiny, who, like all people called Tiny, was truly massive and quite cheery.

They drove to the unassuming council house, in Penlan, that Karl had procured for their use.

"Shit," Tiny said, getting out of the car. "You sheep-shaggers actually have proper houses."

"What were you expecting?" Karl asked, slightly confused.

"Dunno," Tiny shrugged, scratching his bald skull. "Wattle and daub huts."

Karl ignored the jibe and instead led them up the path and into the unassuming council house.

"Hey, look at this; you've got electricity as well," Tiny said, flicking the switch back and forth. "Tell me something. Does it still frighten you?"

Karl pushed past him, into the lounge.

"What not even a little bit? Come on, man, you can tell me."

Tiny had gone around the house marvelling at how it was just so similar to the houses you found in England.

Reno had busied himself laying out the plan to Daryl and Batty Boy. "I've got it all set up," Reno had said, while cutting up *welcome to town* lines on the table. "Mardy will be all on his own when we grab him."

"How did you manage that?" Daryl asked, leaning forward.

Daryl was the oldest person in the room and had a few grey hairs creeping into his precisely trimmed beard. He also had very alert eyes, which he was using to look intently at Reno.

Karl wasn't meant to say how the plan had come together. Emily had been very specific about that. He wasn't to mention her to the gangsters from **[REDACTED]**.

✻

"Whatever you do," she had said, while round Karl's flat, "don't mention that you are working with a woman."

"Why?" Karl had asked.

Emily had sighed. "Look, I know the type of people who will

315

be coming down here. And as soon as you say you are getting help from a woman, they think you're not a proper man, which will make us look bad." Emily had appraised Karl for a moment. "Do you understand?"

Karl had nodded.

"Good. Now hit me."

"No, I'm not hitting you."

Emily sighed another one of her exasperated sighs. "You need to hit me if this plan is to work."

Karl had hesitated before closing his eyes and reluctantly clocking Emily in the face.

*

"How did you manage that?" Daryl repeated, still leaning forward.

"I've been busy banging this guy Mardy's wife," Karl said, smugly. "I tell you she is hooked on me. She's left him, left him in a right state," Karl sneered. "So when the time is right, she'll ring him up saying she wants to meet to talk. Just them two on their own and then we turn up instead of her."

Batty Boy laughed. "You've got a woman to help you?"

"Yeah, I got the bitch wrapped around my little finger."

"Ok, when we've got this Mardy Davies, what's the plan?" Daryl wanted to know.

"He's got a boat. We go for a little sail and drop him off somewhere."

"Whoa, whoa, whoa, I'm not a fucking sailor," Batty Boy cautioned.

"You don't need to be, I've been out on it before."

Daryl ignored Batty Boy. "Doing a similar kind of 'drop off'?"

Karl paused, remembering back to his final job interview.

*

He'd been standing with Mardy and Danny, puke covered and scared. Stockard Clifton-James, crime lord, heroin dealer and owner of the biggest second-hand car franchise in the city, was lying in chains on the pitching deck, spitting insults at them.

Stockard was a big man, corpulent from years of good living. He'd fought back, when they'd appeared at his front door, but what had been muscle was now just fat and they'd quickly subdued him.

What had taken more time was torturing the combination to the safe out of him. They'd had to break all his fingers before he'd given it up.

With the safe empty and bags of clothes packed it would seem to all the world that Stockard had disappeared to warmer climes, rather than lying on this sea-swept deck.

"You gotta cut him first," Danny had said, handing Reno a vicious-looking knife. "As the body decomposes, it fills with gas and can actually float to the surface. Hence the need to stick him a good couple of times."

Reno had gingerly taken the knife off him.

"After tonight, I am never going to dirty my hands again," Mardy said to Danny, as Reno moved, hesitantly, forward and Stockard Clifton-James rained down curses on their mothers.

*

"Doing a similar kind of 'drop off'?" Reno mumbled, before shaking away the ghosts. "Yes, it was a while ago."

"Ok, we'll leave it at that for now," Daryl said. "Just one thing, I don't like working with women, so, for now, you keep an eye on her."

*

Everyone wanted him to look out for Emily, Karl thought, putting his seat back into position. So look for her he did. He looked across the road and saw her coming out of the police station. He looked as she crossed the road and got into the car.

He tried to ask her how it went with the policeman, but instead she lit a cigarette, inhaled deeply and ordered him to drive.

14

From his office window, Brogan watched Emily cross the street and get into a car.

He hared down the stairs towards his own vehicle.

Brogan nearly hit a bus as he tore out of the police station's parking lot and snuggled into the traffic, seven cars behind them. He'd dropped back further, as the traffic thinned. He recognised Reno's car and guessed they were heading to the new flats down the marina. One day all the old docks would look like them.

Brogan had parked way down the street and watched as Emily got out of the car with Reno. They jogged up a flight of stairs and disappeared into one of the flats.

Brogan knocked the engine off and sat there ruminating. He knew that one day they would be coming from **[REDACTED]**.

He'd worked out the identity of their scout years ago. He just hadn't expected it to begin like this, with Emily betraying her husband and ultimately betraying them all.

It hurt him.

Hearing the tape Emily had produced hurt him too. He'd recognised Mardy straight away, but oddly, it had taken a few seconds for him to recognise his own voice.

It was an old conversation, discussing how they had taken over the drug supply to the city's university.

It had been a few years ago. A spate of students had ended up in hospital from dodgy ecstasy. Brogan wanted the supply controlled, limited quality assured.

It had not come over on the tape that way.

It was not good.

"He's mad," Emily said, stopping the tape and leaving it on the table. "He's doing too much coke; he's bringing it in by the kilo. He's going to force your hand; he's got a load of these tapes. They're stashed away in the safe. He's got to be stopped."

"I will have a word with him," Brogan said, just to say something. He needed time to think.

"No. It's out of your hands. He's going to be stopped, that is a given. It's the after part that will concern you." Emily ground her cigarette into the paperclip holder.

"The after part?"

"That's right," she said, suddenly looking so much different from the girl he had once loved. "When Mardy is out of the way, we are going to have to work together to resume the status quo."

"What do you mean 'out of the way'? Are you going to kill him?" Emily just smiled at this.

"And what? You want me to help cover up his death?"

"You've helped me before, John."

"We were different people back then."

"I saw the way you killed my father. That was instinctual, something like that doesn't change."

"How do you intend to stop Mardy?" Brogan asked, changing the subject, wanting to get away from that night.

"You don't need to know that, John."

"I am going to need to know everything, before deciding whether to help you or not."

She lit another cigarette. "I don't see how you have a choice."

"Emily, there is always a choice."

320

She shrugged. "It doesn't matter. Karl Reno is covering that part of it."

"Karl Reno?" Brogan snorted. "You have made a big mistake trying to take on Mardy with him."

"You're right, Reno's an idiot. He will serve his purpose for a while though. I've also got help from outside."

"Who?"

"Some men are going to come down from **[REDACTED]**."

Oh, you stupid woman, Brogan thought. *You've actually opened the door and invited them home.* He massaged his temple. "Emily, this is a very dangerous game you are playing. How do you know these men aren't going to just waltz in and take over the place?"

"It's a one shot deal for them. They get paid and then they leave. Just like a gardener or a handyman."

"These sorts of people are not like gardeners or handymen."

Her look showed she thought they were.

"You can keep the tape by the way," Emily said, getting up to leave.

They both knew it was a hollow gesture; there were more.

She stopped in front of him, her eyes softening. "Look, John, you have twenty-four hours to decide what to do. But things need to change." She put her hand against his cheek for a moment. "Things could be good between us, John."

The touch had meant nothing to Brogan.

*

Brogan sat in his car, watching the flat, trying to get those two lines of hers out of his mind, *"I saw the way you killed my father. That was instinctual, something like that doesn't change."*

She was right, something like that doesn't change; it festers and fights its way to the surface.

That one phone call years ago that changed everything.

Mardy had been on the phone; he had been scared.

They'd been seeing each other – Mardy and Emily. They'd been seeing each other for a while. No one in the pub had known about it, not even Brogan.

Daddy dearest knew though. He'd caught them in her room. He'd caught them busy "courting".

Now, Mardy could handle himself, but Daddy had boxed professionally and Daddy kept a bat under the bar.

That's when Brogan had got the phone call.

He'd got to the pub to find Emily's father, skull cracked open, on the floor in a pool of blood.

Mardy was battered and in shock, one of his eyes was dilated.

"Help me," Emily had begged. "He was beating up Mardy; I hit him with the bat and he cracked his skull on the table." She collapsed onto him sobbing.

Brogan felt betrayed, he felt devastated.

He was going to walk away.

She must have sensed it; she gripped onto him tightly. "He hit me too," she sobbed.

"Stop crying," Brogan said, gently returning the hug.

Brogan hadn't been in the uniform for very long, but he knew enough to doctor a crime scene.

"Emily, I want you to start straightening the place out. We are going to have to clean up this blood as well. You," he said to Mardy, "are going to need to clean yourself up, but first, we're going to have to move the body."

With a great effort, they dragged the corpse through into the bar. He was heavy; it took time. Brogan opened the trapdoor to the cellar.

"Will the cleaning lady be in tomorrow?" he asked Emily.

She nodded.

"Good, we will let her find him. It will look like he missed his footing and fell through the open trap door. "I'll be on duty tomorrow and make sure I'm the first policeman on the scene. I can control things then, smooth things over." He turned to Mardy. "After we have done this, we will need to clean up here. Then get yourself around to Danny's to get an alibi. You don't tell him about this though."

Mardy nodded dumbly.

"Now help me get him through the trapdoor."

They pushed and they twisted the body, trying to get it through. It was no good.

"Right, if we try—" Brogan jumped, as the body gasped and started moving.

"He's alive," Mardy said, sounding relieved. "Quickly, Emily love, get on the phone, we'll get an ambulance. We'll just tell them that he—"

Brogan picked up the bat and pushed them both out of the way and proceeded to cave the man's skull in.

That had been the first person he murdered. And he remembered, at the time, feeling an incredible release, of what? Anger? Hatred? Pleasure? Yes, that was it; for the first time in his life he'd felt pure pleasure.

✷

Now, Chief Inspector Brogan could feel the need for that pleasure rising within himself again.

✷

Twenty minutes later, Karl Reno came out of the flat alone and drove off. Brogan followed.

Emily had been lying earlier. The men from **[REDACTED]** weren't coming down. They were already here. And they were just the advance party.

As Brogan pulled out of the new marina complex, a voice squawked over the police radio. *"Attention all available units, James Carter's car has been found."*

15

As always the café was deserted; most people in Swansea regard meals that don't contain meat and some form of potatoes with suspicion.

Pragnesh Lankhani tried to let his mind relax to nothing. Normally he found it was an easy exercise to achieve. However, after the events of the last few days, it was an impossible task.

Pragnesh Lankhani had been a Hare Krishna for fifteen years. Never before though had he found his beliefs tested to such a level.

Was Pastor Morris right to use such violently direct methods against the Society? I mean machine guns? But what were the alternatives?

Some of the younger Hare Krishnas had called for action, a few even arguing that Pastor Morris was right.

Pragnesh Lankhani had been adamant though. They would not, could not, use violence. He felt in an inextricable position. He wouldn't endanger any of his members by going to the police directly – the Society's power and influence were something to fear. However, he couldn't see any alternative. So it would be tonight that he would meet with his fellow Hare Krishnas and decide a course of action.

He would also tell them the worrying information he had found out about Pastor Morris.

*

The café had internet access and one of the younger men had shown him how to use it.

After a number of frustratingly fruitless hours of visiting websites and church directories, he still hadn't been able to find anything on Pastor Morris. Not on any list or website or search he tried did Pastor Morris turn up.

Tired of staring at a computer screen, Pragnesh Lankhani had spent just as long on the phone, pillar to posting his way around every church-based organisation he could think of.

Pastor Morris didn't seem to exist.

Perplexed, he had tried to meditate for a while, but without success. His eyes kept on wandering back to the computer in the corner of the café. Pragnesh Lankhani, intrigued now, went back and sat down at it for another hour of searching in vain.

Just as he was about to give up, he stumbled across a website. It was gaudy and nut-run, containing badly written articles, outlining stories of Christian shame and salacious secrets.

One of the articles contained a picture of Pastor Morris.

Pragnesh Lankhani froze; according to the article the pastor was dead.

*

Pragnesh Lankhani opened his eyes, as the wind chimes over the door did their thing.

Two men, in workman's overalls, entered the café and looked around. Pragnesh Lankhani brightened up; finally, some customers. He smiled at them warmly as they approached.

The taller of the two workmen came up to the counter and smiled back.

"Would you like to see a menu?" Pragnesh Lankhani asked.

The taller man pulled out a laminated ID card and held it between unusually well-manicured nails.

"No, thank you, sir," the workman said, in a surprisingly posh accent. "We're here to check the gas."

One of the good things about being a Hare Krishna is that disappointment doesn't last that long.

Pragnesh Lankhani led them through the back of the café and down into the basement, where the gas boiler was. They thanked him and he went back to watching the café upstairs.

Twenty minutes later, after stopping for a few moments to tell the Hare Krishna that everything was fine, the two workmen left the café. They didn't notice Donald lying low, camouflaged and largely pigeon free, in the waste ground.

16

Reno squealed to a stop outside the unassuming council house.

He'd dropped Emily off at his pad. She'd be staying there until tomorrow, when the plan would be set in motion.

He had spent a frustrating fifteen minutes trying to get her undressed. She'd told him, in no uncertain terms, to stop pawing her; there'd be time enough after.

He'd given up on that idea and instead cut up a nice, big, fat line on the table.

Karl had then left to pick up Kieran.

Dance music was pounding out of the unassuming council house, making it not so unassuming. *The bunch of stupid cunts*, Reno thought, *this isn't professional*. The last thing he wanted was a neighbour calling the police to complain about the noise. And then there was the smell. He could smell it as soon as he got out of the car. Skunk hung heavy in the air.

He'd put a stop to this in a minute.

Firstly, he had to get rid of the annoying voice in his ear. "I said I'm still fucking looking," Karl snapped, rolling his eyes in exasperation. "What music?" He switched the mobile to his other ear. "Ok, ok, for fuck's sake. Where will you be this afternoon?"

Reno listened for a moment before cutting in. "I'll buy some grapes and a big bunch of flowers for him after I find the woman. Ok, how's that? Now stop calling me." He switched his phone off.

"Is Danny pissed off?" Kieran asked, sounding concerned.

"The fucker's always pissed off. Who gives a shit? It won't matter soon anyway," Reno laughed, heading for the front door.

"Who are you taking the flowers to?"

"Ivor, that's who." Reno was feeling great. "You know what I'm going to do? After this is all done, I'm going to go along to the hospital and give him a nice big bunch of flowers, and then tell him he has been banished and he has twenty-four hours to get out of the city." Karl laughed. "That is, of course, after I've told him what has happened to Danny and Mardy."

Reno was taken with the image of that muscle-bound fuck's stupid face changing, as the truth sank in and he realised he'd been banished from the city.

A smile glided across Reno's face as he repeated the word *banished*. By tomorrow he'd have the power to banish.

"Should we ring or knock?" Kieran asked, bringing him back to the front door they were standing at.

They knocked.

They knocked five times, louder and louder, hammering away, until finally the door opened a couple of inches, leaving them staring into Tiny's chest.

Tiny looked down on them, glaring at Kieran. "Who the fuck's this?"

"He's with me," Reno said, trying to push through the door, the chain and Tiny.

None of which budged.

Tiny just continued to glare. "I said who the fuck is he?"

"This is Kieran, he's with me. He was driving my car yesterday, remember?"

Tiny considered this for a moment before nodding and closing the door, as if to take the safety chain off.

The door stayed closed for over a minute.

"Perhaps you should banish him," Kieran suggested.

Reno glared at him, before he started hammering on the door.

Tiny opened the door again, this time fully and he let them squeeze past him.

Kieran, all cockiness gone, kept his eyes to the ground.

The aroma of skunk grew stronger as they reached the lounge. Tiny was walking down the hall behind them and pushed Kieran into Reno as they reached the door. The force of Kieran cannoning into the back of him made Reno stumble forward into the room.

Inside, the room was Gorillas-in-the-Mist smoky.

"Hey, here they are," Batty Boy said from the sofa.

17

Brother Dowling had gone missing that afternoon. Or at least, that was when someone realised he was missing.

It was only after lunch, when Brother Dowling didn't show up, that Pastor Morris began to worry. One of Brother Dowling's most annoying traits was his incredible attention to punctuality. *"Like it was the eleventh bloody commandment,"* as Al had once said.

An hour later, Dowling still hadn't shown up or answered his phone.

The pastor wanted to seek Al's council, but Al had taken the minibus up into mid Wales to visit an old army colleague. He was picking up something special for tomorrow night.

The pastor decided that they would have to call there.

Pastor Morris knocked on the front door of the little terraced house, while Jason and Muppet scooted down the back alley.

There was no answer or movement within the house. The pastor knocked again, louder now.

The door was opened.

Muppet was standing the other side of it, eating a bit of cake.

"No one's here," he said, cheerfully spraying crumbs at the pastor.

"How did you get in?" the pastor asked, pushing past him.

Muppet and Jason shared a look.

"The back window was... well, is smashed," Jason said sheepishly.

Without turning around the pastor knew that Muppet was smirking.

The house smelt of body odour and sour milk.

There was no sign of Brother Dowling at all.

Back at the chapel, Pastor Morris paced uneasily, smoking cigarettes. Smoking them quickly, lighting one off the butt of another. Al wouldn't be back for hours and now Brother Dowling was gone.

Pastor Morris feared the Society had taken him; it was the only explanation for his disappearance. That could mean just one thing. It meant that they hadn't taken the bait, hadn't gone for the Hare Krishnas. It meant that someone had found out that it was his little band that had shot at them, which in turn meant his plan hadn't worked and they were all dead.

More time, that was all he had wanted. They were so close; Al would be back later with something that should stop the Society in its tracks.

One more day, that was all that was needed. That and to find out where the Society was going to meet next.

Being given another day, well, that was always up to God, whereas finding the location was up to him.

So, with a new purpose, he ground out his cigarette and left the office.

Pastor Morris was going home to visit mum and dad.

rogan had followed Karl Reno for half an hour, watching as he picked up one of Mardy's people, a Kieran something, Brogan seemed to remember, before driving out into the shanty towns and parking up outside one of the unassuming council houses.

Reno had obviously gone to check on the **[REDACTED]** crew. Brogan had smiled at this. Karl Reno and his little helper would be stuck there for a while.

He turned the car around and headed out of the city to check on the progress of the James Carter investigation. Brogan had driven out onto the Gower making good progress until, down one of the many narrow country lanes, he came across the traffic jam.

Brogan pulled into a siding, got out of the car, dug around in the trunk and changed into his galoshes. He then walked up to the front of the traffic jam, tasting exhaust fumes as he went.

Stone and Keyes' souped-up, powerful-looking green car was badly parked alongside two police units.

The side of the road fell away down a steep bank. Two uniformed police officers were milling about at the bottom of the hill, next to an upturned car.

"Jones," Brogan shouted down to one of the policemen. "Get up here and get this queue of cars moving."

Jones stared back at him, bovine-like, until the other policeman gave him a prompting shove. He made his way up the bank and ambled past.

"Are you aware of the term *career ceiling*?" Brogan snapped after him, before carefully negotiating his way down the slope. "Where are the two detectives?" he asked the second young policeman, when he'd made it to the bottom.

"They had an argument and headed off into the woods."

"What argument?" Brogan asked impatiently.

"Stone... sorry, Detective Stone reckoned the fugitive has headed into the woods. There was a trail of blood, see, and so Detective Stone wanted to track him, but his partner said Detective Stone couldn't track something to save his life. Then Detective Stone said—"

"So they have gone off into the woods," Brogan summarised. "What have you two bright sparks been doing in the meantime?"

"Guarding the car, sir."

"That's it, just guarding?"

"Yes, sir." The young policeman nodded, embarrassedly. "Detective Stone said for us to stay here and *'guard the car or something'*."

"Well, let's concentrate on the *something* bit of that, shall we, son?" Brogan sighed. "Get back up the slope and get on the radio. You will need to ask for a dog team, a recovery truck and also, I want the helicopter up and grid searching the area. Tell them it is thick forest so they will need the thermal imaging gear. If anyone at the other end says the helicopter is not available, tell them I say it is. Also, I want you to check if any cars have been reported stolen in the area. This James Carter is going to have to keep on moving."

The young policeman nodded, his face working hard as he tried to make a mental note of all this information.

"And finally, get everyone you can out here, we are going to check every building or residence within three miles of this spot. If Sergeant Johnson back at the station gives you any grief about manpower, you tell him I said this gets priority. Do you understand, son?"

"Yes sir," the policeman said eagerly, before turning and scrabbling up the bank.

Brogan called after him, asking in which direction the detectives had gone. He then headed off into the woods after the two errant policemen.

The undergrowth was thick and it was hard going. After five minutes, Brogan was about to give up and head back to the road. It was then the woods started thinning out and he saw Stone and Keyes off in the distance. They seemed to be arguing, Stone prodding his large partner, pointing in his face, looking mad.

Brogan stopped, trying to hear what they were talking about. But he was too far away. He moved forward as quietly as possible.

Forward, closer, *damn*. The snapping twig made the detectives swing round and straighten up, both looking guilty.

"What are you two doing out here?" Brogan blustered, wading through the last of the bushes. "You left two inexperienced policemen back at a crime scene, with their collective fingers stuck in their collective asses. There is a dangerous criminal at large, but it has been up to me to organise everything and now we've lost a lot of time on him."

"Well done for organising everything." Stone smiled. "You've got a chopper up I presume and a dog team."

"Someone had to do it."

"And I'm glad it was you."

"Detective, I don't appreciate your flippant attitude."

Stone shrugged at him flippantly. "Listen, right," he said. "We assessed the situation, saw the trail of blood and followed it out into the woods. At the time that seemed like the best thing to do."

"And did you find anything?"

"Nope, the trail peters out back there."

"In that case, Detective, I suggest you accompany me back to the road in order to wait for the dog team."

Stone glared as he brushed past his superior officer.

19

The prodigal son returned.

His mother had gone puce, before fainting, bringing down the crockery as she fell.

His father, bless the old bastard, had just said, "You look well, for a dead man."

Pastor Morris had smiled at him coldly.

*

After leaving the city and getting into the country lanes, a feeling had started to well-up inside Pastor Morris. It had been nerves. He had been nervous. Nervous to the point of having to stop the minibus, as he thought he was about to be sick.

The country lanes were busy even at this time of year. He had been stuck behind a caravan for four and a half miles. Finally, when the caravan had turned off, Pastor Morris had driven straight into the tail end of a traffic jam.

At the top of the lane, an assortment of vehicles was parked, including a haulage truck, ambulance and three police cars.

As the pastor inched past the incident, he saw the two detectives who had been looking for Trish.

The smaller of the two detectives was pointing and gesturing into the woods.

Other officers in uniform were scrabbling down the steep bank.

The pastor saw Chief Inspector Brogan standing at the side of the road. For a moment their eyes locked.

After clearing all the police, he was able to pick up some speed again, before, finally, coming to the turn off. As he came through the trees, he noticed his birthplace hadn't really changed. If anything, it was slightly smaller and oh yes, the wolves were new.

*

Eventually, when his mother had come to, she went into overdrive, making up for all the tea and cakes she hadn't baked for him in three years.

Pastor Morris, nee London, sat with his father in the living room. It was the same as he remembered it; the same polished brass on the walls, the same fire burning in the hearth and the same silence. "The wolves are new," he said.

"Aye, diversification is the word they used."

"Diversification." The pastor nodded slowly, as if he'd never heard the word in that context before. "Diversification," he repeated. "Is that what you call letting out the old quarry to the Society?"

His father looked at him, not a tell on his face, before sighing and staring into the fire. "It's tradition, son. A lot of people don't understand that."

"Tradition?" the pastor snarled. "What they do is… is murder."

His father shook his head at him sadly. "Son, the people up there protect the traditional ways. I watch the news and you know it scares me. We are living in a lawless society and they protect us from it. I've read the stories about all these people committing crimes and, son, I mean dreadful crimes and being let off scot-free."

"Or getting taken on one of these expensive foreign holidays, apparently to rehabilitate them," his mother added, entering the room laden down with a tray of tea and scones, "at the expense of the taxpayer no less."

"So you think it's ok for those using your quarry to be judge, jury and executioner?"

"Well, son, there are actually a few judges involved." His mother smiled, pouring the tea out.

"It's murder! They are murdering little more than children up there." He reached into his pocket and took out a photograph, placing it on the tray of scones. "That is a picture of the last girl they murdered."

His mother picked it up gently, looking at it for a long time.

"Her name was Trish Reed and she was homeless," the pastor continued. "I helped look after her and she died." From nowhere he felt tears welling up. "She had a family who loved her and a boyfriend who was ill, but was getting better." He looked at his father. "What *dreadful crime* did she commit?"

The old farmer met his gaze unblinking. "It is not our place to question that."

Pastor Morris looked away, turning back to his mother, his tears flowing freely now. "How do you think her mother feels? How did you feel when you thought I was dead?" He took the photo out of her unresisting hands. "How do you think the mother of the next victim will feel?"

"Oh Franklin, maybe he's right, I mean—" she said to her husband.

"No." It came out quietly, but laden with conviction. Franklin London stared directly at his son. "What happened to you brought shame upon this family and how did you deal with it? You ran, pretended to be dead and then what? Changed your name? Hid and skulked? Son, a man would have dealt with those accusations; he would have stood up for himself."

Pastor Morris saw that his mother was crying now too.

His father leant over and held her hand. "You didn't call, you didn't write, you break your mother's heart and now you turn up here wanting help against a group of people you don't understand. I am sorry, son, but I want you to leave now."

"But Franklin—" his wife started to protest.

"No, I have said my piece. I want you to leave this house now."

"I know the Society, Father. I know the Society well. It was they who framed me. It was they who brought shame on this family and forced me to run, forced me to hide and skulk. But I am not skulking anymore."

"But the paper, the news, all those terrible things that they reported about you, they—"

"They were all lies, Mum, every word a lie. I, and others like me, fought against these people. But we lost. The Society has decimated our ranks. They are insidious and full of guile. I mean do you really think what they said about me could have been true?"

His father shook his head searching for words. "Son, I... I..."

"Oh, son, I knew it must have been all lies," his mother gushed, hugging him hard.

20

Carter was still in the wind.

The helicopter had been up, grid searching in vain. It was gone now as it needed to refuel.

So far, the door-to-door searches of all the farms had brought up nothing.

The sniffer dog had arrived, for what good it did. It followed Carter's trail for about half a mile and then started whining and lying down, the damn thing refusing to go any further. The dog handler said he'd never seen it act like that before.

Stone was still swearing at him when Brogan had left.

Back at his car Brogan radioed the station to hear that young Suzie Gorman was still in surgery.

After that, he'd driven back past the unassuming council house to check if Karl Reno's car was still there. It was.

Emily and Karl Reno, eh? The pairing made him angry, the pairing made him hurt. For the time being he pushed those feelings away. Brogan felt confident that Emily's promise of twenty-four hours to decide had been valid. So for now, that could go on the back burner, along with his anger. There would be time enough to vent that soon.

At the moment, he wanted to get back to the death of Trish. The whole thing was wrong. It screamed it.

Despite what Doctor Llewelyn had said in the morgue, Brogan was sure he had evidence of her being restrained. Also, Brogan couldn't get the upcoming meeting with the fire inspector, Ryan Accord, out of his mind – *"These are powerful people you are dealing with."*

Ryan Accord, to all intents and purposes, was a very flawed man; well, he had one flaw, a love of marriages and children. He'd had loads of both, which is where his problem lay. It was like a compulsion to the man.

Ryan Accord was a bigamist. He had three families in different parts of the city. A situation that, Brogan was sure, led to constant comic incidents and close brushes. Brogan though had no interest in the *Carry On Ealing* comedy, screwball antics of the chubby little fire inspector. What he did have an interest in was the financial pressure three families put Ryan Accord under. And what he would do to make the three ends meet.

One of Accord's incomes came from the falsification of fire safety reports. For many businesses in the city, a couple of grand bung was a lot cheaper than completely rewiring the premises and introducing fire doors.

That was Brogan's lever on him. He'd used it three years ago and had no problem letting it hang, sword of Damocles-like, over his head today.

The fire was the key to Trish's death and Brogan wanted as much information on it as possible, which is why he pulled up outside the council offices. He wanted to check something out, something that had been overlooked from the detectives' investigation.

Brogan *"badged"* his way past an overweight security guard and made it to the planning office just before five.

The place was deserted, except for a drip of a youth in an overly large and badly fitting suit. The young man had stared at him blankly as Brogan explained that, *"As this is police business, the office would damn well stay open past five."*

Brogan had said what he needed and the youth, who by now Brogan thoroughly disliked, had disappeared for ten minutes.

He finally returned with the schematics to the burnt-out building and a thin, dog-eared file.

Brogan commandeered a desk in the corner of the office, before spreading out the blueprint. It took only a cursory glance to tell him he would find nothing of use in it. He neatly refolded it and turned to the file.

Checking these details was a minor thing and probably a waste of time. But it was one of the many loose ends Keyes and Stone had left flapping in their investigation. Brogan hated a loose end.

It was just another example of the sloppy approach that the two detectives had taken to this case. When investigating a suspicious fire, one of the prime suspects is always the owner of the building, insurance jobs being a common crime. The detectives hadn't even broached this line of inquiry.

Which was why Brogan now turned to the file. The file listed all the previous holders of the deeds of covenant. It was three pages thick. The history of the building went back to 1886, with the original owners being listed as a Mr Sullivan and Mr Chaney, directors of the Belgium–Congo Trading Company. Brogan was interested in times more modern though and turned to the last page of the file, to the current owner.

He stared at the name for a long time, his mind working, trying to build connections. Trying to make sense of it.

Mardy Davies' name stared insolently back at him.

21

The front of the café was dark now. They had closed at six o'clock, after the afternoon's customers, an old hippy couple, had finished their plates of tofu and left.

Pragnesh Lankhani, after two hours' meditation, had eventually managed to let his mind relax to nothing. He now felt refreshed and ready for tonight's meeting.

The twenty members of the sect were standing next to their seats, waiting for the vegetarian feast to start. Pragnesh felt sure that he could persuade them to follow him. He had decided, during his meditation, that the best way forward would be to tell the truth. To tell the truth to as many people as possible. He had called a press conference for the morning, contacting as many branches of the media as he could think of, from the local paper to the national news. He intended to lay out everything that had happened. Everything, even Pastor Morris' little secret.

Pragnesh Lankhani was about to motion for everybody to be seated, when an urgent pounding on the metal fire door stopped him.

Everyone shared looks.

Pragnesh Lankhani got up and went over to the door. He pulled it open.

"Good evening," one of the two purple-robed figures said. His accent was very posh and very familiar.

Between the two robed figures, his hands clamped tightly in theirs, stood a pear-shaped man.

The pear-shaped man had a rough cloth bag over his head.

"This is a present from your friend in the newspaper business," the second hooded figure said, before pulling off the cloth bag.

Both of the robed figures took off, at full pelt, down the side of the building, towards the road.

Pragnesh Lankhani speechlessly watched them go, robes flailing, before turning back and looking into the puffy, blistered face of the man they had left.

Pastor Morris had referred to this sweaty man as Brother Dowling. Pragnesh Lankhani noticed the glazed look on his face.

Brother Dowling, dopily, looked down into his hand. "They told me to hold this," he said, his speech heavily slurred.

He opened his palm to reveal something.

Pragnesh Lankhani followed his gaze, squinting, making out a load of wires and a small circuit board.

"I am sorry I let it go this far," Brother Dowling said.

The Hare Krishna hardly heard him; he was remembering where he knew the posh accent from. They were the two men who had come earlier to check the gas boiler.

The gas boiler!

He turned to look back into the café and started to say something. Some word of warning.

But it was too late. In the last split second of his life, Pragnesh Lankhani was awed by the brightness that surrounded him.

22

Brogan sat in a booth in the back of the ice-cream parlour; his seat overlooked the car park.

It had started raining heavily as he left the council offices. He'd been tempted to find a payphone and ring Mardy to arrange a meeting. Find out *exactly* why his name was on the deeds to the burnt-out building. Find out *exactly* how he was involved. Brogan had decided against it for now, at least until after he saw the fire inspector.

He decided that also as he hadn't eaten all day and needed some food. Getting to the meeting place early, he'd wolfed some gammon and chips, before spurring the waitress on to clear the table. It wouldn't be the done thing to discuss a police matter with someone over a pile of dirty dishes.

Brogan had also turned down a look at the dessert menu, as the same went for discussing official police business over a Knickerbocker glory.

Ryan Accord arrived; he shook off his coat and left it hanging by the door. He was dressed in his civvies and looked a lot smaller out of his padded fireman's clothes.

Seeing Brogan, he beelined it over to him looking furtive. "Damn it, John, why did you have to sit right by the window? Anyone could see us," he said, sitting down low in the booth.

"Why are you so nervous?" Brogan asked, shooing off the approaching waitress.

"Look, you don't have any idea what you are dealing with here. I shouldn't even be talking to you about this."

"Talking to me about what?"

The fireman sighed and stroked his moustache nervously. "What did the autopsy say?" he asked.

"That she had probably died from smoke inhalation."

The fire inspector shook his head. "No, they must have got to the pathologist too. Look, John, if you want me to tell you what's going on, I will, but you must realise how dangerous this is."

Brogan gave him a long stare. "Ryan, you must realise how dangerous I am."

Ryan Accord paused for a moment, arranging his thoughts or perhaps making a decision. He let out a long sigh before beginning. "The girl was burned somewhere else before being moved. There were no traces of fatty deposits on the floorboards underneath her." He saw Brogan's confusion and explained. "When a candle burns, it drips wax; when someone burns, if there is enough heat, their fat isn't that much different to candle wax. There were no fat deposits around the body. There should have been, but there weren't."

"Why didn't you mention any of this before?"

He paused. "They got to me. Got to me with the same threats as you used, threatened to tell my families about each other and bring to light my... my interpretation of building fire codes." He paused again looking out of the window. "They wanted the same thing as you did three years ago. Cover up a deliberate fire. Write it up as accidental and I did. The only difference between what I did for you and what I did for them was that this girl was innocent. What had she done? I saw her picture in the paper, sweet-looking thing."

Brogan remained silent, letting him talk, letting him confess it all out. There would be time enough for questions later.

"Two men came to me the day before the fire," he continued. "They told me what to say and what to do. They said if I went along with it, they'd straighten out my financial problems and that in the next round of fire station downsizing, my job would be safe. I told them where to stick it, but they produced a load of paperwork, proof of payments from shop owners, stuff stretching back fifteen years. What could I do?" He shrugged. "But seeing that girl's picture in the paper… my conscience kicked in. I haven't been able to sleep since."

He seemed to run out of steam.

"Who were the men?" Brogan asked.

"I haven't seen them before and I haven't seen them since."

"Where were they from?"

"They said they were members of a society. The Society, they said. From the way they talked and their manner, it was like they controlled everything in this city. Do you know, one of them said I should be honoured to help them?" Ryan Accord looked ready to cry. "That was the word that got to me, *honoured*. I should be honoured to help them? Honoured to help them get away with murder?" He lapsed into silence, staring at the quick of his nail.

"You'll give a statement?" Brogan asked.

"They said they can kill me if they need to."

Brogan shook his head, trying to pull off a reassuring smile. "This is my city, not theirs; I can protect you."

The fireman nodded. "I'm on duty tonight. I need to think about it; what'll happen to my families?"

"We can protect them too," Brogan said. "Come in with me now, we'll get a statement down."

"No, I need to think about it. I'll be in contact tomorrow."

Brogan was about to tell him that wouldn't be possible, that this was going to be done tonight, when the fire inspector's beeper went off.

"Look, I'm on call; I've got to go, there's a fire." He stood to leave.

Brogan debated whether to follow him outside, slap the handcuffs on and take him down to the station. But then he backed down. The logistics of protecting Accord's three families, at such short notice, was immense.

He decided to let the fire inspector go until tomorrow.

With hindsight, Brogan would come to regret this fatal decision.

23

They were deviating from the plan. They should be driving around, familiarising themselves with the city's layout. That's what Karl Reno kept on saying.

Batty Boy had said, "We'll do it later."

Reno had wanted to leave; he wanted to go home and see Emily.

Batty Boy had said, "Stay here for now; we'll go over the plan later."

That had been two hours ago.

Reno had gone upstairs for a piss earlier and when he'd come out of the bathroom, Tiny had been waiting on the landing. Even though it had remained unspoken, Reno now realised they were prisoners here.

Kieran seemed quite oblivious to this. He and Tiny were getting on like a house on fire.

"Hey Batty Boy, have you got any pop or anything?" Kieran had asked.

Batty Boy had bristled. "You don't get to call me Batty Boy. You get to call me Winston."

"Why do they call you Batty Boy then?" Kieran asked.

"None of your business."

"Go on, tell them," Daryl said.

Batty Boy glared at him, before turning back to Kieran. "Because of dumb fucking luck. I had to dress up as a faggot on my first hit."

"What, a hit like killing someone?" Kieran asked, wide-eyed.

"No, I was once in a boy band," Batty Boy had said sarcastically, wanting to put an end to the subject.

"Go on, tell them properly," Tiny chimed in. "Tell them how you cut your teeth."

Winston/Batty Boy glared at Tiny.

"Don't be shy," Tiny said.

"Just leave it."

"Go on, tell them, it's funny. Sod you then, I'll tell them." He turned to his audience. "This is funny," Tiny said, before going on to guffaw his way through Batty's first hit.

*

It had been three years ago. Winston, as he had been known at the time, had been nineteen, coming up in the business.

He'd been granted an audience with I-Knows. An actual audience.

He'd gone to London. I-Knows was in the middle of expanding his empire northwards. It was taking longer than expected. I-Knows and the family had been tied up in an increasingly violent gang war for the last six months.

The Thai restaurant, where the audience was to take place, had been "acquired" as part of this expansion. It was situated off a main thoroughfare with its run-down exterior belying the plushness inside. Winston was met by a gaggle of pleasingly deferential oriental waitresses.

He had been ushered through to a back room. Winston's brother was waiting. He was lighter skinned than Winston, to the point he could have almost been mistaken for white. He had short-cropped hair dyed blond and was well dressed in a tailored *Ted Baker* suit.

Winston's brother had made the introductions.

I-Knows sat there, flanked by his lieutenants, resplendent in a white suit that probably cost more money than Winston would see in a year from his car thefts.

I-Knows had regarded him in silence. His expression unreadable behind those large, out-of-place sunglasses he wore.

There was something larger than life about him, something that made him fill up the entire foreground. Winston oddly started thinking how he looked like a comic book villain, like something Batman would have to face. That thought combined with his nerves almost made him laugh out loud.

Finally, I-Knows spoke, his voice deep and full of authority. I-Knows asked Winston what he would be prepared to do in order to serve him.

He told I-Knows anything.

I-Knows said he wanted Winston to kill someone.

Winston asked who.

I-Knows said a powerful and important man.

Winston said, "I'll do it."

*

Winston stood shivering in the biting wind.

Winston had the target's details memorised – photo, car description and number plate. As it was his first hit, he had been walked through every detail carefully. He had been told how to act, where to stand and how to dress. Winston was sure they were taking the piss.

Winston's two teachers, his brother and Tiny, were probably laughing at him now, parked as they were on the other side of the canal, ready to pick him up after the job.

Chris Dyer had a secret nobody knew. Chris Dyer was gay. It was a fact he had kept well hidden over the years. No one would have guessed, not his wife, Laura, or his colleagues on the force.

Winston had spent two freezing cold nights, in a crappy part of London, mincing up and down along Canal Street, dressed in a cut off t-shirt and denim shorts. He spent his time telling the other rent boys and occasional punter to *fuck right off.*

Until, finally, the target turned up.

The grey car crawled its way down the street, stopping by that blond, effeminate fucker who had tried to step up to Winston yesterday, faggoting on about it being his corner.

Winston, throwing a glare across the canal, stepped out into the headlights and did a little curtsy. The car pulled off towards him, Blondie cursing it from his spot.

It drew alongside Winston, the kerb-side passenger window already rolled down.

Winston squatted down to look inside the car.

"You're new," Chris Dyer said, his features lost in shadows.

Winston tried to pull off a smile that showed alluring coyness. "Yeah, I'd love it if someone could show me a good time."

The car light came on as the hit opened the passenger door.

Winston studied the man he was going to kill. He looked older and fatter than in the photos.

"I know a place to go if you want a good time," Chris Dyer said. "I've often gone there with boys and we've always had a good time."

The place that Chris Dyer knew was, in fact, an alley running behind the gas works.

"This is the place?" Winston asked.

"Oh no, this is the place," Chris Dyer said, pulling his flies down and exposing himself.

"That's a hell of a small cock," Winston laughed.

The policeman turned angry and started to say something, but Winston reached over and slit his throat with a speed and a dispassion that would have made his teachers proud.

The look of anger on the hit's face turned to one of utter incomprehension.

He didn't fight or try and grab at Winston; he just sat there, holding his throat in shock.

As he had been told to, Winston reached across and dug into the hit's pocket, pulling out his wallet. It contained twenty pounds.

"You cheap, dying motherfucker," Winston had huffed. "My ass is worth a lot more than this."

He got out of the car, wiping the handle and few surfaces he had touched with his t-shirt, before jogging down the alley.

A car was waiting to pick him up. He got in the back.

"Hello sailor," Tiny had said, before pulling away.

"Is he dead?" Winston's brother asked.

Winston nodded. "I cut through to the jugular."

"And you took the wallet?"

"Yes, and wiped everything I'd touched."

"Good, you did well. How do you feel?"

Winston had shrugged; he'd felt nothing. His brother kept on staring at him.

Winston shrugged again. "Confused. I-Knows is smart. Why didn't he just blackmail that copper over the rent boys? Why kill him?"

"He called I-Knows a nigger," Tiny said. "What else was he going to do?"

Winston had sat back and looked at the streetlights going by.

A week later, his brother had been sent away to lay down the foundations of another expansion. Winston missed his brother; he had been smart and ambitious, which was probably why I-Knows had wanted him out of the way.

Because of the circumstances surrounding Chris Dyer's death, the subsequent investigation was low key and played down in the press. A week later, when a rent boy, known on the street as Blondie, was found hanging in his bed-sit, the murder victim's wallet under his pillow, the case was unceremoniously closed.

Chris Dyer was forgotten.

*

Forgotten by all except Tiny. "Apparently our man in the Met reckoned they found him with his dick out, reckoned he was killed after having had sex," Tiny said with a laugh.

"Yeah, we said blow him away not blow him," Daryl joined in. "Isn't that right, Batty?"

Batty Boy just glared at them. He hated them both. Tiny, the fat fuck, was an idiot and Daryl was too far up his own ass to be believed. Anyway, they wouldn't be around for long. His brother would be here soon and they would be able to put their plan in to action.

An hour later the doorbell rang.

"Now's a chance for you to reacquaint yourself with my brother," Batty Boy told Reno as he got up to answer it.

This was the first time Batty Boy had set eyes on his brother in three years and he was shocked by his appearance, with his pale skin now turned into rainbow shades by the severe bruising.

Karl Reno was seated facing the door to the lounge. He was the first to react to the newcomer's appearance.

"What are you doing here, I thought you were banished?" he spluttered, as Zach the Mac entered the room.

24

I t was quiet and customer-free when Alistair got back to the house. Clancy was on a night shift, so only Ebin was around. His door was open, a reggae song coming out of the amp connected up to the tape deck.

Alistair leaned against the doorframe and watched his friend illuminated by the epileptic light of the TV, the *Rainbow Road* flying by.

Alistair entered the room and perched on the arm of the settee. Ebin didn't take his eyes off the screen until he finished the race and put the controller down. Alistair pretended not to notice the worryingly fast lap time. The bastard had probably been sitting here all day, racing over and over again, just to bring up the idea of having a race and beating him.

Ebin looked up. "How was university? I thought you'd have a traffic cone on your head by now."

Alistair flopped down onto the sofa. "I must have left it in the kebab shop."

"How did it go?" Ebin asked. "Days out, her staying over, this is very serious all of a sudden."

"I should say, I've just met her parents."

*

The train had been almost deserted when it pulled into Swansea station; Alistair's mind was still reeling from what Maggie had asked him. He hoped she'd come back to his for the night and then the next night and the one after that.

"Oh God, I didn't think they'd be here, I forgot they were meeting me off the train," Maggie breathed, seeing the figures walking towards them across the platform. "Just agree with everything I say," she cautioned Alistair out of the corner of her mouth.

The parents were upon them now.

"Mum, Dad, this is my friend Alistair."

"Your friend Alistair, eh," the woman said, raising an eyebrow disapprovingly.

Maggie's mother was well dressed, with the same black hair as her daughter. Only it had been clawed back into a severe-looking bun. It was a good word, severe, it summed her up well. That and bitch.

Maggie's father was a few inches shorter and a few stone chubbier than his wife, with thinning hair. He was attempting to make Alistair wither under an ineffectual glare.

Alistair smiled warmly and offered them his hand, which was pointedly not taken.

He felt stumped, unsure what to say. *"Hey, how's it going? I'm the guy ploughing your daughter,"* probably wouldn't be good, so instead he settled with, "Hello, it's lovely to finally meet you both. Maggie has told me a lot of nice things about you."

"Oh, has she? Well, that would be a first, wouldn't it, Margaret?" the woman said icily.

God, already Alistair hated that one.

Silence filled the station, an uncomfortable long silence.

That stretched.

And stretched.

And stretched.

"Look, I'll see you later, Alistair," Maggie said, before planting a long kiss on his lips. Her hand rested on his cheek for a moment, before she turned and walked off with her parents.

"God, they sound weird," Ebin said, after Alistair had finished his story. "They were probably pissed off she'd been out all night being deflowered by an oik like you."

"Yeah, well I thought that, but how would they know?"

"Oh they're parents, they know alright," Ebin said knowledgably. "What about the rest of the day, how did that go?"

"It was good." Alistair thought for a moment. "It really was good, at least before I met her stupid parents. She asked me something on the way back as well."

✼

They had been on the train coming home, sitting next to each other, with university brochures spread out on the table, legs intertwined the way that new boyfriends and girlfriends do.

Maggie had been quiet for a while, pensive almost. "I want to ask you something," she said, biting her bottom lip and looking away, in that cute as a button way she did.

"What?"

"You know, I got two copies of all of these. If you wanted to take some to look at in more detail."

Alistair had smiled. "Thanks, but you need A-Levels and all that junk to go to university."

"There're ways around that. I saw how you looked the other night."

"What do you mean?"

"Up on the roof, when I said I was going away. I caught the way you looked, even though it was only for a second."

Alistair started to speak.

"No, let me finish. I've been picking up the courage to say this all day." She turned, intense now, no smile, no twinkle of the eye, just dead serious. "Believe me, the best thing we can both do is get out of the city." Her features softened again. "And you know the way you looked on the roof, that's how I'm starting to feel. I know it will be next year and all, but what do you say, we could become students together."

*

"What did you say?" Ebin asked, passing a joint.

"I said I'd like that, I think I'd like that a lot," Alistair said. "I need a change; I'm done with carrying blocks of pot around in the rain and having wet feet all the time." He laughed. "I've got a hole in the sole, you know."

As if on cue, Johnny Nash came on the stereo, singing *"I can see clearly now the rain has gone"*, filling the room, sound-tracking Alistair's life.

Ebin smiled, putting his head back and closing his eyes. "You'll be leaving as well, just like that Jewish cunt."

"Mordechai's not Jewish; it's just that his parents are weird." Alistair shrugged.

Ebin turned to look at him. It could have been a trick of the TV light, but his eyes seemed red, in that about to cry sort of way. "Fuck you all, eh? Fancy a race?"

25

Brogan parked outside the hospital. It was late now, but he knew the morgue would be open, death being a twenty-four-hour event.

As he went down the ramp towards the morgue, Brogan thought about what the fire inspector had said. Ryan Accord had talked about a conspiracy, a lot of people involved and culpable for the death of Trish, all of them nameless.

Brogan realised he did have one link to these faceless people. It was for now flimsy, but it was there. Doctor Llewelyn. He had taken on the autopsy of Trish personally. He had also been lying. He had lied well, even to the extent of using a prop and it was that prop that Brogan was going to find.

Brogan stopped at the last set of double doors and peered through the glass. Normally at this time there would only be one person on duty.

The attendant was slumped behind the admissions desk, seemingly asleep. Brogan recognised the kid. Taking a moment to remember his name, Brogan left and went outside to the bank of payphones. He dialled a number, getting through to the hospital's switchboard and asked to be put through to the morgue.

The phone rang six times before it was answered with a slurred, "What?"

"Hello, is that Clancy?" Brogan said, using the kid's name,

sounding friendly. "This is Nurse Ratchet here from geriatrics. Unfortunately, we've had another patient pass away tonight and I need someone to come up and bring the body down to the morgue."

"We don't collect them, we just book them in."

Brogan sighed, annoyed that his ruse had not worked. "We're really short staffed up here. It would be really helpful if you could help us out this one time."

"I'd love to, but we don't collect them, we just book them in."

Brogan kept his temper in check. "I understand that, but it would be really appreciated. There's even a load of food up here. One of the old codgers hit eighty-five and his family brought in party food for him. It's only going to go to waste."

There was a pause. "What's there all together?"

"Let's see, we've got a load of sandwiches, there's jelly and birthday cake."

"Are there any of those cheese and pineapple things on a stick?"

"Let me check… yep, you're in luck."

"Ok, has the doctor signed off on the stiff?"

"Yes, he did it about fifteen minutes ago."

"Cool, I'll be up now."

Brogan hung up the phone and went back down into the morgue. Again he peered through the double door and saw that Clancy had already left.

Brogan hurriedly walked past the admissions desk and down the corridor, stopping at Doctor Llewelyn's office.

It was locked.

Brogan pulled a small leather wallet out of his coat; it was a set of lock picks. He hadn't needed to use them for years, the door took time. Inside now, he put the light on and hit the filing cabinet. More time lost, before he popped the lock.

The filing cabinet slid open.

Flick, flick, flick, he pulled the file, no time to look at it; this was coming with him, if his theory played out, this was evidence.

Relock the cabinet.
Knock off the light.
Relock the door.
Down the corridor and out of the mortuary.

26

They were all in the operations centre.

Donald stood ramrod straight by the weapons table. Everybody else was gathered in a semi-circle around him.

Jason and Muppet were looking openly nervous. They could feel things spinning out of control; *or at least if they can't, they're fucking dolts*, Pastor Morris thought, too tired, even, to chastise himself for swearing.

"So what exactly did you see before the explosion?" the pastor asked, massaging his temples.

They had found Brother Dowling.

*

It had been earlier on in the evening. The pastor had been sitting at his desk thinking about seeing his parents that afternoon.

His mother had been on his side, she always had been. Even when he was a kid she'd tried to moderate the beatings, knowing that one day he'd just up and leave.

"Oh son, I knew it couldn't be true," she had gushed, hugging him hard.

His father had started mumbling something about the papers not lying. The old bastard didn't scare anyone anymore though; he was little more than bluster now.

His wife had shushed him. "Franklin," she had said, fixing him with an ever so serious look. "I brought our son up to be honest and if he tells me he didn't do those horrible things then I believe him."

"But we haven't heard from him for—"

"Franklin, I will not share my house with any man who thinks my son is a liar."

His mother stared at her husband until he had looked away.

She turned back to the pastor. "Right, dear, that's settled. Now Franklin, your son wants to know where the Society will be meeting tomorrow night."

His father had whined out a few protests, but grudgingly he had started speaking. "They try and vary where they meet. They pay handsomely for the use of an area for the night. I think they like the idea of including as much of the local community as possible. But that's the problem. If you are lucky enough to have your land used, you dare not tell anyone about it, at least until after they have met."

"And none of your friends talk in the pub? Come on, I know what gossips the people out here are," the pastor said.

"No, not now. Someone shot at the Society during their last ritual. It scared them. I heard a lot of the people want to quit and go back to something safer, like fox hunting. But the powerful members have vetoed that idea."

"Where are they meeting?" Pastor Morris pressed.

"No one will say." His father had shrugged. "People are scared. I know members are turning against members. All I know is they have beefed up security for the next ritual. They have got some outside people in to help."

"Who?" the pastor asked.

"I don't know; they've kept that quiet."

"What security? How are they making it safe?"

His father hadn't said any more and Pastor Morris could tell that he wasn't lying.

At the door his mother had hugged him goodbye and told him, "After everything those horrible people did to you, I hope they get what is coming to them."

And those horrible people would get what was coming to them and they would get it in spades.

Urgent knocking had brought him out of his ruminations.

A mop of dreadlocks followed by Jason's head popped around the door. "Donald's on the radio, he wants something. What's a *dust off*?"

✳

They had picked Donald up in the minibus; he had emerged from some bushes and dived into the van. In the distance, the shapes of firemen could be seen running back and forth, backlit by the café's structure fire.

Al, having got back from his supply run earlier in the afternoon, sat in the driver's seat. He was grinning widely, supping up every detail of the scene across the waste ground. "Gouranga!" he muttered, before putting the van into gear.

Al's good mood had evaporated as they started to debrief Donald back in the hostel.

"Are you sure he is dead?" the pastor had asked.

"The ambulance people zipped the body bag all the way to the top," Donald answered, not a trace of sarcasm in his voice.

"Why was Brother Dowling there?" Jason said nervously. "If they killed Dowling they'll be coming for us next." He was scared; you could hear it in his voice.

"They might not know about us," the pastor said. "It's a set-up. The past altercation between Aled and the Hare Krishnas is public knowledge. So I think that's why they left Brother Dowling there. When the police come to look for suspects, we'll be top of the list. They probably even left Brother Dowling with some incriminating evidence on him."

"Either way we should cut our losses and scarper before it is too late," Jason said.

"No, by this time tomorrow, things will be finished one way or the other," Pastor Morris said.

"But if the Society doesn't come after us, the police will. I say we go." Jason turned towards Muppet looking for support.

"Yeah, man, we should book," Muppet agreed.

"You want to know what I think?" Gavin said, speaking for the first time since being rescued, all drug addled, from the car boot.

Everybody turned to look at him. He was sitting on the makeshift operating table. His ruined face all but hidden under a mummy's wrap of bandages. "It's not about good or evil, that's just a big old clumsy metaphor. I'll tell you what it's about; it's about us against them, Class War. They have it all but still want to take." He made eye contact with everyone, clear eyes, all lucid and with it. "Trish was homeless, she had nothing, but that wasn't good enough for them. They wanted to take more so they did and they did because they could; it's condoned and accepted so they can take. But not anymore. I think we should try to even things up a bit."

Jason and Muppet had looked at each other before nodding uneasily in agreement.

"This would be a good time to gather in prayer," Pastor Morris said.

He held out his hands and they were taken by Al on one side and Donald on the other. Gavin held Donald's hand, while Jason and Muppet reluctantly joined the circle.

Pastor Morris prayed for the soul of Brother Dowling and to give them all strength for the trials to come. He had prayed and he had prayed, but for the first time ever, he had found no solace in the act. After saying amen, he felt totally alone and isolated. Even in his most trying times, he had not been forsaken by his God before.

Wrapped in his own thoughts, he hardly even heard Al saying, *"So it begins."*

27.

I t was three in the morning and Brogan wasn't asleep. How could he be? He'd been betrayed. Mardy, his childhood friend, had been taping him. All those conversations, everything they had discussed. And now Emily, the stupid, stupid girl, had invited them into his city.

He'd been thinking about it since the ice-cream parlour. And now, as he looked at the kit laid out neatly on his bed, Brogan knew he'd decided.

Brogan started loading kit into his bag. He was adding the silver duct tape when an insistent ringing on the doorbell stopped him. Brogan threw a blanket over the bed, before going downstairs.

Brogan went into his lounge where, lying wide open on the table, was the file he had taken from the mortuary. Brogan had read it three times cover to cover. He hadn't found anything about that hemp bracelet Doctor Llewelyn had mentioned when looking at the same pages.

Llewelyn was involved, Llewelyn was culpable; Llewelyn was the link, his way at getting to the Society.

One thing at a time though.

Brogan went to the front door and opened it. Stone and Keyes blocked up the doorway. Stone had a sneer dallying across his face.

"Detective Keyes, Detective Stone," Brogan acknowledged them, trying to look nonplussed. "I trust that to be disturbing me at this hour it is urgent."

"Nice slippers," Stone said, pushing past him into the house.

His big partner followed, eyes downcast.

They both smelled like a bonfire.

Brogan trailed after them into the lounge. "What is the meaning of this intrusion?" he demanded.

Stone was facing the mantelpiece looking at the clock.

He turned, a wolfish smile plastered across his face. "We're here to wish you a happy retirement."

"Excuse me, Detective?"

"You are looking into the death of that scrubber," Stone said, any pretence at civility gone. "We filed our report all nice and correctly. Everything corroborated. Everything pointing to an accidental fire, but no, that wasn't good enough. You start to look into it yourself, looking for something that isn't there."

Brogan stared at the detective in disbelief. Keyes was behind him, standing against the door.

"I am your commanding officer. I have every right to supervise your work." He moved slightly to keep them both in his field of vision. "Now, I demand you get out of my house and we will continue this conversation at my office in the morning."

Stone spat out a laugh. "You don't get to demand anything." He pulled a tape recorder out of his pocket and put it on the table between them.

It was a similar model to the one Emily had played earlier and, like earlier, a similar conversation came through the little speakers. He recognised his meeting with Mardy the other night.

"We'll hit him tomorrow then, give him a chance to sell some of it in the interim. I don't want my men focusing their questioning on any areas that aren't strictly relevant to the case. Does he still sell amphetamines?"

Stone hit the fast forward button.

"Now for the money."

"Here's your share of the monthly takings, John."

Brogan found himself wanting to laugh; Mardy was going to ruin everything.

"Oh dear." Stone tutted. "To the untrained ear, this could smack of police corruption."

Brogan stared, tight jawed, at the tape recorder.

"This is the offer," Stone continued. "You leave this case alone and tomorrow you hand in your resignation. You could cite health issues or wanting to spend more time preparing for your sex change operation." He laughed at his own joke. "Actually, the offer is dependent on you giving that reason in your resignation letter. Isn't that right, Keyes?"

His partner didn't join in with the laughter.

Brogan regarded the two detectives for a long time, calculating, deciding. "So now the Society owns you both?"

"You know about them?" Keyes asked, sounding surprised.

"Of course I know about them. I'm a... what was the phrase? A very busy detecteve," Brogan said, running with it. "Do you think that something like this can go on in my city without me knowing? Without me gathering evidence and names? This whole *Society* is about to come crashing down and, believe me, detectives, you don't want to be associated with it when it does."

Stone clapped slow and hollow. "Well done, you found out about them. That little prick of a fire inspector filled you in, eh? Did he go on to say how powerful and ruthless they are? I hope you got it all in writing and got him to sign it, before the accident tonight."

"What accident?"

"It looks like he crashed into a tree while responding to a fire. He was killed instantly by all accounts."

Brogan went cold.

"He had a chance, you see," Stone continued. "They knew all of his dirty little secrets and offered to keep them safe, just like they are doing with your corruption. Listen, John, these are not bad people; they don't want to see upstanding members of the community die, unnecessarily. That is why they've given you this out. It wouldn't be hard for them to turn around and cut the brakes on your car or have you found in a burnt-out house. But they don't want that. So come on, resign, walk away."

Brogan felt deflated. His bluff had been called and he was responsible for the death of someone. In the situation he did the only thing he could think of which was to bluster. "Corruption, eh? It is not corruption, son, it is policing. I have saved lives and kept this city safe. This is my city and I have protected everyone in it the best way I can." He turned to look fully at Keyes. "When was the last time someone died from a drugs overdose? When was the last time anyone was arrested for possession of heroin or even cocaine?"

The big detective shrugged.

Brogan nodded at a little victory. "Those problems don't exist in my city, I ensure that. And you know the best thing about what I do, Detective? No one dies, whereas you are murderers. I knew you were looking for Trish when she disappeared, you were following the same trails as me, but getting there quicker. I was impressed." He smiled, before his face turned hard again. "When did it change? When did you go from trying to solve a murder to participating in it?"

The big detective looked away, his jaw flexing.

"What did they pay you?" Brogan pushed.

"A life," Keyes said, looking back, determined, steeled. "They offered to save Stone's kid, they found her a donor."

28

Emily Davies had fallen asleep on the couch around midnight. She'd drunk more than she'd intended to while waiting for Karl to show up.

There hadn't been much else to do.

Bored of waiting for his return, she had gone room to room. Karl's flat was small but expensive. Its interior reflected his juvenile personality. In the lounge there was a large, framed poster from the film *Scarface*, along with an oversized television and a computer games console. The bedroom wasn't much better; he had a Playboy bedspread reflecting off the mirrored ceiling.

Emily had sighed at this.

An inspection of his drawers had revealed a stash of sex toys and pornography.

She had toed that drawer closed.

After unsuccessfully trying to phone him again, Emily had settled down on the couch, got the TV to work and started tucking into his scotch.

It was now she awoke, all disorientated and confused.

It took a few seconds to get her bearings and realise that she had been woken by the door buzzer.

She got off the couch and unsteadily made it to the intercom. "Karl?" she asked, pressing the button.

"No, it's me."

"John? What do you want? It's… it's four in the morning."

"I know. I had some visitors, which means I'm running late. That is why I have to be quick, let me in, Emily."

She hit the switch to open the door and went to meet him on the landing.

Brogan was dressed in black trousers and a black sweatshirt.

"What do you want?" she asked.

"Get me a drink and I'll tell you."

"You drink now as well, do you?" she said, going into the kitchen.

"Oh Emily, you're going to be amazed at the things I do," Brogan said walking behind her, slipping on a pair of latex gloves.

29

I t was late now. Ebin had gone to bed in a mood, having had his ass consistently red shelled. Alistair retired to his room.

He sat there, nicely stoned, his mind wandering. He realised that he was being changed.

The brochures she had got him were fanned out on the bed. *Prospectuses*, Alistair corrected himself. Brochures would be for someone going on holiday; these were prospectuses for someone who was going to go to university.

There was something about the glossy pages that kept on drawing him towards them, kind of like an academic magpie.

There were loads of really captivating pictures. Bristol was looking sun drenched, with all the clean-cut student twats looking radiant, either with their heads back laughing at some collective joke or captivated by some academic pursuit, such as staring down a microscope or poring over books in the library. *Pawing or poring*, Alistair wondered vaguely. One thing he knew was he'd have to buy a rugby jersey or a checked shirt to fit in.

And that was one big question: would he fit in? University wasn't the sort of place that you should go with a boyfriend in tow. Maggie could meet someone nice and he didn't want to be calling her new friends twats and bringing her down.

But then Alistair thought about her smile and he realised everything would be alright.

Everything would be alright. This made Alistair feel happy,

genuinely happy. It wasn't as if he had been unhappy before. Most of his days involved pissing himself with laughter, that and coughing, but that wasn't happiness; happiness was what surrounded him now.

He was going to go to university with Maggie and everything was going to be alright.

Everything was going to be alright.

And that should have been the first sign that it was all going to turn to shit.

THE FINAL DAY

†

They had come later than the pastor had expected. He watched on the monitors as three police vans drew up outside the hostel, spilling forth policemen. Al sat next to him in the office, eyes glued to the screens.

"We've got four coming round the back, in cover formation," Al said, pointing at dark shapes moving through the bushes in the cemetery.

The pastor didn't know what that meant, but he did notice the sub-machine guns they were carrying.

"It's not too late for you to hide, but you'll have to come now," Al said.

The pastor looked at him from a world away. He shook his head. "No, we are so close to the end we dare not tip our hand. The Society will get suspicious if all the police found was an empty church. They might become cautious and change this evening's meeting place." Pastor Morris stood up. "I will face them."

God had not forsaken him. God had come to him in a dream, as He had done in biblical times. The dream had been confusing. There had been a man and the man brought redemption, redemption for all. The man also brought terrible vengeance; the man was a harbinger of death.

The dream had stayed vividly in Pastor Morris' mind when he awoke; it stayed with him along with an incredible feeling of peace. For he knew God would be on their side in the events to come.

"Are you sure? We should go and hide," Al repeated.

"No, this is the way God has willed it."

Al glanced nervously at the monitors. "Look, say this isn't God's plan. Say they just arrest you and take you to the police station, what then?"

"Then you go and snatch up that paper editor and you have my blessing to do whatever is necessary to find out where they are meeting," Pastor Morris replied. He got up and left the room, not a single shake in his hands. "This is as God has willed it."

2

"We've found someone," a voice crackled over the radio.

"Where?" Stone barked. He stood with Keyes in the middle of the hostel's deserted dormitory.

The front door had been wide open when they had arrived, all the lights burning bright.

The message came back.

"In the church? Right, we'll be there now," Stone said into the radio. He looked at his partner before turning and walking out of the hostel.

They headed around the building, climbing over bloody sniffer dogs as they went.

Keyes followed in his partner's wake, feeling drained and empty. It had been a sleepless evening.

*

Last night they'd been sitting in their office in silence. The tension was palpable, as it had been since Stone had asked for his favour – *help me save my daughter's life.*

Stone's mobile phone had rung; he answered it, listened for a moment before leaving the office.

Keyes had heard him from the corridor say, *"No, look, this isn't part of the deal, I'm not doing that."*

After further mutterings that Keyes could not hear, Stone came back in. "We've got to roll, there's been an explosion."

Keyes noticed his partner's hands were shaking. He was going to ask what was wrong, but the *ring, ring* of the office phone stopped him.

"Yes," Keyes said, answering the phone.

It was Sergeant Johnson; the old fart sounded stressed. There had been an explosion, the fire brigade was on site and they were pulling out bodies. Johnson had done the rounds of senior officers, but Stone and Keyes were the only ones left in the building.

They had rolled.

Even from a distance, the fire lit up the skyline. There were three tenders lying abreast, laying down water. It had been a big blast. The body parts strewn around the area testified to that.

Keyes and Stone were pointed in the direction of the crew chief.

The crew chief, a powerful-looking man in his fifties, started to brief them. "There was an explosion earlier on, we only got here after the fire had taken hold."

"What was it, some sort of gas explosion?" Keyes asked.

"No way, it wouldn't be gas," the fireman said, absentmindedly rubbing his hand over his face, leaving soot streaks. "Outside of the movies, I've never seen an explosion this big."

"What is this place?"

"It was that Hare Krishna restaurant; God knows how many people were inside."

Shouting off in the distance drew their attention away from the fire. *"Medical officer, medical officer."*

The man lying in the waste ground was beyond the help of any medical officer.

"Shit, he must have been thrown seventy-five feet," the crew chief marvelled.

Stone knelt down by the body. "Hey, we know this guy, it's… what's his name? Richard Dowling."

"Who's that?" the crew chief asked.

"He works in… used to work in a homeless hostel, the Mount Pleasant one."

"Why do I know that name?" the crew chief mused out loud.

He thought for a second. "Wait, they were the idiots who pulled that arson attack on the Hare Krishnas a while ago; my engine dealt with the call. I reckon that could be a clue for you."

"Could be," Stone said, looking up at him.

"Look, what's that in his hand?" the crew chief, now in full Jessica Fletcher mode, wanted to know.

Stone prised open Brother Dowling's fingers.

"If I'm not mistaken, it looks like some sort of crude detonator," the crew chief said. "Look there's even a safety switch on it."

Stone shot an amused glance at his partner. "Could be a clue," he said.

They had left soon after that. There wasn't much that could be done until the fire was out. The crew chief had told them that as soon as the fire inspector turned up, they could start the preliminary investigation into the cause of the fire.

"I paged him over an hour ago. He should be here by now."

"Call us when he is," Stone said.

"They did this, didn't they?" Keyes said, in the car on the way back to the station.

Stone looked at him; sometimes it was easy to underestimate his big partner's intelligence. "What do you mean?"

"You know what I mean, this Society, they did this, didn't they? That phone call you took was from them. You knew about the explosion before Johnson rang."

Stone sighed. "You're right, they did this."

"Why?"

"They reckoned the Hare Krishnas had found out about them."

"So what? They decided to blow them up?"

"Yes, pretty much."

"And the sweaty guy from the church? The one conveniently holding a detonator?"

Stone was silent for a long moment. "They needed a patsy."

Keyes shook his head, his voice barely under control. "Are they that arrogant? Do they think they can just kill people so blatantly?"

"Yes, yes, they do," Stone snapped. "They think they are above the law. And while they have my daughter's life in their hands, they are."

He waited for a reaction from his partner. Nothing came, but it was there, contained just below the surface.

Stone continued. "So first thing tomorrow, we are conducting a raid on the Mount Pleasant Hostel for the Young and Disenfranchised. We are going to do it by the book and we are arresting everyone in there and charging them with murder."

"Fuck," Keyes exploded, putting his fist through the passenger window.

Glass waked out behind the car.

*

They had done it by the book, followed protocol.

Protocol said get everybody.

Milling around in the police station's car park were the region's bomb squad, the dog handler, still shame faced about his mutt's failure to pick up Carter's trail, and reluctantly the Tactical Operations Squad, or TOSsers as Stone called them.

The TOSsers stood together in the corner of the yard, smug and aloof, because they were the ones who had the guns.

Spazhead, their leader, leaned against the van, a Death's Head tattoo just visible above the neckline of his body armour. His second-in-command, Cave Troll, stood next to him. Cave Troll was short, squat and, like the rest of the TOSsers, shaven headed.

Keyes glared over at them – *get back to your basement, you fascist fucks.*

Stone was going through the pre-operation briefing. "This is going to be done by the book. The Tactical Operations Squad will go in first, to sweep and clear the church." He stared over at Spazhead. "Once you've done that, I want you to fuck off back to your basement to wait for the next call out." He turned away dismissively. "Then I want the place swept by the bomb squad supported by the sniffer dog. Ok, any questions?"

The assembled police officers remained silent.

"Right, in that case everybody get in vans and let's go hit the church," Stone ordered.

❋

Keyes and Stone picked their way through the overgrown graveyard and entered the chapel.

"He's been like that since we got here," one of the policemen said, gesturing at the pastor who was praying in front of his guano-covered altar.

"Well, fucking stop him."

The older policeman put his finger to his lips to hush Stone, gesturing around the dilapidated church.

"For fuck's sake," Stone muttered, as he walked up to the pastor and loudly cleared his throat.

On the second clearing, just as he looked about to kick the pastor, Pastor Morris rose, acting like he was seeing all the hubbub around him for the first time.

"Pastor Morris?" Stone asked.

"Can I see some identification, Officer?" the pastor started to say.

Stone grabbed him by an arm and shoved him against a pillar.

Keyes put a restraining hand on the older policeman's shoulder, before lumbering off towards his partner.

"Fuck that son shit," Stone was snarling into the pastor's face. "What the fuck have you lot been up to?"

The pastor winced at the use of language and the spittle that landed on his chin. "My son, I…" he started to say before stopping himself.

"We've just spent half the night outside what was left of the Hare Krishnas' building." Stone was shouting now. "That sweaty lump that works for you was there, all charred."

"Calm down," Keyes ordered his partner.

Stone ignored him.

Stone shook the pastor. "Why did you blow them up?"

Keyes shoved his partner away. Stone turned on him, ready to swing, but stopped as he saw Brogan striding towards them between the pews.

There was an unreadable expression on the Chief Inspector's face.

3

anny opened his armour-plated door and was surprised to see Alistair standing there smiling. Danny looked up and down the street, checked his watch, before shrugging and letting him into the council house.

"Congratulations," Danny beamed, showing his gold tooth. "I think this is the earliest anyone has ever turned up to collect the stuff. Are you bucking for a promotion or something?"

"Nope, I gave in my notice, remember? I'm off to become a contributing member of society," Alistair said happily, as he sat down.

Danny stopped short, his eyes narrowing. "You saying I'm not a contributing member of society?"

Oh God, he's going to turn and go nuts, Alistair thought to himself. "No, Danny, you contribute a lot of things… er, I mean look at this estate, who do people turn to if there's a problem up here?"

"Me."

"Exactly, you're like the giant, cropped-haired gift that keeps on giving."

Danny carried on staring at him.

And staring at him.

And staring at him.

"You're right," he said eventually. "You can say it with a bit less lip, but you are right. People do look up to me on the estate."

Phew, Alistair thought.

Walking away from Danny's to start the day's deliveries, Alistair was full of smiles. He had just a short time left doing these runs and he hadn't had a vampire dream for what felt like an age.

Obviously, if he knew how the day was going to unfold he would have started running now. Instead he tunelessly whistled a song to himself, while thinking about all those prospectuses he'd looked through.

Alistair already knew something about the student life. Call one of the day was Ian Fenton. Fenton was a student and, as far as Alistair could work out, seemed to be doing a degree in knocking out pot from his little room in the university halls.

The campus, as Alistair would start to call it, rather than, *"the place where all those twats live"*, as Ebin did, was through Singleton park and overlooked the sea. There was a security fence around the perimeter of the campus and the entrance was blocked by a big, high gate with an electric key pad on it. This had always seemed a bit pointless to Alistair, as all he had to do was wait for a student to open the gate and follow them in.

Over the two years of Fenton's arrangement with Danny, Alistair had been able to walk around the university grounds and even the halls without ever being challenged. Sometimes this made him wonder if he actually bore a passing resemblance to the passing students.

The Halls of Residence were modelled on seventies' tower blocks. The only difference being the lifts worked and rarely smelt of piss. Today though, he had to straddle a load of vomit, as he travelled up to the twelfth floor.

The lift door opened onto a small, black and white tiled corridor. Ian's room was the third along. Alistair liked getting there early, as it was important to take every given opportunity to annoy students.

"Who's there?" a voice answered his knock.

"Me," Alistair said, not recognising the kid who opened the door.

Fenton was sitting in the room's only chair, a red-eyed king, sitting over his subjects. Behind him, there was a large window that had probably the best view in the city – you could see the coastline crescenting off into the distance, hugged by the sea.

Alistair recognised one of the three others crammed into the room, a slightly annoying guy who was as overfriendly as he was acne covered. Alistair always seemed to bump in to him in town and could never remember his name.

Fenton himself had short hair and three days' growth of matching ginger stubble. All the students worshipped Fenton and Fenton, in turn, tried to live up to this gangster image he had fostered. Alistair personally thought he was too big for his boots. Alistair knew people that would hold him down and shit on him for a laugh. Well, Lettuce, Ninja and Kieran to be precise.

That had been two years ago and had been the clinching argument for Fenton to enter into a business relationship with Danny.

*

Danny had come up with the new business plan at one of the monthly AGMs he held. They were going to branch out into supplying pot to the students, or *rich wankers* as Danny had called them. He had it all worked out on his whiteboard.

"Why bother? You sell loads of the stuff anyway," Lettuce had commented.

"There are wheels within wheels working," Danny said, tapping his nose conspiratorially.

Danny outlined the plan: Alistair looked most like a student, so, despite his protests, would have to go undercover around the university buying drugs.

When he found someone selling, he would report to Kieran and that little prick Karl Reno. They would ensure the person decided to buy only from them.

It had seemed to be a good and well-illustrated idea at the

time, but had degenerated into Ninja and Kieran holding down Fenton while Lettuce pooped on his face.

*

Fenton had been in the middle of telling a story when Alistair had knocked on the door. He restarted it for Alistair's benefit. There was always space made for Alistair, after all, he was the one who brought the drugs to the dealer.

"You know Frank, lives down the corridor?" Fenton asked lighting up a joint.

Alistair nodded; they'd met him a couple of times. He was a tall and lanky kid who could have even been described as spindling, if Alistair had owned a thesaurus.

"Well, yesterday was his birthday, so we took him out and got him well pissed."

Fenton used COCKNEY words as often as possible, even though he was from Barnsley.

"While we were out, two of my mates stayed behind and moved all his stuff down to a room at the bottom of the building." He paused to re-light the joint. "Well, after we've carried him home, we put him in the lift and went up and down, a load of times until he is completely disorientated and has even thrown up."

Alistair had some of the sick on his shoe.

"Then we put him to bed." Another pause, partly for effect, partly to take a toke on the joint. "So at eight in the morning, we burst into the room downstairs, calling him a cunt, and asking what the hell he'd been doing last night. It was so funny. He was mumbling, saying, *'What are you talking about?'* And we say, you know damn well what we're talking about and we don't want to share a landing with your sort. So then we grab him and throw him out of the window, which he thinks is on the twelfth floor. The soppy git falls just under three feet and lies there on the grass for five minutes screaming his head off."

Fenton roared at the memory.

And despite all his prejudices Alistair had to admit, he might quite like student life.

4

"What the hell do you think you are both doing?" Brogan exploded, covering the distance to the altar in a couple of strides.

Stone unhanded the pastor and turned to face his superior officer. "Hello sir. We weren't expecting you to grace us with your presence this morning."

"Really? Well, I'm afraid you were mistaken," Brogan said, before turning to the pastor. "Pastor Morris, I can only apologise for this disgraceful treatment from my men. I would be grateful if we could go somewhere to discuss urgent matters."

"We can use my office," the pastor said, in a surprisingly calm voice.

"Thank you. You two, I want you to wait here until I return," Brogan ordered the detectives.

"Sir," Stone snapped. "I thought you would be otherwise engaged this morning. Weren't you meant to be drafting a letter?"

"I will talk to you later," Brogan said, before turning on his heels and leaving with the pastor.

*

Brogan had been much too busy to draft any sort of letter. He had sat unnoticed in his car watching the raid on the church unfold.

His time last night, with Emily, had not brought him the peace it should have. What he had done should have sated him, but instead Brogan felt wound up, as tight as a drum.

He sat in his car until the Tactical Operations Squad had trooped out of the church and Detectives Keyes and Stone entered the hostel.

Leaving the car, Brogan approached the Tactical Operations Squad. He carried a folder; it contained their new mission.

The Tactical Operations Squad were gathering around their van, swapping high-fives. Brogan disliked dealing with these sorry men intensely. They were, without exception, bad policemen, stupid, incompetent and racist – all the attributes that someone entrusted to uphold the law should not be. Unfortunately, being stupid, incompetent and racist were not enough to get you fired from the police force. So instead, they had been given weapons training and a room in the basement. Down there, ignored and inactive for weeks at a time, they had formed their own clique, a clique within a clique, their personal ideology leeching into their police work like the job was litmus paper.

Most of them now just used their National Front nicknames. Nicknames like Spazhead or Cave Troll. Brogan found them all incredibly distasteful, but the assignment he was going to send them on was vital.

*

The floorboards creaked underfoot as Pastor Morris led Brogan up a dusty spiral staircase to his office. At one point, they had to push themselves against the wall to let the bashful dog handler and his charge come down.

"Nothing up there, sir," the dog handler had said, by way of conversation as he squeezed past them both.

At the top of the stairs, Pastor Morris entered his office and sat behind his desk.

"It's not really coming along," Brogan said.

Pastor Morris looked up at him for a moment, seemingly wondering what the policeman was talking about.

"The church. It doesn't seem as if they have done a lick of painting since the last time I was here."

One of the monitors showed the inside of the church and the unfinished white wall.

From his seat the pastor shrugged.

"It must be a test of your faith," Brogan continued, "spending years working for something, or at least your idea of what something should be like and then..." He trailed off.

"I trust you are not solely talking about interior decorating."

"Trish is dead," Brogan sighed. "And I did nothing."

"You were one of the only ones who cared for the poor thing." The pastor tutted. "When you first came to me, I asked why you cared. Do you remember? You said because someone has to."

"Well." Brogan smiled sadly. "I thought it sounded good at the time and it was better than telling you the truth."

"The truth?"

"I used that girl as much as anyone." He paused, staring at the monitor, watching Stone and Keyes talking to a young policeman. "As much as those who killed her."

The pastor froze – *those*. Brogan looked different now; there was a madness there, a madness that belied his stature and his conservative appearance. It was the same madness Pastor Morris had seen in Al when he was about to torture the press man, a controlled madness, as flat and dangerous as a knife.

"*Those* that killed her?" the pastor asked.

Brogan nodded. "I used to own this town, Father, in so many ways and on so many levels, you would be truly impressed. And I have done some terrible things to get to this position of power, but I have protected this city for a long time and I have sacrificed a lot in order to do so. In ways you wouldn't know."

"I wouldn't count on it," Pastor Morris mumbled.

"You're right, that is why I'm here," Brogan said, sitting down, leaning forward, making eye contact. "Father, I am being corralled, driven to do something that I would never be able to square with my conscience."

"The answer is simple then. Refuse to do it."

Brogan smiled at him, a thin, sad, little smile. "Oh, they haven't left me a lot of wriggle room. Either I do what they ask and spit on everything I have ever worked for or I go to jail or end up dead."

"And you feel you need my help?"

"I feel I need to talk to someone who went through the same experience."

"I don't understand," the pastor said.

"My superior officer sees himself as a forward-thinking visionary," Brogan answered. "Those were his words by the way; one of his forward-thinking visions involves computers. He's invested a lot of the budget in computers and training up a lot of us old dogs to use them. I had to go on one of these training courses, you see. That internet was new to me. It's an amazing tool as long as you've got the patience to use it. And, Father, I have an awful lot of patience."

"Even though these surroundings may look backwards, I've heard of that at least," Pastor Morris reassured him.

"Good, good. You are not on it by the way," Brogan said, without taking his eyes off the pastor. "Do you know I searched and searched for you and nothing? There is just no mention of a Pastor Morris in any of the records I looked at, nothing at all. I was ready to give up, but something just made me push on. And then I found a story; it was in a news archive. It covered the death of a pastor, a pastor originally from this city coincidently." Brogan was staring at him intently now. "It was not a very pleasant story to be honest; the pastor was accused of abusing young boys in his care. He was due to be arrested, but on that very night he disappeared, disappeared without a trace. Initially the investigating officers thought he had absconded to the continent. That was until they found his clothes on the beach." Brogan paused again, evaluating Pastor Morris. "It was eventually ruled as a suicide."

"What was this man's name?" the pastor asked, his throat dry.

"It was London, Pastor London," Brogan said. "There was a picture that accompanied the story; the picture looked an awful lot like you."

Pastor Morris leaned forward; he felt calm, God's love surrounded him, fortressing his being. "And if you found this man, London, would you turn him in?"

"If he was guilty, in a heartbeat," Brogan said.

A heartbeat past.

"Are you guilty, Pastor London?"

"Am I guilty of those charges I was accused of? No, no, I am not. Detective, I was in a similar situation to you. The people we dance around and have not mentioned once had me in their clutches." Pastor Morris sat back in his chair, formulating what he needed to tell this man. He decided everything. "My involvement started while I was in seminary school. Now, Detective Brogan, I was an exemplary pupil. I came to the attention of some people in the church. I was put on, let us say, an intensive training course. After I had finished my training, instead of being given a parish or a missionary posting, it was deemed that God was calling me in a different direction, giving me a different purpose." He paused. "I believe that the Church is there to offer people both spiritual and physical protection. In the Church there was a small group of us who covered the physical aspect of that protection. They are, or rather were, called the Brethren. I was honoured to be included amongst their ranks, for a short period, before their downfall."

"Their downfall?"

"Detective, there are powerful forces set in direct opposition to the Church. For centuries the Brethren were tasked to deal with these forces. We were free ranging and, as God is my witness, we were powerful."

Detective Brogan looked around the dilapidated room. "*You* were powerful?"

"Yes, before our downfall. The forces ranged against us were insidious in their cunning and myriad in their influence. And they operate at every level of society, even in the Church," Pastor Morris said sadly. "Our ranks were decimated in a short period."

"How?"

"In innumerable ways. For instance, do you really think there are that many paedophiles in the Church?"

"Yes, pretty much," Brogan said, after a moment's consideration.

Pastor Morris looked at him coldly, before continuing. "Chief Inspector, I am not joking, these people are very powerful. They have in the past gone under many different names, but today they are known as—"

"The Society?"

Pastor Morris nodded.

"Why didn't you come forward?" Brogan asked. "Why didn't you tell anyone earlier?"

"They are myriad in their influence."

Brogan turned to look back at the TV monitors. Keyes and Stone leaned against the pews. "But now you trust me? Why? I could be working for them; I could be a member of this Society."

"Oh, I know what you are, Chief Inspector, and I know what you are capable of doing."

Brogan broke eye contact for a moment, staring off into the events of last night. "Then you should run, Pastor London."

The pastor smiled. "In truth, I'm all run out. It is going to end tonight."

"What do you mean?"

"You'll have to let me finish the rest of my story, Detective."

Pastor Morris started at the beginning. Way back in the beginning. The history lesson went like this:

"The story of the Society goes back to the dying decades of the nineteen-hundreds. Tell me, have you heard of King Leopold II of Belgium?"

"Please remind me," Brogan had said, a trace of impatience creeping into the reply.

"Well, King Leopold II was a remarkably evil man. He has been compared to Attila the Hun and even a forerunner to Hitler. He was ambitious. He saw that every other European country had colonies spread across the world and he in turn wanted his share, so King Leopold II set out to colonise his own piece of Africa."

"The Congo Free State."

"Very good, Chief Inspector." The pastor smiled, obviously impressed. "It was a brutal colonisation, murder, mutilation, rape and genocide. No one knows how many people died, but estimates range up to fifteen million."

"You are losing me, Father. This happened over a hundred years ago."

"Yes, but those events resonate even today. There was one man who was involved in the founding of this 'colony', a Henry Morton Stanley."

"Henry Morton Stanley?"

"Yes, he was best known for finding Livingstone. He was given control in the Congo and he set about dividing and conquering the country. Terrible punishments were received for the most minor of things. Somewhere in this turmoil, the Society began." Pastor Morris looked off into the distance for a moment. "We tried to stop it at its inception, but failed badly. Stanley returned to Wales, married and became an MP in London. But that knowledge, the knowledge of how powerful fear is, stayed with him and he started to share it with people."

Brogan massaged his temples. "So you're saying that some secret society has been killing people for the best part of a hundred and fifty years and no one has noticed?"

"Well, granted they're not the oldest group of their type, but they are one of the most powerful."

Brogan shook his head. "Father, two days ago I would have laughed in your face, before having you arrested for the murder of twenty-one Hare Krishnas. However, recent events have changed my view of all this. Now I don't know if this nonsense all started in some jungle, way back when. But what I do know is that it is happening in my city and I do not like it. Now, I know that you are involved up to your neck, but what I do not know is how far you would be prepared to go to stop them."

Pastor Morris met his stare, matched it, eyes glittering in the poor, office light. "Detective, I have almost everything in place to crush them, to clean out your city."

"Except?"

The pastor looked away, his cheeks flushing. "Unfortunately, we have yet to verify the location of where they are meeting tonight."

"Oh, that's an easy one," Brogan said, sitting back in his chair and steepling his fingers. "But in order for you to find that out, Father, you are going to have to sit through my confession."

"I am not a Catholic. I cannot take a confession," Pastor Morris started to say. But he was too late, Detective Chief Inspector Brogan had already started talking, telling him about last night and the murders he had committed.

5

C all two was Warren.

Call two was where Alistair's day started to turn to shit. Alistair normally took great pleasure in calling in on Warren. Out of all of the deliveries on his various runs, Warren shone as an atoll of calm in a sea of insanity. Or as Danny described him, *"the most chilled out spade you'll ever meet."* Warren was a big, bald, slow-moving guy who had one of the most circumspect outlooks on life Alistair had ever come across.

They were sitting in Warren's lounge drinking coffee. Warren offered him a joint out of the large lump that had been brought round.

"No, I won't, thanks," Alistair said, still quite stoned from leaving Fenton's tower block.

"Well, that's unusual." Warren smiled.

"Yeah, man, you're looking at a whole new person. I'm giving up running around delivering this crap."

"Well, good for you. What are you going to do instead?"

"Just straighten my head out. I've got this girl now and you know she's… she's brilliant. I'm going to apply for university and everything."

Warren breathed out a massive cloud of smoke. "Hey, that's great, I didn't know you had any A-Levels."

"I haven't."

"Aw, man, you need grades to go to university; you need grades to do anything." He shook his head. "Take where I work. There's someone there who's got less experience but more qualifications, so they're above me. They're shift coordinator, which means that I end up leading all the crazies around by the hand and cleaning up after them, while this person spends her time doing paperwork in the office."

"Nope, I'm twenty-three. I don't need grades. They'll let me in because of my life experience."

Warren looked at him quizzically.

"No seriously, I'll have to do a foundation year, learning how to do maths and punctuation and stuff, but it'll be cool. It'll be good to start learning something again."

"That's really good, what're you going to study?"

Alistair hadn't had to think about this question very hard. "Geography," he said.

Warren had nodded his head approvingly.

"My girlfriend reckons I'll have to get more job experience than this though," Alistair said, thumbing at his little black bag.

"Hey, if you need a reference, let me know and I'll say you've been working up at the hospital or something."

"Thanks, but I'm going to try and get a job somewhere over Christmas and hopefully stay on through to September."

"Good for you. She sounds like a nice girl."

"Oh, she's wicked. Hey, I've got a photo if you want to see it," Alistair said, pulling his wallet out of his bag.

The photo had been taken in one of those little booths on Bristol Station. Both shoved in together, all kisses, smiles and goo.

Warren took the little square photo off him and looked at it, the smile dropping from his face. "What did you say her name was?"

"Maggie, why?"

"You know she used to be a patient up at the hospital, right?"

6

"Time to wake up," Zach said, toeing Karl Reno in the ribs. Reno sat up, all fug headed and confused. The room was a mess and stank stalely of skunk. Kieran was sitting at the table, watching Tiny roll a joint.

"I need to go home to have a shower and get changed," Reno said.

"Yeah, man, you pong," Tiny commented from the table.

Kieran had laughed at this.

Zach looked at his watch. "You haven't got time for that now."

*

Seeing Zach the Mac, Big Boy Z, etc., turn up at the house had been a shock for Reno. Zach had hugged his brother for a long time before shaking hands with Daryl and Tiny. All smiles, all of them swapping hearty backslaps.

Finally, as if seeing them for the first time, Zach turned to Reno and Kieran. "I bet you two are surprised," he said, the words coming out with difficulty, due to his broken face.

"What are you doing here?" Reno asked open mouthed.

"Hell, I was the scout. Can you believe that, a three-year scouting mission in this shitburg?"

"Scouting what?"

"What do you want done with them?" Tiny asked, ignoring Reno's question.

"The honkies can chill at the pad for a while," Zach said, before laughing and slipping out of his pimp jive accent for the first time that Karl had ever heard. His accent was replaced by a well-educated one. "We still need their help for a while."

Reno had noticed Tiny placing his bulk in front of the lounge door at this command, so had sat down on the couch.

"Now we'll have a nice night," Zach continued. "So why don't you knock your mobile phone off and put it on top of the television."

"So as not to be disturbed," Tiny said.

The enforced imprisonment had been conducted politely but firmly. The rest of the evening had gone by with them all smoking superbly strong skunk and doing lines of coke. Whenever Reno had brought up the subject of planning for tomorrow or going home, Zach had just laughed it off, saying it would be better for them all to stay in one place for now.

"Yeah, mission security and all," Batty Boy had said.

Reno had laughed along with them, feeling that he was losing control of the situation slightly. At some point in the evening, he had lost control completely and had passed out under the table.

He had blearily drifted awake at one point, everyone else unconscious around the lounge. He was about to sit up when he saw Batty Boy and Zach stir; they both got up and sneaked out of the house. Karl watched them go before extracting himself from under the table and getting to his mobile phone. He tried Emily at his flat three times, each time getting no answer.

*

The two brothers had been gone for a long time. Now, in the harsh light of morning, Karl wished he'd taken his chance and run. It was too late for that now though with everyone awake.

He wanted to go back to his flat and make sure Emily was

alright. But again, in a firm way, Zach had said, "You haven't got time for that now."

"Yeah, it's time to get suited, booted and strapped up," Tiny said, from the table, lighting a joint.

Zach had looked at Reno. "Do you know what getting strapped up means?"

Reno shook his head no.

"Show him, Batty."

Batty went out of the lounge and could be heard fiddling about in the little alcove under the stairs. He returned to the room carrying two large duffle bags.

Tiny cleared the table – backhanding takeaway cartons and detritus onto the floor.

Batty Boy started laying out the bag's contents.

"Shit, man, that's a load of guns," Kieran said, transfixed. "Wow, you've got machine guns, pistols and look at those. Are they real pump-action shotguns like in films and stuff?"

Tiny had laughed at this. "Sure they are, heft one up. It's not loaded yet."

"Right, it's time to go over the plan," Reno said, in a vain hope of wrestling back some semblance of control. Behind him Kieran made shotgun noises.

"Oh yeah, we forgot to mention the plan has changed," Zach said, sharing a smirk with his brother.

7.

"**Y**ou look like you've seen a ghost," Ebin said, regarding him from the couch. "I mean, you hear people say that quite regularly, and all, but you really do look quite pale. Are you sure you're ok?"

Alistair didn't say a word.

"I'll take that as a yes then. Right, make me a coffee and I'll tell you a secret."

"Look, fuck off, I'm not in the mood," Alistair snapped.

Ebin stared at him dolefully. "Milk and two sugars, or I won't tell you what I know about your little girlfriend."

"Oh for fuck's sake, you know as well?"

"Well, fine, if you're going to swear," Ebin huffed. "She came round earlier to see you."

"What did she want?"

"I asked her again if she fancied hopping on the good leg and doing the bad thing, but she was all weird."

"What did she *fucking* say?"

"Ask her yourself, she insisted on waiting in your room."

Alistair hit the stairs two at a time.

"I never did like that girl," Ebin shouted after him.

Alistair burst into his room thinking for a moment it was empty and Ebin was having a wind up, but she was behind him standing against the wall.

"I'm glad you're back," Maggie said, making him turn.

She looked stunning.

"There's not much time and I need to tell you something."

"I've been out delivering pot," Alistair said, his voice sounding distant. "I'm working my notice period." He half-smiled at this.

Maggie stepped forward taking both his hands in hers. "That's great, but look this is really, really important."

"It's been a busy morning," Alistair said, talking over her, still in that miles away voice. "I had to make a couple of deliveries."

"Listen, Alistair, it's—"

"My last call was interesting. There's this guy Warren, he's a really nice guy. He works up at the nut house on the hill."

Maggie froze.

"I showed him your picture, he recognised it, said he used to work with you, when you were a patient."

The colour slowly drained from her face, her hands going limp before falling away. "What did Warren tell you?"

*

"I can't tell you much, man, patient confidentiality and all." Warren had shrugged by way of explanation.

"Look, you've just told me the girl I've bared my soul to has been lying to me since we met," Alistair said, feeling like he'd been shot. "You can't just say *'oh it's patient confidentiality'*."

"I shouldn't have even told you that she'd been a patient."

"Look at the picture again, are you sure? She said she'd been away travelling."

"I don't need to, man, it's her."

"At least tell me why she was there." It came out as a plea.

Warren regarded the end of his joint. "Ok look, it was some sort of family tragedy she took badly."

"What, badly enough to go into a nut house?"

Warren sighed. "Do you like this girl?"

"I think I love her," Alistair said, the words shocking him as they came out.

"Then you don't need me to tell you anything. Go and talk to her."

*

"What did Warren tell you?" Maggie repeated.

"Nothing, he said I should ask you."

Maggie smiled at him sadly. "Warren was a nice man." She gestured to the bed. "You're probably going to want to sit down."

8

ogs, TOSsers, the bomb squad, everybody was heading away from the church.

Stone nursed his injury while Keyes drove.

"I don't like it," Keyes said. "Brogan's smart, he's not going to go away, not over one tape."

"Fuck him, he's over and he knows it," Stone said, still massaging his wrist.

Keyes lapsed into his own thoughts for a while, too lost to notice their new tail, bird-dogging them seven cars back.

Keyes finally turned to his partner. "He may be over, but he was faster than you."

*

Chief Inspector John Brogan had indeed been faster.

"Everyone out," he commanded coming down the staircase and back into the chapel.

"But, sir—" Stone had started to protest.

Brogan ignored him. "You," he shouted at the nearest PC. "Get on your radio and call a desist to this operation. I want everyone out of here."

"But, sir, twenty-one Hare Krishnas were murdered last night and the evidence points to—"

"I said out," Brogan roared, taking everyone aback. "Now."

The police trailed out, all except Stone and Keyes.

Stone waited for the last person to leave the chapel before turning to Brogan. "Listen, pal, I don't know if your memory is going or whether you thought it was some sort of bad dream last night, but me and him were there and we did tell you today was the day you resign."

Brogan stared at him.

"Look, you little shit," Stone continued, punctuating his words with hard fingered pokes to the senior officer's chest. "You are over or did you forget about that tape? You corrupt fuck."

"I have not forgotten about our conversation last night nor have I forgotten about the sort of men you are." Brogan produced a plain white envelope from his pocket. It was mottled with poke-shaped crumples. "This is my resignation letter, Detective, and I will give it to the superintendent at the end of the day. But until it is formally accepted, I am your senior officer and as such you will obey my commands and you will not lay your grubby little fingers upon me. Is that clear?"

"It gave the sex change as the reason, did it?" Stone crowed.

Brogan turned to leave.

Stone grabbed him. "I said did you put the— ahh."

Brogan had, in a breath, grabbed Stone's wrist, twisted it back and kicked out a knee.

Stone crumpled, his arm twisted and ready to break.

Keyes lumbered forward on instinct.

"Detective Keyes," Brogan bellowed. "Come any closer and I will take his arm out of the socket. Detective Stone, do you know the kind of trouble you can get in for trying to assault a superior officer?"

"Step forward, get him," Stone ordered his partner, a crazy smile flecked across his face.

"Enough of this," Keyes rumbled. "None of us like being in this situation, but this is the situation we are in. You two fighting isn't going to make any of us feel any better about it. So Chief

Inspector Brogan, please let my partner go. And Stone, we've won, for what good it does, your daughter's going to be saved, so stop acting like a prick about it."

Brogan released the prone detective. Silently Keyes helped his partner up and they left the chapel.

*

Stone was still pissed off though. A car, with three men in, cut them up. Stone leaned over and with his good hand kept the horn depressed.

"Look, enough ok?" Keyes said, dragging his partner's arm away.

"Come on, let's pull those pricks over," Stone said. "We can use them as stress balls."

Keyes rolled his neck, muscles bulging.

"See, you're stressed. We'll pull them over and you can be the bad cop. Come on, it'll be great."

"Look, stop being a prick, ok?"

Stone held up his hands in mock surrender, before changing and looking serious. "You're right, you know. What you said back in the church. None of us like this, doing this. It's not me and I know it's definitely not you." He stared out of the car window, formulating, searching for words. "Hey, you know, I haven't said thanks for going along with this yet."

"You don't have to; I'm not doing it for you."

"Well, thanks from Megan then." He bent his wrist back, flexing it, wincing. "And you know, as soon as she's fixed up, we're going to take all of those fucks down."

Keyes shook his head. "They'll have thought of that."

"Sure they have, but look at the two of us; they'll underestimate us big time," Stone said, starting to laugh one of those stupid infectious laughs that you get when nothing is actually that funny, but it's better than breaking down into tears.

His partner joined in.

Their tail was still snuggled unnoticed seven car lengths behind them, when Stone's phone rang. He answered it wiping tears from his eyes.

"Hello." He glanced at his partner. "No, we didn't arrest anyone, our boss stopped us."

Keyes mouthed, *"Is that them?"*

"Yes, we played him the tape," Stone said, holding a finger up to silence his partner. "Yes, he's going to give in his notice today."

He was silent for a minute listening. "You want us to what? No, listen, that wasn't part of the deal, no, listen, I... you're serious? Shit ok."

Stone hung up the phone, looking tired and drawn. "You'll never guess what they want us to do now."

9

Kieran had wanted a gun. Daryl had said, "No, you don't get one; you just go along to give directions."

Kieran had been quite stoned when they left the house; Daryl had told him to sit his ass in the back.

Kieran had given directions badly. "Shit, man, left by there."

Tiny had bullied his way across the lane and headed up the hill, cutting in front of traffic as he went; behind them a car horn honked long and angry.

They had parked up at the bottom of Danny's street and hunkered down low, watching the armour-plated door. Watching and watching.

"This is stupid," Tiny said, looking at his watch for the thirtieth time. "We've been here for ages, let's just go and get him now."

Daryl had shaken his head. "You know the plan, we wait for the phone call."

*

"Right, here's the plan," Batty Boy had said.

They were all sitting around in the lounge drinking coffee. Batty Boy was doing the talking as Zach's speech was still all mouth-twatted and drug-slurred.

"I-Knows wants them together at the same place. So Tiny, Daryl and Kieran, you go get this Danny fucker, and me, Zach and Reno, we'll sort out meeting I-Knows and getting the copper."

"Wait, that's not the plan," Reno said. "Besides who the fuck is this I-Knows cunt you are talking about?"

Daryl flung his coffee across the room hitting Reno in the face, making him claw and screech. In a second he was standing over him, dragging Reno up by his sodden collar, their faces inches away from each other.

"You do not speak of I-Knows in such terms," Daryl spat, his rage barely held in check. "I have killed better men than you for less. I-Knows is our leader, he is our master and he is our purpose and you should be honoured that I-Knows is coming home."

Batty Boy shared a quick glance with his brother before separating them. "Yeah, in short, the plan's changed," he told the quivering Reno, before turning back to the others. "Now, we'll have to coordinate it so we get them all at the same time. So you three wait for my phone call before you grab this Danny."

"What about what's his name?" Daryl asked.

"Mardy Davies? He'll be last. We'll use his big pad to go to work on them all."

"What exactly are you going to do to them?" Reno said, his former cockiness all but gone now.

Batty Boy glanced at Zach. "We'll let I-Knows show you when he gets here. He's got big plans for those three."

"But why? How does he know them? Why does he care?"

Batty Boy glanced at Zach. "Those three wronged I-Knows in the past and I-Knows doesn't forget being wronged. Especially when he sees the remnants of that act staring back at him each time he looks in a mirror."

*

Sitting in the car was boring, Tiny spent his time tutting and looking at his watch, while Daryl was busy giving Kieran last-minute instructions.

"So you're going to go up to the door and knock. There's a peep hole in the door, right?"

Kieran had nodded.

"Stand up close to it, use your head to hide the view, me and Tiny will be standing either side of the door out of sight. When this Danny opens up, you step through, as you would on any other day. Say something like, *'how's it going',* then keep on walking, me and Tiny will be right on your heels. Now this is the important bit: you need to get between Danny and the door. If he's quick he might try to slam it; if he does, you act like a human door jam. If he manages to close it, we're screwed."

Tiny turned fully in his seat, to give Kieran his best I-hate-whitey stare. "Just so you know, I'd shoot through you in a second."

"It's normally not locked," Kieran said, a slight quaver in his voice.

Tiny burst out laughing. "This one's a funny fucker, anything else you haven't mentioned?"

Kieran took a moment to decide. He'd figured out last night that Reno was way out of his depth and they were both caught up in the middle of something that was going to end really badly.

"Well, there is one thing," he said, deciding it was time to suck up to someone new. "Danny's got a safe."

This pricked up their interest.

Encouraged, he pressed on. "Now while we're kidnapping him, why not clean that out as well?"

Tiny glanced at Daryl. "Why didn't you mention it to Zach and Batty Boy?"

Kieran picked his words carefully. "Well, I was going to, but they seemed so intent on going through the plan, I thought it might be an unwelcome distraction."

A big smile spread across Daryl's face. "I think you're right, mentioning the safe to anyone else might, well, distract them. You'll be ok, Kieran. That is if you keep your shit together, especially later, in front of I-Knows, when we start going to work on those three fuckers. If you can do that then you'll go places. But, if you screw up, then Tiny here will shoot through you in a second."

Kieran had smiled weakly, wishing, not for the first time, that he had never listened to that little prick Karl Reno.

"Who's that?" Daryl asked, as a figure walked quickly along the street, down the steps and knocked rapidly on Danny's door.

"Oh that's Alistair; he's one of the delivery boys. The guy's an idiot."

10

Alistair, lugging his life in his bag, was banging on Danny's door. He was going to pick up some scarper money and run, *"Please, do it for me,"* ringing in his ears.

She'd confessed. She'd started and hadn't stopped; everything came out, confessional big time.

Alistair banged on the metal door, loud rat-a-tat-tats.

Danny opened up. Danny was drunk; midday on was happy hour in the Howells' household. "Oh, it's you." He grinned sloppily. "Here to drop off the money?"

"Something like that," Alistair grunted, as he walked past him.

"What's in the bag?"

"Clothes mostly. It's strange, but when you boil it down to what you actually need, it's just a bag of clothes."

Danny looked at him oddly. "Sorry, mate, I'm not following."

"That's it, twenty-three years on this earth and my worldly possessions fit in this," Alistair said, absent-mindedly tapping the tennis bag.

"Nope, I'm still not following. Here, do you want a drink? You look a bit odd."

Alistair stared around the lounge, as if he'd just come to, before his eyes settled on Danny. "A drink? No, I think I'll be fine. What I do need though is my money."

"What money?"

"What I'm owed for the last three years."

Danny put a fatherly hand on his shoulder. "Listen, Alistair, all this quitting nonsense. That's all it is, nonsense. You're good at the job, why not have a little think about it for a couple of weeks before deciding?"

"I need my money now. I've got to leave town."

"Leave, but why?"

"Because she's left me and I have to get out of town."

*

That had been the first thing that Maggie had told him as they sat together on his bed.

"I can't see you anymore," she said, holding his hand tight.

"Why not? If it's about you not mentioning the institution then that's fine. We can—"

"No, I haven't been…" She paused, letting go of his hand, eyes resolutely floor-ward. "Look, I'm sorry; I planned out what I was going to say and now… I lost someone I was really close to; it put me in a bad way for a long time."

"Bad enough to go into a ment… into a hospital?"

"Yes, it was my sister. She went off the rails a bit, broke away from the family and got into all sorts of drugs."

"How did she die?" Alistair asked, going cold inside, wanting to be wrong.

"From a heroin overdose."

"Did I know her?"

"Yes."

Alistair felt tears welling up inside him. "It was Ceri, wasn't it?"

"Yes, she'd talk about you often when I saw her. Whenever she saw Mum and Dad, she'd be boasting about this guy she had wrapped around her little finger, who'd get her all the drugs she needed. Ceri only said it to spite them."

"Is that how she saw me? As the guy who got her drugs?"

"That's what she said. The drugs changed her, it wasn't… that

413

wasn't the real Ceri." She paused, choking up. "And then the drugs killed her and we all blamed you, the guy who'd got her into drugs. But what could we do? We went to the police, but they weren't interested."

"I didn't get her *into* drugs; she was already in the life when we met," Alistair started to say.

But Maggie kept talking, eyes on the floor, looking back into the past. "I started going off the rails and they hospitalised me. You see my parents have connections, enough to get me institutionalised. My mother couldn't face the scandal of another daughter going the same way. It was my doctor, while I was in the hospital, who introduced them to the Society. He had studied medicine with Dad at university. God they loved the Society. My mother always had been a social climber and you can't get any higher than becoming a member of that. It took a year of waiting before it was their turn."

"Their turn?"

"Yes, it's the reward for when you become fully initiated."

"What? Fully initiated? I don't understand."

"You can pick someone who has wronged you in the past. And as long as the other members believe you have been truly wronged, you can exact revenge."

"Revenge? Revenge for what? What's this Society?" Alistair said, trying to hold her. She flinched him off, wanting to get through it all.

"They got your friend Trish last. She'd ruined some woman's fur coat or something. So they burned her alive."

A raft of emotions hit Alistair; he didn't, couldn't, believe what he was hearing. Part of him hoped it was an elaborate way of being dumped, but deep down he knew it was true and God did he feel sick.

"They killed her over a fur coat," Maggie continued. "Over something as trivial as that."

"Who did? Look, we'll have to go to the police. They'll be able to help."

414

Maggie laughed humorously at this. "There's no one we can tell, everyone is involved. All you can do is run."

"Why? Why should I run?"

Maggie turned looking at him for the first time since she had started speaking. "Because you're next. I tried to tell them you're innocent, but it's too late."

Alistair couldn't focus, his head reeled. "Because of Ceri?"

Maggie nodded. "They want you dead. Hell, I wanted you dead, until I got to know you."

"Why? Why did you first meet me in the pub if you thought I'd killed your sister?"

"The Society likes it that the whole family is involved. They made me spy on you."

"That's all it was, spying?"

Maggie shook her head, taking his hand again, squeezing it tight. "Yes, for all of the first hour, then I saw you weren't the person I imagined. You were decent, probably the most decent person I had met in three years. Even by the time you told me about her, I knew that you hadn't been the one to kill her."

"What did your folks say to that?"

"Mother and Father had already put their case to the Society and it had been decided. That's it, there's no way to un-decide it."

"So what? Now this Society kills me?"

"No, because you're going to run."

"Run where?"

"I don't know, anywhere. You've just got to go now. Please, do it for me."

"What about you? What are you going to do?"

"I've got to go."

"Wait, look, let's get out of here together for a while. We can work something out. I know some policemen."

Maggie leant forward, kissing him hard, tears welling up. "No, you've got to run. Please, do it for me."

And then she got up and rushed out of the room.

"Because she's left me and I have to get out of town," Danny repeated. "Oh is that it? Just a girl? I'll tell you this for nothing, mate, what you need to do is—"

"Look, I don't have time for this crap. I've got a bus to catch. I'll take whatever you've got on you now and get the rest some other time."

"Listen, you little shit. You can't just flounce in here expecting a load of back pay. I'm not a fucking bank."

"Well, you've got a fucking safe."

A mad expression crossed Danny's face, stayed there for a second and then flickered out. "Listen, mate," he said, smiling again now. "I know you're owed money, but it's not as simple as going in the safe; it'll take time. Let's have a joint and you can fill me in on what's been happening."

"Fill you in?"

"Yeah, mate, you're not looking a hundred per cent."

Alistair shrugged; it was as good a plan as any. In all honesty, he didn't even have a long-term plan. He'd grabbed a bagful of clothes, pocketed his cosh and left. An hour or so here would give him a chance to calm down and think. After all, he was in Danny Howells' house; nothing bad could happen to him here.

Danny smiled and refilled his glass. Danny drank his spirits out of a pint glass.

He turned as someone started knocking on the door.

Danny gave Alistair a *criminal's work is never done* roll of the eyes, as he ambled out into the hall.

"Oh hello Kieran... Oi, who the fuck are these guys?"

11

"This is the hard man, is it?" Tiny asked, smacking butt into gut.

They had chosen the pumps.

"Best way to cover a room," Tiny had explained earlier. "Now it's an obvious thing, but stay clear of the business end of these, there's a wicked spread on them."

Danny doubled over not making a sound.

They had come in fast, Tiny and Daryl barging through Kieran, barrels up into Danny's flabby neck, Danny only managing to get off the cheap reply of flinging his drink over Kieran.

Now the tableau unfolded.

Danny pushed himself up straight again, looking mad, looking like he was going to charge. The black guys covered him from different corners of the room, too far apart to be got in one go.

Alistair, hands away from his body, in a *this is fuck all to do with me* stance, was sidling towards the door.

"Right, where's the safe? Open the safe," Tiny shouted, riding the upper hand.

Danny ignored the order and instead turned to Kieran, anger radiating off him, his nostrils flaring bull-like. "You stupid little shit. You're doing me over for the contents of the safe? Do you know what'll happen to you?"

Kieran looked away.

"Where's the safe?" Tiny repeated.

Danny laughed, turning to him. "Sure, I'll show you the safe, just so you can find out what'll happen to you after. Come on, it's in the kitchen." Danny gestured.

"Slowly," Daryl ordered.

"Yeah, yeah, I know how to do this sort of thing, mate."

"I'll be off then," Alistair said, heading towards the door.

Tiny turned, covering him with the shotgun.

"I've got a bus to catch and I can tell you guys have all come to an agreement. You're going to rob Danny now and later he'll try to track you down and kill you."

"Oh fair enough, if you're running late for the bus." Tiny winked, before driving the butt of his shotgun deep into Alistair's stomach.

Alistair went down gasping out coughs. "Ow, what was that for? That really hurt, you fucking asshole. God you could have ruptured something."

Tiny turned to Kieran. "Bring this idiot into the kitchen as well. Think you can handle that?"

Kieran dragged him up.

The five of them were crammed into the kitchen, Danny happily pulling back lino, shotguns on him, Kieran holding Alistair by the scruff.

"Right, lads," Danny grinned, hand on the safe. "You're sure you want what's in here? This is your last chance to disappear."

Alistair remembered last time he'd been in the kitchen.

Danny started to open the floor safe.

Alistair frantically started to dig through his pockets.

Danny opened the safe.

Alistair found what he was looking for, turned, sparking the lighter.

The flame sheeted blue, too hot to see.

Kieran, all booze soaked, went up screaming.

Tiny and Daryl turned. Shotguns snagging.

Danny came out of the safe, smiling jollily, gun a-blazing. Alistair dived back into the lounge, eardrums bursting. Behind him shotguns blasted off.

12

They met in a car park outside town, Zach, Batty Boy and Reno, standing in a row by their car, all deferential-like.

They'd briefed Reno earlier. They'd briefed him in list form. *"Firstly, it's a great honour to meet such an illustrious figure as I-Knows. Secondly, don't speak unless he speaks directly to you. Thirdly, never ever question why I-Knows does something. If he offers you his ring to kiss, kiss it… yes, that's right, like the Pope."*

A big, expensive car pulled into the car park. Batty Boy nudged Reno who was playing with his mobile phone.

"I can't get through to Emily," Reno said.

"You're not going to," Batty Boy replied.

"What do you mean?"

"You'll find out. Now put that away. I-Knows is here."

The car pulled up in front of them. Three men exited and stood there, each of them wearing incredibly well-tailored suits. Two of them took up position with their backs to the car, hands in jackets, looking out, while the driver opened the passenger door and then stood back.

I-Knows was here.

I-Knows was a monster of a man with a shorn head that seemed to glister in the drizzle. His white suit was even more expensive-looking than his lieutenants. The only thing out of place were the sunglasses he wore; they were large and about two decades out of fashion.

He walked forward, his cane tap-tapping on the ground, the driver a few steps behind him.

I-Knows held out his hand. Batty Boy and Zach both immediately kissed his ring. He proffered it towards Reno. It was gold and chunky. Reno, after a moment's hesitation, followed suit.

I-Knows nodded in approval at the three of them before speaking; his voice was deep and disconcerting, like a slowed down record. "You have done well. Zach, you especially have shone and at great cost to yourself." He clasped Zach with both his hands, turning his head gently, looking at all the injuries. "I have suffered in a similar way and I-Knows knows your pain. It can linger and stay with you until you can take it no more."

He let go of Zach and walked past them to look at the vista.

The car park was situated on a hill. There were a few graffiti-scarred picnic benches facing a view that stretched seven miles down the valley to the city and the bay beyond.

I-Knows stood there, breathing deeply, arms stretched out in a Jesus pose.

He finally turned back to his entourage. "It is good coming home."

13

Kieran had a look of pure surprise frozen onto his face. Alistair had been staring at the shotgun-desiccated body for a very long time. You could see all his insides.

The kitchen was worse. Peeping round the corner, Alistair had wanted to throw up. Wanted to throw up and then run, but one thing was stopping him. The question of his scarper money. The safe was full of it and everyone was dead.

No one would have to know he'd been here. What had he touched? Nothing, this time at least. But he'd been round loads; how long do fingerprints last? Shit, he didn't know. Never mind, at least they wouldn't find any fresh ones.

What to do? What to do? Right, stop, take a couple of deep breaths, count to twenty and then start thinking. You've got time; none of the neighbours would be calling the police. Round here they just let Danny get on with it.

Alistair peered out of the front window. The street was quiet, no curtains were twitching. He locked and then dead-locked the front door.

Right, scarper money. Standing on tiptoes outside the kitchen he could see into the floor safe just past Danny's almost headless body.

There was a lot of money in it.

Alistair found his bag and then gingerly stepped into the kitchen. The skinny black guy was closest to the door, lying face down, his shotgun pointing out towards Kieran's body; he had two bullet holes in his back. Alistair guessed he'd turned to see why Kieran was screaming and his shotgun had gone off when he'd been shot. Alistair stepped over him, careful not to put a foot in the pooling blood.

Climbing over the fat man was more difficult; he was a hell of a big lad and was lying wedged between the cooker and the sink. He'd obviously taken some stopping; Alistair counted three holes in his chest and one in his head.

And then there was Danny; Alistair held back the puke. They'd redecorated the back wall with lead shot and brains.

Alistair got past them and finally reached the safe. Grabbing a tea towel he gently removed the top layer of money, which was all covered with gunk and gristle, before shovelling the rest of the stash into his bag.

Severance pay.

He then replaced the bloodied money, shouldered his bag and got to the back door.

It had always struck Alistair as funny that Danny had the big metal door at the front and just a normal back door.

It was unlocked.

The fresh air felt good on Alistair's face after the cordite smoke and blood stench that had just filled his nostrils.

Alistair closed the back door and waded through Danny's unkempt garden, jumped the wall and was away down the alley.

It was a few minutes later, as he headed down the big fuck off hill from the estate, that the shakes started.

Alistair was sick in a garden, retching loads.

Not even noticing the car skidding to a halt and reversing.

Not even noticing the sound of car doors being opened.

"Hey Alistair, just the guy we've been looking for," Detective Stone said, clamping a hand onto his shoulder.

14

-Knows' car followed them as they crawled their way through town. It was a beautiful car; it looked out of place on the rain-washed streets of Swansea.

Reno had been silent and pensive, sitting in the back, starting to feel scared. He wanted to see Emily. She was strong, stronger than him; she'd know what to do.

They turned onto Mumbles Road, the traffic lessening as they headed for Mardy's house.

"What's going on exactly?" Reno finally asked.

Batty Boy looked at him in the rear-view mirror. "What do you mean?"

"Well, you told I-Knows that we were going to wait in the mansion until Mardy and his wife got back. That's not the plan. Emily was going to go back to her husband and keep him there until we arrived."

"I didn't exactly say that. I said there'd be no one at the mansion, so we'd have to wait." Batty Boy smirked across at Zach.

"Look, where's Emily?"

"Now listen, boy," Zach said, turning uncomfortably in his seat. "You wanted to get into the big league and this is it. Now here's what you're going to do."

Zach explained what he wanted Reno to do.

"So I just pretend to be speaking to her?" Karl said unsurely.

"That's right."

"But where is she?"

"Look," Batty Boy snarled. "If you do ever want to see her again, you're going to do exactly as we say. So stop asking fucking questions."

Ten minutes later, both cars pulled up outside the gated drive to Mardy's mansion. Batty Boy leaned out and swiped a card through the reader; the gates opened smoothly.

"Where did you get that?" Reno asked.

He was ignored as they drove around to the back of the house, parking the cars out of sight behind the garage.

Batty Boy used a set of keys to open the front door. The seven men entered the house and stood in the reception area.

"Batty Boy, check upstairs to make sure no one's home," Zach ordered, before turning to Karl. "Reno, ring your bitch, see how long before her and the husband come back here."

Reno hesitated for a moment before nodding and going into the other room.

Zach turned to I-Knows. "Sir, this is the home of Mardy Davies. I hope you will be content to wait while we pick up the policeman."

I-Knows entered the lounge. "Truly vile, but it will suffice for now," he said, while seating himself in the middle of the sofa. He turned to one of his lieutenants. "Buenos Mad Dog, go and find the kitchen. I will have a cup of tea while I wait."

Batty Boy came down the stairs. "It is all clear," he told Zach.

"Good, go and bring the car round to the front of the house."

Reno came forward, head down. "I've just spoken to Emily. They will be back in forty minutes."

"That will give us enough time to pick up the policeman," Zach said. "With your leave of course, sir."

"Wait." I-Knows raised his finger; he looked at Reno. "Before you leave, I want to know why you have decided to betray so many of your own people."

"I never meant for this to happen. I only wanted rid of Mardy.

I didn't expect all this," Reno said, gesturing to all the dangerous-looking men filling up the room. "Why are you here anyway? What has Mardy or this copper done to you personally?"

The atmosphere in the room suddenly changed. *"Thirdly, you must never ever question why I-Knows does something."*

I-Knows stood up.

His lieutenants reached into their jackets.

I-Knows approached Karl.

Karl backed away.

Karl bumped into the wall.

I-Knows came closer, inches now from Karl's face. "You dare to question I-Knows' motives?" he asked, his voice low. "You who are nothing to me?"

"Er… sorry, I was just, um… wondering why you have come here yourself."

I-Knows put his head on one side, his eyes hidden behind the dark, out-of-fashion glasses. "You ask why I have come here. I have come here to take back what is rightfully mine."

"What?"

"Something I have coveted from afar for a long time."

Karl shrugged slightly, the word *coveted* lost on him.

"I have come to reclaim my city. For years I have wanted to come home. However, my plans for expansion led me in a different direction. But this city was never far from my thoughts. I even sent a scout, in the form of Zach, to live among you and worm his way into your ranks," I-Knows said, putting the emphasis on the word *worm*. "And my little scout did well in his worming. He found out that this city was run by a man who hurt me in the past, the only man who has ever bested me. He watched this man, watched him consolidate his power and watched his empire grow."

"What, Mardy Davies?" Reno asked.

"No, you stupid boy. The man who hurt me is now a policeman, a Chief Inspector Brogan."

"Why, what did he do?"

I-Knows reached up and removed his glasses. One of his eyes was lifeless and marble white, bedded in a crisscross of scars.

15

The ladies of the Central Hotel watched with sullen eyes as Alistair was marched past the reception desk.

Detective Stone went up to say something to the clerk.

Detective Keyes held Alistair's face against the wall while they waited for the lift.

They rode the lift in silence, before walking down a dimly lit corridor and stopping at room 302.

Detective Stone pulled out a set of keys and opened it. "This room is rented by the constabulary on a permanent basis," he said, by way of explanation before pushing Alistair inside.

The room was small, the décor reminiscent of a used teabag.

Detective Keyes handcuffed Alistair to the rust-flecked radiator.

Alistair gave an experimental but futile tug at his handcuffs, while scanning the room for an escape route. He needed to get out of here before someone found all the bodies at Danny's house and the policemen looked in the bag. He had at present one thing going for him. Stone's pat down of him had been cursory at best. He'd missed the cosh.

Think, Alistair thought. Surely he'd seen enough films to escape from anything. He needed a tunnel, a motorbike or a syringe of chemicals to hold against one of their necks. That or a gun… next time he had a chance he would actually take a gun.

Detective Stone opened the bag and whistled. "This is an

awful lot of money, young Alistair, and a lot of clothes; anyone would think you were going to flee the city."

"I was."

"Why? Because of what Maggie told you? Don't look so shocked, kid, these are powerful people," Stone said, throwing himself onto one of the two single beds in the room. The bed sagged in the middle. "They found out what Maggie told you and they can't have anyone outside their circle knowing."

His big partner just paced, looking at his watch, looking angry.

Stone glanced at Keyes for a moment, before turning back to Alistair. "So we were tasked with finding you and picking you up. We'll chill out here for a while and then take you out nice and early for the ceremony."

Ah, that's why he was here.

*

"Hey Alistair, just the guy we've been looking for," the nasty little one had said, getting out of the car.

For a second Alistair had thought about running, but he'd been unable to outpace them last time. Stone was a fast fucker. That had been a year before. Alistair had been on one of his runs when he noticed them following him. Twenty yards back on either side of the road.

Alistair had thought he was about to be done over so had cut down an alley before breaking into a run.

What a crap alley – it ended in a garage door.

Nowhere to go – shit, bollocks, fuck, Alistair had thought, before turning slowly, hand on his cosh.

Both the men were standing at the end of the alley.

"Hey, how's it going?" the smaller of the two asked, walking forward.

"Why you running?" the huge bugger asked, coming closer.

"Why are you chasing me?"

"We want to see what's in the bag."

Coming closer.

"That isn't any of your fucking business."

"We bet it is."

Coming closer.

"That's close enough," Alistair said, swinging his cosh.

He didn't manage to connect with either of them; he just managed to spin on his own axis before falling over.

"Stop laughing at me, you cunts," Alistair said, from his prone position.

"That was pathetic," the bigger of the pair said, wiping a tear from his eye.

The other one was rummaging in the bag. "Tut, tut, tut," he said, pulling out the cellophane-wrapped packages. "You're in a lot of shit, unless, of course, you want to make a deal."

Alistair had been a rat bastard ever since.

*

"Thanks for the tip on Carter by the way," Stone said, from the sagging hotel bed.

"He beat up an old woman. I'd have reported him to the police even if I wasn't working for you."

"You're a good kid, Alistair, which is why it pains me to have you here like this." Stone gestured towards his pacing partner. "It pains him more though."

"You could let me go, say you couldn't find me," Alistair said.

"I'm sorry, we can't."

"Why not? You're meant to be policemen, for fuck's sake. Why are you working for them? You should be out there arresting these assholes."

The policemen shared a glance.

*

430

Stone had been sitting in the doctor's office. The NHS furniture was cheap and functional. Doctor Fletcher sat opposite them behind his desk. He was a chubby, balding nothing of a man, or at least that had been Stone's impression all those months before when he had taken on little Megan's care.

Stone sat with Lucy. They held hands; she looked, as always, tired and drawn, but she was smiling. Smiling for the first time in a long time.

"That's just incredible news, Doctor. When will you be able to start the procedure?" she asked.

"Soon, hopefully very soon," Doctor Fletcher informed her. "We have a bone marrow donor lined up. We need to obviously run a few more minor tests to ensure full compatibility with Megan, but I must say it is all looking extremely positive. Dependent, of course, on your husband's full cooperation."

"Excuse me?" Lucy had said, after a pause.

"Dependent, of course, on your husband's full cooperation," Dr Fletcher repeated before holding up his hand as there was a knock on the door.

A mean-faced man entered the office, regarding the couple coldly.

"Ah Doctor Llewelyn. I believe you know Detective Stone already. I'd like to introduce you to his lovely wife. Lucy, I'd like you to meet Doctor Llewelyn."

Doctor Llewelyn didn't offer his hand or smile at the introduction.

Lucy flatly returned his stare before turning back to Doctor Fletcher. "My husband's cooperation? I don't understand what you are talking about."

"Yes," Doctor Llewelyn said from his position by the door. "Your daughter's life is dependent on your husband's cooperation."

"What—" Stone started to say, but was talked over by Llewelyn.

"Detective Stone, at this juncture it is very important that you do not speak or stand up or try and put on any of that bullish police

431

act that you like so well. The same goes for you also, Mrs Stone. If you love your daughter and want her to live to see Christmas you need to sit quietly and listen to what I am going to tell you."

Stone started to rise, but his wife pulled him down, the strength of her grip turning his knuckles white.

"Thank you, Mrs Stone," Doctor Llewelyn said, coming to sit on the edge of the desk facing them, invading their personal space. "Now it is important that, firstly, you understand that we are all law-abiding citizens and believe completely that the police are a cornerstone of our society. However, your investigation into the death of Trish Reed must stop here and now."

Stone started to speak, but his wife had told him, with more venom in her voice than he had ever heard, to *"Shut the fuck up"*, swearing for the first time in their twelve years of marriage. And so Stone sat in silence, holding Lucy's hand, as Doctor Llewelyn went on to explain how he would now be working for the Society.

*

"I'll pay you to let me go. I've got money to pay," Alistair said, having given up on the idea of finding a motorbike in the small, mothball-smelling room.

"I can see that. But we can't, I'm afraid," Stone said glancing over at the bag, sounding sad, his normally irritating level of cockiness all but gone.

Fuck them then, Alistair thought. *I'm not begging. I wouldn't give the bastards the satisfaction.* "Can I at least have a pillow?"

Stone threw him one over as his phone started ringing. He looked at his partner for a moment before pulling it off his belt and answering it.

"What?" Stone's face changed. "Alright, thanks, I'll be right there."

"Who was that?" his partner asked.

"That was Johnson; the hospital rang about my daughter. They want me there right now."

"Did they say why?"

"Johnson didn't know, just said it sounded urgent."

"I'll watch him, you go."

Stone got up and made for the door. He stopped, reaching under his shirt and pulling out a gun.

"What the hell is that?" Keyes asked.

"The gun we got off that guy on the waste ground." "Why are you carrying it?"

"Look at what we are doing," his partner snapped. "Carrying a gun is the least of our worries."

"Well, I don't want it."

"Look, I'm not going to take a loaded gun to see my daughter in hospital."

"Just leave it on the fucking table then."

"I'll look after it if you like," Alistair offered.

16

It had taken Buenos Mad Dog about ten minutes of rifling through the kitchen before he found the tea bags and a decent enough cup and saucer. Buenos Mad Dog had been with I-Knows for years and still got stuck making the tea.

His task completed, he carefully carried the drink back into the reception area. It was deserted. Hearing voices from the side room, Buenos Mad Dog pushed open the door to find I-Knows, Bam-Bam and Roy sitting in a hideously gauche lounge.

He gave I-Knows the tea.

"Where's ours?" Bam-Bam demanded straight away.

"In the kettle."

"Well get it," Roy said. "You never make us any. I mean if you're making one cup, it's just as easy to make three."

"Well, if you made the tea occasionally you'd—"

"Silence," I-Knows ordered, bringing an end to the squabbling. "I will not sit here on such an important day as this, listening to you three act like children. Buenos Mad Dog, you are the most junior person amongst us so, as such, you can make the others tea."

Junior person indeed. Buenos Mad Dog tutted to himself as he left the lounge. Buenos Mad Dog was, in fact, the fourth most senior member of this family; it just happened to be the other three sat in the lounge. No one else thought he was junior. Those boys from south London hadn't. All chained up, begging like women, as he'd gone to work on them with that electric sander; junior nothing.

They could whistle for their tea, he thought as he climbed the stairs.

Buenos Mad Dog was going for a snoop. As a kid he'd started out with a bit of B&E. Even now he got an incredible buzz from prowling someone else's house.

There were five doors leading off the landing; he went room to room tossing drawers.

Three rooms down and nothing of worth; door four was locked tight.

Buenos Mad Dog pulled out his wallet, removed one of his many platinum credit cards and popped the lock. He took a moment to congratulate himself for still having the knack, before opening the door.

Buenos Mad Dog stared in horror at the scene in front of him.

The bedroom had been turned into an abattoir.

17

Chief Inspector Brogan watched as Detective Stone came running out of the hotel, jumped into his car and tore away through a set of red lights.

Sergeant Johnson must have gotten hold of Stone quickly. Brogan had only rung the front desk five minutes earlier, sounding like a concerned doctor, using a handkerchief to mask his voice.

He could take on one of them, but both would have been stretching it.

Brogan picked up the radio. "Alpha One, this is team leader over."

"Come in, team leader," a static-filled voice crackled.

"I am requesting an update on the situation," he said, hoping that Zach had completed his part in the plan.

"The car with your informants has left the grounds. We are waiting on your go command."

Brogan knew he should have been there at the finish, possibly with some witty comment to I-Knows, just like you would get in a film, but in truth Brogan didn't watch many films. He had no real history with I-Knows anyway, other than having attacked him to protect his late mother's possessions when they were children. That had been a lifetime ago; he hadn't thought about that incident for years.

*

That was, of course, until Zach had first appeared in the city.

Mardy had mentioned him one evening. *"I've even got this man I use, a guy I know, called Zachariah Plum. He's a good man; I've started using him to look after some of the girls. He's got connections down in* **[REDACTED]** *and can get us an introduction."*

Brogan had, at the time, agreed to Mardy's plan. He had done it unwillingly and with a great deal of hesitancy, but he had not done it blindly. Brogan had run a check on Zachariah Plum and his so-called *connections*.

The bane of a senior police officer's life was the propensity of training courses and seminars one had to attend. Pain though they were, it was an excellent chance to – what is it in management speak? – to network. Brogan knew police officers throughout the country and they knew him.

At those weekends, proper coppers stood out to each other, like islands of decency in a sea of management types.

Brogan had reached out to one of these men, a senior detective from **[REDACTED]**. The detective had promised to get back to him as soon as possible.

It had taken a couple of days, but he finally returned Brogan's call.

"I've checked out this Zachariah Plum. He's well known down here," the policeman had started to tell Brogan, after the brief niceties were out of the way. "He's got a long old rap sheet from when he was a kid, burglary mostly."

"Anything more recent than that?" Brogan had asked.

"Nope, he hits nineteen and that's it."

"You are saying that he has started toeing the line?"

"What this guy? God no, this is the good bit; I mentioned your man's name around and one of my colleagues recognises it, and starts getting interested. This Zach has been MIA for a while now; my colleague assumed he was one of the Disappeared?"

"One of the Disappeared?"

"Yeah, look, this is talking out of school," the detective said. "My bosses will never admit this publicly, but we have got a serious organised gang problem down here. There's one gang in particular, the Farrell family."

"The Farrell family?" Brogan asked, the name sounding familiar.

"Yeah, these are very serious guys. Apparently there has been some internal wrangling for the last few years, but that has been sorted out now."

"Sorted out? What do you mean?"

"The head of the family goes by the name of I-Knows, real name Jesse Farrell."

Brogan went silent at his end of the phone, childhood memories coming back in Technicolor.

"I-Knows," the detective continued, "has apparently done some spring cleaning. Some of the top people in his firm have disappeared. Rumours are they've disappeared permanently."

"Have their families contacted you?" Brogan asked.

"That's the thing. The people who have disappeared are I-Knows' own brothers."

"What, you think this man has killed his own brothers?" Brogan said incredulously.

"Like I said, these people are serious."

"So where does Zach fit into all this?"

"One of the people who went missing was Zach's father, I-Knows' cousin. We assumed father and son were in the same hole, but now he's shown up in your town?"

"No," Brogan lied. "His name came up in a drugs investigation we are running, but it's not a current name, more just background."

"Listen, I've been up front with you," the detective said, his tone changing, having sensed the lie. "So I expect the same courtesy."

"Like I say it's an old name and probably not related to anything. If it is I promise I'll be back in touch," Brogan said, finishing the call.

He sat at his desk for a long time after that, thinking back to his childhood and Jesse Farrell, or I-Knows as he now seemed to be called.

*

Well, bye, bye, Jesse, Brogan thought, sitting there now opposite the hotel. He probably wouldn't ever see him again; at least not after the briefing he had given the Tactical Operations Squad.

"I repeat, we are still waiting on your go command," Spazhead crackled over the radio, desperate for some more action.

"Ok, everyone be careful," Brogan said, into the radio.

"Go command acknowledged."

Brogan switched off the radio and pulled out from his parking spot. He drove down the alley that ran around the back of the Central Hotel and got out of the car. Checking no one could see him, he opened the boot.

Brogan wore a set of the white overalls and shoe covers that were usually used for keeping crime scenes intact. He put a coat on over them.

Looking around again he pulled out a heavy duffle bag and slipped a gun into his coat pocket.

It was the second time he had dressed like this today. The first time had been outside Mardy's mansion, well before dawn, with Emily hogtied on the back seat.

The clothes he'd been wearing then, along with the safe full of cassette tapes, were now in a black bag ready to be burnt.

He had all of those pesky, incriminating cassette tapes now.

All except one.

18

"Where's my tea?" Bam-Bam asked.

"Upstairs," Buenos Mad Dog said hollowly.

"What's it doing upstairs?"

"Wait," I-Knows ordered, seeing the look on his lieutenant's face. "What's wrong?"

"Upstairs it's... oh God, it's horrible."

Bam-Bam and Roy looked at each other, before pulling their guns, suppressed Uzi 9mms, and rushing upstairs.

I-Knows picked up his cane and followed after them.

Bam-Bam and Roy stood looking into the room as I-Knows got to the top of the stairs. He strode past them into the midst of the slaughter.

"This is the man and woman we have been waiting for," he said.

"How do you know? They've got no heads," Bam-Bam's voice came out weakly.

I-Knows dragged his eyes off the scene and turned to the door. "It is time to go. We have been set up."

"There are people coming up the drive," Buenos Mad Dog shouted from downstairs.

I-Knows pulled out his gun from an underarm holster and unsheathed the rapier from his cane. "Get to the car," he ordered.

19

The four of them crossed the lawn in a cover formation, guns up.

Spazhead had hoped they'd make the distance, from the tree line to the back of the garage, before being spotted. But, as the first suspect ran around the side of the building, he realised they hadn't been fast enough.

"Police, police, police," he shouted, while sprinting at full speed.

Target 1 was nearly at his car when he saw them and fired a short burst of machine-gun fire. It was rushed and high, bullets mosquitoing overhead.

They returned fire, still moving forward, rounds Swiss cheesing their way through the car.

Target 1 was thrown backwards with multiple tags.

"Cover him," Spazhead ordered one of his unit, while gesturing for the other two to follow him in a wide circle around the garage.

Thirty yards in front of them, the back door on to the patio was flung open and three more black men bundled their way out.

Spazhead's eyes locked with the first man out, Target 2. A look of hate passed between them before the target started firing, getting off a short-controlled burst, covering the other two's retreat back into the house.

To his right, Spazhead saw Boz go down, tumbling head over heels.

Spazhead returned fire, no spurts of three, body-body-head

combinations, but straight out, empty the clip, fully automatic; Target 2 was ripped apart.

Spazhead shifted his sights to the doorway. Identifying and then firing the rest of his magazine into the short-lived Target 3. The stupid prick didn't even try to get out of the way, just spread his body wide, taking all the tags.

As Target 3 crumpled into the house, Spazhead remembered back to the briefing. *I-Knows never travels alone; he will have bodyguards.*

*

Chief Inspector Brogan had pulled up after they had cleared the church and were taking off their gear. He made them gather round and had duct-taped a series of photos to the side of their van.

Spazhead didn't like Brogan; the man was nothing more than a weak, little paper pusher. But hey, two jobs in one day, great stuff. Normally they were stuck in that basement for months at a time.

"We have had concrete information telling us that this man, I-Knows, real name Jesse Farrell," Brogan said pointing at a photo, "has recently entered the city. This man, I-Knows, runs a criminal organisation based in **[REDACTED]** and has, over the last five years, been expanding northward into London. The Metropolitan Police believe that his gang is responsible for upwards of thirty murders during this time." Brogan looked around at the officers. "Gentlemen, this I-Knows has been successful in his expansion into London and it now looks like our fair city is next on his list."

"Why do you think that?" Cave Troll wanted to know.

"My source puts him at the residence of one Mardy Davies, a local businessman and possible small-time criminal."

"Who's your source?" Spazhead asked.

"I will come to that in a minute. I-Knows never travels alone; he will have bodyguards. His bodyguards will be heavily armed. Most likely it will be these three men," Brogan said, pointing to the other pictures on the van. "I've got the files for you to read through. You will notice from I-Knows' file that he has never been convicted of a crime. He is too smart and too able to afford very good lawyers. He has, to date, gotten off on charges of murder, blackmail, assault and rape. By all accounts, he indulges in unusually violent sexual practices with white women."

A shared bristling went around Spazhead's men.

"Now getting onto my source, he will be with them when they return to the house, but will leave soon after. His car and all the passengers are to be left unmolested; I want you concentrating on getting these four men. To capture them would be a big feather in all our caps."

*

Brogan had said there were four of them; well, there was only one of them left now – I-Knows, Target 4.

Spazhead threw himself against the wall, next to the back door.

Gaz hit the wall next to him.

Boz lay unmoving on the lawn.

"Officer down, officer down," Spazhead shouted into his radio.

"Moving in for evac," a voice from the support team crackled in response.

Next to him Gaz whooped approval.

Spazhead ignored him. "Bravo Team, Bravo Team. Position?"

"We're at the front door," Cave Troll, the leader of Bravo Team, came back.

Spazhead shouldered the MK7 and drew his pistol. "Ok, there is one in the house, watch out for us. Everyone in."

Gaz whooped again.

They entered the house, Spazhead on point, sweeping each room, left to right.

Kitchen clear.

Dining room clear.

Into the hall and face to face with Bravo Team.

Spazhead gestured for them to take the upstairs while he took the ground floor, Gaz on his six.

They entered the lounge.

A big man, Target 4, Mr I-Knows himself, stood there smiling, arms away from his body a pistol and sword on the table two feet away.

"Look at me, look at me," Spazhead ordered.

Gaz moved to the left, covering him.

"Get down onto your knees. On your knees."

Target 4 smiled at him benignly, before complying.

"Put your hands behind your back."

"Now you be careful where you point that gun," Target 4 said, before complying with the order.

Gaz moved in behind him, cuffing his wrists and giving him a punch in the back of the head. "Less lip."

From where he knelt, I-Knows turned awkwardly to look at him. "Officer, I am handcuffed and not resisting arrest; what you have just done constitutes an assault. I will take your name now."

"Fuck you," Gaz said, illustrating the point by giving him the finger.

"Sarge, get up here," Cave Troll was on the radio.

"Gaz, cover him," Spazhead said, before marching upstairs.

Bravo Team stood on the landing, looking pale; there was vomit on the carpet.

"What are you bunch of woofters doing just…?" He trailed off.

*

"Upsetting, was it?" I-Knows asked, as Spazhead and Bravo Team entered the lounge.

"You did that to them?" Spazhead felt sick.

"I have done nothing illegal. For now, until I have liaised with my brief that is all I will say."

The scene flashed through Spazhead's mind.

He has never been convicted of a crime.

"Also, I wish to be interviewed by your Inspector Brogan."

The lower half of the woman on the bed legs spread wide.

Unusually violent sexual practices with white women.

Spazhead looked at Cave Troll.

Breasts flayed off, no heads, no hands.

Cave Troll caught his look and nodded.

It had been decided.

Spazhead turned to I-Knows. "You're not going to need a brief."

"Alright, who wants to take one for the team?" Cave Troll said, picking up I-Knows' gun from the table. "It's an awfully big gun, Sarge."

The smile fell off I-Knows' face. "Officer, I demand that I am escorted out of here and—"

"Gaz, stand over by the door there, will you?"

It took Gaz's mental process a couple of seconds to catch up. "No way, Sarge."

"Over by the door."

"Oh, come on."

"Gaz, you are wearing a bullet-proof vest, it won't go through it."

"It might," Gaz said, looking panicked. "At least let me put on another one as well then."

Cave Troll shook his flat head. "No, there needs to be a lot of bruising for it to look real."

Gaz reluctantly went and stood by the door, his eyes squeezed shut.

Cave Troll took aim.

"Officers, I demand that you stop this now," I-Knows said, hysteria entering his voice.

"Ready, Gaz?" Cave Troll asked, sighting down the gun.

"Just fucking do it."

"Officer, I swear I had nothing to do with what happened upstairs. I have been set up. I promise that—"

"Wait," Spazhead ordered. He leant in close to I-Knows. "Why should I believe you?"

"We have only been here for half an hour, I swear, the bodies upstairs aren't that fresh."

Spazhead was about to say something when a message came over the radio.

"Sarge." It was one of the support team. "We've checked out their car. There are two heads in the boot; they're wrapped in plastic."

Spazhead shook his head at I-Knows. "Looks like you're shit out of luck, pal."

Cave Troll shot Gaz in the vest and a second later Spazhead put two bullets into I-Knows' face.

"Could you stop pacing?" Alistair asked. "I've got enough on my mind without having to watch you walking back and forth."

Keyes looked at him, before, sheepishly, sitting in the room's one chair.

"You don't seem happy about this situation," Alistair said.

Keyes was silent for a moment before looking at his charge. "I'm not," he said. "How much did she tell you, your girlfriend?"

"Enough? I didn't think it was true originally, I just thought it was a really elaborate way of dumping me. She was in a mental home, you know."

"I didn't believe it either. I thought Stone was winding me up."

"It still could be a wind-up." Alistair smiled sadly.

"I'd like that," Keyes said.

"So what are you getting out of it? Money?"

"That's the second time I've been asked that."

"And how did you answer?"

"A life."

"A life?"

"Stone's kid is really sick; they'll save her."

"Well, I suppose it's a better reason than money."

Keyes looked away for a moment. "And is your girlfriend special?"

"Yes, you know, I told someone today that I loved her."

"And do you?"

Despite everything, Alistair smiled. "Yes, I do. She showed me that I could do better than this."

"She must feel the same way about you."

"I talked to her earlier and can categorically say she doesn't."

"She must feel something, because telling you to escape like that has signed her own death warrant."

Alistair froze, his jaw working, trying to get words out, coming up empty.

Keyes saw the look on his face. "You really didn't know?" He seemed surprised. "You can't go against this stupid Society, but that is just what she did. They are going to sacrifice her in your place."

"You're lying."

Keyes shook his head. "Her dad is a doctor; he's the one who made the offer to save Stone's daughter. He rang earlier and said we had to pick you up. Her parents don't want her to die; they were hoping to present you to the gathering and, I don't know, barter for their daughter's life."

"She is going to get herself killed for me?" Alistair asked, not believing it.

"That's why we've got to take you there."

They sat in silence for a long time.

"I'll make you a deal," Alistair started to say.

The detective looked up at him.

"Open these handcuffs," Alistair finally said.

"Listen, I'm not happy about this, but I'm not letting you go either."

"That's not the deal." Alistair paused for a moment, wanting to get the pitch right in his mind. "You and your partner are a pair of nasty bastards, but I doubt you're murderers. So, I bet being reamed like this must really get under your skin. I'm also willing to bet that after they've fixed Stone's kid, you'll want to get revenge on them."

Keyes was looking at him intently.

"I mean," Alistair continued, "have you ever known your partner to carry a gun?"

Keyes shook his head. "What's the deal?"

"I'll go with you willingly. So what they do to me won't be on your conscience."

"And in return?"

"When you get even with them, you leave Maggie out of it."

"What about her parents?"

"Her parents? Oh, you can fuck them in the ear."

The large detective smiled at this before reaching into his pocket and tossing a set of keys across the room. "If you try any funny business, I'll break both your arms before handcuffing you back to the radiator."

Alistair gave him his sad little smile. "No funny business."

Both of them jumped as there was a knock on the door.

21

Brogan had waited until he got his breath back before knocking on the door. There was no point in panting orders.

The decision about Keyes' fate had indeed been hard reached. Keyes was basically a good man, if not a bit easily led by his partner. But one fact swung it: he was prepared to let a murder go. And that to Brogan had been the deciding factor in his decision.

The big detective was surprised to see him standing there, dressed in a white SOC suit and carrying a gun.

Brogan shoved his gun into Keyes' face. "Back up," he ordered, pushing the silencer hard into Keyes' gullet, forcing him back. "Turn around by the window and kneel," his voice belying arguments.

Once Keyes was knelt down facing the window Brogan scanned the dower room, now made smaller by the three people in it.

"Alistair, are you ok?" he asked.

"Not really," Alistair said, looking at the unfolding scene in front of him.

Brogan threw a set of handcuff keys onto the floor. "Undo your cuffs and stand up."

Alistair very slowly did as he was told.

Brogan's gun was still hovering inches from the back of Keyes' head while, with the other hand, he dug into his bag, pulling out some handcuffs. "Put these on him."

"Fuck off, he's massive," Alistair said, trying to judge the distance to the door.

Brogan swung the barrel of the gun to point at Alistair; it was hypnotising. "I am not going to repeat myself."

"Ok, ok," Alistair said, before cuffing the big man's unresisting hands behind his back.

"Now, put the key I gave you on the bed and handcuff yourself back to the radiator," Brogan ordered, still keeping the gun on him.

"I could just wait outside," Alistair offered, still eyeing the door.

Brogan gave him a look.

Alistair shrugged and went back to the radiator. "How do you know my name anyway? If you're here to rescue me, it's a pretty crappy attempt."

"How do I know your name? Good question, I should tell you that, it will put everything I am about to do in perspective," Brogan said, putting the handcuff key into his pocket. He turned to the kneeling policeman. "Detective Keyes, I want you to get to your feet and sit on the bed."

The big man, all handcuffed up, did this with some difficulty.

Content that everyone was where he wanted them, Brogan continued to speak. "It all revolves around you, young Alistair."

"What does?"

"Everything I am and everything I am about to do to this so-called policeman stems from your actions."

"Hey, they were the ones that brought me—" Alistair started to say, but Brogan talked over him.

"I've been with you for years, you see, keeping an eye out for you, protecting you and so forth. I was even the one that got you a job with Danny. Even the same type of job as you had been doing previously. Except, of course, that the product you mule around now is not going to cause anyone to die from an overdose."

"What are you talking about?"

"Oh come on, you know perfectly well what I am talking about, I can tell from your tone of voice." Brogan turned his attention back to Keyes. "I'd watch young Alistair here, if I were you. He can turn very violent."

"I don't know what you're talking about," Keyes said.

"That is why I am explaining," Brogan snapped. "You see, Alistair, I was there when you attacked that despicable heroin dealer, Moses Jones. Moses was trying to run, wasn't he? He knew people would be after him for selling that poison. But you stopped him. I saw you wrestle him back into the house."

"You were involved in that?" Keyes asked Alistair.

Brogan ignored him. "I saw the state that you left him in. He was very badly hurt, too hurt to actually be scared of me. Can you imagine that? He showed no fear at all. Even after I had spread around the petrol, even after I had put the barrel of this gun up to his eye, even after I pushed the barrel into him so hard his eyeball burst, nothing. No fear at all, just this small weak smile. Goodness knows what you did to him, young Alistair, but you did something to me as well."

"Look, he had it coming and—"

"It was odd," Brogan continued, speaking almost to himself. "I'd never had such a real craving for something before, but this sleazy, dying piece of nothing did not deem I was fit to be feared. The cheek of the man, even at the end, he died without a trace of it."

"You, you were the one who killed him," Keyes said. "You had us looking for that used car salesman, thinking he'd disappeared to the continent, but it was you. You killed them both, didn't you?"

"I bought them both redemption from their acts, Detective, as I am going to do to you."

"Fuck you, you murderer, I'm placing you under arrest," Keyes said trying to get up.

Brogan regarded Keyes with a look of thorough disdain. "You honestly thought I was some weak-kneed paper pusher, didn't you?" he said.

Keyes stared back at him radiating hatred.

"Is that what you think?" Brogan's voice was getting shriller.

"You think you can walk into my house and order me around, then tell me to retire from my city? My city?"

The gun was inches from Keyes' face now.

"And kill a girl. You think that you can get away with killing a girl and that I won't do something about it? In my own city?" Brogan's voice was pitching hysterically. "Well, do you?"

"Go fuck yourself, pal."

The silencer turned the weapon's report into nothing more than a whisper.

Keyes started screaming, one of his ears was shredded-deaf and powder-burned to fuck. Brogan shoved the barrel of the gun into the cavity, twisting, scraping, dragging the big man off the bed and back onto his knees. Pushing him forwards, forcing him facedown onto the floor, choking him on carpet, choking him on his own blood.

"Where is the tape you had of me? Where is it?"

Keyes said something through the blood; it sounded like *"Fuck you, fairy."*

Brogan turned him over. "Where is it?" he demanded, twisting the gun in the gristle, making Keyes squeal out *"Fuck you"* more clearly.

Brogan stood blood splattered and furious.

And then there was calm.

Brogan seemed to subside.

"Detective Keyes – David, David, look at me," he said, rolling the quietly whimpering detective over.

Keyes was pale, shock setting in fast.

"It will be over soon, but I need to know where that *fucking* tape of me, talking to Mardy Davies, is." Brogan caressed the big man's hair. "And David, I need you to look at me, so I can see that you are afraid and that you know you have done something that is wrong, so very wrong."

He fired again, this time close up. The bullet entered Keyes' stomach just below the rib cage.

The report was muffled.

Brogan put the barrel into the hole, twisting it, gouging it, repeating, "This will redeem you," over and over.

"Jesus. What the hell are you doing?" Alistair shouted, from the radiator.

Keyes gurgled, weakly shaking his head, *"No, don't."*

"How does that feel?" Brogan asked, grinding the weapon in the hole.

"I'll tell you everything," Keyes sobbed, spasming up blood.

"I know, I know," Brogan chided. "You'll tell me everything, but that will be later. For now, I'm just going to…"

He stopped and turned, as Alistair rose up behind him and turned very violent.

22

The churchyard, for want of a better description, was as quiet as the grave. The pastor checked the bank of monitors for the final time, before he turned them off and left his office.

Pastor Morris was no longer scared; Pastor Morris was no longer lost from the Lord.

He now knew where the Society would be meeting and, having taken Chief Inspector Brogan's confession, knew that God did indeed move in mysterious ways.

*

He'd tried to explain, to Chief Inspector Brogan, he couldn't do it, at least not in a semblance of something that meant a jot to his religion – *"I am not a Catholic. I cannot take a confession."*

But the policeman had already started talking, already started outlining the bloody life and times of Chief Inspector Jonathan Brogan.

"I have in my time, Father, killed a number of people. In truth I wouldn't know where to start," he'd said, glancing at the bank of monitors. Stone and Keyes were pacing between the pews. "But there was only one person I killed that made me feel truly guilty. And that is the only person I need forgiveness for."

Again Pastor Morris tried to say something, but Brogan ignored him.

"You see, there was a disease in this city. Drugs were ravaging it, tearing out its heart. Something needed to be done." He sighed, a thin smile cresting across his face. "A large shipment of heroin briefly came into my possession." He paused, searching for the right words. "I ensured that it became contaminated. There were a lot of deaths, Father. But it cleaned out the disease; my actions saved a lot of lives."

"How many died?" Pastor Morris asked, stunned at witnessing a callousness that outstripped even his own.

"How many? Nine within the first week."

"How weren't you found out?"

"I ran the investigation. We concentrated on finding the suppliers."

"And you killed them as well?" Pastor Morris asked, already knowing the answer.

Brogan nodded before continuing. "I offered them redemption for their acts, Father."

"You offered *redemption*? What do you think gives you the authority to do that?"

"Because it is my city," Brogan said, as if it was the most obvious thing in the world.

"And who can offer you redemption?"

"Oh, I think I am way past that point now."

Pastor Morris leant forward, green eyes intense, voice taking on that hell and brimstone baritone. "No, I don't believe that, it's never too late. The Lord will always take you back into his fold. But you must want it. You must pray for it. You must realise your sins and feel the guilt, and seek the forgiveness that the Lord offers you. And that, my son, will save you."

Brogan looked away, seemingly startled by the ferocity of the pastor's conviction. He spoke again, softly now. "There were two people who became caught up in it all. One of them died from the heroin and the other saw her boyfriend hospitalised for a long time."

"Trish?"

"Yes, they were the only two that made me question my actions, made me feel guilty. Is that enough, Father? Is that enough for forgiveness?"

The pastor pondered for a moment. "Well, it's a start, I suppose."

Brogan sat silently considering this. He seemed to brighten, push away the ghosts of the past. "A start." He nodded. "Well, that will do for now, I suppose. And, in turn, I will tell you where you can find the Society."

"How do you know?"

Brogan laughed humourlessly. "I think that is definitely a confession for another day."

*

Down in the operations centre, everyone stood around, uneasily, waiting for the off. Their little band was down to six people now, including Gavin who still didn't seem right after his run in with the two detectives.

There was a crudely drawn map of the slate quarry spread over a table. The area the quarry covered was massive, the extraction of slate now being undertaken on a scale that far outstripped previous decades.

"They've gone for a quarry again," the pastor said, looking at the map. "Except this one is still in use."

"But it's so big. Where do you think they'll conduct their *ceremony*?" Jason asked.

"Well, there's only one entrance. We'll put Gavin and Donald on the Sixty here," Al said, pointing at the map. "I want the Society penned in the kill zone."

"Are you sure they can handle it?" the pastor asked, looking over at the Sixty, which was wrapped in plastic.

"They'll have to; it's the best way to stop any of the Society escaping when we blow the charges."

"And the charges? Where are we going to set them? The place is so big they could gather anywhere."

Al's trip to the back of beyond had proved very successful. On one of the tables lay two duffle bags rammed with enough explosives to turn the chapel into a smoking crater twenty times over.

"Well, that's the thing; there are not enough explosives for me to cover the whole area. I'll have to see exactly where they have gathered before I set them," Al said.

The pastor looked once more at the map and sighed inwardly. Al was right: it was an awfully big mining operation and they would need to lay the explosives right under the noses of the Society.

"It's time to go," the pastor said. "But first, I think it is right and fitting that we should pray."

Pastor Morris knew the Bible, he knew a hundred prayers, but oddly the one that came out of his mouth came from a film; the prayer seemed fitting. He didn't know why it popped into his head; he hadn't thought about the film for years. It had been one that his dad had taken him to the cinema to see when he was a child – the story of *Cromwell*.

The prayer was simple, the prayer was felt from his heart – "Oh Lord, how busy I must be this day, if I forget thee, do not forget me."

listair didn't come out of his daze until he'd walked through the open door and climbed over the mountain of mail. He was out of breath and sweating heavily, unable to remember walking up the big, winding, fuck off hill to his house.

He was pretty sure he'd just killed another human being.

*

Handcuffed to the radiator, Alistair had recoiled at the torture that was going on in front of him.

He'd forced his shaking hands to un-cuff himself, using the key that the big detective had given him.

He'd forced himself up, scrabbling in his back pocket until his sweat-slicked hands had found the cosh and then came out swinging.

The madman had started to turn, but hadn't been fast enough; thwap, thwap, thwap. Collapsing under a volley of blows.

"Get him off me," Keyes begged, weak and quiet.

Alistair pulled the limp form of Brogan away, smacking him on the back of the head again for good measure.

Alistair looked at the big detective. He wasn't in a good state.

Keyes blubbed quietly, bleeding out life.

"Where's Maggie?" Alistair asked.

Keyes coughed up blood, red and frothy, eyes staring at nothing.

"God help me, I am going to wake this cunt up and let him carry on," Alistair threatened impotently. The cracking noise that followed his third swing hadn't sounded too clever.

Keyes' eyes fell on him, unfocused, tears welling.

"Where is she?"

Keyes said something, quiet, imperceptible.

Alistair leaned forward, gently wiping blood from the dying detective's lips, asking him again.

The answer came out slow, raspy, weak. "The quarry out in the Gower."

Alistair took a second to place it. "What, the massive one?"

He'd been there once on a school trip. They all had to put on yellow hard hats and stand in front of a cliff as the teacher pointed out different layers of strata. Two of the kids had been caught trying to steal blasting caps from a shed.

"The massive one?" Alistair repeated, slapping Keyes who was slipping out of consciousness.

The detective tried to nod.

"I'll ring for an ambulance."

Keyes shook his head slowly, gripping onto Alistair's arm with the last of his strength. Final words time: "Tell Stone to get them for me."

Keyes' grip went limp.

In a daze now, Alistair collected his bag, shovelling in guns, Stone's from the table and Brogan's from the floor. They weren't going to get him for lack of shooting back.

The second gun was still slippery with blood, the end where the bullet came out all gunked up with, what could only be described as, bits.

Alistair booked, stumbling down the stairs and out across the hotel lobby.

He got some funny looks from the washed-out ladies smoking in the foyer and the skinny guy behind the front desk shouted something after him.

Alistair just kept moving, pushing his way out into the cold, dying afternoon.

*

Watching one man twist a gun barrel around in a freshly made bullet hole, while you are trying to unlock some handcuffs with shaking hands, would affect everybody at some level. And it was only now, as Alistair was halfway up the stairs in his house, did his brain reset itself and click back on. Rebooted and ready to save his girlfriend.

The open door.

Well, not completely open, but it hadn't been locked, which Ebin was normally quite good at; it was one of his few nods towards security.

Alistair stopped halfway up the stairs and strained his ears to listen. The house was quiet, quieter than he had ever noticed, unnervingly quiet.

Alistair put the heavy bag down and unzipped it, not taking his eyes off the top of the stairs; he scrabbled around for one of the guns. He found the sticky one first. It was one of those six shooters, like Dirty Harry had used, but not as big. It was more like the sort that the fat guy from *Beverly Hills Cop* had used. Alistair assumed there were still bullets in it. He wasn't sure how to open the bloody thing to check.

The house was still emanating silence as Alistair walked up the stairs, barrel first. By the time he got to the landing his arm was aching; guns are really heavy.

He put it down by his side.

There was a faint noise coming from Ebin's room as he inched along the corridor.

The TV was on, snowing static.

Alistair carried on, up the next flight of stairs, past his and the weirdo's room.

461

On up the last set of stairs to Clancy's room.

This is where Alistair was aiming for. He needed to find the car keys and then work out how to drive. It couldn't be that difficult.

"What are you doing with a gun?"

Alistair spun round, raising the gun and pulling the trigger.

There was a loud silence as nothing happened.

Nothing, except for Ebin standing there, looking shocked, his face beaten into mush.

24

rogan came to, sucking threadbare carpet. Something wasn't right; he passed his hand back and forth in front of his face, seeing it, not seeing it, seeing it, not seeing it.

He'd lost the vision in his right eye.

Pulling himself up and stumbling to the mirror, he saw the pupil was big, un-dilated and filled up with blood. Brogan turned his head slowly, the back of his skull was mashed in, punctured out of shape.

Jesus fuck.

His phone started ringing with an annoying chirp, chirp. He tried to answer it, all thumbs, all butter fingers.

"Hello" – Right ear nothing.

"Hello" – Left ear an answer.

"It's me, where are you? We're waiting." It was Zach on the line, wanting to know if I-Knows' reign was over.

Brogan looked at his watch; he hadn't been out for too long.

"I will be there in twenty minutes."

"What?"

"I will be there in twenty."

"You sound drunk, have you been drinking?"

"What? No, I have not."

"Why are you slurring your words so badly then?"

Brogan looked at himself in the mirror. "That does not matter. I will be there in twenty," he said, before closing his phone.

He turned to look around the room. Keyes' large body was on the floor, his face a sickly clammy white, the blood around the bullet hole already starting to congeal.

The room would be awash with forensics. Alistair had disappeared and Brogan still didn't have the tape. Tape first, forensics second, Alistair last.

The tape – Keyes had put it back into his pocket after playing it last night. Brogan went straight for the jacket, hitting lucky three pockets in.

On to forensics. Opening his bag, Brogan pulled out a cheap plastic petrol can and liberally covered Keyes' body, splashing what was left over the walls.

The Central Hotel had not had a fire inspection for years; they paid a lot of money to make sure of that.

Brogan walked down the back stairs, away from the smell of smoke.

Now for Alistair.

25

Brogan didn't sound too good," Zach said putting down the receiver.

He and Batty Boy stood at a payphone in the car park by the sea. Reno stood away on his own. Very much on his own.

"What do you mean, didn't sound too good?" Batty Boy asked. Zach shrugged.

"He should be here by now," Batty Boy said, getting impatient.

They had been waiting in the car park for over half an hour. Batty wanted to know what had happened to I-Knows and if he needed to start running.

"He'll be here in twenty minutes," Zach said, acting the picture of calm even though underneath he felt far from it.

He was more nervous now than when they had been driving away from the late Mardy Davies' mansion.

*

"Did you do it?" Zach asked his brother as they crunched gravel down the drive.

"Yep, man. I didn't even need to pop the lock; one of them must have left the boot open. I just dropped the bags in and closed it again."

"That's good," Zach said relieved.

It had been earlier that morning. Everyone had been fast asleep in the non-descript terraced house as Zach and Batty Boy had crept out to go and meet Brogan.

They had met in a park ten minutes' drive away. The place was deserted, a low mist hugging the grass.

Brogan had parked a little way away from them. He exited the car carrying a duffle bag. He looked smaller than Zach remembered him.

Batty Boy must have been thinking the same. "This is the one you're scared of?" he asked incredulously.

Zach shushed him. He was indeed scared of this man.

This was the man who had almost killed him.

*

He hadn't been in the city for that long, but as I-Knows had instructed him, he was making inroads into infiltrating Mardy Davies' organisation.

Zach was already on good terms with Mardy. Mardy liked his pimp get-up and he had taken over the running of the stable.

He'd been trying to sell Mardy on the idea of buying drugs from his connection in **[REDACTED]**. "*Seriously, man, the people I know down there can get you anything.*" Mardy had been reticent though, not biting. Zach couldn't understand it; there was a lot of money to be made in drugs.

It had been a couple of nights later when Danny Howells phoned "*wanting to discuss a bit of business*".

Danny was just out of prison; Danny was in with Mardy – Zach was making inroads.

They met up for a drink. Zach must have been slipped something. He came around all tied up in the dark, feeling sick, his world moving up and down.

"He's awake," he heard Danny say from somewhere above him.

"Get him up on deck then," an unfamiliar voice said.

Danny came down a short set of wooden steps, lifted Zach to his feet and chivvied him out into the light.

Zach squinted in the sun. It took a moment to realise there was no land around him, just a small, fifteen-foot-long boat and a lot of ocean.

The second man was facing away from Zach, driving the boat. He knocked off the engine; they drifted.

"Do you know who I am?" the man asked, turning to face Zach.

Zach had shaken his head no.

"I will ask the question once again, and only once, because I cannot abide liars. Are you ready? Do you know who I am?"

"Yes," Zach said. He'd never seen the man up this close before, only through binoculars. Being here, tied like this, he knew even the truth probably wouldn't save him.

"Good, go on."

"You're a policeman."

"Go on."

"Your name is Jonathan Brogan."

"Very good, Zach, now, why do you think you are in this predicament?"

"Hey, man, I don't know, I work with Mardy, you know. Hey, I ain't been messing with his women or nothing like that."

"Oh come on, Zach, please drop that stupid accent. You know it is not about *messing with any women*. Try again and this time, try and get it right."

Zach, despite the ropes, tried to front up to the policeman. "Look, I don't know why you crazy assholes have brought me out here like this."

Brogan sighed and rubbed his face before shaking his head. "I cannot abide liars," he said to Danny. "Throw him over the side."

Danny, grinning merrily, started to tie the anchor around Zach's legs. Zach tried to kick him off, but to little avail.

Brogan turned away and started looking over the side of the boat. "There's about three-quarters of a mile of water underneath us here," he said conversationally. "It is quite a depth."

"Hey, look, guys, what is it you want? What have I done?"

"Oh come on, Zach, you must know that at least."

Zach thought quickly. Maybe they were bluffing; maybe it was indoctrinate the new boy into the gang time. But that didn't feel right. So far, from what he'd found out, Brogan stayed away from the business end of the gang. He and Mardy only met discreetly.

"I'm here because of I-Knows, aren't I?"

"Bingo," the policeman said. "Now, does Mardy know who you are and who you are working for?"

"No. Why?"

Brogan hadn't answered.

Zach's mind raced, making connections, striving for a way out. One connection made: Brogan didn't trust Mardy, that's why he wasn't on the boat with them. Brogan might think Mardy was in league with I-Knows.

"That was all I need to know," the policeman said, eventually. "Danny, carry on."

"Wait, wait," Zach begged. The truth came spewing out. "I-Knows badly wants to take over this city. I'm here as a spy for him, to get a feel for the lay of the land."

"Are you feeling it?" Danny said, slapping him across the back of the head.

"Danny," Brogan cautioned. "Let him continue."

With difficulty Zach got back to his feet. "I-Knows is planning to come and take over the city and he also wants revenge on you two and Mardy."

"Why? I've never even heard of this stupid-sounding prick," Danny said. "Fuck him, let him come, we'll give him a nice boat ride. Fuck this, John, give me the knife I'll do him now."

Brogan picked up a knife from where it lay and passed it to Danny.

"It's not a case of just drowning you, son." Danny was close behind Zach now. "We have to prick you full of holes first. So in a week or so your body doesn't fill with gas and rise to the surface."

"You need me," Zach said. He addressed Brogan. He was the one in charge. "When I-Knows comes, it will be in force and you won't know when that'll be. He knows all about you already, I told him about you. So you need me to warn you when that day will be."

Brogan seemed to be looking amused at all this. "Why? Why would you tell us? And it better not be to save your life."

"Ok, ok, you want to know the truth. When he comes down, I'll help set him up. I'll even plant evidence on him. It'll be a feather in your cap."

"That is very nice of you, thinking of my career like that."

"No seriously, I want his business. I don't give a shit about this stinking city, I want what's rightfully mine."

"Hey, watch what you say about Swansea," Danny said, poking him with the knife.

"Ow, look it's the truth. When he comes down here, it'll only be with a few of his men. I'll give you plenty of warning, help you set them up."

"Again, why should we trust you?" Brogan asked.

"Because the son of a bitch killed my father, so one day I want the same done to him."

"Hey, John, I'm getting seasick now. Let's get rid of him and head back."

They hadn't though. Brogan seemed to understand what Zach said; Danny had been unhappy, but had gone along with it. Zach had heard Brogan tell Danny not to mention this to Mardy.

As the boat chugged its way home, Brogan came up to Zach. "You work for me now; you come to me when the time is right. And just so you know, you owe me your life."

*

"Why's it taking him so long?" Batty Boy asked again. "He said it'd be twenty minutes over half an hour ago."

"He'll be here soon, just stay calm, ok."

"It's difficult to stay calm. We've got a car with two dead bodies in it parked around the corner and for all you know I-Knows could be alive and coming here right now."

"No, you don't know this Brogan. He'll have dealt with I-Knows."

Batty Boy stopped his pacing. "Fine, we'll wait. So what's the plan when he gets here? Do we pop him or not?"

"Look, I don't know."

"Well, when will you know? After he's turned around and arrested us?"

In truth, Zach wasn't sure; it hadn't been part of his original plan, but his original plan had gone to shit after leaving Mardy's house.

*

After leaving I-Knows in the mansion, Zach had repeatedly tried to contact Daryl and Tiny on their phones. He was going to tell them that the plan had changed – bring Danny to the unassuming council house.

Zach had something special lined up for Danny.

Zach needed insurance to keep him safe from Brogan. That insurance would be Danny.

Back home, in the countryside outside **[REDACTED]**, was a special farm. The farm was a long way from anywhere and underneath one of the outhouses was a series of cells. This was where I-Knows held certain people. People he wanted kept alive. There was one bloke who apparently had been there for twelve years. That would be Danny's new home, living indefinitely in a five-by-seven foot cell, as insurance against Brogan trying anything.

That was the plan at least, but it was hampered by Daryl and Tiny not answering their phones.

He had thought about bringing them in on the demise of I-Knows, but they were too loyal to their master.

470

That meant that there was only one thing for them. There were two body bags in the back of the car with their names on.

"Shit," Zach said. "Right, we'll have to go to Danny's house. Turn left at the next junction."

Ten minutes later they were cruising down Danny's street.

"Hey, there's their car," Batty said.

It was empty; they double parked and checked the house. Peering through the window Zach saw legs and blood – *Shit, there goes the plan.*

They had climbed the back fence.

The back door was open. The kitchen was a mess.

They made Karl search through Tiny's pockets to find the car keys, slapping him away from staring at his friend's body.

They had bagged up Daryl.

They had bagged up Tiny – *get in there, you fat fuck.*

Batty Boy brought Tiny's car around to the back of the house.

They'd got hernias squeezing the two bodies in the boot.

Back in the house, they made Reno put a shotgun into Danny's hand and then put one into Kieran's hand, barrels facing each other. It was a poor cover up.

They drove the two cars out of the estate calmly, Zach thinking up a new plan, weighing the pros and cons of just capping Brogan.

26

I t was getting dark as Al parked the minibus down a rutted track, deep in some woods.

The pastor checked his map; they were about three miles away from the quarry. It was going to be a hard slog across country, lugging an awful lot of heavy equipment.

He checked his watch. "Do we have everything we need?"

Al was shouldering one of the duffle bags; he patted it gingerly. "This little lot will be more than enough."

Pastor Morris smiled and moved away from him slightly.

"What about the victim?" Donald asked, coming up behind them.

"We're not going to let them burn anyone," the pastor said, unable to meet Donald's keen stare.

He shared a look with Al. It had already been decided that Donald would be away from the action, in case his noble streak kicked in. They both knew that the six of them couldn't do a lot of saving today. Today was for killing.

With Al on point, the little group headed off through the woods.

27

while ago, Clancy had given them all an impromptu driving lesson in a deserted car park. Alistair still remembered some of the basics: how to change gears, how the indicators worked and to never, under any circumstances, let someone in a BMW out.

Even after such an intensive course, driving out of the city had been a stressful affair. He'd already lost a wing mirror and the fucking gears were a nightmare. There had been some really bad screeching noises coming from the front of the car. Clancy was going to be well pissed off at him.

As the traffic had dropped off, Alistair more or less had it down. As long as he didn't have to try and find reverse.

Outside of the city, night started coming in fast. Alistair tried to put the headlights on, but only managed to get the windscreen wipers to work. Operation Ivy filled the car, speaker-rattling loud.

Alistair parked up in a lay-by a mile shy of the quarry. He was seriously lacking a plan, feeling scared and starting to wish he'd accepted Ebin's offer to come with him.

*

"Is that a real gun?" Ebin had asked. His voice was distant and he looked concussed from the obvious beating he had taken.

"Yep."

"Why didn't it go off when you tried to shoot me?"

"I didn't try and shoot *you*. I didn't realise it was you and I've no idea why it didn't fire," Alistair said, looking at the gun. "Ah, here we go, this little flicky thing is on. I suppose that must be the safety."

"I'd be careful with that then."

Ebin wasn't in a good way. There had been one time a couple of months ago when Alistair had spilt coffee on Ebin's foot. Ebin had demanded he be taken to the burns unit down in the hospital and had gone on about the incident for weeks. Nearly getting shot was a lot more serious than a minor scalding, but, as yet, he'd failed to raise any comment.

"What happened to your face?" Alistair asked, helping Ebin to sit down on Clancy's bed. He sat next to him.

"Oh, my face? There were two men here earlier. They were the same ones who smashed up Donald's room. They said they were policemen and were looking for you. I said that I didn't know where you were and they started pushing me. I told them *I didn't truck with no trash*, in one of my funny accents and then they beat me up." Ebin was looking at the floor, looking sadder than ever. "So I told them you were at Danny's house. Sorry about that."

Alistair put an arm round him. "Don't worry, they didn't find me," he lied.

Ebin gave him a tired little smile. "You fancy a joint?"

"No, I can't. I've got to go and somehow save Maggie."

"A joint for the road then. There is always time for that."

Alistair smiled at his friend. "Come on then, but it'd better be quick."

As they left Clancy's room Alistair picked up the car keys off the table.

Downstairs Ebin started rolling a joint; he did this slowly, dropping baccy everywhere. "You know you could forget about Maggie," he slurred, not even noticing the mess he was making. "There are plenty more fish in the sea."

Alistair was up pacing. "I can't, I've got to go."

"I'll come with you then, back you up."

"Thanks, but I've got to do this on my own. Besides, you don't seem in a good way. Look, I'm going to leave this bag here under your bed. If, for some reason, I'm not back by the morning, take it and go to visit Mordechai at university for a couple of weeks."

Ebin didn't answer; he had passed out. Alistair checked his pulse, before putting him in the best semblance of the recovery position he could remember. As he left, Alistair grabbed the big chopping knife from the kitchen and, after one last look around, headed for the door.

✻

He'd never got his joint for the road, which was probably a good thing; Alistair was going to need a clear head for the rest of the evening.

He just couldn't shake this all-pervading feeling that he wouldn't be seeing Ebin ever again.

Sitting there in the lay-by, he fought to shake that feeling off. He was going to save Maggie and everything was going to be alright; except, he didn't think so. Whoever these people were, they were powerful and he was what? Sitting in a stolen car with one wing mirror.

He needed to come up with a plan to save Maggie. A plan to ensure they could leave and would not be chased. Not tonight, not ever.

He thought back to Trish and their last time together outside the Coach House. He thought of Maggie. He thought of the people he would be facing tonight and he forced the hate to build. He let the hate consume his body, fire off every fibre and down every nerve ending.

Right, you idiot, start thinking.

28

'll be there in twenty minutes." It had taken him thirty, driving badly, slewing across lanes.

The roof of the hotel was already smouldering as he inched his car forward to the mouth of the alley. He saw Stone sprinting across the road, ignoring car horns, pushing past the thronging whores and into the building.

Brogan floored the pedal, pulling out into traffic like a drunk; more car horns, the radio spitting out panicked talk.

He'd told them to meet him in the car park by the sea. Zach and his brother, along with Karl Reno, were standing there waiting for him. They looked on edge.

In the distance, a thunderstorm was rolling in across the bay, dubbing out the horizon.

Brogan, unsteadily, got out of the car.

"Shit, man, you've got a massive hole in the side of your head," the younger brother told him.

Zach shushed him. "What's happened to I-Knows? Are they dead?"

The radio had been alive with rapid chatter on the way over:

"The fucking bastards were using armour-piercing rounds."

"Officer, this is control, maintain radio protocol."

"The fucking bastard. He had the wrong sort of ammo."

Brogan nodded. "They all died, but killed two of my men in the process."

"They've killed a lot more than that in their time," Zach said.

"You did as I told you then? Put the heads in their boot before leaving?" Brogan asked.

Batty Boy smiled proudly. "It only took a second."

"It was you who killed Emily," Reno said, finally seeing everything.

Brogan looked at him, with his one working eye. "Oh yes, and believe me it took time."

✶

Mardy had been wearing a dressing gown when he answered the door. It had taken Brogan five minutes of ringing the bell before he surfaced. Mardy reeked of alcohol and was half asleep. He never even asked why Brogan was dressed in a white SOC suit and how he had gotten past the front gate.

"What?" he slurred instead.

"I've got someone for you in the car."

Mardy had stumbled out of the house and sworn, as his bare feet landed on the gravel.

"That's Emily," he said, seeming to wake up a bit. "You brought her back! Is she asleep?"

"For now, yes," Brogan said as he came behind him with the chloroform-soaked cloth.

Emily and Mardy had woken in the master bedroom, sitting facing each other, sitting taped to chairs, sitting on plastic sheeting, dressed in their underwear.

Brogan stood between them, off to the side, dressed in his white jumpsuit.

Mardy tried to talk, tried to talk through the tape, his mouth and nose hurting badly. Chloroform blistered, like they never show happening in the films.

"This is not going to be an easy time for any of us," Brogan said, turning his head slowly to look at them both. "We all go back such a long way that this hurts me. It really does hurt me. But I have got to leave you both looking just right. And it will not hurt me as much as the betrayal I have felt from both of you." He turned towards Emily first. "Now, Emily, let me see if I have got this right. You have grown tired of Mardy. You think you are smarter than him and deserve to be in charge of everything; I can understand that. But what I do not understand is why you had to come to me in such a way, blackmailing me like that. You knew the torch I used to hold for you and now I feel that you have just spat on it."

Emily had been staring at him with a mixture of loathing, fear and anger. Now her stare softened. It turned into a smile.

She tried to speak, the tape making this impossible.

Brogan went up to her, kneeling down to be at her eye level, his fingers on the tape's corner.

He stopped and shook his head slightly. "I'm sorry, Emily, there really is nothing you could say that I want to hear. You will just come out with sweetened niceties to try and save yourself, but neither of us will believe them and, to be honest, we both know you are better than that." He caressed her hair gently before standing and turning to Mardy.

Emily thrashed uselessly at her bonds.

"But Mardy, it's you I am puzzled at and I must say very hurt. The tapes of you and I talking are turning up everywhere. Are you giving them out as prizes?"

Mardy stared back not breaking eye contact.

"Now I have found a lot of tapes with Emily. Do you know where she was by the way? She was, I suppose the term is, shacked up with Karl Reno. Why you ever trusted that boy is beyond me. But back to the tapes. Now, I am sure I have most of them, but I cannot be completely sure, because, between her and two of my detectives, everyone in the city seems to have a copy. So I am going to take off your gag and you are going to tell me exactly what you have been up to and how you are involved with the Society."

Brogan came forward to remove the gag. He stopped. "And Mardy, just so you know, this is your only chance to come clean. It is your opportunity to find redemption. If you do not want to take that opportunity then it will be a long and painful evening. Or what is left of it," Brogan said, looking at his watch.

Brogan removed the gag.

"Fuck you, do you know what I'll do to you when I... mmm mmm."

"What did I just say?" Brogan shouted, spitting mad, having replaced the gag. "I said not to do that, but you wouldn't listen so now... now you are both going to pay."

He snatched up the duffle bag that had been lying on the floor and shook the contents out onto the bed.

Brogan threw the bag to the floor and picked up one of the implements from the bed. It was a saw, small and glistening, more suited to the operating theatre than sitting in a tool box. "This is on your head," he said to Mardy, his voice shrill, waving the saw in his face.

He turned to Emily.

He sent her and the chair crashing to the floor.

He started low, starting below the ankle, below where she had been tied.

Mardy tried to look away. Brogan stopped what he was doing, grabbing electrical tape, taping his head in position.

He went back to Emily, starting on a new bit.

Mardy had tried to close his eyes.

"This is your doing; you are going to watch this," Brogan said.

Mardy stayed eyes scrunched up. Brogan went back to the bed. Brogan chose a scalpel. Mardy screamed and thrashed as Brogan cut off his eyelids.

Emily had taken her time to go. She had stopped screaming towards the end, blood loss and shock numbing her to the worst of it.

Mardy too was silent now. He just stared at the space where

she had been. Behind him Brogan put the body on the bed. It took him a few journeys.

He came back to stand in front of Mardy. He was breathing heavily, bathed in blood. "Now I am going to ask you again to tell me about the tapes and about the Society. I hope, for your sake, you tell me everything straight away or it will be harder going for you."

Brogan removed Mardy's gag and Mardy, in a quiet, defeated voice, told his story.

Mardy had been recording their conversations for over a year. He'd speculated heavily that the council would invest money in the docks, gentrify them. Mardy had bought up as much property down there as he could. He wanted to go legitimate. As soon as the docks were redone, he could cash in and get out of *the life*. The tapes were insurance in case Brogan hadn't let him.

Nothing had been happening down there though. He had all his money tied up in derelict, useless property, while the council just stalled.

Mardy had tried everything; joined one social club and then another, tried to network, offered bungs this way and that. He had, somewhere along the lines, been offered a place within the Society. Mardy had been desperate for it, would have done anything.

"Being a member of the Society is to be a member of the elite," he said, hollowly, his eyes bulbous without the lids. "But it has its price. I had to get rid of that girl's body once she had been burned. Normally the people who we take aren't missed, but she was. Everyone was nervous. The police were looking for her, asking the right questions, getting close. It was noticed that she was gone. I was given the task of making it look like she'd died in a fire. I had to sacrifice one of my buildings for that."

"Was it much of a sacrifice? You could get the insurance, you still owned the land."

Mardy shrugged. "You know me, John, I'm a businessman."

"Go on with your story."

"We'd bought off everyone we needed to; the fire inspector was cheap, your two policemen also had their price."

"Stone's daughter?"

Mardy nodded. "And then there was you. How do we buy you off? I said we couldn't. I mean look at you, John. You've got nothing, you haven't even got your sanity anymore. All you have got is this city and your job. That is what they wanted to use."

"By making me resign? I don't understand."

"No, that was Stone. We told him just to present the options to you, but he said he was going to make you resign. The other members of the Society were happy with that."

"So that is why they had a copy of one of your tapes?"

"It was the only one left. I got back to the house to find Emily gone and the tapes missing. I was scared; you don't let the Society down. It was then I remembered there was that one tape, the most recent one. I'd been drunk and left it in my coat rather than in the safe. I gave it to those two cops. They used it on you."

"So that is the only tape left?"

Mardy nodded again.

Brogan asked some more questions about the members of the Society and where they met. Mardy answered them all. He didn't lie or posture; he just answered everything in that empty voice. He listed names, lots of names. Doctor Llewelyn? Yes, he was one; he'd lied about there being any hemp fibre on Trish that *hippy, earth-child type's* wrist.

Eventually Mardy had lapsed into silence. Everything admitted, everything out.

"It is time," Brogan said finally.

Mardy had looked at him and said, "You remember when we were kids? Who'd have thought it would have ended like this, eh? Do it quickly, yeah?"

And in memory of their childhood friendship, Brogan had done it quickly.

481

"You didn't have to kill her," Reno said almost to himself. "Why did you kill Emily?"

"It's done, shut up about it," Zach cautioned him.

Brogan nodded. "Mardy and his wife betrayed me, went against me. They tried to undermine everything I have done for this city. So yes, I did that to them."

"But—" Karl started saying, only to have Brogan put a hand up to silence him.

"There was another reason as well." He turned to Zach and his brother. "It was a warning to you two. You now know what I am capable of and the depths I will plumb in order to protect this city. I am sure you will keep that in mind when you leave for the last time."

Batty Boy's smirk at this little speech withered away under Brogan's mad-eyed stare.

"And now it is time for us all to leave," Brogan continued. "Karl, you will come with me as I have one more chore to complete tonight."

Karl was visibly shaking now.

Batty Boy pushed him. "Go on, son. You've got your city now."

Karl edged forward, eyes on the floor.

Brogan motioned him into his car. "I think you will need to drive."

Reno got in and sat behind the steering wheel, like a good boy.

"Before I go I will need a gun," Brogan said to Zach.

Zach and Batty Boy shared looks – *this guy's a lunatic*.

Brogan kept his hand out.

"Shit, give him your gun," Zach finally said.

Batty Boy handed it over.

A tense moment slid by and then Brogan turned and walked around to the passenger door. He was leaning heavily on the car now.

Zach called after him, "You can trust that our future plans do not involve encroaching on your territory." He turned his head up towards the heavens, the first drops of rain falling, big and heavy. "Besides, I'm sick of the fucking weather you people get down here."

29

The howling coming from the yard was increasing. Franklin London looked out of the kitchen window. The thunderstorm was getting closer. Lightning always riled the wolves up, but tonight it was different. The farmer felt it.

His wolves had been anxious all week. Pacing, ears down, nasty. Geronimo, the big alpha male, had even snapped at him during feeding time, causing parents to pull their children back.

Franklin was going to give it another couple of days, before calling the vet in to give them all check-ups.

"Thunderstorm's coming," he told the wife. "I had better go and check on the wolves."

She looked up from her knitting and smiled. "Leave them tonight, Franklin. You know how they get."

She had been in a good mood ever since seeing their son.

"Best do it before it starts raining," he said, while taking the shotgun down from the cabinet.

His wife put her knitting down. "Now what are you doing with that?"

"The wolves seem quite anxious. I'm worried there could be a fox about," Franklin lied; the tracks he'd seen around the cages didn't belong to any fox.

"A fox? Don't be silly. No fox would come near a pack of wolves."

Franklin left the house before his wife could say anything else.

Squinting through the darkness across the yard, he could see the silhouettes of the wolves a hundred yards away. Rapidly pacing back and forth, howling loudly.

Two of the wolves started fighting with each other, their yelps and growls cacophoning around the yard.

Franklin started walking across to them.

Just out of sight, a shape came away from the barn.

Franklin froze, the hair on his neck prickling. He looked around – nothing.

Franklin had lived on the farm his whole life without ever feeling nervous, but now, just fifteen feet away from his house, he cocked both barrels of the shotgun.

Getting closer to the cage, the alpha male lunged for the fence, its weight making the wire groan.

Behind Franklin, a shape crossed the yard, passing through the light, spilling out from the farm house door. A shadow fell across the farmer. He swung around, gun pointed in front of him, breathing heavily now.

The noise of Geronimo hitting the cage, again, made him turn. Some of the wire meshing started to come loose; it fell away leaving a hole.

The wolf squeezed through it, looking at the farmer, a low growl coming from deep within its soul.

Suddenly the wolf stopped; its tail down.

Franklin turned slowly, the noise behind him drawing him round. It was a strange noise not dissimilar to a squeaking, rusty swing.

Franklin turned in time to see a shadow disappearing behind a pile of tyres. He let off both barrels, turning them into confetti.

He cracked the stock of the gun and pulled out the shells.

The squeak-squeak was getting closer now. Behind him the wolves cowered, ears down, howls turning to whines. The farmer saw a shape dispatching itself from behind what was left of the tyres.

The used shells fell to the floor as he scrabbled through his pockets for more.

The shape took form, massive, blood-matted and with a set of wheels.

He saw his wife come to the door and let out a scream.

Dog bounded forward.

Franklin went down backwards into the sucking mud.

The last thing he saw were the jaws of Dog ripping back and forth while the howling of the wolves filled his ears.

30

The slate quarry was a massive scar on the landscape. The owner, being a member of the Society, had enough clout to literally bulldoze through the concerns of environmentalists and expand his operation ad nauseam.

Nestled at the other end of the quarry was the processing factory. It consisted of three buildings connected and interconnected by chutes and walkways. They might have looked tiny from this distance, but the largest one measured over six storeys in height. They were lit up by multiple lights now, acting almost like a beacon in the darkness.

This is where Donald and Gavin were heading. Or rather, they were heading to the other side of the structures. Heading to get in position by the long access road, ready to block it off when the time came.

They skirted the quarry, sticking close to the rusted, gap-filled fence. Eventually they made their way down through the slippery, steep woods and found a ledge in amongst some rocks, several feet above the gravel track that ran up to the quarry.

"This will do," Donald whispered. He had found it hard going in the dark, especially carrying the M-60, or *"that gun like Rambo used"* as Jason called it, which kept getting tangled in brambles and shrubbery. Gavin collapsed exhausted behind him; he was loaded down with an AK-47, with bandoliers of M-60 ammunition crisscrossing his skinny chest.

Parked up alongside the track was an array of expensive-looking cars, mostly 4x4s or Mercedes. After setting up the gun and stringing the ammo belts, they sat and waited. Donald caressed the cold metal of the Sixty, his mind's eye alight with shredding metal, exploding gas tanks and avenging Trish. Gavin rocked back and forth next to him, knees pulled up to his chest.

A loud rustling in the bushes made them jump. Gavin spun round raising his torch, but Donald stopped him.

The silence of the woods was permeated with a low growl. Something was there, something big. Donald silently reached for his knife, but was dazzled as the woods were lit up spotlight-bright. Several shapes retreated away from the light. Their departure was accompanied by a squeaking noise, like an un-oiled gate in the wind. Donald shared a look with Gavin before turning around.

The source of the light was a car, a battered, old, out-of-place-looking car.

The car had pulled into the work's entrance and was driving up the track. Donald forgot about the shapes; he was all business now.

The car was coming up the gravel path slowly, rattling loudly, blasting out music.

Donald pushed the machine gun's stock snug into his shoulder.

The car was thirty yards away.

Twenty.

Down to ten.

Two hooded figures appeared from nowhere, flagging it down.

The car ploughed to a halt. One of the sentries bent down, head into the car, words were exchanged. Donald couldn't hear what; loud discordant music drowned them out. The hooded figure stood back going for the handle; there were two flashes in quick succession.

The hooded figure flew backwards, sprawling into the bushes.

The other sentry stood up washboard straight. Two more

flashes were accompanied by the noise of breaking glass. He went down unmoving between two Land Rovers.

The car sprayed gravel as it sped off up the track.

31

Upon killing a man, Alistair felt nothing. It was odd; he thought he would have felt a twinge of something.

Never mind, maybe with the next one.

He turned the gun and fired two more shots through the side door window, the soft thump, thump of the silencer barely audible above the punk rock.

The second figure crumpled out of sight.

Nope, nothing.

He floored the accelerator, bouncing and buckling the car up the track. So far everything was going to plan.

He'd finished working out his plan in a lay-by on the way here. Alistair wasn't stupid; he couldn't just go blundering into this mess unprepared.

Firstly, the guards. He'd guessed there'd be guards and rightly enough, two of them had come out from behind bushes waving him down, standing either side of the car.

"Hi, I'm here for the sacrifice," Alistair shouted over the music – *Try and bluff your way in.*

"Listen, you can't come in here, this is private property," the hooded figure had shouted back, while leaning down putting his head through the window.

"Can you just tell me how many of you I'll be dealing with up there then?"

"Listen, you'll have to get out of the car and—"

Try and bluff your way in and if that doesn't work, start shooting – it wasn't a very complex plan.

32

Al was out of breath when he returned from laying the charges. He crawled, snake-like, up a cut in the rock face dragging wires after him.

"I'm not getting any younger," he puffed. "Right, I've set up the explosives in amongst some of the gravel piles and below the cliff face opposite. Once we connect the wires and blow this thing, the whole lot will come down and the gravel should act like shrapnel. I reckon the kill zone will be about one hundred and fifty feet."

"Is that going to be enough?" the pastor asked.

Al looked down at the gathered masses below. The Society were conducting their ceremony close to the processing factory, in the lea of a large rock face. They had electrical lights hooked up to a generator and there was a long trestle table with food and drinks on it.

Around the quarry, groups of the purple-robed figures stood chatting. Even from their elevated position, the occasional snippet of conversation or laughter floated up to them.

In the centre of the gathering was a pyre, with a stake in the middle.

"It should be." Al nodded, while he commenced to connect the wires to the plunger. "Ok, now listen. If anything goes wrong, someone will need to get to the plunger and then all you need to do is pull out the safety bar and then depress this lever twice; click, click and boom."

"In that case, let's blow it now and get out of here," Jason said nervously. He was lying next to Muppet. They weren't happy.

The pastor shook his head. "Not yet. I want to make sure we get them all."

Below in the quarry something was happening. The Society got into two lines, a rhythmical chant starting up. Across the quarry a white-robed figure sluggishly moved; she was young, with black hair. She was also held on both sides by two members of the Society. They led her up to the pyre and started lashing her to the stake. The figure struggled languidly, but to no avail.

"I'm going to blow this thing before they set fire to that poor girl," Al said.

Behind them in the woods a twig snapped.

They all turned.

"Pastor Morris!" Detective Stone growled, sighting down the shotgun. "This is unexpected."

33

"You knows him?" one of the moron farmers asked.

"You *know* him," Stone snapped. "*Know* him. Not *knows* him. Christ, now shut up and cover them."

The inbred had muttered something in Welsh before raising his shotgun and doing what he was told.

All Stone felt at this present moment was hatred. Hatred for the situation he was in, hatred for the fucking idiots he'd been put with and hatred for this dishevelled group crouched in front of him. He felt his finger tighten on the trigger. With a mighty effort he fought back the rage, fought back the urge just to continue squeezing and eviscerate Pastor Morris and those weird, intense eyes that seemingly bored into him. It was not the way. It was not what Keyes would have wanted.

*

Detective Stone had made it to room 302, despite the heat and the smoke; he'd shouldered his way in. He saw what could only be Keyes' body on the floor. There was nothing he could have done. Keyes was long past saving.

Stone coughed his guts up outside the hotel, a ring of people jabbering at him. He pushed them away, muscled through them, finding Vince, the scrawny desk clerk. Lifting him up, shaking him, laying on slaps.

"What happened?"

Vince stuttered out an answer. "I d-d-don't know."

Vince got more slaps. "I... I saw that kid you were with. He left and then the place caught fire."

"Fuck! And you just let him go?"

Vince nodded.

Stone laid the cunt out.

People backed off, leaving him to pace, leaving him to curse, leaving him to make plans for what he was going to do to Alistair.

In the distance sirens were approaching.

"Detective."

Stone didn't even hear.

"Detective."

Stone turned to look at the chubby man standing there, the instigator of this nightmare, the man who held his daughter's life in his hands.

Doctor Fletcher stood there in person. Options flashed through his mind.

"You couldn't bring us Alistair, could you?" Doctor Fletcher said. He looked away for a moment, seeming to hold back tears. "That's it then, there's nothing more we can do to save her." He turned back to Stone, barely constrained hatred behind his eyes. "It's time to come with us now."

Stone had muttered about his partner, pointing to the building, tears in his eyes.

"Detective, it's your little girl you need to worry about now."

Doctor Fletcher had made him drive out into the country. They had driven in silence, pulling off the road and up a track. There Stone had been introduced to a group of heavy-set, ruddy-cheeked, local farmer-types.

"You are with them for the evening," Fletcher said, not even looking at the detective.

*

Sentry duty; they'd given him fucking sentry duty, still numb, covered in soot, his eyes still red from the smoke and the tears. It was another way for the Society to hammer home the fact that they were in charge, the fact that they owned him, the fact that if they wanted to they could make him kneel and kiss their shoes.

"It's like with the hunt, see," Dai One explained, as they walked the perimeter of the quarry. "It's not just the posh people in their pretty red coats and all. There's a lot that goes on behind the scenes, chaps looking after the dogs, watering the horses, digging out the fox."

The inbred mongoloid spoke slowly, like he had to think of every word before he said it. Stone wanted to smash his face in with the butt of the shotgun he'd been given.

"Apparently, right," another one of the sheep-fuckers started to explain. He'd introduced himself as Dai Two and spoke even slower than his friend. "The last time they had a roast, someone attacked them. Shot at them like."

"Which is why we all got employed and have to come up here wandering through the woods, see."

"It's good money like, but—"

Stone put his hand up to shush them. He pointed through the bushes at the four figures kneeling down overlooking the sacrifice.

They sneaked up behind them, the mongoloids loud and heavy; a twig broke, the interlopers turned.

*

Pastor Morris' eyes had never left the detective's.

"It saddens me to see this, Detective," the pastor said, moving his hands away from his body, backlit by the works below. "It means I was wrong about you and your large partner." He tutted and shook his head. "I am so rarely wrong about people." He started to get up. "Was I wrong about you, Detective Stone?"

His eyes are weird, flashed through Stone's mind. They glinted, despite the lack of light; they hypnotised, they pulled him in.

"No, Father, no, you weren't wrong about me," he wanted to say. He

wanted absolution from the terrible things he'd done, forgiveness for his partner dying. *"No, Father, no, you weren't wrong about me, I'm going to bide my time, Father."*

Pastor Morris put his hand on the gun, not needing any force to lower it, Stone unresisting, looking away, unable to make eye contact. "I know you're waiting to be forgiven," Pastor Morris said gently.

Stone caught a glimpse of loose wire, saw the shape of a plunger. "Yes, Father, I'm going to bide my time."

Screaming and the revving of an engine broke the moment.

They all looked down into the quarry; a car was flying around the open ground trying to hit people.

Everyone watched open mouthed, everyone except Al. He'd seen the policeman clock the plunger. He couldn't get to it in time.

He could get to the policeman though, get to his gun.

He lunged forward.

"Al! No!" the pastor yelled.

Dai One let off both barrels of his shotgun into Al's chest.

34

The car sped up the track between two huge buildings and out into a wide open space. There were a lot of people there.

Alistair drove around in sweeping circles, going for side swipes, going for multi-death kills. Robed figures flew out of the way, sprawling and falling over each other.

Alistair parked the car deep in a trestle table; food sprayed everywhere.

In a second he was out of the car, pistol into the air letting off a shot. It was Stone's gun from the hotel – no silencer on this one. Its report echoed around the area.

Everyone dropped, covering their heads, shaking – *cow them from the beginning.*

Maggie was in the centre of the circle tied to a stake, dressed in white, knee-deep in kindling – *kind of arousing*; Alistair shook it off.

"I want the girl."

"Who the hell do you think you are?" one of the figures demanded, rising from the floor. He wore a robe of richer purple than the rest overlaid with a yellow sash. "You can't come in here threatening us. Do you have any idea who we are?"

Alistair shot him in the face – *the first person to speak was dead; cow them good.*

Their leader went down twitching out life.

Alistair drew the other gun, adrenalined up, cool as fuck. "Take your hoods off, take them off now, I want to see who I'm dealing with," he ordered.

The dressed-up idiots exchanged looks.

Alistair shot the closest two people to him, blood sprayed on others – *these bastards killed Trish; they don't get the right to hesitate.*

Hoods were ripped off fast.

"Right, now untie my girlfriend."

Two of the de-hooded figures rushed forward pulling at the ropes, hugging her off the pyre. Alistair recognised them. The Society were actually making Mum and Dad watch their daughter burn. Maggie pushed them off, screaming insults, rushing towards Alistair.

Alistair wanted to hug her, tell her he loved her, tell her what he was doing right now wasn't the real him. But they weren't safe yet. He shoved the big chopping knife into her hand. "That's for protection, now grab a hood."

Maggie looked at him.

"Grab a hood," he repeated. "Right, the rest of you throw your wallets and purses over towards the car. Do it now."

Everyone was quick to respond.

"Maggie, gather up as many as you can."

"You're actually robbing them?"

"No. I'm collecting IDs." He spoke loud enough for everyone to hear. "So once we leave here if I ever get the feeling any of these fucking pricks are trying to track us down I'll find them and do them. Do you all understand?"

No one answered. Alistair fired twice, two more people jerked backwards spouting blood, the shots echoing around the quarry.

"Do you all understand?"

Hasty nods and "yes, sir, yes, sir" – *leave them cowed, leave them cowed good.*

Alistair quickly evaluated how the plan was going; Maggie had gathered up enough wallets, he had a bullet left in each gun and the car was still running – *save the girl, kill the baddies and boogallo.*

It was time to boogallo.

"Alistair, watch out," Maggie screamed.

Alistair turned in time to see Detective Stone striding towards him fast, laying down punches, rock hard and spot on accurate.

Everything exploded red.

Stone was shouting, "You killed him, you killed him," stripping Alistair of guns, throwing them away.

onald didn't know what to do. The pastor hadn't mentioned anything about driving a car up into the middle of the gathering. He hoped that it was Al, bravely going off to save the sacrificial victim. He wasn't sure though and as the minutes passed, Donald became increasingly anxious.

He would have asked Gavin's opinion, but Gavin was busy rocking back and forth muttering about what had been in the woods.

A shot rang out from up in the quarry works.

"I'm going to find out what's going on," Donald said.

Gavin stopped his rocking. "You can't leave me here on my own. There're things out there, they're here to wreak their vengeance."

"No, I won't be long. If only I had a disguise, I'd be able to—"

More shots rang out from up in the quarry.

Donald froze as another car started coming up the access road, its double row of headlights blinding them.

The late-comers drove yet another 4x4. This one was resplendent with bull bars, at just the right height for moving cows and killing children. The vehicle slowed and pulled up six feet away from them, Donald covering it with the M-60.

A fat woman opened the passenger side door, hen-pecking her husband about tardiness. She was in mid-stream as she struggled to get out of the car while trying to slip a purple robe over her head.

In the distance another shot rang out.

The fat woman never saw what hit her. Donald had covered the distance in two bounds, grabbed the woman by her ample scruff and slammed her face into the doorframe. Donald started slamming the door on her. There was a crack of bone and the woman's body had gone limp long before Donald stopped his assault.

The driver was still in the car desperately trying to undo his seatbelt while, at the same time, restart the engine, his flight instinct overloading with fear.

Donald calmly let the woman's body slide to the floor before drawing his knife.

The man stopped his scrabbling and just stared, transfixed by the blade. Donald climbed into the car, ignoring the impudent slaps that landed on him and started going to work on another one of Trish's killers.

When he had finished, Donald dragged what was left of the two bodies up into the woods.

Gavin stared at him open mouthed. "What are you doing? We were meant to wait for the explosion."

Donald dropped the bodies in front of the M-60, like sandbags, bloody, carved-up sandbags.

"I am going to reconnoitre," he said, pulling the purple robe off the woman's head.

Brains fell out like puke.

"You can't leave me here in the woods with them," Gavin whined, looking at the bodies.

"You know our mission, soldier," Donald snapped. "You stay here with the machine gun and shoot at anything coming down the path."

Gavin started to say something, but stopped.

Donald nodded as if the matter was settled. He hid the AK-47 under his slightly short and blood-soaked robes before heading up the track towards the quarry.

36

So close, goddamn it, he'd been so close. That was all that went round in Alistair's mind as he lay, hunched on all fours, hocking up blood.

"He's dead!" The woman speaking sounded posh, sounded shocked. "They're all dead, you've killed five people!"

With a mighty effort Alistair pulled himself to his feet. *Jesus, Stone punched hard.* "No, I've killed seven of you fucks." Alistair tried to smile; he could feel his face forming into a deranged grin. "I took out another two down by the entrance as well."

"You killed Dai Three?" someone with a strong Welsh accent yelled, the accent sounded out of place amongst the rest of the Society.

Alistair looked up at a heavy-set man lumbering towards him. The man roared an insult before starting to whale on Alistair.

Now it was Stone's turn to stop a beating. Though vastly outsized by the ham-fisted yokel, he had, in a second, put the man onto his knees in an arm lock.

"He's mine, he killed my partner," Stone said, in a low voice that didn't court argument. "He's mine," he repeated, louder now, letting everyone know. "Now go back and guard those three over there," Stone ordered pointing at Pastor Morris and his little band.

"You have no right to decide that his fate lies in your hands," a grey-haired man said, bending down and gently removing the hood from the yellow-sashed body. "He has killed members of this Society. He has killed our leader, that is an insult to us and the greatest crime that has been perpetrated here today."

Stone snorted in derision.

"Do you have any idea who this was?" the grey-haired man continued. "This man was viewed by many as one of the leading clinical psychiatrists of his generation. It is an insult to us all that his life was cut short by this... this ragamuffin."

Alistair hocked blood on the body – *call me a ragamuffin indeed.*

"What insult? What Society?" Stone guffawed. "You're just a bunch of rich pillocks fucking about in the woods."

"You need to know your place."

"Know my place? Know my place? You fucking lunatic, this isn't the sixteen-fucking-hundreds. I'm not a feudal serf. I'm a policeman and this bastard murdered my partner."

"I didn't kill him," Alistair piped up, back on his feet again.

Stone turned.

"I didn't kill your friend, but I know who did."

"What? Who?" Stone said, coming close, looking nasty.

"I'll tell you, but not like this."

Stone shoved him over, was on top of him again – slap, slap, slap.

They grappled; they collapsed in a heap, wrestling badly, like Saturday night at the taxi stand. Alistair pulled him close.

"Before he was killed, we made a deal," Alistair whispered. "The deal was simple. When you took revenge on them, you left Maggie out of it."

"How did you know we'd get revenge?"

"David wasn't a bad person. Neither are you."

"How did you know his first name?"

"Maggie's life for his killer."

"Who killed him?"

"When you get her out of here I'll tell you."

Stone broke the clinch, grappled on the floor for his discarded shotgun, before dragging Alistair up to his feet and shoving it into his face. "You'll tell me now."

"Promise to get her out of here," Alistair repeated.

Stone stepped away from him, shotgun up, barrels cocked – click, click.

Everything was a tunnel now, just Stone and the shotgun. Maggie's cries, in the background, miles away.

Stone stared at him. "You killed my partner." The look on his face put him beyond reason.

A movement in Alistair's periphery.

Stone saw it too, his features changed.

He shifted the shotgun.

"What are you doing here?" he asked in surprise.

onald's disguise seemed to be working. He had crept up the gravel access road, under the monolithic buildings and across the quarry towards all the activity. Donald had sidled his way into the midst of the unsettled crowd as nonchalantly as possible and didn't like what he saw.

Pastor Morris, Jason and Muppet were kneeling in a line heads bowed, two huge, ruddy-looking farmer-types standing over them. There was no sign of Al, but there were a lot of bodies though. Donald counted five, lying prone and immobile. A few of them were being hugged by sobbing women.

In the centre of the group two people were struggling with each other, rolling around, quarry mud matting them.

The figures got up, one dragged by the other. Donald recognised the victor. It was the policeman who had stabbed him. He was shouting, *"You'll tell me now."*

Donald hesitated, unsure what to do. He felt one of his headaches coming on strong, coming on fast. He desperately looked at the pastor for some sort of guidance. Pastor Morris was staring directly at him through the crowd. Pastor Morris looked serene, his green eyes glistening in the generated light.

Pastor Morris smiled and nodded.

Donald knew what to do. He flung back his robes and started to raise his machine gun.

The detective saw this and turned, looking surprised, mouthing some words Donald couldn't hear.

Time slowed down.
Gunfire kicked in.

38

listair was down. Alistair was hugging the floor, gunfire filled his ears, echoing and rebounding back off the quarry walls.

Stone had turned the gun away from him, something over Alistair's shoulder causing a distraction. That had broken the spell. Alistair's survival instinct kicked in. Alistair had hit him on the nose.

It was a really lousy punch, but enough to put Stone off balance. His shotgun fired, the barrel blast shredding into the crowd, hooded figures dominoed down. One of the figures was holding a machine gun and looked weirdly familiar.

The hooded figure with the machine gun was sagging, going down on his knees holding his stomach, deflating. Deflating for a second, before coming up on one knee into a firing position.

Alistair hit the ground, gunfire filling his ears. People started screaming.

Alistair desperately looked around for Maggie, looked through fleeing legs and falling bodies. She was nowhere to be seen.

He was grabbed from behind, turned over and someone fell on him.

Face to face with Maggie.

"Oh God, are you ok?" she said.

"Yeah, just about, what about you?"

Her reply was a kiss.

Despite all the mayhem around them, she kissed him. She kissed him and it was a great kiss, making everything else fade into stillness.

"I think we should try and get out of here," Maggie said, breaking the moment.

"Sounds good."

Hand in hand they pulled each other to their feet.

Alistair scrabbled on the floor for one of his guns, Maggie pulled him away – *no time, let's go.*

Unarmed now, they zigged and zagged away from the gunfire.

Not looking back.

Not caring who fell around them.

Not seeing the people following.

etective Stone had taken a bullet, taken it low. He was down, gut-shot and thrashing. Only one thought pounding through his mind. Not revenge for his dead partner but Megan, little Megan in the hospital bed with tubes coming out of her.

Lying there in the mud, Stone knew there was still one thing he had to do – kill her doctor. They'd already found her a bone marrow donor. It was easier to find a new doctor than a new matching donor. It had just been the threat of it not being put in Megan that had him here, working for them. And if he could get the doctor, there'd be no one to turn around and say, *"No, it can't go in; this child is in an inoperable condition."*

Stone pulled himself up into a sitting position – *here doctor, doctor, doctor.*

The quarry was a shambles. People running and falling everywhere, lots of them heading for the access road trying to get back to their cars.

Stone spotted his prey.

Stone unsteadily got to his feet.

People shoved Stone, trying to get past him.

He lost sight of the doctor.

With the shotgun used almost as a crutch, he headed after him – *here doctor, doctor, doctor.*

Desperately looking around, Stone couldn't see him. He did

see someone else though. Pastor Morris was climbing up out of the quarry. Stone knew where the pastor was going and despite his pain knew if he didn't get out of here quickly he was dead.

40

"No, not this way," Maggie shouted over the noise and screaming. "Come on, up here."

She hauled him away from the access road, which was becoming thronged with people. Instead, they pulled each other up the side of the quarry.

Maggie was smart, choosing the lowest side of the quarry to go for. After a fifteen-foot climb, they were able to drag themselves onto a wooded plateau, with an uninterrupted run through the woods and onto the road and freedom.

Hand in hand they ran.

"Margaret. Margaret, stop this instant."

The voice came from behind them, sharp, commanding. Maggie's mother was pulling herself upright. Dishevelled from the climb, carefully placed makeup overlaid with quarry mud and scratches.

"Mum, what the hell are you doing?" Maggie exclaimed. "Get away from me."

"Margaret, listen to your mother," her father panted, coming into sight over the lip of the quarry. He too was bright red from the exertion; Daddy was looking on the brink of a coronary.

"Margaret, you are coming with us. Come on, we are going home."

"Going home with you? Are you both mad? You'd have let them kill me."

"No, we tried to stop them, tried to get your… your so-called boyfriend to come in your place, but he wouldn't."

"But he did," Maggie said. "And now we are leaving together."

"No," her mother shouted. It came out high pitched; it came out in a plea. She pulled something out of the recesses of her robe.

"Oh for God's sake," Alistair muttered, recognising the gun. It was one of his, the one with the silencer on it – *he had a bullet left in each gun.*

"Look at the mess you've caused you… you little turd," the mother spat. "It was meant to be our big night tonight. Our choice of who should face the Reckoning and it should have been you. You were the one who killed my baby, killed my Ceri." Her face turned to venom. "I've seen you still selling drugs, still doing nothing. A thousand of you aren't worth one of my daughters." She raised the gun pointing it at Alistair's head – a *bullet left in each gun.*

Alistair let go of Maggie's hand and stepped away from her. The cow was right. He had killed Ceri and this was how it should end.

"Stop," Maggie ordered her mother. "It was you who killed Ceri. If anyone is to take the blame, it's you. You pushed her away; you were the one who disowned her when she came back home wanting help. It was all you. So if you want to turn the gun on anyone, turn it on yourself."

"Oh Margaret," her mother said, face creasing and collapsing into her husband's arms, wailing loudly.

He hugged his wife, there there-ing her. Very gently he took the gun from her unresisting hands. He looked at it for a second, before aiming it at Alistair and, without hesitation, pulling the trigger.

41

Stone had found the climbing hard; he had slipped a couple of times, the pain in his stomach burning now. Just one thought spurring him on – he had to save his daughter.

He finally, and lung-burstingly, got to the top of the climb. Looking down, he saw how the basin had descended into carnage. On the opposite cliff he half-noticed the pastor's progress. Stone couldn't have given a shit.

Keeping low, he moved forward, dragging his sorry, shot-up ass behind some bushes. Moving forward bush to bush. In front of him four people stood; the doctor that bitch of his wife, Alistair and some girl.

He moved closer, staying low, getting within hearing range. The woman held a gun.

The woman had suddenly started crying, her husband moved forward, had taken the gun and raised it.

Stone sighted down his shotgun. He had time; there'd be a speech first, there was always a speech. He had time to rush the scene, put both barrels to the base of the doctor's skull, shout "freeze!" and pull some full-on Hollywood cop shit. Before lining them up and executing them all.

But there was no speech.

The doctor just pulled the trigger.

42

On the opposite side of the quarry, Pastor Morris scrambled up the steep scree slope, the muscles in his legs burning.

He glanced down. Below him Jason and Muppet were in a desperate hand-to-hand battle with their captives, the two burly farmers.

One of the farmers held Jason's dreadlocks in a meaty paw and was smashing his head into the rock. Muppet was doing a little better. He had one of the farmers on the floor and was head-butting him, screaming, "Get some, get some."

Pastor Morris turned and clawed his way up the last twenty feet of the hill, getting there, ready to collapse from the exertion. But he knew Al wouldn't look kindly on such weakness.

Al was there now, lying at the top of the slope, his lifeless body blood-soaked and still.

Pastor Morris knelt by him and gently closed his eyelids, before rolling the body out of the way. In his last act of selflessness, Al had fallen on the detonator, using his body to hide it from his murderers.

Pastor Morris fumbled, connecting the detonator wires; he turned back to the quarry.

The kill zone was still full of people, members of the Society trying to run or trying to hide.

Donald had stopped firing. He lay on his back, holding his stomach in with one hand while trying impotently to reload with the other.

Muppet was down now, motionless being punched.

Jason had fought free of his assailants. He was looking up, looking at the pastor, shaking his head, mouthing the words, "No, don't, not yet."

"I'm sorry," Pastor Morris said, a tear coming to his eye – *Oh Lord how busy I must be this day, if I forget thee, do not forget me.*

43

The hollow click of hammer on nothing rang loudly in the clearing. Maggie's father turned the gun, looking at it, looking surprised.

"Did you know the gun was empt—" Maggie started to ask, stopping when she saw how pale Alistair had gone.

"No, I thought I'd fired five times rather than six," Alistair said, distantly. "I guess in all the excitement I must have forgotten."

"Right, you fuck-heads, *this* gun is actually loaded. So everyone, hands up," Stone said, leaving his cover and dragging himself into the clearing, the shotgun's spread covering them all.

"Oh come on," Alistair said, exasperatedly.

"Shut up," Stone ordered, leaning against a tree, wincing. "Doctor, I'm afraid I'm going to have to shoot you."

"What? Wait, who'll save your daughter?"

"The donor is already at the hospital and there are other doctors. Look at it down there." Stone shook his head. "You'd need my help to sort this mess out and the only way you'd get that help is through my daughter. You wouldn't operate tomorrow. You'd put it off, keep me in thrall to you."

"No," his wife said, stepping forward. "We'll cover this up ourselves. You're not the only policeman we use. We've got people on the paper. We'll find a way to cover this, we always have."

"Not this time."

"You'll need my help with that at least," the doctor said, pointing down at Stone's stomach.

"No, I'll be alright. It's not even hurting anymore," Stone said, cocking the shotgun.

"Wait I… I…" the doctor started, getting hysterical.

But it was no use. Stone calmly raised his shotgun and let off one barrel into the doctor's chest. His wife screamed and collapsed with him, gathering her husband into her arms, life blood gushing out of him and over her.

Stone came closer. "I'm sorry, it's for my daughter."

She looked up from her husband, shock and hatred etched into her face.

Stone emptied the last barrel into it.

Stone cracked the shotgun.

Maggie, poor orphan Maggie, charged, screaming.

He smashed the barrel into her face. She went down.

Alistair was coming forward too.

Stone pushed in two new shells.

Alistair reached him, grabbing the gun; they wrestled, both pulling at the weapon, stumbling backwards towards the edge of the quarry.

Stone, face like a fiend, had Alistair by the hair, trying to force his head in front of the barrel. "This is for Keyes."

Alistair, fighting for his life, brought up a knee.

Stone gurgled and sagged.

Alistair pulled the shotgun free.

Turned it around.

And then light erupted all around them.

44

The force and power of the explosion made Gavin snap out of his trance and move forward to tackle the gun.

He ignored the two bodies piled up in front of him and instead sighted down the M-60.

People were running and stumbling down the access road, filling up his crosshairs.

Gavin closed his eyes tight and squeezed the trigger, holding it down until the belt ran through empty.

Carefully, he opened his eyes. The air was thick with gun smoke and the retch of cordite.

Not a soul moved.

Gavin got up, scrambled down to the road and ran as fast as he could.

45

Reno drove, Brogan lolled – eyes closed, skull blood-matted, pale as death. He'd been out for a while now, mumbling about bringing redemption.

Brogan had tried to explain it to Karl earlier. He'd pointed to his right eye. It was bright red, capillary burst and full of blood. "I see them in this eye, the ones I killed, that's all I see. I'm a bringer of redemption, that's my job, that's what I do. And they're thanking me for it, lining up and thanking me for freeing them."

Karl hadn't understood the mumblings though; he'd tried to ask Brogan what he meant.

Brogan had just given him a horrific look and smiled. "I've probably got God on my side too. Now drive."

"Where?"

"I've got one more person to free. He is a little way from here though."

"Where? Who?" Karl was getting more afraid. He knew he was in over his head and this... this lunatic, the person who had actually murdered Emily and Mardy, was probably the only way out for him, provided Brogan didn't die from his head wound first.

"At the slate quarry, you'll see them all."

"What slate quarry?"

Brogan had explained and Karl had driven, all the time trying to get his brain to think of a way out of this terrible mess.

For a second, the horizon blazed into light accompanied, a few moments later, by a sound like thunder.

Brogan stirred, sitting up straighter in his seat. "We're here," he said.

46

Alistair came around, still gripping the shotgun, not even sure if he'd been out, his head ringing, able to hear bumpkus.

Stone was nowhere to be seen.

He called out for Maggie – called and called.

Then he started crawling, feeling for her. Foliage slapped him in the face, cutting at him. He found her foot. Oh thank God, it was connected to the rest of her body.

Maggie wasn't moving. Even in the poor light, Alistair could see the blood coming out of her ear. He panicked, called her name, shook her, blew air through her cold lips into her still body. Then he stopped, counted to ten, tried to control his heartbeat, tried to calm down.

Refocused now, he felt her neck with a shaking hand. There, there was a pulse. It was weak and fluttering, but he was sure it was there.

Something crashed in the bushes behind him.

Alistair spun around, peering through the darkness, shotgun out in front of him. Something was there, a shape low in the bushes, no more than thirty feet away and then it was gone.

Alistair snatched Maggie up, the limpness of her body making it hard, making him scared for her. He pushed on, heading towards the road, heading towards an ending.

Behind him there was more crashing in the bushes. On each side of him now there was rustling and movement. Alistair stopped, looked around desperately, trying to keep the heavy shotgun up with one hand.

Catching sight of a movement out of the corner of his eye, he gulped back his fear and pressed on, ripping his way through the undergrowth, half-dragging, half-carrying Maggie, before coming face to face with something.

Something big, something that growled low and menacingly.

Something that Alistair recognised.

And then it was gone, leaving only a squeaking noise in the air.

47

Stone pushed his way through the woods, spurred on because he knew everything was going to be alright. The wound in his stomach had stopped hurting a while ago. A lot of people who deserved to be dead were dead and, most importantly, there was nothing to stand in the way of little Megan's operation.

He stopped against a tree, wheezing, trying to catch his breath; the going was hard, harder than it should have been. Just two more witnesses to dispatch and then he could go get himself all patched up. He'd be waiting ready to greet Megan when she came out of the operating theatre.

The last two witnesses would both be moving slowly as well. The girl had taken a pretty bad knock and it wasn't much fun dragging someone through all this. Stone saw a movement in the bushes, thirty feet in front of him, and realised they were hardly any distance ahead at all. He smiled to himself and pushed off the tree, knowing soon everything was going to be alright.

He burst through the last of the undergrowth, tumbling into a small clearing. Painfully, Stone dragged himself up onto his hands and knees, coming up to eye level with... with a thing. A squat and blood-matted thing. The thing was growling low and primordial, steam rising from its flanks.

In great pain, Stone threw himself backwards, crawling away, his body feeling leaden. The thing moved forward, accompanied by a squeaking noise.

Stone tried to get up; his legs weren't working for him though.

Shapes came out of the bushes either side of him; crazily enough they looked like wolves.

Stone backed into a tree – nowhere left to go.

Stone let out an involuntary moan.

48

The horrific scream close behind them made Alistair turn and peer into the woods. Then there was silence – no more machine guns, no more screams, no more explosions, no nothing.

Alistair was worn out, his limbs feeling all weak and useless from the exertion of half-carrying half-dragging Maggie while lugging the shotgun. There'd been numerous occasions when he'd nearly just left it, especially while trying to get Maggie through the quarry's perimeter fence. However, there were still two bullets in the thing and they weren't out of here yet.

Finally, they hit the road.

The road itself had been illuminated by an unknown light. Now that he was closer to it, Alistair could see they were a pair of car headlights. The car was forty feet further up the road, doors open, engine running, looking inviting.

Alistair gently lay Maggie down within the cover of the woods. Her breathing was shallow and rapid. He knelt next to her, stroking her hair, knowing that they had to get out of here. She murmured something he couldn't hear.

Alistair wavered for a few seconds, unsure what to do. Deep down though he knew there was only one real way forward.

"Ok," he whispered. "You gotta wait here for me; I'm not going to be long."

Reluctantly leaving Maggie, Alistair stole into the woods,

intending to circle around to the back of the car rather than blundering up the road with all the headlights in his face.

It took him five minutes, creeping as quietly as possible, to circle around the car. He squatted now in the shadow of a tree checking it out. It was parked on the side of the road in the entrance to an old, abandoned, tumbled-down farm, a place that Alistair recognised. God, had it only been a few days ago that he'd held Maggie's hand under the comet shower?

Well, there'd be more times like that, Alistair thought as he stood up and came out of the woods slowly, the shotgun stock snug to his shoulder.

He reached the back of the car, feeling exposed, feeling like it was a trap, but forcing himself on. He checked out the car – back seat empty, no one in the front, keys in the ignition.

Right, jump in, speed down the road, get Maggie in and let's go.

"I was right," the voice said, making him spin. "You have come for redemption."

"I thought I'd killed you," Alistair croaked, gawping at the ghastly apparition standing in the headlight beams.

49

Brogan hadn't been killed by anyone, but he damn well looked like he had, illuminated now in the headlights like something created by John Carpenter.

Alistair raised the shotgun.

"I knew you would come," Brogan said, his voice slurred, slowed down, off-putting. "You know we both need saving."

"Fuck off. Go on, fuck off down the road or I'll kill you," Alistair said, his voice coming out high pitched and shaken up.

Brogan shook his head slowly, one eye unfocused and blooded.

"Look, fuck off or I really will kill you," Alistair shouted, more convincingly this time, he thought.

Brogan turned, looking down the road and gestured.

Karl Reno came out of the bushes, hefting Maggie in front of him like a shield.

"Put her down," Alistair screamed, coming forward. "Put her down." No clear shot; nothing that wouldn't take out Maggie.

"Alistair, we both need to be forgiven," Brogan slurred from behind him.

"No, I need Maggie," Alistair said, swinging the gun on Brogan. "And if I shoot you that only leaves one person standing in my way."

Brogan clicked his fingers and Reno had a gun up against Maggie's head.

"Reno, you bastard. If you do anything I'll… listen, mate, Karl, what are you doing? We're friends, yeah; we can both walk away from this... this freak. Come on, you and me, eh? What do you say?"

"Shut up," Karl said, speaking for the first time, his voice sounding different, that supercilious air gone. "I'm sorry, Alistair, this is my only way out." Reno just sounded young and scared. "There has been a lot of death. I brought it here. Brogan will protect me."

"No, Karl, there's me. We can work this out."

"Alistair, you need to put the gun down now," Brogan said calmly. "You've got to understand I'm trying to save us both."

Alistair ignored the freak, instead concentrating on Reno. "Come on, Karl; let's get out of here, eh?"

"Alistair, put your gun down or I'll kill her," Karl ordered, sounding more like his old self – the cunt.

Alistair stood there weighing up his options, looking at Maggie. She mumbled something, her eyes still closed. He gently placed the shotgun on the car bonnet. Never taking his eyes off her.

Stepping away – the gun still within grabbing distance.

"Step back further," Brogan told him, coming forward, walking with a weird gait, picking up the shotgun. "Karl, make the girl comfortable in the car. I am going for a little walk with Alistair."

50

The going had been slow, Alistair carrying a torch, walking five feet in front of Brogan, shotgun at his back, Brogan slurring out a blue streak, a lot of it incoherent shit about *"redemption"* and *"needing forgiveness"*.

Alistair recognised the path they walked up. It was the same place they had seen the comets, his first, kinda, proper date with Maggie. That seemed like a lifetime ago now.

Maggie was back on the road, tied in the car, Reno guarding her. *"If you harm her I'll kill you,"* Alistair had promised. Delivered flat, delivered serious. Reno had winced. Close up he looked broken.

They crested the hill, heading for their destination. That odd stone building they had sat on once. Alistair was scared, his mind racing, trying to think of a way out of all this, hitting dead ends over and over again.

"This is where it ends," Brogan said, as they got closer.

"What, this is where you shoot me?" Alistair asked, his voice defiant.

Brogan stopped, agitated. "Damn it. Have you not been listening? I cannot make that choice, only you can."

He prodded him on.

aggie woke up, all grog headed and bound, her head aching like a brain haemorrhage. She started panicking. It took a couple of seconds for events to catch up with her. The onset of emotions overloading her system; both her parents were dead, Alistair was gone and she was, where?

She fought it all back.

With a lot of difficulty, she pushed herself up and tried to look around, her eyes growing used to the dark. Maggie recognised it as country dark. *Oh God,* she thought. *They've got me. They're going to try and burn me again. Where's Alistair?*

Maggie awkwardly looked through the car window desperate to see him. She froze, seeing a figure in front of the car. The figure was pacing back and forth, the cigarette glow illuminating some of his features. The man smoked fast, nervously; drag, drag, drag.

Maggie didn't recognise him. Unsure if that was a good or bad thing, she sank down low again and started scrabbling in her sash. It was awkward, but after a wrist-breaking minute, she managed to get a finger on the knife Alistair had given her.

For everyone there is always hope.

52

The torch light did nothing to warm the small interior of the shed. Brogan was sitting slouched in one corner, shotgun on his lap. Alistair was squatting in the other corner, watching the gun, licking his dry lips, thinking about Maggie.

"You know this evening hasn't gone to plan," Brogan said eventually, some light coming back into his eye. "After I killed Detective Keyes, we were going to wait quietly for Stone and he'd have gone the same way." Brogan gingerly felt the top of his head. "Then a couple of days later, they would have found your body with a bullet in the ear accompanied by a note saying that you were so consumed with guilt for killing those policemen that—" Brogan winced. "Well, you catch the drift."

For a second, a glimmer of hope came into Alistair's head. He pushed the shapes in the forest and that scream out of his head. "You haven't killed Stone though, he was there working for the Society. He gave me this," Alistair said, pointing at a random bruise on his face. "And I told him what you had done to his partner and he said he was going to fuck you up. Now listen, I know where he's gone so I could take you—"

"Stone is dead, you silly boy," Brogan said, suddenly becoming more animated.

"How? How do you know that?"

"Remember the little love tap on the head you gave me? Well, that changed everything. I can see them now, the ones who are dead. I can see Stone and I can see Keyes and I can see so many of them." Brogan pointed at his right eye; it was blood-filled, unfocusing, dead-looking. "That's all I can see in this eye, the dead, and they are telling me that it must end here."

"Oh boy," Alistair muttered.

Brogan stood suddenly, raising the shotgun. Alistair jumped up as well – *this guy is fucking barking.*

The end of the shotgun was grabable, so very grabable.

"I have killed so many people," Brogan continued. "And I thought there was no way of saving myself. But I can save myself through you."

"Look, you're not making sense," Alistair said, eyes on the shotgun.

"I am making perfect sense. You see, Alistair, you were the one who made me into this... this form I inhabit now. It was your actions three years ago that did that and now we have the perfect opportunity to wipe the slate clean and start again."

"Me? Fuck you?" Alistair shouted. "It was you who poisoned that heroin; you were a vicious psychopath way before I came along."

"Yes, but you were the one who gave it to an innocent."

Alistair subsided a little, leaning back against the wall. He sounded tired now. "I didn't kill her. Ceri was a lot of things, but she wasn't an innocent. She wanted those drugs."

"And you could have helped her stop wanting them. Don't you see, Alistair? You were in the rarest of positions. You could have saved someone you loved. Think about the power in that. But you are not that kind of person, are you? You wanted her to need you for something; you wanted her to need you to get that grubby little drug."

"No, you don't know anything about me."

"But, Alistair, I do. I know that you would do anything to go back and rewrite that mistake. Wipe the slate clean, actually save someone you love."

"I didn't kill her," Alistair repeated, feeling oh so tired now. "Maggie doesn't think so, she said it."

"What do you think, Alistair? To actually have saved someone, to turn around to Maggie and say, 'Yes, I was the one who saved your sister'," Brogan laughed. "The family would have invited you round for tea rather than trying to sacrifice you. Trish would still be alive as well; in fact, none of this would have happened."

There were tears in Alistair's eyes now as Brogan continued.

"You see, Alistair, we must all take responsibility for the decisions and the mistakes that we make. And this is it, I am offering you a chance to redeem yourself, to show you are truly sorry and then we can both find forgiveness." He came forward pushing the shotgun into Alistair's unresisting hands.

Alistair looked at it, for a moment not seeing it for what it was, before raising it and pointing it at Brogan. "Well, that was a very stupid thing to do."

Brogan shook his head. "No, Alistair, still don't you see? I'm trying to save you. You can make up for all the hurt and wrong that you caused. I'm offering you a chance to save someone you love."

Alistair stared down at the shotgun. "What if I just shoot you and then go shoot Reno?"

"Maggie will be dead before you have a chance."

"What do you mean?"

"You can save Maggie's life."

"I was going to do that anyway."

"No." Brogan glanced at his watch. "If Karl doesn't hear a shot in another two minutes and then have a call from me on this phone, he will shoot Maggie."

"Hear a shot? Fine, I can shoot you in the leg now."

Brogan shook his head, holding the phone in plain sight.

"What, you expect me to turn this thing on myself?"

"You understand," Brogan exclaimed, his smile horrific, his one good eye glinting with seeming joy. "You'll save someone you love. That will be your redemption."

"That's one option, the other one is you ring him and tell him to let her go."

"No, we need to be saved."

"Ring him," Alistair ordered, the shotgun inches away from Brogan's face.

Brogan didn't move.

"Right, I'll ring him then. Give me the phone."

"Do you know his number?"

"Reno's a coward. He wouldn't kill someone in cold blood."

"You are right. Karl is a coward, but he is afraid of me. He will do it, unless you redeem yourself."

Alistair lowered the gun. "Sod you. I'm going to go and get my girlfriend."

"You would not make it in time."

Pacing now, back and forth, gun down low, tears in his eyes.

Brogan talking. "You need to do this, Alistair; you'll be saving Maggie, resetting the balance for our actions. We'll be forgiven."

"No, there must be another way? There's always a way out of things like this."

"There is one other way," Brogan said. "You can just walk away, like you did before. Leave Maggie, let her die. You've killed someone else you loved before, you got over that soon enough."

"No, I've never got over it," Alistair mumbled, as he slid down the wall again, back to the squatting position, gun between his knees, slick in his hands. "And what about Maggie, what about her? Would you let her go, would she be safe?"

"You would have my word on it." Brogan looked at his watch again. "One minute to decide."

Alistair stared at the shotgun then at Brogan. "You can't be serious?"

"It's the only way." Brogan smiled in the first flushes of triumph.

"I can't."

"It will save someone you love."

Alistair looked back at the barrels, his mind racing, trying to think of a way out. Brogan seemed to have every angle covered.

"I can't," Alistair said before he started to sob.

"You must."

Perhaps Brogan was right; this was the thing to do, to atone for Ceri, to save Maggie.

Alistair put the shotgun under his chin, the barrels feeling cold on his skin.

Time was running out. Brogan had covered every angle.

He closed his eyes and put the shotgun in his mouth. Finger on the trigger.

His mind was shutting down from fear, but he was convinced if he could save Maggie this was the right thing to do.

Then it dawned on him – Brogan had covered every angle except one.

Brogan had forgotten all about Maggie and that was a stupid thing to do.

She had a knife.

He had a minute.

In one fluid movement Alistair rammed the shotgun into Brogan's stomach.

Brogan went down, a look of incomprehension shocked across his face. Alistair stamped the phone to pieces as he charged out into the night and down the hill.

"No, Alistair, no, you can't," it was begged out as a scream behind him.

For everyone there is always hope.

A NEW DAY

1

listair and Maggie sat hand in hand on the bonnet of their new car.

Swansea lay seven miles away down the valley, looking peaceful and still. It was last look at home time; they both knew they'd never be back.

They'd survived and everything felt good.

*

Alistair had pelted through the woods at breakneck speed. He'd found Maggie struggling with Reno, their silhouettes throwing up mad animal shapes in the car headlights, the knife between them.

She'd stuck Reno with it once, twice, going for three. Alistair pulled her off. There'd been enough deaths.

They turned the car around and drove, leaving Karl scrabbling in the road.

They'd driven back to the city. Driven home. Grabbed the scarper money, given a pile to Ebin, told him to get Clancy and to disappear for a few weeks. *"Go and see Mordechai or something."*

They'd left. Found an out-of-town hotel, paid cash, hit the room and washed each other clean. Then they slept deeply, not quite the sleep of the righteous, but close enough.

In the morning Alistair hit pay dirt in the boot of Brogan's car. He found the tapes.

They dumped Brogan's car and then bought their present heap. Cash and chivvying meant the guy didn't ask questions.

*

Alistair and Maggie had survived and everything felt good, even the drizzle misting down on them. Maggie had her head on his shoulder, one last look at home and then they kissed.

They'd talked about getting away. Getting away and not being tracked down. Maggie knew the Society well; she had told Alistair everything about it. Named every name. A plan had formulated.

Alistair got up and went to the solitary phone box. He dropped in a load of change; he'd be in there a while.

All the time looking at her.

2

Brogan and Reno had made it back to the city, having taken a car from the quarry. The doctor in the hospital's casualty department had been visibly shaken by the damage they'd sustained. He wanted to admit them. Brogan flashed his ID and told him, *"You can keep Reno, just bandage me up."*

The doctor had insisted. Brogan had said, *"No, I'm feeling better now."*

The police station had been a buzz of activity when Brogan walked in. One detective was confirmed dead in the hotel fire; his partner was missing. Another two bodies had been found with shotgun injuries up in the shanty towns.

Sergeant Johnson grabbed Brogan as he headed for his office. "Are you ok, sir?" he asked, doing a poor job at hiding his look of shock.

"I am fine, Sergeant. Is there something important you wanted?"

"Yes, sir," Johnson said, before proceeding to fill him in. "The chief superintendent has been in all morning, overriding all the different investigations; he seems more concerned about closing off the roads around some slate quarry out in the sticks. They were digging up there and hit a natural gas pocket or something. Big whoop, we have deaths to investigate."

Brogan didn't move, his jaw working silently. "Sergeant," he said. "It is not your place to question our commanding officer, ensure that the quarry is secure."

Sergeant Johnson shook his head in disgust as the mealy-mouthed little paper pusher stalked off.

Brogan sat behind his desk, formulating a plan. Wondering what had happened to Alistair and that girl, wondering what to do about the Society.

The phone rang.

It was Johnson again. "Sir, there's someone on the line wanting to speak to you. I said we were very busy, but he was insistent. Says it was about the offer you made him last night."

"Put him through."

Brogan recognised the voice, tried to speak, but was talked over.

"No, you had your chance last night and you failed. Now it's my turn. We are leaving the city for good. We've got those tapes you seemed so keen on and everything else you had in your boot. None of them will ever see the light of day again unless you come looking for us or I see either my name or Maggie's in the paper linked to this."

Brogan was silent for a long time. "I understand," he said, eventually.

"Good. Now listen to me. I know that fucking *Society* will be coming after me and Maggie. That will be for us to handle, but last night you talked about needing forgiveness. Well, if you really want to be forgiven for your past actions, you are going to make the activities of the Society public. Now this is how you are going to do it."

3

Martin Chandler hadn't been at the ceremony last night. His robe had remained hanging in the open wardrobe, as he wore out the carpet pacing back and forth looking at it.

He'd spent the night going out of the room, coming back in, physically unable to put it on and leave the house.

The memory of being led through the woods and the feeling of the drill by his eye and that calm, calm voice close to his ear had scared him ridged. Scared him to the point that he couldn't do it. He couldn't put on his once-beloved robe and go to the ceremony.

He realised now that this cowardice had probably saved his life.

All morning his phone had been ringing, the events of last night unfolding as they were retold in confused staccato by the few people who had survived. They rang up panicking, looking for advice, looking to see if he knew who had survived – *"I've rung and rung the Chumleys and there's been no answer."*

All of them confused, all of them scared – *"But, oh God, the police. They'll find out what we've been doing."*

And Chandler didn't know what to say to his friends or what would happen to any of them. He stood there now, pacing as he had last night, debating whether to just pack and go to the airport.

The phone rang; he snatched it up.

"Martin Chandler?" the speaker sounded old and cultured.

"Yes, yes, who is this?" Chandler stuttered.

"We are aware of what has happened. A group of our associates is currently travelling down to you. They will take control of the situation and will make it go away. They are on route as we speak and will be there in less than two hours."

"Who is this?"

The man sighed, long and deep, before continuing in a tone that would be saved for a dullard child. "At the moment my name is of very little importance, Mr Chandler. The matter that is of significantly more importance is a quarry full of corpses dressed in their best sacrificial robes and the associated spotlight, which will then be turned onto our Society. Now please, no more inane questions as time is of the essence."

"What do you want me to do?" Chandler asked, suddenly feeling a lot happier.

"You have all done enough damage down there, so at present very little. We have secured the site of the massacre ourselves. For now, all that we require from you is to contact everyone who survived this outrage and tell them not to speak to anyone until my associates arrive. Is that something that you would be able to handle, Mr Chandler?"

"Yes, yes, sir. I'll do it right away."

"Good," the voice said before the line went dead.

Elated now, Martin Chandler felt he could relax. He froze when he heard the doorbell ring. *God, they do work fast.*

He rushed through the house, brushing his hair with his hand, opening the door and going pale.

Detective Chief Inspector Brogan stood at the door smiling; he pushed past him into the house. "I am here to discuss with you the exclusive that is going to appear in your paper tonight."

Chandler started to say something, only to be slugged in the stomach.

He sank to his knees.

Brogan leant down, close to his ear. "Martin, this is it, this is your chance for redemption."